SAVAGE EARTH
NIGHTMARE FACTORY

By
JK Franks

This book is a work of fiction. The characters, incidents, and dialogues are products of the author's imagination and are not to be construed as real. Any resemblance to actual events or persons, living or dead, is entirely coincidental.

For Noelle

Who convinces me daily that goodness still exists and heroes are not just make believe.

War does not determine who is right
- only who is left.
— **Bertrand Russell**

PROLOGUE

Banshee came out of the darkest corner of the sky, silent and deadly, riding the glide-path programmed by computers thousands of miles away. The war-torn terrain was pock-marked with craters and darkened by fires. The team's approach was tight, but they didn't need much space. Banshee Team rode the night in bullet-shaped capsules opening at over sixty thousand feet to eject their human cargo into the cold night air.

The thin wind screamed past his body at just under 500 miles per hour, but that would slow considerably in the next few minutes. *One more drop, one day closer to getting the hell out of this.*

Fifteen minutes earlier, I'd been aboard the orbiting battleship Hermes.

"Master Sergeant, did I just hear you make a disparaging remark about Ramiro's sister?"

I had to stifle a laugh. "Absolutely not, LT. I hold the corporal's siblings in the highest of respect. I simply stated that I didn't think it was right for her to be pinned up on his bedroom wall like that."

The entire squad broke out in laughter, as they all had seen the centerfold someone had tacked over the man's bunk the prior day. The lieutenant tapped his comms and listened intently. He then looked up, all humor suddenly erased from his face. "We're on in three, people.

Lock into your coffins and remember to check your O^2. Review the mission brief as the objective has changed... again."

I groaned along with many of the others as I stared at the ceramic-composite shell of the orbital deployment pod, or ODP. What we all collectively referred to as, yep...our space coffins. This is my sixth rotation with the spacers, and I hate it as much now as the first. While Hermes was the newer class of battle wagons that Space Force had, it was still just a smelly, cramped, troop carrier. The advantage of a combat deployment vessel in LEO, or Low Earth Orbit, was you always had the high ground. One of the Alliance ships could be over nearly any spot on the globe within forty minutes and boots on the ground within another twenty minutes, assuming all went well. It often did not... go well. That was the problem.

The LT slapped the outer casing, making me wince. "Sergeant Kovach, you good?" the muffled sound nearly lost inside the suffocatingly tight pod that was essentially just enough insulation to keep me from burning to a crisp during the initial part of reentry. My gloved fingers found their way inside the control slots, where I grabbed the handles and braced for launch.

"I'm a fucking Space Force Ranger. What in the holy hell am I do..."

The rest of my complaint was cut off by the ballistic launch out of the firing tubes. What had been an onrush of muffled noise was suddenly replaced by an absolutely total silence, a silence that only the cold vacuum of space could offer. I was moving away from Hermes at tremendous speed, me and the other half-dozen members of Drop Team Banshee. We first have to cancel orbital inertia before the pods' built-in maneuvering thrusters would center us for trans-orbital ballistic insertion down onto the target vectors.

Today's fun little trip was coming via some nameless hellhole on the African continent, again assuming all went well. While Hermes was a Boeing Aries class battleship, the personal launch pods were designed and manufactured by a subcontract outfit in New Mexico that reportedly had already gone bankrupt from the many lawsuits of failed deployments.

I passed the time going through my loadout trying to see what ridiculous inventory the ship's AI had selected for today's mission.

Months earlier, we had dropped into a blizzard in the Italian mountains without cold-weather gear of any kind. I hated the bastard AI. Pretty sure it felt the same for me.

I felt the pod's thrusters kick on and off in rapid succession as it attempted to orient the small craft correctly. Apparently, today the internal gyros were not cooperating, as the thrusters fired again in a longer and even more jarring sequence.

"What we bringing to the party today, Sergeant?" The woman's voice was crystal clear despite traveling at ballistic speeds in her own pod a few kilometers away.

I triggered the squad channel. "Rocks and pointy sticks, probably, LT."

She laughed.

I gave them all the weapons load-out, "Our Standard issue Glisson MK4 Rattlers, one MK5 for Darko, and several of the Apex disruptors. Think you can hit anything with those?"

"Don't worry about me, Boss. What was it your old man used to say? 'The only thing you should feel when you shoot an enemy is recoil.'"

I cringed inwardly. Yeah... my father was an absolute legend in the Corps' Special Forces. What Dad had mostly told me was if I ever found myself in a firefight, I should find a 'real' Space Marine and give him all my ammo. Colonel Jackson 'Bones' Kovach had been highly decorated and much beloved by the corps. That had not made him great father material, but his misfit of a son was now Master Sargent Kovach, and yes, I still very much admired the man.

A massive jolt rattled my teeth as I felt the braking jets come to life. "Damn, never gets easier." Outside, the shell protected me from the thickening atmosphere as the craft slowed from thousands of miles per hour to just a few hundred. The pods would not take the drop team all the way down, as its role was simply to protect the humans during the initial descent phase. Somewhere around 65,000 feet, the canister would release us into the cold, thin air high above the target and then fire off to a pickup spot somewhere safe. If everything works correctly. Many Space Force operators had cratered into the surface, still locked inside their coffins. Those drops were called smear bombs, as that was all that was typically left of the soldier inside.

I pushed the thought away as the sound of one of the drogue chutes deploying slowed the pod even more. I braced myself for the shock of bitterly cold air as the warning alert sounded. My hand cramped as I held onto the control handles while the bullet-shaped pod fired to slow all momentum and in the same maneuver, ejected its human cargo into the dark blue, morning air. I had eight minutes of terrifying freefall before knowing if my battle suit's own systems were flight worthy.

Reflexively, I reached back to ensure my rifle was still slotted into its magnetic receiver on my back. It's like a baseball player touching the brim of his cap or licking his fingers. It means nothing... and it means everything. My heads-up display assured me it was locked into place and of its current ammo count, but I liked to be sure. I flipped through the map overlaying my field of vision. The GPS had shaded much of the view in red, presumably enemy territory. The U.S., China, and Russia had all been fighting proxy wars for years, starting one military brushfire after another in little shithole countries like this.

The Rapid Drop Teams were incredibly effective for Alliance Command in putting out the brush fires. I was second in command of Team Banshee, behind my best friend, Lieutenant Rollo 'Hinge' Hanson. We were all elite members of various special forces in the revamped Alliance organization, primarily the U.S., Great Britain, France, Korea, Canada, and occasionally Germany. The Alliance boasted forty-two countries, all in a mutual defense pact, but the Power-Five, as they were called, provided most of the soldiers, funding, and decision-making.

After the various Crimean Wars of the 2030s, followed closely by the near melt-down of the remnants of oil producing gulf-states where my dad had become legend, wars had adapted to a new, smaller landscape. No longer was it two brutes battling for supremacy. Now, with a flick of a button, even an individual could start a cyberwar that might quickly escalate to real bullets flying. Hackers, criminals, and even a few third-world city-states had been terrorizing the planet for the last three decades. Now the threats were getting worse; computer hacking had paved the way for bio-hacking. Corporate research labs had been the first targets, then exotic defense technologies divisions.

Before those in charge had caught on, many of their secrets were available to the highest bidder, and now... well, now, the planet was being overrun by terrorists trying to outdo each other with the deadliest, most menacing shit imaginable. Banshee no longer felt like a special operations fighting force, but more of a global SWAT team. *We're meter maids with automatic pulse-rifles.*

I was relieved to feel the big silk wings of the canopy fill out overhead. The glider wings' semi-flexible composite ribs locked into place, providing a highly maneuverable and silent descent system. Instinctually, I looked to verify that all the drop team's icons were green on my heads-up display.

Pulling back on my control lines, I saw Hinge moved forward and lead the flight of lethal nightbirds through the still black, early morning skies. We were following a river that glowed in blue outline on our map overlays. Far below, I could see the chalky white marks of rapids and swells that humped up as they climbed from deep water to shallows and then curled over the hidden boulders on the riverbed.

Banshee lined up in perfect formation, one to my left and the rest on a wedge to the right. There were five of them, apart from Hinge and me. The mission brief told us we'd be more than enough for this gig. My HUD displayed the world below in various shades of green. The diminished remnants of an ancient volcano bordered the lush valley to the south. It looked more like a trash dump to me, but the nav system called it Mt. Kickapoopoo or something similar. I didn't speak the local language, but that's what my mind tagged it as.

Our target was a suspected subterranean compound in this overgrown patchwork of jungle nothingness. Today our band of well-armed meter maids was going after Abdul Feraz, a suspected bioterrorist who had developed a component supposedly capable of delivering an even more lethal version of some shit that I couldn't care less about. Don't get me wrong, I hate the bad guys. I just now question if we're doing any good. Maybe we just make the problems worse, you know? Whenever we take one of the bastards out, someone else, usually someone even more crazy, more brilliant, more greedy steps in to take over.

Soldiers wondering if they are making a real difference must be a universal truth. Had I known going in that the owner of the covert research lab was actually just the front man for a group of other even worse assholes who had their fingers deep into the global industrial, military black market, would I have acted differently? Maybe. None of us knew this backwoods tribal fucklord was a key member of something called the Third World Coalition, an assemblage of angry extremists busy acquiring the kinds of fun shit that would allow them to do extensive damage to our modern way of life. Okay, even meter maids stop real criminals some days. Sadly, this was not shaping up to be one of those days.

CHAPTER
ONE
BANSHEE

The ground underfoot was loose gravel, and despite the sound-deadening boots, the ability to move undetected was going to be tough. The CO motioned me to take Bayou and go right. Ramirez, call sign Robot, Danny 'Halo' Jenkins, and a late addition filling in for Priest was a British SAS officer named Walter Highsmith whom they'd been calling Bond for lack of a real call sign. They all took the opposite side. Banshee had one more asset, that would be the spooky-ass shooter named Smith, or more often, just Darko.

"Darko, you are overwatch," Hinge said, looking back toward the shadow standing just inside the tree line. "Halo, check the tablet, make sure we didn't set off any alarms."

"Roger, LT," the man said, getting into position before slipping his battle computer onto his left arm.

I should probably point out that I am not the most patient man, not even just a little. My palms were getting sweaty inside the tactical gloves, and I was getting those damn itchy, crawly feelings up the back of my neck again.

"Hey, Boss," I whispered into my tactical comms.

"What is it, Prowler?"

"Just my spidey-sense, Hinge. Something doesn't feel right," I answered. All RDT jump squads were given various cocktails. Some to fight off infection and fatigue, others to make us hyper-aware, improve eyesight. And some guys, like me, well, we occasionally picked up on shit a few heartbeats before everyone else. Hinge and I had been together for five full rotations, and beyond that, he was my best friend, so yeah, he didn't dismiss my feelings. Sure, it could be nerves or paranoia, but we were fucking space monkeys. We didn't get nerves.

"Everyone, Prowler has an itch. You know what that means. Watch your flanks, people!" Hinge called out.

"Hey, Sarge, your old man ever get the bad JuJu out in the field?" Bayou asked from twenty yards away.

I saw her scanning with a precision that was nearly unmatched among operators at any level.

"Shit, Bones never felt nothing, he gave other people nightmares, didn't he, Dog?"

"Cut the chatter, Ramirez!" the lieutenant called out. "Head in the game..."

The man's words were drowned out by a massive explosion in the jungle off to my left. I knew Bond and Robot would have that, so I swept my weapon in the opposite direction, mirroring my partner as we looked for targets. My finger moved instinctively to the trigger, and my heart skipped when I saw the creatures hunting us.

Lieutenant Debra 'Bayou' Riggs is a shooter, one of the absolute best, trained by none other than the absolutely, freakishly perfect legend of a sniper named Pearson West. Still, she was the number two trigger-puller in our squad. Second to a man who is the personification of deadly from a distance. Darko was locked in and methodically put lead down range on target again and again. On my HUD, I saw both shooters lighting up separate targets coming out of the mouth of a cave we hadn't even seen until then.

"What in the holy..." The only intelligible words that came to mind.

They were dark-skinned, vaguely humanoid, but had grotesquely misshapen heads. The body's upper torso was massive with sharp ridges of bones that do not occur naturally in most humans I've met. Their arms were similarly oversized, ropey muscles cording along each forearm, ending in a fist carrying a double-headed ax. The metal weapon was covered with intricate engravings that looked less tribal than maybe

Celtic. Stupid to be thinking about the warrior monster's artwork, but I'm easily distracted. Just one of the many fine traits that make me special.

"Shit, Boss, this is a genomics lab," Halo said as one of four snipers put two into the closest beast man on his right. Part of the skull exploded, but the thing simply sagged to one knee and never let go of the weapon. The other one came toward me with a speed that would have seemed impossible for anything that large. One of the thick arms lashed out as a fist caught the side of my helmet before I even got the Rattler raised to fire. An instant later, a massive arm was wrapped tightly around my chest.

"Shift left, Prowler!"

I heard Bayou's voice, but my mind couldn't have distinguished left from the color purple at that moment. I felt rather than saw a round hit the beast in the chest and—it bounced off. Yeah...it bounced off. Admittedly, she was using the rail gun, not the pulse rifle, but the sheer kinetic energy of one of those rounds is incomprehensibly high. It should have left a bloody trail of creature; instead, the damn thing had me in a one-handed death grip. My suit systems were beginning to fail. Warnings were going off all over, the million-dollar battle armor seconds away from being scrap parts. I could feel the thing's chest was indeed rock-hard, but the abdomen moved in and out when it flexed or moved.

"Coming in!" Hinge said.

The creature still had me immobilized. I did everything I could to free just one of my arms. I felt an impact that was so close I first thought the round had hit me. Blood spattered across my visor. Another head-shot on the beast from one of my team. It flared back, and with my newly freed hand I grabbed for my fixed blade knife. I was okay with a gun but brutally wicked with the German made vibrasonic blade. The only problem was my angle was bad. My own body was shielding me from hitting anything truly vital. Still, I stabbed, then slashed, trying to gut the creature. I felt a flinch, but the death grip didn't loosen.

"Need help, Prowler?"

I heard Robot ask. "Nah...I'm goo..." Pretty sure I briefly passed out then.

Hinge stuck the Rattler under the chin of the boney beast and unleashed a plasma burst that seared off the front half of the face. I was released instantly. My CO looked at me as I struggled to breathe for the first time in what seemed like weeks.

"Clear!" one of the others yelled.

The lieutenant offered me a hand up, then abruptly let me go as soon as he had my weight in his grip. He laughed and walked off.

"Asshole!" I yelled at his retreating form.

"Saved your life... again."

"Did not," I replied, knowing full well he had.

"Boss, why did Command not bother to tell us this was another one of those damn bio labs?"

Seemed like every other mission was getting to be something like this. Gene editing had been around for half a century, but these bootleg labs were now beginning to make designer monsters. Some had no human DNA in them. They were supposedly based on a synthetic DNA; the lab geeks were calling it XNA.

"Command tells you only what you need to know, which is where to fight, where to shit, and where to sleep," Hinge added, staring at the open mouth of an enormous cavern.

"That's just wrong, man," Bayou said, using the toe of her boot to roll the remains of the creature's head back and forth.

"See anything else hiding in the dark, Boss?" I asked, moving up in a covering position while I tried to catch my breath and regain a fraction of my combat effectiveness.

He shook his head but was uncharacteristically quiet.

Pulling back out of the cave, he held a hand to his temple, a reflexive but totally unnecessary sign he was talking to someone on a private channel. More shit from RDT Command, I was sure. The polarizing tint on his visor hid his mouth. Otherwise, I could have seen the level of shit he was probably giving them. This was supposed to have been a 'cake-walk' – right?

"Some days, I wish you were still the one in charge, Prowler," he said, looking at me with a grin.

We both knew that wasn't true. Hinge was a natural leader and a brilliant soldier. I had jumped rank on him, more than once actually, but my extracurricular activities kept me dropping those same ranks faster than picking them back up. I had a habit of being reckless and not following orders I disagreed with. A fact that I cared little about but infuriated my father to no end, I might add.

"Careful, you know who is watching."

"You're up, Bayou."

Riggs hit me on the shoulder as she passed. I fell in, rifle up, sweeping the opposite side of the corridor. Hinge moved up on our six.

This part of the mission we were ready for. Hell, we were the best at. Banshee was always tops in the RDT mission reports. Tops on kills, tops on intel recovered, and tops on fewest casualties. Space Force doesn't give out medals for just showing up... well, that's not true. Some of the fleet officers get the shiny bits for doing nothing, but the Drop Team is the toughest job in the service and the one with the shortest life span.

At one point back in World War Two, tail gunners in bombers supposedly had less than a one in four chance of getting home. RDT teams weren't all that far behind that, mainly because in the early days we tended to have 100% losses. These days it was better, but we still took our licks. Condo was our last guy to buy it, his pod augured in a hundred miles from the target LZ back in December. Before that... let me see. Oh yeah, the Danger Twins both got caught in the same explosion when they unknowingly tripped a proximity mine while rescuing some civilian hostages in Mexico City.

Banshee had been basically the same guys for almost a full three-month rotation. This was the last drop for this cycle, and some guys always thought that was bad luck. I put little stock in luck. I trusted my blade, my armor, and my Glisson Mark IV Rattler.

Suddenly, without warning, another of those fucking beasts came charging at us. Bayou lit him up with a steady stream of impactor rounds, but I'd already seen how ineffective those were up close. I switched to something that would raise the gore level appreciably.

The twin plasma flechette rounds punched out and through the angry creature. The next two cleaved part of the head from the neck. It still ran for a half dozen more steps before wobbling then crashing down to the dirt.

"Carnage rounds, really?" Hinge asked as he bent to examine the thing.

I caught motion as two more of the things entered from the far side. Bayou was already engaging. I turned back briefly to check on the others and saw the animal I'd just downed twitch.

Then one of the incoming monsters' arms flailed wildly, hitting Hinge full force on the chest plate. He flew backward, impacting a rock wall with a thud that reverberated through me. His broken body sagged to the ground. Rollo 'Hinge' Hanson's health symbol on my visor went from green to red, then black.

Something hit me from behind at nearly the same instant. I knew it was one of the other beasts.

"Bond!" I weakly yelled for Highsmith. "Check him!" I was down on my knees, my vision tunneling toward darkness, but I could see my friend's face. He was gone. I knew it. Couldn't accept it, but I knew it. *Fuck this*, I thought. *Nothing is worth all this crap.* I brought my knife out and into the chest of the thing that had just attacked me. Arterial blood sprayed everywhere. The thing fell on top of me. My armor registered 583 pounds of dead weight. *Shit, Hinge... Rollo was gone.* The thought jarred me from what I should have been doing. "Fuck this!"

"Up, Prowler," Bayou said. "You're in command now."

She was cold and professional. Two things I loved about her until that moment. She was right, though, our CO being KIA was not our mission. "Fuck! Okay, on me."

"He's gone, Prowler," I heard Highsmith say.

CHAPTER
TWO

Bayou was the second highest ranking member of Banshee, but Drop Teams like Banshee tended to ignore things like that when it came to actual mission command. They wanted whoever could get the job done. I had traveled the rank ladder up almost to captain but was on my way back down, lazily enjoying the double chevrons of a Master Sergeant.

Rollo was gone. Whatever these things were down here had killed him. I wanted the person who had spawned these evil bastards into existence. Now that I was the commanding officer, the mission objectives automatically uploaded into my HUD. I scanned them, stopping on the fourth objective.

"No fucking way!" I said.

"What's that, Prowler?"

"Nothing, Bayou. Fall in on our six, leave the Dark Man to look for monsters." She was always my number two on missions I led. I trusted her fully whether or not I liked her right now. Still, I couldn't tell her what I'd just read.

The lab was laid out in very well constructed separate rooms all branching off the main tunnel. We'd raided several genomic workshops over the years. The Third Gulf War had been the beginning, not the end, of the freak research being done by back-alley labs and superpowers alike. Genetic research was now the single biggest line-item expense on half of the developing nations' budgets. Some of these were noble pursuits in that they only wanted to make something better and hopefully profit from it. Like a facility in western Canada that had created a cold and drought resistant wheat. Others, such as one Banshee had seized in India, were editing the human genome. They were in the business of making copycat humans. By purchasing stolen DNA samples, they created a line of women to look exactly like celebrities from years past. They did this by a specialized gene therapy done on very young girls. The epigenetic changes were hard to regulate and apparently quite painful. Many of the girls died in the process or went insane. A few who survived to sexual maturity were then deployed to seduce and entrap rich or powerful men and women.

These genetic code slicers were some of the worst of humanity. While I disliked my job, putting these assholes away had always been satisfying, and today would be even more so.... except for that fourth objective. **4. Secure the lab and key personnel, and keep scientific research intact at all costs. Do not question but hold for HVT exfil.** *Hammer teams...fuck!*

High-value targets for Hammer Industries. We were not working for those guys. Not on my watch. I saw a red notice flash into my visor and brushed it away with a gesture. I didn't give a shit what the TOC had to say on the matter. "It's payback time, bitches!"

I tossed a frag grenade into every room we passed. In the final lab, a room easily 100 yards long, was row after row of clear polyglass tanks, all filled with a greenish yellow liquid. My HUD kept flashing red, but identified the liquid as a growth medium, and as I got near, I could see the shadowy figures inside. Shit... these weren't more of the bony Neanderthals we'd been fighting. Not yet, anyway. They weren't using young girls like the lab in India. No... that would have been too predictable, too acceptable now. Nope... these assholes were using babies. They were turning human babies into freaks.

I moved up beside one tank, Robot close behind. I motioned Bayou and Halo to the other side. The baby in the tank rolled over and stared at me. I couldn't look away. The mangled face had off cheekbones and a brow ridge that was already grotesquely enlarged, but the eyes and face were still that of a child.

"Prowler, this is Command. Secure the lab and stand down."

I'd fucking secured it. *Yeah*... Command was thousands of miles away, but they monitored every away mission. They would know about Hinge, they would have seen all of this. They would have seen my trail of destruction getting to this central lab. I was going to have some 'splaining' to do.

A man stepped out, his hands raised.

"Are you in charge?"

He nodded, a smile creeping across his dark face. "I am doct..."

My gun fired without me pulling the trigger. No, that wouldn't work. His head just fell off all by itself. *Nah*, that was no good either. Shit, I had no good reasons for why I had just killed the man. Then I looked around at the hundreds of fish tanks full of hybrid children, and I no longer cared about objective four, the military, or the scientist, or my career. Dad was going to have a shit.

The explosions started along the back wall and raced toward us. "Clear, clear, clear!" I yelled. The bastard must have had some sort of dead man's switch. He was going to bargain his way out by promising not to destroy the place. I saw Bayou make it into the tunnel just as the explosions reached the row of tanks I was nearest to. I heard screams of children, babies. I saw parts of them flying by me. Blood mixed with the artificial amniotic fluid coated me and every surface. I was just going to make the exit, then I slipped on the wet floor just as the last two rows of tanks went up in a massive fireball. I felt something hit me in the stomach and part of my armor disintegrating under the force.

My last sight was of a steel rod and what my addled brain thought might be a baby's leg—both objects sticking out of my abdomen at odd angles. I felt hands grabbing the drag handles built into the shoulders of my battle suit, then my world went white and soundless.

CHAPTER
THREE

The morphine hit with the force of a hurricane. I felt movement then my mind was somewhere else entirely. This couldn't be death...it looked too much like junior high.

"Sit down and stop talking, Mister Kovach!"

Mister. How could she make something as polite as that sound so filled with venom and hatred?

She had been my eighth-grade teacher. Ms. Vanderhal. A onetime Teacher of the Year in Suffolk County, but that had washed away along with all her humor and humanity. The lesson had been to debate the merits of both sides of the discussion on using genetically modified food stocks in an attempt to alleviate world hunger. Beth Simpson had opposed it, saying God would take care of his faithful and nothing artificial could be condoned by any good Christian. They all knew she could have substituted good Republican instead and made the same argument. Both groups were still denying the climate change was in any way man-made.

I didn't care. I'd made my point loudly. "Do starving kids care about how the food they get was made?" That was back before the commercial food synthesizers, but still... it was such a stupid debate. If I'd only known five years later, my dad would be fighting a brutal war that broke out over those same topics. Most wars had been fought over things, stuff that one side had and the other wanted. Sometimes over purely ideological reasons, but even then, resources were a key factor. Just over sixty years into the 21st Century and the planet was ripe for a new kind of war. One fueled by corporate greed, government overreach, dwindling resources, and sheer panic as mass casualty events escalated worldwide. It started out with a dozen different names. The Okyuk uprising in southern Asia. The Basque independence fighters in Spain, The Crimea Liberation Occupation. Ten years later, they were collectively known as the PetroChem War or Gulf War 3. Eight years of the most constant global fighting since World War Two.

The reason was simple enough: the 'haves' like the U.S. and Western Europe had what the others wanted. No, not wanted...needed, with much of the formerly fertile agricultural regions quickly becoming drought-riddled, arid wastelands. Drought resistant grain crops became a staple. These could only be grown by using genetically modified seeds. Seeds that were patented to just a few companies. Those countries that couldn't afford the seed licenses, which were often ten times as much as the original, began to starve. At the same time, OPEC disbanded as the need for crude oil disappeared almost entirely. With most of the easy reserves pumped dry, no one could afford to go after the more difficult pockets of petroleum. Most of the developed world made the final moves away from fossil fuels, although too late to help the planet. The former oil capitals who had spent a century of wealth on personal excesses instead of anything more lasting, like education, research, and infrastructure, quickly saw their empires collapse. The Islamic world, which was directly tied to the billions brought in by the oil wells, fractured into more and more radicalized offshoots.

By 2047, clean water was nearly as scarce as food in three quarters of the globe. Yet the U.S., in its seemingly protected isolation, felt none of that. Americans existed in a bubble of presumed freedom, safety, and isolation. We watched the world burning from one skirmish after another with an abstract interest, like watching the World Cup after your team has been eliminated. *It had all come screeching up to our doorstep a few years after Ms. Vanderhal's history class,* I thought. *Man, had it ever.*

That was why we're now part of the Alliance. Supposedly a global alliance, but more accurately, it was what NATO had morphed into. It wasn't a bad organization, although it was fraught with infighting and distinctly unequal variations of equality. It also ignored vast swaths of the planet it deemed too unstable, too uncivilized, or too expensive to add. Like almost every instance of power in humanity's past, it was great if you were a 'have' and it sucked if you were a 'have not.' The countries that were in seemed to make sport of exploiting the lower tier states. That's why the TWC, or Third-World Coalition, came into being. They were a loose confederation of groups, some countries and some religious, some ideological zealots with a wide array of goals but one focused target: The Alliance Nations.

CHAPTER
FOUR
KOVACH

"That is the offer," the man said. No hint of any expression on his face.

This was no offer. Say yes to the enhancement or die. Sell my soul to the military industrial complex for as long as I am useful... or breathing. "And if I refuse?"

The older man offered a sad smile. "You will die, Mister Kovach. The trauma your body has endured may already be too much."

Dr. Reichert had pulled me back from the comatose state to offer me one chance. Not for redemption, but for life and the ability to serve once more. "Put me back under," I growled.

The man's head shook sideways, one time, very slowly. "That is not one of my options, Son. To be honest, if it wasn't for the legacy of your father, we likely wouldn't even be having this conversation. You disobeyed a direct order, your CO was killed. Invaluable intel was lost."

That fucking stung. I suppose it should have been obvious, but my damaged brain wasn't working optimally. "You can't prosecute a dead man, right?" Technically, I realized that wasn't actually correct, but... well... fuck it. I'm not at my best right now, ok?

The man had nervous hands; he was fiddling with a small black object, moving it from hand to hand. I didn't like nervous people; seemed to me they were usually hiding something, and this ass clown probably had all the secrets. I thought I recognized the logo on his ID badge.

"Master Sergeant, the choice is quite simple. Do you want to live?"

What they had described so far didn't sound like much of a life. They wanted to experiment on me. Not just keep me alive because, well, I knew I was a fucking mess. The blast had scrambled my insides, turned many of my internal organs to jelly. It had sloshed my brains around dangerously and apparently destroyed major parts of my nervous system and left at least one arm nearly useless. That, along with the burn damage, broken bones, and, well... I was barely alive, anyway. The tubes running in and out of my body and the numerous monitors were doing the actual living. I was just along for the ride. I was definitely going to sue the maker of my battle armor. Hammer Industries—yeah, they gave me a defective suit.

"We could patch you up enough to stand trial," the doctor said, stiffening as he glanced around the room. "Your court-material could be done by holoconference, and we could transfer you to Leavenworth after your conviction. Doubt you'd make it more than a month, but it's an option."

Not even an 'If convicted,' I mused. The man was quite confident, or more likely had already been told what the outcome would be. No one cared to even hear my side of the events. Hinge was gone, Banshee was being broken up. All of it had gone sideways when that fucking lab blew up, and yeah, some of it was my fault—okay, a lot of it. This was why I never held onto rank very long. I tried to remember what was below master sergeant... staff sergeant... no... technical sergeant. *Shit, that would be a pay-cut.* Of course, I'd never been busted more than one rank at a time, but this one seemed a bit more serious.

I was trapped... totally fucked, and we both knew it. My rage was beginning to take over and letting it loose here would only ensure the outcome. I thought again about Rollo. Seeing his face inside that dented tactical helmet. Hinge had given his life for that mission, and all I had done was dishonor him.

As if sensing my crumbling emotional state, the doctor leaned in almost conspiratorially. "Sergeant, listen... this will be a positive thing. You will be one of the most valuable assets in the military, your record will be wiped clean, and you might even get your pick of outposts around the globe. You will be one of the first to have this level of CAE."

Yeah... Combat Asset Enhancements. Nothing sounded ominous about that.

"RDT?" I asked.

The man nodded unconvincingly. "If you wish. In fact, the muscle and calcium blockers will mitigate the normal bone loss and subsequent decreases in muscle density that is normal for those assignments. You likely won't be limited to the normal ninety-day rotations."

"What about my team?"

Magnus Reichert looked even less certain. "Your team?" He checked his data tablet before looking up. "Banshee, right? Some have already been reassigned, but yes, I believe we can keep you with them. In order for them to stay in the same Drop Team rotation as you, they might also require some enhancements. Might be best if we keep that to just you for now, maybe concentrate on dirt side ops for the time being."

I let my head drop in defeat. That would keep me out of most of my team's missions. Shit, they had me; I had no outs. Rollo was gone. Ramirez had taken a round to the neck in a later mission and would likely never see active duty again. Besides, what did it matter? Not like I had a family waiting for me back home. Hell, I barely even had a home, a one-bedroom hunting cabin several hours outside D.C. Being a lab rat... no, a guinea pig for the Department of Defense was my only choice. Slowly, I nodded. "So, what will it involve?"

CHAPTER
FIVE

One of Doctor Reichert's technicians removed the IV and swabbed roughly at the small bead of blood left in its place. "Can I ask you something?" The man gave no response.

"What did you people just do to me?"

"I'd have to check your charts," he replied in a tone that lived somewhere between uncaring and *'You're a piece of shit lab experiment, and why the fuck do you keep talking to me?'*

To his credit, he flipped up the thin data tablet and swiped through several screens; then he ran a rather delicate finger down what must have been a considerable list. "Initial Regenerax bonding and your final Respirosites infusion."

I had no idea what any of that meant. And then he abruptly left. So, I stared down at a body and an arm that used to be all mine and now was clearly... not.

I shifted in the uncomfortable bed, trying to not so much find a more comfortable spot as to find one that was less like an enhanced interrogation technique. Every goddamn part of my body either ached, was on fire, or felt no sensations at all. And before you ask, yes... that included my junk. I knew it was still there, hell, I could see it lying their flopping out of my wispy hospital gown that still passes as clothing in a medical ward.

That reminds me, why in the name of all that is good and holy after all these years, do hospital gowns still offer nothing in the way of comfort or modesty? I needed a second person just to get in and out of mine. Jesus H. Christ on a bike. Okay, back to my penis. It... well, never mind, the thought escaped me as someone else approached. I could tell by the walk who it was.

"Doctor Mengele," I said with as much love and adoration as I could force into my voice.

"Not amusing, Joseph. We are trying to save your life," Reichert said in a tone like he was speaking to a small child.

It was somewhat amusing, *to me at least,* and no... they weren't trying to save my life. They had done that months ago. Now they were seeing just how far they could push a human body before it gave up and said 'Fuck it.' My junk had already done that, apparently. Gave me the proverbial middle finger and opted for the afterlife.

"I can't feel my dick," I said with zero amusing lilt to my voice and with as much sincerity as a line like that could be delivered with.

"Perhaps you should stop trying so much," the doctor said in his precise monotone. "At least until you are more healed."

Did Doctor Magnus Reichert just make a joke? I nearly fell out of the too-narrow bed. "Do you abuse all your patients this way?" I asked.

He smiled and removed his glasses and carefully slid them into the pocket of his lab coat. His other hand held the familiar black marble he always seemed to play with. "You're not my patient, Joseph. You are so very much more."

"What, are we friends now?" my voice literally dripping with sarcasm.

He sat on the edge of the bed and patted me lightly on my arm.

"My dear boy," he began, "you don't understand this, and I'm very sure we wore out any patience you might have had months ago, but yes, I do genuinely like you. I never told you this, but I met your father once."

Shit, who hadn't? Seemed like everyone even loosely connected to the military was aware of Colonel 'Bones' Kovach.

Doctor Reichert continued. "I know his legacy. He was a fine leader, but I must admit I found him to be a bit, how should I say this? one dimensional, singularly focused. I know military leaders have to be purpose driven individuals, but in his case, it seemed almost obsessive."

I had to admit, that wasn't off the mark, but I didn't need a doctorate to figure that out. Try having Sunday dinner with the man. "Where ya going with this, Doc?" They had made it pretty clear already that my dad, or his friends, had a part in me being in this bed instead of in a prison somewhere... or a box.

The doctor removed his hand that had been resting on my exposed arm. "It's just that, well, you are not like that at all."

"Not a good leader, not a good soldier?" I quipped.

"Oh, I don't know about all that. I am sure you are. Your record is filled with considerable accomplishments. What I mean is, your personality is not at all like your father's. You are intelligent, smart-assed, a bit more disrespectful than we expected, but also quite humorous at times. I genuinely like your wit and will miss you once this is over."

Dad could be funny, but generally only at the expense of others. He had a tongue that would slice you into jerky if you left him an opening. "So, I'm not a mindless drone?" I asked. "Wouldn't that have been better for your program?"

The older man stared off down the white corridor for a long time with a look that I can only describe as haunted expression. He took out a tissue and absently cleaned his glasses before responding. "When DARPA began looking into enhanced soldiers, Joseph, they did some abominable things. The human body is amazingly adaptable, it seems. They learned they could turn certain genes on or off with very striking results. I'm sure you remember the fiasco on the so-called cluster of warrior genes back in the late thirties."

I did recall that, not long after the war, a medical lab working with one of the big private military contractors created a serum that boosted the aggression and stamina of its fighters. The cocktail also raised testosterone and dopamine levels, so they fought with a ferocity that was downright scary. Problems occurred later when the PMCs were no longer in that role. Those genetic changes couldn't be reversed. Several of the operators committed murderous acts and were killed or imprisoned as a result. Many more killed themselves either by outright suicide or by engaging in such dangerous activities as to be nearly certain of their ultimate demise.

"You see, every physical advantage we can give you comes with a drawback. If we make you stronger, you will need to stop and eat more. If we make you impervious to pain, you may not realize how much damage you are taking. Even the artificial red blood cells we just added to your system can be a problem."

I looked down at my arm... my real one, comprehending what he had just said. "Artificial?"

"Yes, yes, the Respirosites. They are actually a class of nanorobot, a biological machine of sorts that is much more efficient at transporting oxygen to your body than regular old hemoglobin. Only a percentage of your normal blood cells were replaced, but these will give you many advantages. A significant increase in stamina, better ability at high altitude, or underwater. We estimate you can hold your breath for five or six minutes with no reduced mental functions. Still, too much reliance on them could have long-term consequences, and what remains of your body's own organs will not accept them. I'll have to keep you on a regimen of anti-rejection drugs as long as they are in your body."

"What?"

He patted me again in what I assumed was to be a reassuring gesture. "Not to worry, Sergeant. The dosing pack will be self-administered and only need to be refilled every few months." A chime sounded, and he stood up, unfolded his own tablet from a pocket, and retrieved his glasses again. He scanned something on the screen, nodding slightly. "Yes, very good. Looks like your vitals are settling back down."

I already knew the various sensors' telemetry went to the medical tablets, as there were no monitors nearby. "So, what was it about my dad?" I asked. The man's attention span seemed to have wandered, and strangely, I wanted to know where he'd been going with it.

"Oh yes, yes... my apologies. My point was we can make you a better soldier, but it is always a balancing act of improvement versus cost. Whatever you gain, there will ultimately be a price to pay physically. DARPA never cared about the long-term effects of their super-soldier project, and it doomed them. We have always been a bit more pragmatic —we aren't trying to create monsters, simply give an edge to our fighting force. It's something that has been done for years. Even those dammed Nazis you enjoy comparing me to tried it.

During World War II, they gave N-methylamphetamine and oxycodone to their soldiers like they were Skittles."

"They gave their soldiers meth?" I asked in genuine astonishment.

Yeah," he smiled. "They originally called it Pervitin. Later, they made it into pill form and called it D-IX. It contained five milligrams of cocaine, three of Pervitin, and a nice chunk of oxycodone."

"Holy shit... no wonder they fought so damn hard."

"Exactly, but that was only good for the immediate moment, and I'd have to say probably not even that. Soldiers that high on narcotics cannot be expected to make sound decisions. In battle, I maintain that is the most important enhancement of all."

"Intelligence?"

"Yes, and that is one area where we can help without any noticeable downside. A smarter soldier is a better soldier in every possible way. Despite everything we have done to you, and it is a lot, you will be more durable, faster, have more muscle mass, get sick less often, heal quicker. Still, we are shooting for only about an eighteen to twenty percent increase over an average soldier in purely physical abilities."

He moved the sheet back, uncovering one of my legs, and examined it for a minute.

"Now that alone," he continued, "is substantial. In some ways, you should leave here able to compete with Olympic athletes in several events—running, swimming, high jump. You could probably medal with no additional training, but you won't be superhuman, simply better." He tapped the leg and smiled. "If we can also get a fifteen percent improvement in cognitive abilities, then... then we really have a super-soldier. Thankfully for you, you already had an impressive intelligence level."

"So, not like my dad?"

He smiled. "The colonel was an amazing soldier, but 'are we doing this because you are his son?' I know that's the question you keep wondering about, isn't it? The answer is, absolutely not. At most, they may have brought you to my attention, but if you had not been such a good fit for the program parameters, I would have still turned you away."

The doctor moved up and shone a penlight into each of my eyes before tapping my skull much like he'd done to my legs.

"This, Joseph. This is why you are here."

"So, you're going to make me smarter?"

The man smiled and walked away, leaving me in even more confusion.

"What about my junk?"

CHAPTER
SIX

"Master Sergeant," the doctor began.

This one was new, sort of. I'd had a rotating crop of attendants over the past few weeks. Each of them seemingly concerned only with whatever their particular specialty was. This one... well, I hadn't quite figured out what she was a doctor of.

"We... I," she amended, "don't want to hear about the shit we are putting into your body. That crap is as old as the old Covid pandemic when people were too stupid to get the cure for fear it might be doing something unnatural or unsafe to them."

I nodded glumly; I'd heard my grandad say stuff about that time. He'd lost two uncles to the pandemic back in the twenties, as I recalled. I was just being obstinate and had refused all drugs for the last two days.

"Unnatural as in fighting off an alien invader that was intent on using you for a breeding ground before it killed you, then yeah, it was totally doing that," she added.

She took the data pad and looked at me. "Joe, how much do you weigh?" I knew she could check my charts, but she was obviously trying to make a point.

"Two hundred and five," I responded. She ran her finger across the electronic paper and did some quick calculations before turning the screen so I could read.

"Ninety-eight?"

"Yes, almost half of you is not human. In your case, ninety-eight pounds of alien material are taking refuge within your body. Get used to it. Much of you is simply not you."

The look of shock must have registered as her stoic expression began to soften into a smile. "Don't be alarmed, this is not because of anything we did. Honey, my body is smaller, but the proportions are the same. Just like every other person on Earth." She lay the pad aside. "We all want to believe we know what we're made of. We try to put good things in, but we are an ensemble, a symbiosis of other organic materials and living organisms. This includes bacteria, viruses, fungi, and archaea. The greatest concentration of this microscopic life is in the murky depths of our oxygen-deprived bowels."

"So, you're saying what you put in me is what... natural?"

"No, you idiot, I am saying the complete opposite. It was totally unnatural, but big effing deal—it was beneficial. Just like the other stuff that's already in there. It saved your life, Joe. In fact, it did much more than that."

The woman leaned in, her tone becoming more sympathetic. "Nearly all of your internal organs are either lab-grown or totally synthetic. You were a mess, Joe. Two decades ago, your chances of survival would have been zero. Now we have tools that can prolong, enhance, and in your case, rebuild the human body."

"But the nano meds, those..."

"They are machines, molecular machinery not that different from the organic cells and bacteria that occur naturally. You're also on an upgraded course of Regenerax which is a regimen of nanobiotics, but you don't seem troubled by that. Is one type of nano meds all that different from the other?"

I hadn't thought much about that. Artificial antibiotics had been around at least twenty years. Hell, I remember taking them as a kid when I got a sore throat.

"All this tech is designed to promote healing and keep your dumb ass alive. Some of it will make you more capable in the long run, and that's all the military teams care about, but there will be some trade-offs. I'm sure Magnus told you that you will have to keep taking the anti-rejection drugs for life. That's just the way it is. Otherwise, your body will literally start treating your new organs as foreign invaders. Your body will kill itself to be rid of them." She pulled me close and used her hand sensor on my back to listen to my heart and lungs. Satisfied, she let me lean back. "Joe, it's important you get how serious this is. Take the meds. They will keep you alive."

Reichert had indeed drummed it into me. I would have to take them every few months. He'd explained the consequences in horrifyingly gory detail. Fever, cranial swelling, intense pain as my organs begin to shutdown followed by the most extreme headaches resulting in diminished cognitive abilities, dementia, hallucinations. And just to make the party complete, alternating lower GI issues as my insides try to exit through my asshole. Okay, I mean, he used some fancier words, but that was what I heard.

"What if I'm on duty? Space borne soldiers don't have a drugstore right around the corner."

She smiled. "Make sure you take enough with you. The Space Force will not want to jeopardize anything happening to you, so that shouldn't be a problem, but you can't get this stuff at the local drugstore, anyway. It has to be custom made in one of our labs just for you, Mister Kovach."

So, I was part alien even before beginning this ridiculous journey. That didn't make me feel weird at all. I looked down at my left arm. I knew there was a lot of me that was no longer me. Knowing the military, I was sure there was lots more they weren't even bothering to tell me.

She stood to leave, and I noticed her stop and speak to another woman standing in shadow by the door. They whispered in hushed tones, and just from the other woman's silhouette, I knew I wanted to see more. I was mentally trying to move her into the room. Hey, I was bored. I'd laid in these damn hospital beds for months. I pulled back the sheet to see if any other body part had taken notice of the shadowy vixen... it had not.

CHAPTER
SEVEN

Honestly, I couldn't keep track of everything they were doing. The surgical procedures, treatments, and tests all began to blur. At some point I ran a fever, and oddly, they seemed to think this was a good thing. "So, can I get some aspirin or something?"

The pretty and petite med tech shook her head. "Sorry, Joe, elevated core temp is one of the enhancements."

"Why? You mean I'm going to stay like this?"

She offered a sad smile. I liked this one. She had been friendly at least and, as far as I could tell, completely honest with me. "Kirsten," I pleaded, "can you get Doctor Reichert? This can't be normal." She was taking my pulse; the touch of her skin was awakening parts of me I had feared were completely dead. *Okay, maybe a fever wasn't all bad.*

"Do you feel bad? Are you in pain?" she asked.

Truthfully, I didn't. "Just chills." She made some notes on the screen.

"Expected, you may prefer warmer settings in the future, dress in layers. Once you begin retraining, you will also notice spikes in your temperature. This is all expected, Master Sergeant."

Damn...I liked it better when she called me Joe.

"Part of that is simply the denser muscle mass and cellular boost the treatments have made. Some of it is due to a metabolism shift in your body. One advantage to this is you will probably never get sick."

"How is that?" I asked, now intrigued. She pursed her lips in a way I found incredibly alluring, although that could be mostly because I had been in these med wards for months already. A white room 32 feet by 18 feet, confined mainly to a bed that was smaller than the one I had in basic training.

"Fever is normally the body's natural way of fighting off infections. The fever is not the problem, although persistent or very high ones can do harm. We've improved your body's systems to withstand the additional stress, though."

"So, if I always have a fever, infection can't take root?"

"You remember hearing how bats supposedly caused Covid back in the twenties and a new version of SARS in forty-two?" she continued without answering me. "Bats are mammals but are also notorious reservoirs of all kinds of viruses, many of which are zoonotic, meaning they can transfer to other animals, including humans. For years, researchers couldn't figure out how bats managed to not get sick themselves. They do have a difference in their immune system, but what they found was the bats' metabolism works at a much higher level. This is probably an adaptation that helped them master flight. Higher metabolism means higher core temperatures, and the infections just can't take hold."

"So what? You gave me bat DNA?" She laughed; it was a kind of adorably sexy laugh. The sheet was tent poling around my waist. *Not now, you freakin' idiot,* I thought, glancing down. She followed my eyes down and smiled more and... *was that a blush?*

"No bat DNA. You won't be needing to feast on human blood or anything. Just a slight temperature elevation. You will probably need to eat more often to maintain your weight, and your life expectancy might be slightly reduced, but otherwise, nothing to worry about."

She left me alone with my thoughts again. They were not happy thoughts; I was going stir-crazy in here. Magnus had been around less and less; I had no access to any news from the outside. Now I was being transformed, enhanced mostly against my will, but I had to admit some of it sounded pretty cool. A chill raced through my body as I pulled the blanket up.

~

The next few weeks blended together in my head as a host of unfamiliar faces seemed to come and go. My body ached; my bones ached. At one point, my voice stopped working, and my vision began going in and out. Coming out of anesthesia on the very familiar operating room table, it surprised me to see Doctor Reichert himself. He pulled down his mask, and it shocked me to see how bad he looked. Not just tired, but exhausted. His skin was an unnatural shade of gray, the color of walls in a funeral home. His cheeks were sunken, and his eyes were ringed by dark circles.

"Shit, Doc, you look worse than me."

The man smiled, but it didn't reach his eyes. He just seemed devoid of life.

"Joe, you'll be glad to know we are finishing up with this phase."

He sounded muffled until I turned my head to the other side.

"Whoa, careful there," he said, reaching down to my face. "That side of your head is heavily bandaged. "

I reached up and touched it. Just one side of my cheek and ear were covered. "What was this one?"

He looked contemplative but shook his head. "I can't tell you, and... you won't want to know."

"Is it a bomb? Did you put a bomb in my head like with Snake Plissken?" I knew it was an old reference to a long-lost movie, but hey, it was what came to mind. Besides, my dad made us watch tons of the classics, especially the stupid 2D action movies. Shit, he would walk around quoting those awful cheesy lines for weeks afterward.

"No bomb, and no, you don't have to escape from New York... and I think that was on his wrist," the doctor said, impressing me with his ancient cinematic knowledge and his humor despite his withering appearance.

"Doc, no offense, but you look like you need some of my treatments. You sure you're up for doing surgery and shit?"

Magnus gave a nod to the others, who discreetly left the operating room. "Mister Kovach, you understand, I'm sure, how compartmentalized things are here. It's government and all."

I nodded.

"Well, things are changing, getting worse out there. They want more assets... and yes, before you ask, yes, like you, but we have other defense projects we are working on as well. Not just here. I am sure I am one of dozens, maybe hundreds scattered around the Alliance countries."

I thought I knew where this was heading. "You need to deliver the goods... is that it?"

The man's drawn face nodded slowly. "About the gist of it, my boy. They need you and the rest of our goodies. We are going to have to speed up the next few steps, then kick you out. I'm sure you will miss seeing my pretty face, but we'll be checking in with you."

I nodded, my acceptance of my fate long a non-issue. "So, what else is left? I mean, to do here?"

"Something... unpleasant, I'm afraid."

Shhhhiiiitttt... he was not kidding. The next fourteen days was a constant intravenous infusion followed by long sessions in a modified MRI machine followed by hyperbaric chamber sessions.

"The carbon graphene mesh is bonding with your bones to strengthen your skeletal frame by a factor of five," the rehab tech said as he worked my aching legs. My body trembled. It hurt so much. Not the white-hot agony of a knife wound or gunshot, more the constant pulling apart of every bone in my body at the same time. Even my cheeks hurt. I felt like my head was being wrapped with bands of metal and a demonic blacksmith was hammering each one into place. I'd been through hell up to this point, but this was the worst month of my entire life by far.

Finally, they left me alone and let me sleep, and man, did I ever sleep. I came slightly awake when someone was replacing an IV bag, another time when I saw an orderly changing my bed. I knew from the smell I'd shit myself. I had zero fucks left to give. I should have chosen to die back on that first day. I don't know how long I was in that state or what else they may have done to me while I was out of it. I prayed to not wake up again because the pain never stopped, it never gave up. It was relentless and being sentenced to eternal hell could not have felt any worse. My body was on fire, my head an explosion of suffering, and my will to go on was gone.

Later... much later, I was wheeled down a long corridor and into an elevator. People had come out of offices to wave to me. Apparently, I was leaving. Reichert had said this phase was ending...*what comes next?*

CHAPTER
EIGHT

I discovered, after a long hover copter ride in a blackout cabin, and yes, if you want to know the full joy of what motion induced nausea can feel like, by all means, please do just that. Anyway... I then discovered, much to my horror, that the last of the scheduled Joe Kovach upgrades was less intrusive, yet somehow even more disturbing.

"Look Dude," the kid said, invoking visions of him with a skateboard and weed stick. "Like, hey... it's not up to me, man. Shit, I wouldn't do it, but you know it's cool and all."

I looked up and yelled loudly, "Can someone find me an adult... someone who speaks English!"

The kid with the surfer boy's speech tried to make eye contact, but totally failed. "Yeah, like they aren't, um... coming. It's just me. They don't have like the clearance and stuff. There was another girl, she used to be here. Cute, Asian, kinda militant look, you know? She helped design and code a lot of this stuff, but like, she bailed. Off the grid and shit. You know, with the politico shit going on and all."

I, of course, had no idea what he was talking about, having lived in a fucking hospital bed for most of a year now. "You're the most qualified person they have?" I asked with as much respect as the situation seemed to demand... which, if you are keeping score, was precisely NONE!

"Oh yeah, Dude, like I have degrees and shit, you know—did my time."

"Okay, Doctor Hotshot, what have you got for me?"

He beamed and unclasped the latch on a silver hardcase he'd been holding. The case was just foam padding with one small object in a cutout placed neatly in the center of the padding. He gently pried it free and held it up for me to inspect. I was clueless about what it was and clearly less impressed than the kid was hoping. It was an item about as thick as an old-style credit card but only a fraction as long or wide.

"Do I even want to know?"

"This is the coolest thing ever, Joe," Surfer Doc said smugly.

So now I had gone from being Dude to first-name basis with this Mister Nerdnick 9000.

"And where does that go?"

"In your anus," the kid said, trying to stifle a laugh.

"You know I can kill you even without my enhancements."

"Sor, I mean, no...no, sir. It actually adheres to the base of your neck... maybe just a bit farther down." As he bent behind me to study his subject closer, I felt his fingers mapping out the vertebrae of my spine.

"Just sticks onto my skin? That doesn't sound like you people. Ya'll like surgical implanting stuff. In my ass would actually not have surprised me."

"Well, it sticks rather permanently," the kid said in a tone of genuine apology. "The adhesive, if you want to think of it as that, is new. It bonds at a near subatomic level to be like... you know, totally accurate. The contents of the neural card will imbed in your skin over time, and the filaments are self-routing. Most of it is wireless, though."

"What the fuck is it?"

"Oh, brain stimulator, comms array, and data retrieval and storage."

"It's a computer?" I asked.

"No." He suddenly looked more uncomfortable. "Joe, you're the computer. Your brain, I mean. You have been on a cocktail of neural enhancers as well as the transcranial electrical stimulation therapies. You also have the uploaded comms block from our Biological Technologies lab. This little beauty just ties it all together and allows us to go live, ya know?"

"I'm the computer. Did you happen to see my ASVAB scores, Son? My father actually cried when he saw them they were so bad."

"Yeah," he snorted. "So, I suck at tests, too. Like this one time in grad school..."

I snapped my fingers in front of him. "Focus, Lawnmower Man."

"Oh, um... yeah. Okay, well, you are getting smarter, but that stuff is just taking effect. I believe Doc Mags may have even done some epigenetic changes, but you won't be like genius level IQ or anything... at least probably not. More like, you know, it's specialized knowledge battle tactics, survival skills, and shit."

This kid was about to realize the human version of a hard drive crash. My fist kept clenching and unclenching with every sloppily assembled sentence he spoke. The trigger was if he started another sentence with 'so.' I quickly decided that was my kill command. My father was an absentee for most of my formative years, but he made damn sure we knew how to fucking speak the English language to someone. "Scuse me, Chuckles, any chance there is a grown-up around I could speak to? Someone who hasn't been hitting the meth pipe?"

"Huh?" Captain Oblivious said before continuing, "Oh, hey, like nah, man... sorry, no, not anymore anyway—right?" He chuckled nervously. "Anyway, soon as this is synched up, you'll understand better."

The surfer dude, doper doctor kid, moved again to my back, pulled down my hospital gown, and did something between my shoulder blades. I felt a coldness, then a sensation of intense burning, but within ten or fifteen seconds it was gone.

"So, what? I can pay my bills through this, surf the internet, play Halo X?"

"Nah," the kid said. "Well, maybe. I mean, it does have some games loaded, and yeah, you could probably play the online versions."

"So, my brain is going to be on the Internet?" *Shit, now I was starting sentences with so! Sorry, Dad.*

"Nah, just the root bios. But in time, you'll figure out how to access it."

"Which one?" He knew what I meant; the Internet had evolved over the years. The original web now came in multiple flavors. Most adults like myself only accessed via the Blue line. It was more restrictive, actively policed for trolls, viruses, spammers, and such. You could only access it via a verified address that was as personal to you as the old social security number. While you could assume any public persona you liked, if you crossed the line, did something wrong, you would be fined or worse. The internet provider could and would immediately tell the governing body who was responsible where you were and withdraw the fines from your digital wallet. Therefore, behavior, while still anonymous, was much better than it once was. Anonymity no longer equaled unaccountability.

"Oh, like for sure. Like we have it programmed for Blue. You can add your personal IP address at boot-up. Ya know, in truth, the core level AI can access all of them, even the old www or dark web if you needed it to. Built-in standard and Milcrypt text and SatCell comms of course. Battery should last indefinitely; it literally draws power from..."

I cut him off. I had seen the old Matrix movies. More of my dad's favorites. "That's okay, I got it. I'm a human battery."

Wearable computers had been around for decades, and personal AIs had been a growing fad, but this was neither. It was more. Still, I couldn't sense anything.

"How do I turn it on?"

Surfer Doc was scrolling through his tablet, humming some inane pop tune at the same time. "Huh? Oh, yeah... it's on, Dude. So, you see, right now, it's just synching up and installing hot patches, you know? Like to some bugs we found." He quickly punched something on the screen. "And the interface is like pretty intuitive and stuff—you'll know when you see it."

He should have said 'hear it.'

"Hello, Joseph."

A light tone had preceded the unbelievably sexy voice. Still, it scared the piss out of me. Then I realized I had not actually heard it, not aloud anyway.

"Hello," I replied.

"Oh, so you don't have to speak aloud, the system is tied into your speech, auditory, and optic nerves, so you can say it mentally or just think it. It will take a while to integrate fully, but within, say, forty-eight hours, it should be fully functional."

"Then this thing is running wires throughout my brain?"

The computer AI answered, "Not at all, Sergeant Kovach. We use synthetic nerve bundles to tap into your existing systems as needed. These are biologically indistinguishable from your body's own network of arteries, neural, and nerve pathways."

I knew exotic biotechnologies had come a long way, but this was an off-the-charts level of tech.

"Pretty amazing stuff, huh?" Surfer Doc said.

I had no answer for that. My body was clearly not my own, and I was feeling more tricked out than the latest Ford pickup and a lot less useful. "Does it... she have a name?"

"I can be programed with one," she answered. "Whatever name you prefer."

Surfer Doc smiled, apparently reading her response from the tablet screen as well. "Yeah, they have an evolving personality code that adapts to the user. We typically leave them blank for installs as some people prefer to just think of them as a tool, like a PC or Smartcomm, you know?"

I nodded. "But even those had AI interfaces. Hell, Siri, Alexa, Doris, and Prime have been around for decades. Let's go with Ada."

"Ah, your third-grade teacher," Surfer Dude said, looking at his tablet. "Damn, she was a looker, Dude. Little Kovach was a playa."

"Fuck me, kid. How much info do you have on me?"

"Sorry, Joe, I actually revealed that," Ada said. Your memory centers lit up with that name and history, which I then cross-referenced with your old school records.

Shit... I thought. *This is going to be...*

"Fun?" Ada said in a tone that was somehow both upbeat and foreboding.

CHAPTER
NINE

I was still at what they referred to as Delta Site a week later. Seven days and the only other live person I had spoken with was Surfer Doc, whom I eventually learned was named Jace. And, of course, he would be. And where was Delta Site, you might ask? I have no freakin' clue; the government, military whatever, loves their little secrets.

I was still getting accustomed to Ada, and although as odd as hell as it was the first few days, it was amazing how quickly I got used to having her there. "Ada, can you show me a tactical terrain map of the area?" I asked again, in a slightly different way, just to see if she could slip past the handler's firewall.

"I can give you an example terrain map of any coordinates you select. I am not privy to your precise location."

"But you are here with me?"

"Not exactly, you are a single remote node. I am a distributed network AI. My presence, or virtual consciousness, resides on many servers and network connections. Due to security concerns, I, of course, cannot offer anyone maps of those geographical coordinates either."

The system was smart, and through some trial and error, I found I could actually see the records she often pulled up. The image simply appeared in my field of view, like a floating window.

One I had her search for was the obituary for Hinge. He and I were closer than brothers; I should have been there to say goodbye. The fire at the terrorist lab was so intense they hadn't even been able to tell his remains from any others. The obit post was disappointing, as there were less than a dozen comments on it. Such was the fate of Tier-1 operators, it seemed. No one cares for us; we are nameless and meaningless other than for the brutal tasks we are called to perform.

"Ada, do you know what else they're going to do to me?"

"Yes, Sergeant, I am fully briefed on your enhancement schedule. Would you like me to summarize?"

"I would," I began, then amended, "just let me know what's next." I found out early on her summaries could sometimes take hours.

"You are entering the final stage. Next, you will be transported to a combat simulation center for advanced war-fighting, tactic, weapons, and hand-to-hand. You will also undergo a rigorous PT regimen, all designed to get your enhanced musculature, skeletal, and mental facilities working together at an optimum level. After that, you will undergo RDT requals."

"Shit, requalification." I hadn't even considered that. No way Space Force would let me back on a Tier-1 team without it, though. The thought of going through hell week again nearly made me cry.

Ada's itinerary had seemed very clean and orderly. The reality turned out to be anything but. The next twelve weeks were spent in a muddy section of what I thought was North Carolina designed to make Army and SF Rangers puke their guts out. I spent four hours running drills with the more advanced special operations teams, then another five or more working with an individual specialist. Each of these guys focused on a separate area of my retraining. As a former ground-pounding Ranger, I had gotten all the basics down at Fort Benning. Advanced navigation, fast rope, lifesaving, defensive driving, demolition, jump training, and, of course, marksmanship. Mostly what I learned down there was how to do all that when I was suffering from blind exhaustion, extreme hunger, and the certainty that the commanders were trying to see which soldier they could kill first.

The training I was in now made 61 days and the final hell week of my first Ranger tab look like kindergarten playground shit in comparison. My personal demon from the underworld was Captain Lacy Johnson from Arlington, Texas. She was not enhanced, yet she routinely made me look like a fucking cripple when she showed me the 'proper' way to do whatever it was I was struggling with. From field stripping a Glisson 442, to setting up snares, to catching small game, she was better, faster, quieter, and unquestionably the better soldier. That was disappointing to me as I still had the same rating as I did back on Banshee. She knew I was technically Tier-1; she made sure I knew she had zero fucks to give on that point. I was a miserable disappointment to the Army, the Alliance, and probably the entire human race. I had been a massive waste of money, and she would be thrilled if she never laid eyes on me again.

"I think she's getting a crush on me," I confessed to Ada at one point.

"Oh, and why is that, Sergeant?"

"When I fell out of that tree earlier, she didn't make me get up before she made me do the push-ups."

"Yes, her concern is... touching," Ada said with very artificial sarcasm.

I've had martial arts training since I was a kid. None of the entertainment style stuff. My dad wouldn't hear of that shit. "Training you on how to punch without making contact is fucking useless," he'd said. "Might as well be learning to dance the ballet." Not that he had anything against ballet. I also had three years of dance. Don't ask, it was a weird time.

No matter where we were stationed, he'd find someone to 'train me,' a.k.a. beat the shit out of me for money several hours a week. Usually, it was an old drill instructor who would know some tactical karate or kickboxing. I'd spent two years on a base in Thailand getting the shit beat out of me in an underground Muay Thai gym by a man who was barely four feet tall. That angry little ball of human misery made my teen years miserable. What I was going through now put all that to shame. More on the Dragon Lady in a second.

I get it. Much of the training was simply to improve reflexes, muscle memory, and hand-eye coordination. "Get that super brain working in harmony with those super new muscles. The battle is won or lost in your head first."

I'd been in a lot of battles and that was rarely true, but these new instructors were all good. Combat martial arts bear little resemblance to the artistic styles in movies or sporting tournaments. It is ugly, brutal, and efficient. There is no basis of sportsmanship; its sole mission is to use the human body and anything within reach to kill or disable your opponents. To graduate the course, all I had to do was render my instructor for that level unconscious. Easy peasy—right? I was a bad ass drop soldier before, and now I was an augmented and enhanced super soldier version of the original.

It took me three weeks to even land a punch on my first instructor. She was a young, Asian girl probably barely in her twenties. Dragon Lady, as I called her, was on permanent reassignment from hell. I'm not sure which level... had to be six... maybe seven. Wherever the senior demons like to hang out. The Dragon Lady seemed to know every way to attack me that I could not defend. She made me look like a helpless feeb.

There are points in a man's life, correction—a soldier's life, where you just want to chuck it all. Take your DD214 and ring the bell or shit, just hit the road. Of course, a dishonorable discharge can follow you around worse than a listing on the sexual predator website. Still, Ms. Quan, aka Dragon Lady, taught me suffering, humility, and pain on exquisite levels of agony that even the late Stephen King would have been challenged to describe. At the end of one unusually humiliating session, I begged for the paperwork. "Just let me sign."

"This is only day two. Not even breakfast yet," she so rudely pointed out. Then she proceeded to kick my ass for five more hours.

So, leaving wasn't an option. Apparently, the investment in an Enhanced War Fighter was on par with that of a small hypersonic fighter jet. I'd now been out of the game for thirteen months and was beginning to wonder if I had any real value to anyone. Then my dad called.

No, not through my phone. He dialed straight through to my surgically implanted comms headset.

"Greetings, Cowboy!"

"Pops? How did you..."

He cut me off, as usual. My father had two default settings: pissed-off or asleep. Today he was awake, so I braced myself.

"You enjoying yourself over there at summer camp?"

I knew better than to even ask how he knew something as classified as this had to be.

"It's not..." I started, then thought better of it.

"Remedial Ranger School, right? Do they put mints on your pillow every night or just when you request the turn-down service?"

I looked at my battered arms and hands; scrapes covered almost every inch of skin. Blood mixed with mud filled every cut. Dark bruises ran up both arms like a human Rorschach drawing. "Yeah, Pops, having a blast. Heading to the sauna next, so can we make this fast?"

"Ha! Sauna!" It sounded like he covered the phone while he said it.

"Who else is there?" I asked.

"Huh? Oh, no one. Just thought I would check in on you. Things are kind of circling the toilet out here. Not sure you are getting any news and all, but world's getting a damn site bleaker these days. Terrorist attacks, hackers targeting... well, everything. It's nuts."

I could sense another one of the 'Back in my days' speeches coming on.

"So, how are you doing?" I asked, tactically cutting him off from the diatribe he was undoubtedly gearing up for.

"Oh. Well, shit, Son, we are doing great. Me and your mom found Jesus and the dog is shitting gold bars. Seriously, couldn't be better."

I'm sure my face was screwed into a complete mask of unadulterated confusion. Listening to my old man inside my head wondering again what in the hell he was getting at.

"I did follow your treatment; you know... best I could. They wouldn't let us call until now, but anyway, sounded like you were going to be okay. I saw the after action and all. They threw you guys into the shit, Master Sergeant."

He always used my rank when he wanted to talk to me more as a soldier instead of as his son... which, if I am being honest... was most of the time. "We could have done better, I... I could have done better, sir." I didn't want to get into disobeying a direct order, not with this man. Colonel Bones Kovach lived for the rules. No one broke the rules—not fucking ever.

"I'm sure you could, and maybe you could have avoided all this if you had. That ship has sailed, though. Probably best to pay attention this go round."

"We did our best, Dad."

"Your best? Losers always whine about their best. Winners go home and fuck the prom queen."

Oh, shit... he was quoting movie lines again. I didn't remember that one but could see the old Scottish guy saying it.

"Gotta go, Pops."

"Hang on... Joe, I have something. Got you something," he corrected. "It might help with your mental health." He said mental health like it was a venereal disease.

My father hadn't given me anything personally in twenty years. I... I was stunned. When I went to thank him, the connection was dead.

"Ada, did my father hang up?"

"I show no incoming calls," she said in her sexy-ass voice. That didn't surprise me either. He would have the override codes for making encrypted calls now straight into my brain, it seemed.

I heard barking and saw a corporal heading my way, leading a gray, black, and white dog. The younger man handed me the leash wordlessly, then walked away. *My pops had gotten me a puppy?*

"Not exactly, Joe," Ada said internally. "He is an augmented subject, too, also worked on by one of the good doctor's teams. He is a combat dog with several minor enhancements."

I rubbed the dog's ears, something I don't think you're supposed to do with K-9 soldiers. The dog tilted his head and obviously loved it. "Does he have a name?"

"He has a designator, so you may name him much as you did me. However, the handlers have been referring to him as Sumo."

"Sumo?"

"Yes, I am unsure why," Ada offered.

"I like it. Seems to fit, even if he's not an extra-large Japanese wrestler."

Ada helpfully informed me that the word itself meant 'to mutually rush at, or to complete.'

"Sumo it is." The dog leaned in and licked my outstretched hand.

"You ready to go to work, boy?"

CHAPTER
TEN

Seeing my war buddy and friend, Hinge, go down on my last mission had undone me in ways that would take years to reach a level of peace with. Soon, though, I had to admit Sumo also proved much more than just a great partner in battle. He seemed to prefer the solitary lifestyle as much as I did, no doubt for many of the same reasons. Ada gave me a partial rundown on what had been done to him as a puppy. Carbon composite reinforcement of his skeletal structure. Titanium, diamond tooth shields with total replacement of several teeth to improve... well, the stuff dog's teeth normally did, but with increased effectiveness and a bite force that now rivaled that of a small gator. He had an implanted comms unit as well, but no built-in AI, at least not one anybody admitted to.

As we were finishing up retraining and requals, I had the Ranger school armorer work up a custom set for Sumo as well. They routinely did light armor for the standard K9 units, but as part of a Drop Team he would need more. Our body armor had to not only be bullet proof up to and including protection from fragment grenades, it also had to seal itself to outside atmosphere and be rated for space—sometimes, no atmosphere. Toxic gases were a routine occurrence, it seemed. It took several weeks to get Sumo a helmet that worked, and by worked I mean one that covered his head and didn't irritate him so much that he chewed it to small pieces when I wasn't looking.

Ultimately, the armorer, who'd taken a special interest in the husky, created something miraculous; in fact, I wanted one myself. He used an expandable alloy that folded down almost invisibly onto the dog's back armor plating when not needed. The workmanship was incredible.

"It's nothing, Kovach. Just some spare Hammer tech we've been experimenting with."

I thanked him with a bottle of Scotch I managed to get smuggled in, thanks to Ada.

I got my new orders a week after the 14-day requalifications, which were worse than I remembered and less than much of the rest I'd already been through. Still, by the end of hell week part two, I was wheezing, wiping tear gas from my eyes, and rinsing the vomit from the inside of my tactical helmet.

I stared at my data tablet, curious as to where Space Force would send their brand new, high-dollar, experimental drop soldier.

'Remote ops.' Remote fucking ops... which was Space Force lingo for desk duty.

It was work, but not like what I had expected. I didn't go back into regular rotation with Banshee, although I was still nominally in charge of the squad. Instead, I got to help plan, direct, and debrief Riggs and the crew after each mission. Her missions. I shouldn't have complained, but, well... shit. I had a body that was an investment of several million Alliance credits and almost a year of advanced warfare training, and I was filling out spreadsheets and updating budget reports.

Anyone who ever used the term Military Intelligence in a sentence without it being a joke was an idiot.

"Military Intelligence is an essential part of every operation, Son."

"Pops, please." The untraced call had come in during a routine field op that had just gotten dicier. One in which I was about to break ranks and assign myself to the mission.

"I'm serious, it's useful to think of in the context."

"Like jumbo shrimp?"

"It's not just an oxymoron, moron," he said. "Okay, well, it kind of is, but you have to understand, Joe. You are a proof of concept."

I knew there was a joke lying in wait for me, but I bit anyway. "And what concept might that be, Dad? They figured out how to build a super accountant for under two million credits?"

"Don't knock the accounting, kid, the soldiering sure as shit wasn't working out for you."

"Wow, thanks, Dad. Kind of like when you decided to be a farmer and used a claymore to blow up a fox trying to get into the chicken coop."

"Hey, you little bastard, that was no ordinary fox."

"No, it certainly was not, Dad. Pretty sure it was a communist agent from Red China kind of fox."

He got decidedly more distant. "It was red."

"Dad, I'm a weapon, and I am going to help my team. If you can make that happen, great. If not, I'll probably be warming a bed in prison. I appreciate your help."

"You're no weapon, you're a tool."

"Goodbye, Pops!"

Twelve hours later, Sumo and I were dropping toward Banshee team. Not in a ballistic pod, just a traditional glider-chute. The husky swung in a modified harness between my legs. I'd done tons of test jumps with him by now to get used to maneuvering with him aboard. War dogs jumping into combat like this were actually nothing new. Paradogs went back as far as WWII, and Sumo tended to sleep most of the way down. That was how he dealt with stress and geared himself up for battle.

Minutes later, we were on the ground working our way through the sparse forest to Banshee's locator beacon. I felt a surge of adrenaline combined with an eerie confidence that frankly scared me. Something on missions always went wrong; it was why we trained so damned hard not only to get it right but to know what to do when it went sideways.

Banshee had come down here to Belize to liberate a group of hostages from a would-be terrorist. The bastard had then wired them with explosives, demanding the release of a former coalition higher-up who, I knew for a fact, was already dead. Don't ask me how I know this, just accept it as fact.

I moved up into the compound and saw no sign of Banshee. That was excellent because I would have pulled them out immediately if I had. They acknowledged my arrival with a single mic click. I could see each of my team's positions in my HUD anyway.

Ada located the combatants and showed me the structural layout of the surrounding building.

"Multiple enemy combatants, Prowler."

The schematic of the school building updated, and enemy positions were indicated in red. Two red figures were outside in the small village. "Send those to Bayou."

I checked my armor, stood, and began walking purposefully toward the front door of the building.

"Master Sergeant, do you have a plan?" Bayou yelled, breaking radio silence and protocol in the process. I then realized she'd been there negotiating with these assholes for the better part of two days. Her voice was decidedly not in the 'happy to see me' sort of tone. Something had changed in me over the last year, something I felt I was only partially in control of. An aggression, a 'kill them first' attitude toward the enemy... any enemy. Negotiations were bullshit and best left up to the cops and politicians. We were warfighters. "Fuck 'em."

"Sumo, hunt." I pointed my rifle at a wall where I launched a small explosive-tipped round just big enough for him to launch himself through.

"Active jamming is on,"

Ada's words assured me, but I'd already figured out the scam. This was a shakedown. Some of the supposed hostages were more terrorists. That meant the leader would be less likely, or maybe even unable, to blow them all up. Ada and Sumo were now jamming all RF bands they might want to use as a trigger for the bomb.

A cold, steady ripple began pulsing along my spine. I now knew that was Ada activating a higher processing mode required for real-time combat intel. It felt natural and boosted my confidence even more. I kicked the flimsy door so hard it detached itself from the frame and flew off into the blackness. I moved inside, taking one man down. Two more swung out and tried to fire, but Sumo swept in from one side, while I blind fired on the other.

I saw the line of hostages with the embedded terrorists marked in red in my HUD. I used an AI assist mode to send pulse rounds into each of the concealed enemy, and yes, they were unarmed. That was on them; they had made a serious miscalculation. The leader, or spokesperson, or mullah was frantically stabbing at the button on an old-style looking phone. Seeing that wasn't working, he grabbed up a boy from the line of hostages. He somehow managed to suck his entire skinny-assed body behind the kid.

The bearded man began babbling frantically in Spanish. Ada automatically interpreted in real time. He wanted to negotiate.

"I'm just a simple farmer. I just want a peaceful outcome," he said with all the sincerity of a used autocar salesman.

"Look, Paco. You are confused, clearly. I'm not who they send to negotiate. Time for deals has passed. The lady on the fire team outside. The one you have been dicking around for two fucking days. She's the one who could make a deal. I'm just here to make you dead."

Ada whispered the jammer was beginning to break down. The arming circuit would be live in a matter of seconds. Sumo was waiting for the signal, and I could hear sounds of the rest of Banshee closing in. The line of hostages now covered in blood and bits of... less identifiable 'stuff' were all crying. I sheathed the MK4 and removed my sidearm. It was less accurate, but I only needed one shot. It would have to go through the boy but wouldn't kill him... *probably*. That was a coldly logical thought, and the fact I'd had it scared me. I wasn't really going to shoot a kid, was I?

I began squeezing the trigger. The terrorist seemed to realize his time was up and threw up his hands in surrender. I wanted to shoot him anyway.

Bayou slapped my shoulder as she went by and cuffed the man. Halo and Priest made quick work of disarming the bombs and ushering the group, that I could now see was mostly kids, outside.

"They took over the school, killed the administrator and one teacher before taking the class hostage," Bayou said as a way of greeting.

"Darko, get down here." She scanned the surroundings before calling for an exfil.

"Good to see you back in the game, Boss." She then knelt to stare at Sumo.

His blood covered muzzle nosed her uneasily until I signaled 'friend.'

"Welcome to Banshee, Sumo. We must get a battle patch for that armor."

It was bad luck to put a squad logo on a soldier until after the first enemy engagement. I'd say he'd earned it.

That was by far the easiest of all the missions I had over the next few months, and yes, at some point I'll tell you about them, but most are still classified, and frankly, I'm not that sure they are even relevant anymore. I mean, we had our share of pompous dictators trying to oppress in ever more creative ways. A rash of warlords that popped up in Mexico and California that caused some real fucking issues. Then the mess with very targeted M8 cyberattacks that seemed to be aimed at crippling the military's command-and-control systems, as well as compromising almost every citizen's identity in one form or another. From ruined credit to deep fakes of illicit affairs and crimes, every day seemed to bring a new and more absurd headline or conspiracy theory.

Increasingly, Bayou took the team out and played cop. The need for an expensive super-soldier was obviously much less relevant in the current military environment. That, and the fact that my need for the regular med pack dosing had proven to be much shorter intervals than Doctor Reichert had suggested. I could normally make it six weeks, but a few times it was less than four. The variable seemed to be how much I stressed my system. When I crashed, I crashed hard. He had not been kidding about the need to stay on the drugs. My time in orbit became less and less, and an RDT soldier who can't go into space is about as useless as 'tits on a nun,' as my dad was fond of saying.

To imply it was frustrating was an understatement, but I managed to catch up on reading, outfitting my mountain cabin with all manner of counter-intrusion devices, and begin work on a dining table made from a tree that had fallen on my property a few years earlier. Unless Banshee was on a drop mission, Sumo and I were pretty much able to make our own schedule. Other than my regular need for the shots and my dad calling to give me hell every few days, it wasn't a bad time to be me, until it was. I should have been happy about what came next. I am a warrior, and only part of that purpose is fulfilled unless we fight. No one truly was prepared for this, though... no one.

CHAPTER
ELEVEN

The end was my beginning, as they say. It was a Tuesday... shit, maybe a Wednesday. Yeah, that's it; the world ended on a Wednesday. To be honest, I didn't realize it for what it was. Not at first, anyway. Maybe that's the problem with being a career soldier, one conflict starts to look a lot like all the others after a while.

Yeah, I know I probably should have seen the clues, the growing unrest in the world. The heightened military state of so many countries. The growing outcry over gene editing, personal freedoms, and the accompanying political rhetoric, but to me, it was just 'noise.' You know, shit other people get paid to worry about. I was more concerned with getting the table sanded down for a finish coat. The surface was already glistening from the workout I'd been giving it for weeks now. I rubbed the wood, feeling the warmth, smelling the sawdust that floated in the warm summer air. I was due back at the base in D.C. in a few days, and I wanted to get the first coat of sealer on the wood slab before I left.

It seems stupid to me now, but I have a little trouble recalling the precise moment, even though it was less than a month ago. Did I know this was it? Working in my shop, did I understand that the world I had known was hours from disappearing? No, honestly, what I knew that day was that the last of my good bourbon was disappearing. That, to me, was a genuine tragedy. The world? Well, fuck the world. I'd already done my part. Those assholes just want to keep fighting, to keep believing they are just and right, and the other side is evil. Just like all the other dumb sons-a-bitches before them.

So, who were 'they?' What group ultimately did the deed? Who cares? Hell, who knows? That's not entirely true. I could probably take a guess, and yeah, I would like to give 'em some payback. I'm sure my father would know; he seems to know everything that happens anywhere. Like him, I had fought for my country all over the world. One shithole battle after another. Unlike him, I had never advanced far enough up the ranks to avoid people trying to openly kill me.

I ran my hand over the ridge of scar tissue encircling much of my abdomen. Yeah, I had given my all, as they say. But now, I've got to begin again. I needed more whiskey. We also needed food. I rubbed a calloused hand over a week's worth of stubble. Yep... food, that was probably more important. Sumo looked at me with an affirming head nod.

Anyway, when I say it was my beginning, don't read too much into that. It's not like I'm a rock star, badass survivor now, or I was a bum back in the before. It just changed me... hell, it changed all of us. Those who lived to tell the story at least. Bear with me, as it will take some time to unpack it all for you.

CHAPTER
TWELVE
FIVE WEEKS AGO

The wood grain was really starting to pop... to show through. I used the scraper to delicately shape the thick wood a bit more, then ran the ultra-fine sandpaper over it to smooth out the coarseness of my scraping. The slab was oak and eventually would become my dinner table, or something. I liked the feel of wood, the smell of the sawdust. It felt warm to the touch, solid but somehow still alive. If treated right, the dead wood often has more to offer and a longer life than the living tree ever had. I'm not an anachronism, and yes, a 3D printer could spit me out something made of one of the plywood composites in minutes that would look, feel, and perform nearly identical to this, but it wouldn't be the same. There is no satisfaction like working the wood with your own two hands.

I heard a sound from far below, then a cloud of dust rose from the valley road. As was a part of my nature, I eyed the sun's position, then checked my watch. "Only twenty minutes late this time." The lump of dog at my feet ignored the comment. The sound of tires on the dirt road was the only sound as the delivery truck rolled to a stop. The middle-aged delivery man nodded to me in silent greeting before stepping back into the cargo area to retrieve the shipment.

Sumo and I watched from the door of the isolated cabin's small workshop. As usual, the delivery man looked as if he wanted to make conversation, maybe ask what it was he brought to me every six weeks for much of the last year. Realizing again that it would be pointless, the man stayed silent and instead set the box on the porch and passed the tablet over for me to sign. As always, I simply tapped my ident ring to the screen, using an anonymous verification instead of anything traceable.

He left as silently as he had come. I watched until the truck was an insignificant dot far below on the valley road. I knew this delivery added at least thirty extra miles to the man's route, but that wasn't my concern. The contents of the shipping container were. "Sumo, check."

The dog snapped to attention and moved to investigate the container. It was the typical biodegradable rigid foam box used to ship perishable items. Food companies had used them back in the day before technology made shipping luxury steaks and frozen Chicago pizza a quaint throwback. Sumo nudged the box over on its side and sniffed the bottom before giving a small chuff and going back to his spot by the wooden rocking chair on the porch.

I stared at the container, tearing off the nondescript mailing label for the compounding lab just outside D.C. I felt the familiar rage inside taking root, rising up... getting ready to erupt. This was the price; this was the deal I'd made to stay alive... alive and free, I amended. Sighing heavily, I picked up the box and moved inside the house, retrieving a standard handheld scanner from the chipped plastic counter. The scanner showed no tracking devices; the dog had cleared it of any bio-agents, but there could be more.

Yeah, I know my paranoia is almost as bad as my anger. It took a considerable amount of conscious effort to force it all back down to just this level of bat-shit nuttiness.

I was an operator... now I was more of a loose end. One the DOD hadn't willingly let off the leash. To be accurate, they hadn't let me off. The truth was, I relied on them and these shipments to stay alive. My agreement had been to stay hidden, stay quiet, and be ready whenever they called. I was still nominally in command of my team. I got to sit in the TOC and second guess my hand-picked replacement to do the job I should be out there doing.

It's hell being an aging soldier, even worse, being an elite Tier-1 operator who is now mostly used in advisor roles. I'm a Master Sergeant in the Space Force Ranger division. Maybe all of that should be past tense. Like a million-dollar pitcher who just threw his arm out. What's his value then?

Banshee Squad were some of the best. They were my friends; they were fucking heroes, and I should be with them. I'd shown that I could still do the work many times now, but despite my abilities, I had weaknesses as well. Problems that kept me closer to home than I liked to admit. So, my team did most missions without me. I watched remotely, and meanwhile, when I'm not at the base, I make dead trees into beautiful tables that no one but me and my goofy-ass dog will ever enjoy.

In the past year, RDT Command at Alliance Space Force had called me back into the field five times. Number three had nearly ended the dog's life. Fighting against something that still gave us both nightmares. Number five had cost me an arm... again, and yeah... another one of our team... my team, didn't make it back.

Ramirez had been solid. One hell of a soldier. He'd been a key member of Banshee Squad. We'd almost lost him right after Hinge. That had been the mission that brought home my body's absolute dependence on what was in this box. It did so with absolute, horrific clarity. I'm an enhanced super-soldier who is literally addicted to a drug cocktail that has to be specially made for me every four weeks. Six, if we're taking chances. Since most RDT missions are ninety-day rotations, my time on the space side of the service has been very limited since my upgrade. I went up twice and dropped within days both times. When my body begins to fail, I become a liability, not just combat ineffective. Ramirez had stepped on a concealed proximity mine, taking point on my patrol because I couldn't manage. Another fallen brother, another friend gone on my watch.

Dropping the box into my homemade faraday cage, I carefully manipulated a remote blade to slice through the sealing tape. Biological hazard sensors in the cage could detect all but the most sophisticated of agents, and my containment box itself would warn if any tracking devices were present inside the container. Hell, I knew this was overkill, but this level of caution kept me alive. The sensor was going through the BAN's biohazard protocol when my embedded comms went active. The incoming call chime nearly scared the piss out of me. At the same time, I felt a distant rumble coming from beneath me.

"Shit," I said as my onboard AI made the connection.

"Shit? Is that any way to speak to your old man?"

"Sorry," I said. "I was in the middle of..."

He cut me off, "Yeah, no time for chit-chat."

You would have to understand my father. The highly decorated former commander was not a man of patience. He was also the only caller Ada could not block. We still couldn't figure out how he'd managed to hack her system to always give him priority access.

"What's up, Pop?"

"Got a crawly feeling going down my spine like someone is walking on my grave."

Dad tended to speak in cliches as if he was a character in an eighties action movie. And, oh my God, he made us watch them all over and over to the point I never wanted to see another 2D movie of any kind.

"You sure it's not just arthritis?"

"What's that supposed to mean? Are you calling me old? Don't forget, I was the one who got you that goddamn bouncy house for your eighth birthday, you ungrateful shit."

Holy cow, I thought. *Zero to crazy in seven seconds.* "You never got me a bouncy house, Pops." I felt the rumble again, stronger this time, and Sumo was looking around, his internal alerts going off as well.

"Oh, yeah," Dad said, unfazed. "That's right, we got that for your brother. Goddamn, I miss that kid."

"I'm an only child, Pops."

"Well, a man can wish, can't he? Sorry you're pissed about the bouncy house. I'll make it up to you."

"No, you won't."

"Well, let's call this a 'grow the fuck up moment,' Joe. You can't keep being a victim, you know. Hell, everybody had shitty childhoods."

"Dad, I never even wanted a bounc..."

"Can we drop that shit? I had something important to talk to you about," he cut in.

"Your itchy back?" I said, trying to be helpful... or snarky. He ignored me.

"I made some calls. Something big is going down. I suggest you contact your team to get them spun up and prepped."

"Colonel, you're not in my COC."

"Fuck chain of command, Son. I am telling you this for your own good. Go on alert now. This is a Condition Black."

The line went ominously dead.

I tapped at the spot just behind my ear. "Ada, did we lose him?"

"As usual, Joseph, I have no record of the call," she answered.

"Any chance he's onto something? I think we just felt a couple of impact tremors."

Ada is not like most commercial AIs. She's a fully functioning, military grade issue, strong AI that came with some other 'upgrades' after a particularly ugly mission. The same mission that had me addicted to what was in this goddamn box I still hadn't unpacked.

"I believe..." she began. Then, "Sergeant, protocol alert. Status Activation Black."

That was the official Milcrypt Command channel. I realized something definitely was happening. I ignored the scanner and rushed out to the rear of the cabin. Not that I could see much there other than the eastern slope of the ridge below. I lived in an overlooked rural area of dense forest along the West Virginia and Pennsylvania line several hours away from D.C. I'd chosen this spot just for its remoteness and the fact it legally didn't exist on any current map. My address on the shipping labels was a set of coordinates, nothing more.

"Ada, lock down the house. Liquidate all assets, now," I said as I saw high arcing vapor trails far in the distance. I saw a dark blue shape coming fast across the long, green valley. My brain registered what it was before my enhanced eyes even could. *That's an old Chinese Darkstar hypersonic EMP cruise missile.* It was following a 'nap of the earth' flight path and would pass to the south a good ten miles.

"Shutting down all non-essential systems, Joe. All financial transfers are handled. Your crypto accounts are all now linked to hard assets. Ample funds added to your indent ring for emergency purposes." I felt and heard a missile impact, this one much closer. *Shit,* we were under attack. Someone finally had the balls and the stupidity to launch a domestic attack on the continental U.S.

Ada could interpret what my optic nerve had just witnessed. She knew what this meant and probably where the missile was heading. EMP weapons were old but had only been used a few times. They were essentially inert nukes. The destruction was very localized. No radiation, or very little, but total failure of any non-hardened electrical systems. In a country as dependent on electricity as we were, that meant the end.

My life savings would have been instantly transferred onto a more global crypto via a formula Ada and I had worked out months ago. Mostly likely WorldCoin or even the original Bitcoin. Something with a global presence and wide acceptance. Ada would also activate several emergency accounts to secure cash, gold, and some rare coins and hard assets. These would have courier instructions to transfer to specified locations in various small towns. Have I mentioned that I am paranoid as fuck?

"Ada, are you safe?"

"My processor is organic, but my cloud storage and online access will probably go down. So, I will be fine, but likely limited in functionality for you, Joseph. Depending on where this attack is centered."

I saw multiple streaks, and the ground shook again as somewhere off to the northeast got blasted. The impact felt like a minor earthquake. To the east, I could see a blue glow lighting up the darkening sky. The capital, I guessed, had also just gotten hammered. I glanced at the remnants of the shipping label still clutched in my hand. Lab N4, and the Washington D.C. address. The country was under attack, but... realization slammed into me like a gut punch. I likely had just over six weeks to live.

CHAPTER
THIRTEEN
BANSHEE

"Any luck?"

"All comms channels are still down or being routed for priority traffic only."

Ada seemed peeved with me. I couldn't imagine why; I'd only asked her the same question a dozen times. The bright blue glow over D.C. had been joined minutes later by several more in other directions. An enormous one to the northeast that I assumed was New York City. Several more to the south, possibly the naval yards at Norfolk or the state capital. Ada had made some calculations and judged the one that came close to us was heading toward Louisville. Primary targets would likely be financial, government, and military centers. Major cities and transportation hubs next, then possibly more secondary cities. Those assumptions came back to me from my war college days. That was assuming we were now fighting a conventional enemy. As the Petro-Chem Wars taught us, we couldn't really count on that.

"The Darkstar design was an outdated model," Ada had said. Probably purchased on the black market. That might be good news, especially if they didn't have enough of them to hit all U.S. major targets. Still, I had clearly seen missiles launched heading away as well. The United States had responded to someone.

Ada had managed to send an alert to members of my combat team just before the attack. She'd done that just based on the code phrase my father had used. I was still shaken but sat down and looked at the box still sitting in the safety container. Sumo had been pacing in and out the open door. He'd sensed something bad was going down, too. Sitting here in the hills of West Virginia, we both felt useless. As much of a pain in my ass as my dad was, damn, I'd love to hear from him again.

"Keep trying," I said, my mind already racing through what protocols I should follow. The one ever present thought was the ticking clock inside my body. The meds I took were specifically designed for me—for the organ replacements—anti-rejection drugs, then some special compounds to keep the rest of the repairs and upgrades functioning mostly in harmony with my natural body. My doctors had made it abundantly clear what would happen if I stopped taking them.

So far, I'd only had two close calls, the last just six months ago. Banshee Team was in Indonesia tracking down one particularly nasty asshat who had a habit of trafficking in young white girls from America and Western Europe. I was nearing the end of my six-week window when we finally located the douche bag. I called for a replacement team, but Command said it would be a simple snatch. Another cakewalk. Three days in and out.

The cakewalk turned into almost two weeks. On Monday of the second week, I was four days past my expiration date. Until that point, I'd felt fine. I had pretty much convinced myself it had all been a ruse. Something the lab rats and DOD had done just to keep me close and quiet about, well... about stuff. Stuff I'm still not supposed to talk about. Not even to my dog. Definitely not to you.

Hoofing it through that miserably hot jungle, we were closing in on Mister Sunshine. That was our name for the target. Midmorning on that Monday, we came under heavy fire. I knew I'd been shot. Even through the armor, I could tell my shoulder and arm had taken heavy damage. I went down like someone had landed the knockout blow. My vision started blurring, and I had stabbing pains in my stomach, then my heart seemed like it was beating out of my chest. My head felt like it was filled with a thousand bees. Halo and Darkman were standing over me by then, the firefight having moved on. Or maybe they'd killed them all, I didn't know. I heard Halo say, "He's seizing." I felt my body go rigid, then I lost control of every muscle in my body and remembered nothing else for two and a half weeks. It was only afterward I learned that Ramirez, call sign Robot, had taken my place at the front of the spear and then gotten nailed by the damn proximity mine.

Darko, a.k.a Jack Smith, told me later a military drone dropped some emergency meds in once they found our location. Our medic Highsmith got the IV started, but my heart had already coded multiple times by then. They airlifted me out the following morning. After that, it was more desk duty. The new protocols were not to send me out without an emergency supply and never that close to my six-week deadline. Space Command, obviously seeing my limited usefulness, sent me out less frequently. Bayou started taking on more missions without me. Still, the government didn't like giving up on its expensive toys. And yep, that's what I was.

I looked again at the box; I was due for the next treatment in three days. Then, somewhere around forty-five, hell, let's be optimistic, fifty days from now I'd get to recreate that little scene one last time.

"I have a connection," Ada said.

CHAPTER
FOURTEEN
CAROL

The distant boom was quickly followed by a much closer concussive blast, which shattered windows and sent glass shards flying like a fleet of tiny daggers. Carol Reynolds was rattled, but professional enough to remember the crisis plan. Terrorist attacks were a common enough problem that every company had a disaster plan. Even though she was in one of the more hardened data rooms, she got a chill as the lights blinked off. Her hand trembled as she ran a palm around the underside of her desk, trying to activate the emergency data dump.

Bomb, plane crash... whatever was going on, the sensitive data in her department's files had to be protected at all costs. She glanced out of her office through the opening to the outside where the window had been. Jagged fragments of the glass cladding now were all that remained in the frame.

Her son, Lux, would be scared. She tapped her comms to call him, then remembered he was at his dad's this week. Her comm set was dead anyway. She activated the office phone only to see it was dead, too. The system's backup didn't seem to be working either. The entire system was on an ungodly expensive UPS power system that should have kept her computer working, no matter what. Even the emergency power failure alarms on the system were silent. She glanced nervously around the open office. There had been a lot of downsizing lately, consolidating teams.

Now she hardly knew anyone, and most people still worked remotely on Wednesdays; the place had been nearly deserted, but she'd barely noticed —until now.

"The place was attacked, Carol. What are you doing?" She tried talking herself out of the shock of the moment, but her rattled nerves were still trying to piece together something that made sense.

Her ears finally registered the obvious. Everything was deathly silent. Something had happened, a bomb she assumed, but where were the sirens, the car alarms? Hell, where were the screaming people? Her offices were in Virginia, a half-hour flight from the capital. Triple that or more by ground, even on a good day. She checked the other workstations. Everything was dead. Nothing electric was working.

She was trying to make sense of everything or of anything. They had a utility room down by the server racks in the basement. No, she needed to get through to her son. First, she ought to make sure no one here was badly hurt. Ultimately, that one won out in her confused mind, but she still went to the server room. Her office was on the outer wall and had daylight for illumination. The inner offices were a darkened labyrinth. She'd opened the door and called out, but no one answered.

The offices were a maze of overturned furniture, sparking light fixtures and collapsing ceiling panels. One large holowall screen had fallen, crushing a desk, one she was certain had been occupied earlier. *Who had done this? Was it one of the other labs? Had an experiment gone wrong?*

Carol gingerly continued down three floors before she got a response to her call outs. It was muffled and weak but sounded to her ringing ears like a man. The blast damage seemed to have been much worse lower down. The concussion wave must have hit the ground and spread out. *Why am I thinking this?* That was simple, because that was what she did. She analyzed data, she collected the clues; she searched for patterns. Her mind's default state was to try to unravel the seemingly unknowable.

On the floor ahead, an arm was sticking out from a cubicle. She reached to check a pulse, then noticed in horror the limb wasn't attached. The former owner, or what was left of her, was lying in a heap several yards away. Blood coated the downed partitions and workspaces. She had not been the one calling for help.

"Where are you?"

No one responded, but she heard something from up ahead. A sound like fingers on a keyboard was coming from the darkness. She moved toward it, her heart pounding in her chest. *What in the hell has happened?* Wires dangled from the ceiling along with pieces of ceiling cladding. Parts of the back wall of the office seemed to have buckled inward. She wasn't even sure it was safe to be in here. The databanks be damned. If it all collapsed, they were finished. *Did buildings collapse like that anymore? she wondered. Didn't they make them stronger or something after 9/11?*

She found him a minute later. Someone she knew, although not well. He worked in logistics and lived in her subdivision, so they spoke often, although mostly on the comms. "Tom, can you hear me?"

The man just stared at her and touched his ears in incomprehension. "Your hearing is..." She didn't want to say gone, although it probably was. Blood was trickling down from his right ear, and the other side of his face looked like he'd hit the wall behind him hard. "Temporary hearing loss," she said, mouthing the words in an exaggerated fashion. Tom was tapping on a broken keyboard, probably the same things he'd been doing when the blast came. He was going into shock. That much was plain to see. She checked him over quickly; she had rudimentary first aid skills from school, but nothing more. He seemed mostly ok to her except for the massive bruising and a head wound. *It's probably a concussion*, she thought. So, yeah, definitely not ok. Also, his other arm felt... off. Maybe a dislocated shoulder, maybe worse. Well, not as 'off' as the other woman, but it was likely broken.

"I'm going... I'm going to try to get help," she said loudly.

His eyes were looking glassy, but they seemed to finally focus on her. He tried to speak, but nothing came out but a croak. His eyes were darting back and forth. No...not back and forth. Down and back up to meet hers. Down to his hand, the one holding the keyboard.

"Don't worry, you'll be okay."

He shook his head. The movement caused him to wince, and he

looked on the verge of passing out. He looked down again, and she watched his fingers fly across the keyboard. U T R U N G E T O U T

"Get out," she said aloud as she read the words. "Run?" She leaned back. "You need help."

The keys tapped three more times. She didn't need to look down; she knew he was saying it again—Run! Then she remembered Tom no longer worked in logistics, they had moved him to... to special projects.

"Oh, shit!" Her only thought was of getting out, getting to her son. She stood quickly, then leaned back down and patted the man. "Thank you and... and good luck." She felt horrible but was already at the exit stairs as she called out her goodbye. This man knew Iron River's secrets.

She sprinted down the final two floors and down a corridor, the simple marker for Lab J12 the only identifier. She passed more bodies, one of which was a security guard. She removed his service weapon and ammo belt. No one seemed to know what they actually worked on here, but rumors had spread. It wasn't good, whatever the case. She'd developed predictive human behavior models. Feeding millions of data points from unsuspecting people all over the world to refine and improve the models to the point they could be relied on with near precision. Here, systems could tell what people were going to do, say, date, harm, buy, or reject long before the target did.

She stepped over the body of a young woman, possibly a courier. A box lay just out of reach. In one glance, Carol saw hundreds of glass daggers embedded in her tortured flesh. Remarkably, the girl's face was mostly untouched. She'd been pretty, a daughter, a girlfriend, maybe in time a mother. Carol rushed past, offering a silent prayer for the dead. She was a mother, and she had a son to find.

CHAPTER
FIFTEEN
BAYOU

"Where are you?" The comm's connection was fuzzy and kept fading in and out, but at that moment, I was happy to hear from anyone, especially my second in command.

"Non IC," Bayou responded cryptically, indicating that she was not at liberty to say, but she was not 'in country.' That meant Space Command had deployed them early. I was supposed to be in the TOC for this mission, yet, again I had been left out of the loop.

"Good copy, Bayou," I responded. "You're aware we've been attacked?"

"Affirmative, Boss. I was online with Command just before all communications with the CIC went down."

So, CIC might have been taken out. No way they simply lost tactical comms.

"What were they saying?" I looked at Sumo whose ears had perked up at the sound of Bayou's name. She was a dog person and seemed to always have treats, so, yeah... my combat dog now became a big pussy cat anytime she was around.

"Typical half-assed intel that they were willing to share," she began. "They were tracking two dozen bogeys from various origin points. Most seemed to be ship-based missile systems, but they had no known military vessels in any of the launch locations."

"So, submarine?" I asked before Ada cut in, using her two-way audio.

"More likely Merchant Marine ships, Master Sergeant. Cargo ships with hidden launch systems and cruise missiles hidden underneath. A clever bit of subterfuge."

"Yeah, what she said," Bayou stated. She was very familiar with my built-in AI but was not overly friendly with it... her... um, whatever.

"Sounds like a terrorist hit or someone wanting it to look like that. I saw one of the hypersonic cruise missiles, though, an older Chinese model," I informed her.

"Seems like it was a bit of everything," Bayou went on before fading out for a long pause. "Silkworms, Dragon class, some old Russian BKA12s, even a few that might have been French made. Some were obviously carrying nuclear warheads as the interferences with our satellite comms proves that, but others they were tracking, the ones hitting some of the less sensitive targets on the East Coast, apparently had some other payloads."

I thought through those comments, unable to make much sense of it. Missile payloads had gotten incredibly sophisticated over the last fifty years. Cluster bombs, smart bombs, cluster rods, and the increasingly nasty 'special payloads.' "What kind of detonation?"

"Varied, although they just had initial reports before they cut out, so who knows? One near D.C. said a big airburst, then a bright bluish violet light."

I recalled the blue glowing dome I'd seen building over D.C.

"You remember what that sounds like," she added helpfully.

My blood ran cold. I knew, how could I not have recalled it? "Shit."

"Yep, Prowler," she said, using my call sign. "Just in case you missed the freaky bio hack shit, they may be at it again."

"It's banned, outlawed by the modified Geneva Convention."

"Not a conventional enemy, or at least maybe not. They don't have to play by the rules," she said.

"Who was our outbound strike against? I know we bitch-slapped somebody. I saw the launch signatures."

"Unknown, Sarge. Maybe you should run that by the colonel."

She meant my father.

"No luck getting through so far."

"Sorry," she said somberly. We both knew what no contact might mean.

"I have a sister over near Louisville. Can't get through to her either."

Shit, I had forgotten all about her younger sister. "Shit, I'm sorry, Deb. I'll be glad to try and get down there... see if I can locate her."

She seemed to consider that seriously. "I have a question first, Joe... a serious one."

"Okay," I responded uncertainly.

A burst of static cut in so loud Ada had to dampen the signal before it cooked my eardrums. "What point in the cycle are you?"

I knew what she meant but hated that it was even on her mind. We'd been through a lot together, though. "Just got a shipment, so full cycle plus one."

"So, six weeks, maybe seven, right?"

Lieutenant Debra 'Bayou' Riggs was also an enhanced warfighter, although hers were the more standard military upgrades. Blood oxygen enhancers, regenerative compounds, slight epigenetic changes to her DNA for stamina, eyesight, muscle mass, and more. My path had been a bit more radical. Most of my abdomen had been blown away by the enemy detonation, and, well, my enhancements were to save my life. She knew that the cycle I had to take the anti-rejection drugs was carved in stone.

"You don't have time for a road-trip south, Boss. You need to get to the med labs."

She was right; I knew that, but I also had seen the blast. "I don't think the capital even exists anymore. I saw at least one detonation, possibly two in that direction, Bayou. I'm not sure I would find anything even if I tried."

The static was back again, her voice sounding very far away and indistinct.

"I can make it down to see that your sister's okay." I queued Ada, "Do you have her sister's contact information?"

"I do, Joe, the information was updated in the last week."

"Bayou, you there?"

I was met with silence.

"Bayou? Debra? Are you safe? Have you heard from anyone else?"

There was no response, then three rapid beeps signaling the connection had ended.

"Fuck!"

I tossed more supplies into a go bag I'd pulled out of its rack and then added a few more items. I wasn't sure of the destination, but I damn well knew we couldn't just wait around here. "Ada, any geo data on her call?"

My AI responded immediately, "Likely southern hemisphere, Costa Rica or Belize."

"Hmmm...yeah." Both had seen a lot of unrest lately. Insurgents, gangs, and warlords kept moving into the once pristine tropical wilderness regions. Bayou did a lot of solo work, as she was uniquely equipped as a special recon operator. Generally, though, they assigned her to lead a three-man recon team as advanced scouts for larger missions. Sometimes all of Banshee was included, sometimes not. The entire team was due back in a couple of days because I'd been busy prepping the next full mission. A traditional drop mission into enemy held territory, full body armor and the latest fun toys to deliver death from above. Looked like that one was going to be scrubbed.

CHAPTER
SIXTEEN
LUX

Lux Reynolds stared blankly out the window, the video game automatically pausing when he looked away. He hated these trips. He loved his dad, just couldn't stand that they couldn't all just live together like they used to. The miles rolled by with agonizing slowness. The autonomous car was not the issue. It had all the fun and games, just like home. Even there, his mom worked so much she was barely around. Still, knowing she was back home while he was here in this Georgia place made him sad. Every other month, they packed him into a car for the overnight drive where he would spend a week or sometimes a little more in Atlanta, where his dad now lived with his new girlfriend and her brat daughter.

"Lux?" the NanyBot AI named Marcie said softly from the car's speakers. "Are you okay?"

He shrugged his shoulders.

"That's not an answer," her tone growing firmer.

"I'm fine."

He was eight, and like most kids, his parents were not together. Not divorced, because they had never married, but there had been a legal union.

Marcie clearly wasn't buying it. She had undoubtedly already analyzed the tone of his voice, his posture on the seat, and all his vitals from the sensors in the comms unit he wore. She muted the slightly annoying sounds coming from the paused video game. "Would you like to talk about it?"

They'd talked before. It did no good. "I need to finish my homework." School was the one constant no matter who's house he was at. He preferred attending remotely most days anyway, but this was the last of spring week back at his school in West Charles. It was one of the more fun times as they had outdoor games and lots of fun stuff going on, as soon as they finished the biggest test of the year, of course. This was why he was headed back home during the day instead of at night like normal. His parents liked him to just sleep the entire trip. Being in the autocar was safer than being at home, so they never gave it a second thought.

"You are all caught up with your assignments. Your teacher even sent some personal comments back to you on your homework from yesterday. Would you like me to read them?"

He shook his head. "Just leave me alone, please." He made sure the please sounded more like a command. Marcie did not reply. Instead, the ambient light in the cabin shifted to a more subdued blue, and the rest of the interior dimmed. She would try to lull him to sleep now, he realized. Because grumpy kids the world over just needed a good nap to make everything great again.

The hills swept past as the car moved farther and farther away from his dad and back toward home. His gaze shifted to the range of far hills. He noticed an odd color in the distance, more like a bubble of violet light than anything. "What's that, Marcie?"

The AI used the car's internal cameras to follow his pointing fingers and then zoom out. Immediately, the car slowed. The spectral signature of that light matched only one thing in Marcie's memory files. A Sapphire II ballistic warhead, a rare relic of the PetroChem Wars. She placed the likely impact somewhere in Tennessee, possibly near Knoxville. She also now had internal reports coming in of other blasts going off. The AI directed the car to disengage from the highway's traffic pattern and exit the roadway. The car rolled to a stop as several vapor trails appeared in the sky. It was some sort of rockets high overhead.

"I think it is a weapon, possibly a terrorist attack, Lux." She hated being so blunt, but her programming was quite clear on this. She was in an exposed situation; her circuits could be fried if any of these weapons had EMP generators onboard.

Lux's sadness was quickly turning to fear. "Wh...what does that mean?"

Marcie was all business. "No time to explain. You are going to have to be a big boy now. If anything happens to me, you need to know what to do, okay?"

He nodded. "What could happen..."

"No time." Several compartments opened in the car's interior at once, and the passenger door swung open. "Take the bags in these compartments and move away from the car and into the tree line." She had confirmed official reports now that the ongoing was indeed an attack and both nuclear and BioGen weaponry was in play. Even if they avoided an EMP blast here, the internet would go down, and the national WiFi mesh was already phasing in and out. She would be offline in seconds. "Lux, I need you to be brave. Don't stay here with the car."

Lux looked back at the highway, where dozens of other autocars screamed past at incredible speeds. He never realized they went that fast.

"You must find safety," Marcie continued. "Other people. Don't trust the others stranded on the road. They will be desperate. Do you understand?"

Dumbfounded, he nodded slowly. He'd never been without Marcie, couldn't imagine life without her constant reassurance, in fact. She was more a mom to him that his actual mother. "I love you, Lux. Be careful. The small red bag, leave it sealed for at least a day or two. You have other supplies to last, okay?"

He looked around bewildered, "Last... you mean out here?"

Something screamed above the treetops, a shadow of it passing directly overhead, followed by a massive blast several miles away. The car rocked violently from the impact. "Run..." Marcie began before being suddenly cut off as the car itself burst into flame, all the lithium/magnesium batteries cooking off instantly behind the massive EMP wave.

Lux tried to run, to get away, but he was scared and confused. The sounds of other cars crashing and exploding terrified him, and then he heard the screams. "Don't look, don't look back," he told himself as he scrambled on his hands and butt to move farther away from the intense heat. Then he glanced back toward the road and saw some of those that had been screaming. Burning cars with people trapped inside, cars just like the one he had been in minutes earlier. The scene was awful, much worse than anything he'd ever seen. Not even his dad's video games, which he sometimes snuck in and played, showed anything this gruesome.

He didn't realize he was moving, but his body had taken command and pulled him deeper into the nearby woods, away from the fiery inferno. He was shaking from fear; tears and snot cascaded down his face. He kept trying his wrist comms to call Marcie, his mom, or dad... anyone. No one answered. He lay down on the carpet of brown pine needles and pulled his knees up close to his chest. He put fingers in both ears to block out the sounds. The screams had stopped, but the fire and explosions were echoing up and down the highway. Those sounds went on for a very long time. At some point, he fell asleep. That was the only relief he found that day. It only lasted for minutes, or so he thought, because when his eyes opened again it was even worse.

CHAPTER
SEVENTEEN
KOVACH

"Not really looking forward to this, partner."

My dog just looked at me, unsure of what I was thinking. Dawn was just breaking to the east, despite the carnage of the day before; the sky was so brilliant it looked like a painting. I swung open the heavy doors on my shed and looked inside at the rusting contraption. The truth was, I had little use for a car up here. When I was due back on base or scheduled for deployment, a car, or more accurately, a 'vehicle,' was sent to pick me up. There was nowhere close-by to go. Like everyone else, groceries and supplies were delivered to me. I couldn't even tell you where a food store would be. Driving was not something considered nearly as essential as it once had been. My dad had always owned a car, and his dad had quite a collection. What I was looking at now was the last one of those.

Inside the shed was a classic GMC Raider S pickup with the original mechanical steering and manual transmission. In truth, the thing looked like shit, just old and tired. I'd had dreams of rebuilding it, knocking out the dents, maybe a new paint job, but... well, my time and skills were limited and my desire even more so. Now, this beast might be my only way to get to the labs near D.C.

The truck was as solid as they came; the tires looked to be in good shape. The interior was another matter. That was something I should have handled. The double cab originally would have sat five or six, but now the interior only had a well-worn driver's seat. I'd need to find at least one more for Sumo to ride shotgun.

First thing, though, was to find the battery packs and make sure the motors hadn't seized up. I had taken the precautions to line the shed's walls with wire netting, which should have blocked EMP waves, but they'd obviously never been tested.

The battery trays were ancient looking. Bricks of black rectangles seated in neat rows of ten. Each rack held about sixty of the things, and all I could remember was how heavy they were. These old metal and chemical mix batteries were nowhere near as advanced as the modern power cells, but they got the job done. The indicator lights on each rack glowed green, although it was flickering a bit in two of them. Probably a few more weak units as well. I disconnected the now useless charger. My solar power station in the cabin was still working, but the feed out to the shop had been fried.

It took me a half hour to find all of the dead batteries. I didn't have any spares, so I just had to bridge those connections with a bit of wire and solder. How did my solder gun work, you ask? Well, that was a bit of cleverness on my part by actually making a fire, heating the metal part of a screwdriver and quickly using that to melt the metal solder in place without burning me or setting the rather explosive batteries on fire. It wasn't pretty, nor safe, and certainly wouldn't last. I couldn't have been prouder.

"Ada, any outside comms?" Looking at the battery tray, I knew I was simply stalling, but did I mention how heavy these batteries were?

"Nothing yet, Joe. A few mostly garbled reports of attacks around the globe, but no word from your command, any other team members, or your father."

"I'd like to know what else is happening," I said, bending down to clean the spiders and various debris from the battery wells on the truck. Ada began playing a various mix of broadcasts, all very difficult to understand. Panicked voices mixed in with terrible interference made it almost unintelligible.

"Stop. Summaries only, please."

Ada's calm voice replaced the noise with a brutal roll call of the past day's destruction. "This is based on limited and unconfirmed information. Simultaneous coordinated attacks on the U.S. mainland were carried out by a still unknown enemy or enemies. The most apparent targets were political, financial, technological, and numerous major population centers. At least twenty-three East Coast cities were bombed, seven of which were equipped with low to medium yield nuclear warheads, what we normally refer to as tactical nukes. Another five cities were the apparent sites of dirty bombs that were detonated at ground level. Several seismic impact sites suggest possible orbital kinetic strikes as well."

Nuclear war had been the stuff of disaster movies since the 1940s. Dropping a nuclear bomb had been the tipping point of something called MAD, or mutually assured destruction, well into the mid twenty-first century. Then very-low yield tactical nukes, or VLYs, began showing up in arsenals. These were very low yield, with damage limited to less than a mile. Also, radiation mediation methods had improved to the point the ground could often be made useable again within a decade or two. The first admitted use of a tactical nuke was against a warlord in West Africa back in 2042, although most agree that Russia had used them several years earlier on an internal uprising in one of the Crimean states. They had proven so useful that now the globe was a freckled maze of off-limits pockmarked nuclear blasts sites.

"As Bayou suggested, these appear to have been launched from commercial ships," Ada said, continuing with her summary. "Both ocean-going freighters and many that were in port or even at the docks being unloaded. No news is getting out of those cities, but death tolls could well be in the tens of millions."

"What cities?"

Ada began naming them off. Most were East Coast and the ones I would have expected. Some didn't seem to make much sense, though, like Bangor, Maine, a site in rural Virginia, Memphis, New Orleans, Houston, Atlanta, and others. The scale of the attack was shocking. America hadn't been punched like this... well, ever.

"The majority were East Coast, although seven major cities on the West Coast were also partially to completely destroyed," Ada continued.

"Southern Florida was largely untouched other than one of the ten additional Sapphire warheads which struck outside Orlando."

She knew I wanted to know about where my father was. Orlando was only a few hundred miles away. "Any ideas on the payload in the Sapphires?" That had undoubtedly been the blue glow I saw near the nation's capital. What I recalled of those missiles was more legend than fact. I remembered they used an unusual dispersal system, and the payloads' capabilities had a long list of possibilities, none of them good. They hadn't been specifically banned by any of the more recent treaties, however, any payload they would carry likely was. But hell, what good did having a treaty do now?

"Nothing yet, Joseph. As you are aware, they have a surprising variety of possible uses, none of which are friendly to existing life forms. Most likely would be an engineered bio toxin. The proton blast spreads the payload agent over a large area without damaging it. Therefore, sensitive organic or biological compounds can be in the warhead."

I was well aware of that fact; my father had filled me in on their reported uses during the PetroChem War, an ugly affair that nearly brought the entire world to its knees. Still, those were mostly isolated skirmishes, nothing like this. Dad had encountered a few missions where viral agents had been in the payload chamber, but more often than not, the Sapphires were simply a ruse to terrorize the enemy. The brilliant blue flare struck immediate fear that they'd been exposed to some deadly pathogen.

I grunted loudly as I slid the second of the battery trays back into place. Back in the day, there would have been a moveable sled to do this, as they were far too heavy for one man to lift, unless you had millions of dollars in biological enhancements.

Sighing, I sat back, still wrestling with the new information on the attack. I knew countless people had been killed, cities destroyed, families ripped apart, but I was a soldier. My focus was squarely on the enemy. Where were they based? What was their weakness? What assets did we have left, and who in the fuck was in command? I needed to kill people and break shit. That was what I was good at. In response, one of the rusty handles of the battery tray came off in my hand.

The so-called Sapphire warheads were a clue. They were rare, supposedly, all destroyed back in the fifties. They were developed from the original research on a neutron bomb. A bomb that would only kill people but not the surrounding buildings or infrastructure. That technology never panned out; they couldn't get the prototypes to not saturate the blast zone with lethal radiation that rendered the site useless for later occupation. My mind was telling me this was a useful clue, something that might lead to an actual enemy. "Ada, do you have any other information on the Sapphire bombs?"

"A highly unusual radiation signature. Gamma radiation."

I knew virtually nothing about that other than it came from deep space. "Isn't that created in like a supernova or something?"

She answered, "That is one way. There are others, including normal radioactive decay and even lightning. It seems someone has developed a way of generating and weaponizing it."

"Gamma rays are lethal, right? I remember seeing a graphic novel where the bad guy blasts a planet with 'em."

"Lethal in large enough doses, although this one seems to have been filtered or altered in some way. I am relatively sure the population in the immediate blast zone would perish, but beyond that, I am less certain of the result."

I was in the garage until well past Sumo's feeding time, and he was none too happy with the arrangement. He kept pissing on the tires of the old truck, once when I was behind trying to free up a seized mounting bolt on one of the motor mounts. "Ok. Shit, dude. Come on."

I fed the pup and made myself a sandwich. I had supplies to last; my larder was nearly full of freeze-dried or dehydrated food stocks, plus I could hunt and fish. I thought we would be okay for a while, certainly my bigger issue was the medicine. I eyed the vials in the container, debating whether to take them now or wait until I saw the first signs. I decided to wait.

"How long do you think it will take before normal deliveries are back up?"

There was an unusually long pause before my AI responded. "I don't think you fully understand, Joe," she said in a tone a kindergarten teacher might take with a particularly dense student. "The country cannot survive this, maybe the world. These attacks are a crippling blow to all of humanity."

The thought was inconceivable to me. I sat back on the wooden floor, my mind spinning at her words. All night long, I had been focusing on contingency plans, my own survival and how to get to D.C. or maybe to Bayou's sister, but was that even enough? *Could humanity actually die out? How could this happen?* "Even if both coasts were in ruins, wouldn't the country survive?"

"The war is here, Sergeant," Ada answered. "Yesterday's attack and our counterattacks were just the first blows. But—they were damn good blows. This enemy was smart. They hit everyone at the same time. They seemed to know the weak links in every chain. They took out nodes and hubs that control commerce, communication, food distribution, and defense. Joe, whoever was behind this, knew the key points to wipe out. It was a killing blow."

The world as we know it is gone. That was what my AI had been trying to tell me since the Black Alert first came down. I thought about all of my pre-planning, moving my banking around, stocking up on gold that was supposedly in a vault somewhere, probably buried under half a mile of debris now. I was already living in my bug-out shelter, so heading there was out. The food in my storage lockers was a good move, but that probably only delayed the inevitable.

Still, I was a soldier, used to extreme situations. Used to living off the land or going native if required, and I was just about as thoroughly unprepared for this as everyone else. The bombs hit, and the first thing I realize is I must get to civilization for something. *Shit...I'm an idiot. Just like one of those in my dad's old movies. Usually, the dumbass that gets killed off before the first commercial break.*

It was nearly nightfall before I had Grandad's old truck finally going again. The charge rate showed the old cells would likely drain more rapidly than ideal. The cruising range on a full charge was supposedly

500 miles, now that might be cut in half. With no assurances that I could find a working recharging station, that meant I needed a backup plan. That took some help from Ada, but the backup plan consisted of two large plug-in solar mats that I could lay out to catch the sun. They were high-energy rated but still probably could only get a quarter charge per day. That would mean sitting idle somewhere for the primary sunshine hours. Not a good plan for a risky ground journey like this.

Locking my supplies inside the cab after mounting a seat I had built for Sumo, I went to get some rest. Looking out over the valley once more, there were no house or streetlights to be seen. Normally, a few specks of light would pepper the scene. Nor did any of the typical glow of cities on the horizon break up the unyielding darkness. My dad talked about blackouts growing up and the 'grid' being down, but that system of power distribution had been abandoned long ago in most places. Homes now typically had standalone power systems: solar, wind, or even the ultra-small self-contained fusion reactors if you could afford it. Towns of any size had hydro, solar, or more likely one of the larger nuclear reactors. The reactors were safe, cost efficient to maintain, and could supply everybody inside the town and up to fifteen or twenty miles out. Larger cities used the same setups just with a reactor on every few blocks or even on top of individual buildings if they were needed.

Electricity was just not the vulnerability it once had been... or so I thought. As Ada kept reminding me, we were addicted to electricity the same way we'd once been addicted to oil. Every damn thing we did used it, drank it in, and the hungry beast never got satisfied. Even out here in the woods, my cabin consumed more kilowatts in a day than a large family home in the suburbs would have thirty years ago. Everything was more efficient now, but we just had more of it.

We also now use the ubiquitous little square wafer p-cells for almost everything. Over the prior decade, they had gradually taken the place of batteries in most things and were referred to not completely inaccurately as 'reactor on a chip.' The damn things could run almost forever, and a double handful could power a hotel for a week. I had spent much of the day gathering all of them I had. Nearly every weapon I had used one either for the pulse energy power slugs or for the IR targeting scope, lights, lidar, and other accessories. The MK4 would go through p-cells quickly, but it was throwing out bolts of high-intensity energy. Most other items could go for months or even years with no deep recharge.

Sumo came over, bumped my hand, then licked it. He sensed the melancholy mood I was in. I scratched him behind the ear, then right between his eyes. He loved that more than anything. "You ready for this, big guy?" He wagged his tail.

"Yeah, I should have known. You love an adventure." I fed him, then myself, and put us both to bed early. Tomorrow, we begin.

CHAPTER
EIGHTEEN

There was an unseasonable coldness to the morning air, or maybe it was just me. I blew across the steaming cup of coffee knowing it would likely be my last for a while. Travel distances had become so meaningless as I couldn't even understand how close or how far I was from the capital. I liked the remoteness out here, but when I was needed, it seemed like I was only an hour's flight away from anywhere. Of course, being part of an elite RDT squad, you get special perks like transport in one of the ultra-classified TriCraft. One of those would be damn handy right now.

I was wearing the slate blue Rivex base layer of my standard issue battle suit. That was as comfortable to me as a second skin and offered me some basic protection, but I was less enthusiastic about donning my battle armor. It would be hot and uncomfortable, a pain in the ass to wear all day, but I might regret it if I didn't. No telling what I might be facing. In the end, I donned the lower half but left my torso segments off. I placed it just behind the seat where I could slip into it in under twenty seconds. Yes, I knew because I timed myself doing it. I'm a soldier, that's what we do. We practice, we drill, we get shit right before it matters.

Sumo chuffed, a signal that he thought my dressing and undressing activities were pointless, and he was ready to go. Like me, the dog was a warrior. He did not enjoy retirement, or downtime, or whatever the fuck you called much of the last year. The dog wanted to hunt, to fight, to battle evil wherever it was. Right now, he mainly wanted to lick himself, and well, yeah, there was that.

"Come on Romeo, load up."

The dog hopped in, looked at the makeshift seat, then proceeded to move over to my driver's seat. "Not that kind of car, dog, I have to actually drive this thing. If I can still remember how, that is." It took a bit of coaxing, but eventually Sumo relented and lay down on one of the few bare spots in the back of the double cab. I hadn't brought everything I owned but had brought everything I might need.

"Ada, can you lay out a map to the lab?" She can overlay images on my visual cortex with any information I require. Very handy in a lot of situations, but don't say I have a computer in my brain. She's really just a virtual assistant, and she isn't technically in my brain; she resides in the implanted comms link just over my left ear. She does, however, have neural interlinks that extend from my spine into my cranium and can access to the web, and well... shit, okay she's a computer—in my brain. Are you happy now?

As odd as having that enhancement was... is, it is amazing how quickly I got used to it. Within days of her activation, I was relying on her for even the most routine of tasks, and in a couple of weeks, there was no strangeness to it at all. In fact, now I felt handicapped if she went offline, which had only happened once when an EMP grenade went off too close. She was fine, but some of the logic circuits had to be replaced when the squad got back to base.

The cabin was locked down tight; anyone trying to break in would get an unpleasant surprise. As I dropped the truck into drive, though, I wasn't sure I would ever see this place again. It had always been less a home and more of a hiding spot. Truth was that home was wherever Space Command JOC wanted me in-between missions. There is a detachment that career soldiers have. I saw it in my dad. He cared less about the house, the town, or the area than he did his toys. His cars, weapons, and the collection of movie and sports memorabilia. He needed a house to house his stuff, and you could mostly include wife and kids in that descriptor. I don't mean that the way it sounds, but it is the truth. That was just who he was.

I made it a grand total of seven miles before I had to consult the map. Seven miles from my hidden drive was as far as I had ever paid attention when coming in by ground. That was sad and scary. If nav systems were down permanently, how the hell would other people find their way? Printed maps were a thing for museums and retro collections. Towns no longer grew up by interstate highways or train tracks or along the shores of mighty rivers. The highways were mostly the same, but in urban areas, over half the commuters would routinely take an air cab. The rest spend the time in the autocars doing work or relaxing, watching a holoscreen show. Outside was just changing scenery, not places you needed to actually think about.

I crossed over into Pennsylvania as Ada thought it would be less likely to have roads choked with stalled cars. The towns in this area are small and widely spread out, but the highways are also just the typical mountain two-lanes. Sumo and I were on the road less than an hour before we ran into our first issue. An automated logging truck had come to a stop at a bend in the road. Its trailer full of logs was blocking all of one lane and the cab most of the other.

I got an uneasy feeling easing up slowly on the roadblock. This was rural America, not enemy territory, but something had clearly changed in the last twenty-four hours. I flipped the MK4 onto the maglock receiver on my back and felt it click solidly into place before I stepped out. Using combat hand signals, I motioned Sumo to take the right side. I wasn't expecting trouble, but then again...I always was.

Sumo slipped silently through the underbrush along the roadside while I moved up along the left side of the big rig. Several other cars were now visible on the highway beyond. All apparently had come to a stop at the same time; if one of the detonations was an EMP, that would explain the why.

The log truck had no cabin for a driver, just a sloping engine cab covering the main motor and guidance system. The other cars appeared empty as well, but Sumo and I methodically worked our way through the small traffic jam to make sure.

I tapped my left ear for comms. "Ada, do these trucks have a manual bypass like the military transports?" They were similar in size, and I was hoping maybe a similar tech was involved.

"No," she said, grounding my brief enthusiasm. "But they have a remote override. They mainly used it for the loading yards where the yard master has to move around trucks for upcoming assignments."

"That would work. Can you gain access?"

"Working on it now, Joseph."

I'd noticed she'd taken to using my full first name when she was exasperated with me or trying to make a point. Yes, my computerized assistant was getting an attitude. Out of the corner of my eye, I saw Sumo go rigid and make himself smaller in the weeds. I took the warning sign and did likewise, moving the Rattler from my back to a low-ready position. And where was the rest of my body armor? Oh, yeah, sitting in Grandad's pickup right where I had placed it to be tactically accessible. "Stupid, Joe," I whispered as I glanced past the massive truck tire to see three burly men walking down to the road from the woods. All were carrying weapons.

A sound came from the log truck I was taking cover beside.

"I have access to the vehicle. Should I move it now?

I wasn't sure what scared me more, the armed men or my local AI moving this enormous truck just inches away from me. "Not yet. Let's see what our friends want."

"Perhaps you should be wearing your body armor, Sergeant."

"Ya, think?" I whispered really freakin' loud.

"Yes, I do," she responded, clearly not getting my sarcasm. "They are carrying old-style cartridge style weapons. Your armor can easily..."

"Quiet!" I ordered. I needed to concentrate. I could see Sumo was glancing my way, looking for instructions. He was a combat dog, and in our many missions together, he knew how I thought. Problem was, I didn't know if these were the enemy. I gave a quick hand signal to hold position. Despite all the post-apocalyptic holovids I'd watched, it seemed a bit soon for a full societal breakdown, but I had a gut full of artificial organs convincing me to be cautious.

"That's far enough," I said, resting my weapon optics on the one whom I took to be the lead guy.

The threesome had apparently been oblivious to the fact that they weren't alone until that moment. One began raising his rifle. Bad move; my barrel moved to him as my finger applied pressure.

"Whoa, whoa friend," the middleman said, forcing the other's gun down. He slung his own weapon over a shoulder and raised both hands as he took a cautious step my way.

"I said stop." While simultaneously, I gave Sumo the signal to, well... go bad ass. It's a thing he does where he suddenly can make himself appear twice as large and ten times as mean. If the men were surprised to see me, they were literally shitting themselves to see a ferocious-looking devil-hound charging down the hill at them. Sumo slid to a stop ten feet from the three and bared his very impressive set of killing teeth. He's really a people-person kind of dog. Disney will probably make a kid's movie about him one day.

To their credit, the men stopped moving, stopped talking, pretty sure one of them stopped breathing. I rose up and motioned with my gun for the other two to put theirs on the ground. They complied with eager nods. Seeing me in my 'almost' full tactical gear seemed to convince them they might not have the advantage. My brain had already picked out the one I thought might be the biggest threat. An enormous slab of mountain man with a frayed t-shirt that may have once actually fit his body.

The stand-off lasted several awkward seconds before one of them found his balls again and spoke.

"We... we don't want no trouble, okay? Just wanted to see if we could get my wife's car going. She had to walk home after the... uh. You know, the..."

"The attack?" I offered.

He nodded. I slowly lowered my gun back to low-ready but did not release Sumo from full alert. The dog would act independently of my commands if he sensed trouble, and his instincts were even better tuned than mine. I wasn't getting a vibe from these men that they were anything other than what they indicated. Three locals trying to figure out why their car was dead in the middle of the road. "So, you live close by?"

"Yes, sir, not too far," the one on the left said. The middleman turned and glared at him for obviously revealing more that he thought wise.

"Yeah, we came over the ridge, cuts off about five miles. If you aren't going to kill us, can we get busy... that's hers over there." He pointed to a red, two-door Ford in the right lane just ahead of the log truck. "Going to be a long walk back if she won't start."

I nodded; it might be interesting just to see the three large men trying to all fit in the tiny compact car. "Keep your guns stowed, please. My dog... well, he's a might antsy when weapons are around."

"You have any idea what happened?" the middleman, the presumed leader, asked as he ambled toward the car.

I shrugged, "We were attacked, everything electronic is out."

One of them spotted my truck. "That's still working. It wasn't here yesterday."

I shook my head. "Don't get any ideas. It was in pieces when the EMP hit. Not sure how long the batteries will even last."

"No, no, sir. I didn't mean anything. Just smart, that's all, reverting to old tech. I can get that log-truck out of your way if you want," the nervous, smaller man said. "I mean, if it's still functional."

He walked over confidently, now eyeing one of the readouts on the access panel I'd opened. "I used to work over at the lumber yard."

While Ada could likely do this, I nodded. Despite my admiration for the super AI, I trusted flesh and blood a bit more on some things. The man stuck out his hand. "I'm Pete, by the way, my brother, Hank, and the pretty one is called Peanut."

Peanut was the mountain of a man, and I had to smile. "I'm Joe, and thanks for your help. I'm just trying to get through."

The other two shouted greetings as they were already busy going over the motor compartment of the red Ford. I heard the log truck's tires crunching on gravel as it slowly backed up within inches of my GMC before straightening out and moving over to the side of the road. "Nice work, Pete."

He took the compliment humbly. I was beginning to think these were just good old mountain folks. The kind that would help a stranger out instead of shanghaiing him for his old truck.

"So, you some kind of soldier or something.?"

I gave a short nod while motioning for Sumo to stand down. "Something like that."

"That's a pulse rifle, aint it? A Glisson Rattler."

"You know your guns," I replied. His focusing on my rifle was not making me feel better.

"Seen 'em in pictures, you know, online. Never in person—not even at the gun shows over in Richmond."

The envy in his eyes was clear to see. He wanted to ask to see it, but we both knew that wasn't happening. Our little parties had reached a minor plateau of camaraderie. We had essentially committed to not killing each other over a roadblock. That was enough progress for one day. He met my gaze, got the unspoken response, and nodded briefly before heading back to help his friends.

CHAPTER
NINETEEN
LUX | YESTERDAY

"Marcie!" the little boy cried out in a pitiful voice, unnaturally full of despair for one so small. He had run, he'd run until his tiny legs felt like they were going to fall off. Then he ran some more. He was beyond tired, and it was getting dark. "Mom!" Then in softer tones, "Dad." There were sounds after the cars all stopped and Marcie burned up. He heard horrible things, people yelling. A woman crying. Then he saw the people from the highway. Some of them weren't moving... maybe even dead.

He knew dead, knew what it meant in ways only an eight-year-old can. His grandfather had told him about it after Nana died. He showed him an antique watch, one you held in your hand and had numbers and little pointy arms. "It's like this watch, Lux," his grandfather had said. "When it gets too old, too worn out, it stops ticking. It stops working. It's still a watch, but it doesn't serve its purpose anymore. People are a lot like that, too. At a certain point, we stop working, and that is called dead."

Lux didn't like thinking about stuff like that. Nana was pretty when she was dead. The people he'd seen at the highway were not. They were ugly and bloody. One little girl had an arm that was missing entirely. He'd run away from all of that. It had scared him so badly, but now he was lost, and he was terrified.

Deep down he knew this was something big, something Mom and Dad couldn't just fix, but he wanted them here. He'd even take Dad's new girlfriend, Lauren. She and her mean little girl, Alissa. They were the reason he'd asked to go back home early. He was tired of Alissa calling him names and not letting him play with any of her stuff. Worse, he hated knowing his dad was going to take their side against his own son. *It just wasn't fair.*

Thank goodness Marcie had been there to help him. "You're not real," he said aloud like he sometimes did. "I mean, not really." Marcie was kind of like a toy... just a more grown-up version. Still, she was a friend. She took care of him. She was his parent, too, and now she was gone as well.

Lux ran a sleeve across his face, wiping away the tears and his runny nose. Somewhere in the distance, he thought he heard a dog bark. He hoped it was just a dog. What else might be in these woods? "What am I supposed to do?" The child had to rest. Instead, he sat at the base of a tree overlooking a valley far below. He was hungry and so thirsty, but his eyes closed, and he was asleep in minutes.

The sleep was fitful, and he awoke terrified many times. The night was alive with scary things. Lux sat there with his eyes closed for a really, really long time. He heard sounds like trees rubbing their hands together and smaller, meaner things closer to the ground. The root of the tree he had fallen asleep on was hard, and the ground was cold. His clothes felt wet, he was hungry, and he had to pee. He stayed as still as he could, he was way too scared to move.

Lux started shivering. He just knew the snuffling, evil thing he heard would come to see what he was. Maybe see how he tasted. It is really hard to make yourself not shiver. It was a very long time before the animal moved on farther away. He could still hear it, or something else, but it was no longer close. He rolled over and opened his eyes. The night sky was playing peek-a-boo with the tops of the trees. He could just make out the Little Dipper. His mom had lain on his trampoline once and pointed it out to him. "No matter where you are, Lux, just look for that. I will look at the exact same stars, so we will kind of be together."

Part of him knew she just said that to make him feel better about going to his dad's for the summer, but... well, it did make him feel better. She was out there, somewhere. He just had to get back home. He drifted back to sleep, unaware that he, too, was being watched.

CHAPTER
TWENTY
CAROL

The sounds of death seemed to follow her. The moans and the pitiful cries echoed off the ruined buildings. She heard metal clanging, someone trying to get through a door, and in her mind, she recalled her coworker's ominous warning. Her mouth tasted of bile, and she just wanted to get away. To get to her son, but no, he was still with his father in Atlanta, or was he? At least he was safely away from all this. Still, he would need her. He would want to know she was okay.

She stared at the parking garage where her three-year-old BMW was parked. The multi-level structure was now a single story of crushed polycrete. She could see metal rods sticking out where the reinforcements had failed. Her car would be a metal pancake deep inside that mess.

A scream cut through the air from one of the labs to the south. It was almost impossible to tell if that side was as damaged as this end or not. That was the R&D section; she'd never even been allowed over there. Her bosses always referred to it as the 'money-maker' of the entire operation. Iron River was a proving ground for Hammer Industries. She and her coworkers developed all manner of exotic technologies into production-ready military assets. Actual production was done elsewhere. Even after four years, she knew only a fraction of the things going on here.

She wandered through the side streets for an hour until she found an unblocked way out of the complex. Her car always drove her here; she never paid that much attention. *Where are the first responders? Where are the other survivors?*

Carol assumed it was a terrorist attack. If so, her federal contract required her to stay onsite to advise the authorities when they arrived, but everything about this place now seemed off and strange. She wanted to flee, needed to get away. Screw everyone else. She had a son to get to, and he was, well, he was 600 miles away, but she needed to know he was okay and... and he would be worried. She tapped her comms again. Still nothing. She tried calling her neighbor, Damiana, on the local WiFi but still nothing. She used the app to try to connect to Marcie, Lux's nanny service, but it, too, was dead.

She missed the road by the security gate; there were so many downed trees and debris she could barely see the pavement underneath. Cutting through a ditch, she saw a section of downed fencing and walked out of the secure facility hoping to never see it again. Even topping the next hill, a half mile away, she could still hear the cries of the injured and dying and something else. Something was driving her to put as much distance as possible between herself and her workplace.

The walk home seemed surreal. The damage in the valley was less severe just a few miles away. Many of the people who worked at the facility lived in the small neighborhood of West Charles that she and Lux called home. She still didn't know many of her neighbors. All she did was sleep and eat here. It had never been a home. Despite the upscale look, this was a mill village for one of the thousands in the DARPA war machine. Her heart was still pounding as she broke into a run the last half mile. She knew the comms at the house would be working, they had to be. Still... where were all the people?

CHAPTER
TWENTY-ONE
KOVACH

The road gang had looked a lot worse than they were. I was glad they hadn't wanted trouble, but I just seem to be the kind of guy that attracts it.

"We didn't know what da hell to expect when you popped out on us," Pete said as they finished up. His brother-in-law was eyeing the old pickup appreciably. I now understood that Hank was the mechanical brains in the family, Peanut the brawn, and Pete, well, he was the talker. They weren't a bad lot. The kind of people I'd probably want on my side if the shit went sideways. Which it obviously had.

"You think we're going to have trouble?" Hank asked as he placed his toolbox in my truck. Since they all wouldn't fit in the wife's newly repaired car, I offered him a ride back home. It was along the way, and I was hoping to get some local intel as well. Peanut and Pete had already left in the car. I didn't like that as I preferred to keep them all where I could see them but felt we had reached an understanding and maybe a modicum of trust.

"I do," I answered.

He slid into the makeshift seat, and Sumo took his place behind him. Hank looked back warily at the dog but stayed silent. "I might have a real seat for this thing if you want," he offered. "I mean, that's all it needs, really."

"Thanks, I'm not sure, don't know that I'll be taking more passengers. Hoping for just a quick run toward the city, you know?"

"Yeah, yeah," he said, nodding his slightly oversized head. He'd already figured out I didn't want to waste any more time in these hills.

"Any spots I need to watch out for?"

The man scratched his chin and thought about it. "Honestly, yes. The intersection twenty miles up at Johnson's Gap. Natural choke point and well...got some right unpleasant and opportunistic characters that tend to hang out at the package store there."

I knew he meant the liquor store and caught his drift. "So, they'll be pretty well agitated by the time I roll through."

"Hell, yeah. You know the type, short on brains but long on mouth. You'll be fine. Just know every valley round here has some. Most of us will leave you alone if you leave us alone, but we're an independent lot. Now that the law is proly gone, and the power is out, they's likely as not to be getting a bit antsy, ya know?"

"I appreciate the information." I looked over at him. "You ever serve?" Something in the quiet way he talked made me think so.

He just rolled up a greasy sleeve and showed me the tattoo. An eagle over a globe. I smiled. "Semper Fi."

He gave a silent nod. "You're a Ranger."

That was my original training. "Yes," I offered without elaboration.

"Think we will go to war? Will they reactivate the standing Alliance Forces?"

That was a good question. Most 'wars' now were tactical skirmishes. An RDT squad, maybe a platoon at most. The standing national fighting force had been deactivated a dozen years ago after years of annual budget cuts. The rationale was the automated forces, along with Space Force and Navy, could handle nearly anything going on with less manpower and fewer risks.

"I don't think they have the means to reactivate anyone, Hank. Comms are out. I'd be surprised if anything is still standing in Washington, and no one is going to rush to go fight if doing so is going to mean abandoning their homes and families during a crisis like this."

"But you're going," he said as he motioned me into his drive. The home was modest, but neat. The other two were sitting on a porch beside the red car, drinking a beer.

I felt bad letting the man believe that I was rushing to the capital out of a sense of patriotism or duty. "I just need to take care of some stuff."

I saw him eyeing my arm; a patch of bare skin was peeking out from under my base layer. I realized he was focusing in on my own service tattoo. He could only see one edge of the black field of stars with the slash, but that must have been enough. "You're... a drop trooper? RDT?"

We had a bit of a reputation, even among the other branches. Probably especially among them, as officially, we didn't even exist. I rolled my shirt sleeve down to cover the ink. "Just a guy trying to do his part, friend."

He hopped out quickly, reaching back in the open window to shake my hand. "Hang on one second."

He ran into the barn I'd parked near and reappeared seconds later, carrying an old car seat. He placed it in the back of the truck and dug around in his pockets for some bolts and brackets. "That should work for you. No charge, man. Thank you for... you know, everything."

I hadn't done anything except not kill them. I felt bad, but not bad enough to turn down his generosity. I dropped the truck into reverse and waved at them. "You boys stay safe. Thanks, Hank."

Now, if all my encounters would go that well... they wouldn't. I already knew that.

CHAPTER
TWENTY-TWO

Ada fed me directions. As I expected, no damn way to bypass Johnson's Gap. I briefly thought of simply waiting until later and driving through at night. I had night vision that worked reasonably well, so I could theoretically try it without headlamps, but on these mountain roads with stalled cars every quarter mile, well... that seemed risky. My AI could also do it, but that, too, was theoretical, and I knew much of her real-time data processing was still questionable because of the signal outages.

Risk doesn't bother me. I'm a soldier. We make a living getting comfortable being uncomfortable. What I don't like is the unknown. In the Space Force, and even before that back in the Rangers, we never went into an AO without good intel...damn good intel. It was never actually good enough, but honestly, we just liked to complain. The truth was, we generally knew exactly what we were up against. This time all I had was the word of a still untested new friend.

I watched the green dot approaching the red intersection visible in my mind's eye. Ada had dialed back the overlay, but I kept studying it to see if there was another play I was missing. The one addition I had made was to pull over and top off my battle armor. My tactical helmet was beside me, and I could have that on in seconds.

Ada had a limited interface with the old GMC beater, but I got her access to the admin menu. She silenced the artificial engine noise. It was mandatory on smaller roads like these, but I wanted as much stealth as possible. She also hacked into the self-driving mode which was archaic, and only two of the six nav cameras were still attached, but she admitted if her connection held, she could likely handle it if I needed her.

'If I needed her' meant I was injured or hanging out a door shooting, or you know, no longer among the living. I wondered briefly, *if I died, did Ada die?* I mean, she's in my head, at least some parts of her. Her system literally runs off the energy my body creates. Still, it felt odd to even ask, so I didn't.

Sumo was leaning on the old box, looking forward. We'd been together long enough that he sensed my mood. "I'll get that seat put in for you later, Bud." His quick look let me know that was less than optimal and would likely go on my permanent record.

"Prowler, target coordinates should be in view just over the next rise," Ada said, using my combat call sign. She, too, was all business now. I had the Rattler propped on the dash, extra MagPacks lined up beside me, and my service handgun in my lap.

The intersection was at the bottom of a long, straight descent. In the later afternoon sun, I could see the other roads coming into it from each side and an old store the only structure. A handful of stalled cars marked the area, but no people. Everything was still and lifeless. A few cars were partially blocking the road, but I could still squeeze through. "Ada, anything?" I was about to punch it.

"No visible threats."

I looked at Sumo who seemed to concur. That made it unanimous. I pushed the pedal down, and the high-torque electric motor pushed me back into the seat. The old truck still had some life. We blew through the intersection going ninety.

Glancing both ways as we passed, though, I didn't see a soul anywhere. Well, that was anticlimactic, wasn't it?

"There is a vehicle moving to block the road a half mile ahead," Ada said, harshing my good buzz at the same time. In the mirror, I saw another one of the supposedly stalled cars doing the same thing behind. "Shit, they're boxing us in." I rolled the windows down on both sides and donned the helmet. "Sumo, be ready to hunt." He gave an enthusiastic bark. I leaned over and rubbed his armored back for good luck.

"Take the wheel, Ada. You know where I want to be."

I tightened my grip on the rifle and holstered my sidearm. Sumo and I were coming out hot and ready for war. The first shot spider-webbed the windshield just before Ada braked hard and slid us sideways fifty yards from the roadblock. Sumo used the car's momentum to leap out the window and dart to one side. I stepped out of the truck and let it move away from me as my HUD lined up targets. Two were down before I knew I had pulled the trigger. Sumo leapt over a car hood and tore the throat from another.

In all the apocalyptic movies I'd seen, society goes to hell in the blink of an eye. I always thought that was bullshit. Hank and Pete up the road had nearly convinced me I was right. These boys here were quickly letting me know the movies had gotten it right. "You fucked with the wrong guys, boys. Sure you don't want to call it a night?"

A shout of pain followed by Sumo issuing one of his classic growls. The kind that makes grown men's bowels go all watery.

"You shot Steve. I think he's dead."

"Want me to make sure?" I was walking toward the enemy now, sweeping my gun, looking for new targets as I did so. My HUD only showed two other hostiles, then one of those went dark. Sumo had done his job. A round pinged off my shoulder harmlessly.

"You bastard! You killed my whole family!"

I smiled. "Trust me, humanity will thank me. You keep shooting at me, and you'll follow them." I turned my helmet mic up, amplifying my voice.

"Prowler, more coming up from your six," Ada said as she placed an overlay of three more shooters, cautiously making their way up from the intersection we'd just come through. They were using stealth, walking from cover to cover, hiding behind cars and trees to get closer to their friend.

I motioned for Sumo to finish the hunt; he went after the one who'd been talking. I turned and moved back to the truck, turning my back on the one active shooter up here. That seemed risky, but I needed to neutralize the bigger threat coming from our rear. I flipped the selector on the MK4 for a different ammo, one designed for maximum effect. Banshee squad called it 'Carnage' as the charged pulse came out as twin daggers of pure energy connected by a stream of highly charged plasma. The blueish white rounds sliced through whatever it touched. Sometimes not killing is more effective. These three thought they would surprise me. Sadly, the surprise would be on them.

I took aim at the lead man and selected the one on the right as a secondary target, whom I briefly realized was a woman, not that it mattered. I squeezed the trigger, and the MK4 gave a distinctive reverse 'pong' sound as the devastating carnage round left the rifle, and simultaneously the lead man's body was sliced in half. I swung to the next target, and the gun fired another automatically when it centered on the target. She lost both legs and literally flopped to the ground, her torso still upright as blood began to spurt in all directions. Sumo was back at my side, his face a bloody mess. None of it his, though. Of that, I was sure.

"One target left," Ada said. "Do you wish to offer him terms?"

"Nope."

The short man was looking at what was left of his two comrades. I put a standard rail gun slug center mass. He joined the others.

"Threats neutralized," Ada offered unnecessarily.

CHAPTER
TWENTY-THREE
BANSHEE

He used the embedded sensors on the rifle stock to adjust the reticle my tiny increments until the mildots were in agreement with what his snipers brain sensed was right. Darko had lain in this blind for hours, his legs ached from muscle cramps and some tropical insect, probably more of the damn biting ants had gotten inside his suit and was now dining on his flesh, one tiny chunk at a time. Still, he was a frozen statue even from a meters away you would have trouble picking him out of the undergrowth and even less likely to identify him as a man...as a threat. That was just one of the things that made him so good. He could reach out and deliver bad news to an enemy from nearly two miles out in the right conditions.

This was not ideal conditions. In fact, it was horrible, the rain, the wind and heat distortions; plus, he had no idea what he was targeting. It was big...too big. He could see from the movement of vegetation that it had to be larger than a man. His battle AI had already confirmed no local wildlife here that he needed to concern himself with. They were to find the lab, extract the scientist and any data then level the place. The sniper was overwatch, a hopefully unnecessary backup.

"Contact," he whispered quietly. "200 meters south by southwest."

The double mic click let him know Bayou was aware, she and the others would be scouting the fringes to see what the thing was out there might be guarding. Darko zoomed the scope in and out looking for a detail, a shadow, something that might give him what he needed. Then all at once he saw it, something that shouldn't be there. A splotch of gray and brown that hadn't been there moments earlier. *God almighty, that thing is ugly.*

He sent three precision high-velocity rounds into the face before consciously even thinking. He followed the rounds as they covered the distance in microsecond. Each was a direct hit. Hi instructor would have been proud; the barrel had moved so little during the shots that he was still centered on the target...only it was no longer there.

He panned down expecting to see a lump of dead thing on the forest floor. Instead, he saw, then felt a thundering path of destruction heading directly toward him. The thing had zeroed in his location somehow. Clods of dirt, even small trees were sailing out behind the beast as it charged with incredible speed.

The sniper knew his surroundings provided little cover, slightly raised ground, a ravine twenty meters behind. Several small trees to each side. It hadn't been good for a sniper's nest, that was why he was on the ground. It was the best he could manage on short notice. If he couldn't drop this thing, that mistake was going to cost him. *Shit, it's fast!*

One part of him sensed the panicked calls from his fellow soldiers but he was locked in. He flipped the selector to semi-auto. Even though he no longer had eyes on whatever this thing was he could judge its location by the destruction. He pumped energy bolts into the thing as both the range to target and his ammo count steadily ticked down. Finally catching a flash of the animals front quarter, he realized he'd miscalculated horribly. The blur of movement was on him and gone before he could get another shot off. The massive leg stomping down on his chest, crashing through the armor puncturing his heart and snapping his spine. Darko thought about his family, his mom the fact he couldn't feel his gun, his hands. Then he senses the creature sliding and turning for yet another run. He wanted to warn the others. The thundering ground shook beneath his faceplate. He couldn't speak and the shadow of the monster was above him again.

~

The object in her hands felt safe. It felt normal—it was anything but normal. Lieutenant Debra Riggs, combat call sign Bayou, glanced up and out at the surrounding scenery. This mission had seemed just like one more of the dozens she went on every year. "A cake-walk." That was how she had described it to Darko. Now he was gone; it was just her and Priest now. Halo might also still be alive, if the things hadn't also gotten him. "God, what a fucked-up day."

Darkman, or 'Darko,' had been a quiet man named Specialist Jack Smith from Virginia. Now she could find nothing but a bloody spot in the forest. No body, not even his goddamn dog tags. "We don't leave anyone behind." That was Kovach's number one rule. It had been hard-wired into him at Ranger school, and now she couldn't even find an identifiable body part to recover. She'd lost others, Ramirez, a few months back, but this felt different.

The object she had found was an egg, the thick, dark green shell the first sign it was anything but natural. "Definitely not normal," she whispered.

Bayou didn't like leading missions; her specialty was recon. She could slip in unnoticed, verify all the key points, and get that intel back to the clearing force. She liked being invisible; she was good at it, but she could also be deadly. Stealth had its advantages in every mission. On this one, it was the only thing keeping her alive.

Again, she wished Kovach was here. He was the pure essence of a warrior. Even though he would never admit it, he was made of the same stuff as his dad. She outranked him and probably always would, but that didn't matter on special operations teams. Prowler enjoyed disobeying superiors and stating his opinions too much. As soon as he got a rank bump, he'd do something stupid and lose it. She smiled; stupid was not the right word. Normally he did the right thing, the smart thing, it was just often counter to the team's orders.

A sound in the distance got her attention. She took a quick pull of water from the tube down by her chin. "Priest, you get that?"

"Movement," came the cryptic response from Specialist Bishop 'Priest' Taggert.

Her second in command on this 'cake-walk' mission was a few hundred yards farther inland. Acres of thick tropical rainforest separated them. The tall, wiry soldier looked more like a missionary than a soldier, but that wasn't why he'd gotten the call sign. "Talk to me, Priest."

"It's another one, Boss. Yep, the big ones with the armor plating," he whispered back over the Milcrypt comms channel.

"Shit," she said before removing her knife and plunging it into the green egg she'd been holding. This op had gone fucking pear shaped, and now they were rapidly running out of options. Her conversation with Kovach let her know why the recovery craft had never shown. The country was at war; that meant the Alliance was at war. She didn't have time for that now. *Focus on the mission.*

"Light it up," she ordered. Enough being stealthy. She wanted to live, and fuck everything else out here that meant them harm. Goddamn gene slicers and biohackers.

She could hear the distinctive sound of Priest's weapon. Carnage rounds. Good choice, but it would run the weapon's power down even faster.

"Coming your way, Bayou. She's pissed."

His warning was almost too late. The damn thing burst out of the trees again on a straight track in her direction. And it was a big mother, way larger than the one that had taken out Darko. "Holy fuck!"

"Three minutes out!" Priest called. The sound of his voice clearly indicated he was running flat out to give her backup.

Bayou leveled the rifle. It felt inadequate in every way. What she was looking at was a fucking monster. A lab experiment cooked up by pissed off guerrilla geneticists simply because they could. It was as large as an elephant, but had sleek, sinewy muscle rippling underneath hardened bone plating that they already knew made the animal nearly bullet-proof. If any of her partner's plasma rounds had any impact on the beast, she couldn't tell it.

So far, they had fought against three of the mutant creatures; they had only managed to barely wound one enough to score it as a partial victory. She raised her visor and spit her gum out as she keyed the selector switch on the MK4 to full auto. "Cake-walk," she muttered in disgust.

The pulse rifle rattled like an old-style chain gun as it ripped into the charging beast. One round apparently found its mark because the creature slid to a stop. Its two upper tentacle limbs searching its underside for the source of its pain. The massive alligator like head turned toward her, then on past.

Bayou gave a grim smile of satisfaction. She knew it was studying the nest behind her. What remained of it, at least. Not only had these idiot fucking lab rats cooked up a chimera from someone's nightmares, but they also gave it the ability to reproduce. Humanity was doing a lemming style run for the extinction cliffs. Playing God had come too easily for the human race, and now we get to pay the price for all that hubris.

"Sorry, mom," Bayou said as she, too, changed to the plasma cutting carnage round and aimed for one of the tree trunk-sized rear legs. The blast missed but sawed through several actual trees behind the pissed off creature.

"Got her right where you want her, right, Boss?"

In her heads-up display she saw Priest taking up a defensive position on her nine o'clock. "I think she's having some postpartum depression," Bayou said, putting several more carnage rounds on target. One sliced into the massive jaws causing part of its enormous head to peel back.

The enraged beast charged again, desperate to exact its revenge on the lieutenant.

Priest was pumping hundreds of railgun rounds into the thing's underside. Bayou had to let her weapon recharge slightly from the high-power rounds, so she began moving rapidly into thicker cover, her battle armor's servos whining from the additional strain.

"Move your ass, LT, it's right on you!"

She moved between two trees just as the monster rushed by. She could have nearly reached out and touched it. Her finger moved the fire selector to railgun and aimed for a place in the back where the bony armor looked fractured. Probably from where Priest had shot it earlier.

"Watch out!"

Bayou saw movement out of the corner of her eye just before the bowling ball knot of chiton slammed into her head and shoulders. She hadn't forgotten about the old-looking ball on the end of the damn thing's tail. She'd just hoped the tight cover would have kept it from using it. Debra felt the intense pain, knowing the damage she'd taken was severe, and was vaguely aware she was sailing through the air. She thankfully did not recall hitting the tree or the beast approaching to stand over her before it raised its massive foot to pin her limp body to the ground. It's ruined mouth dripping oozing blood and mucus as it drove down for a killing bite.

CHAPTER
TWENTY-FOUR
KOVACH

"Well, that was fun."

Sumo just looked at me, and I was sure Ada was about to suggest counseling... again. "I'm just saying, you know? There are some people that, well... maybe the new world doesn't need." The sudden buzzing nearly made me swerve off the road.

"You're still alive." Once again, my father's voice blasted directly from my secure internal comms.

"Is that a question, Dad?"

"Hardly, Joseph." Interference on this call seemed to overwhelm the connection every few seconds.

"How bad is it down there?" I asked.

"No time for small talk, Son. Ready to go to work?"

I looked at my hands gripping the steering wheel. The bloodstains appeared brown in the fading light. My dog and I had killed half a dozen people in the last half-hour.

"What kind of work?"

"Goddamit, Son, I thought you were a soldier!"

I decided to fuck with him. It was kind of a hobby the two of us had with each other. It was pointless and a time waster, but cheaper than therapy. "I'm tired of soldiering. I want to retire and work with a giant tech company and play golf in Florida like you did."

"Look, Joseph," my dad said with a tone of genuine concern. "I mean this with all the love I have. I mean, I'm no doctor or anything, but you could be a pussy."

"Ok, Pops, you win. What's up? How did south Florida fair?"

"Parts of it are still here. I'm still here. What else matters?"

"I mean, what do you know? You always have sources." He'd gone to work with a tech start-up after he retired from the military. Even now, my dad had to be the best-informed civilian in the country.

"The coasts are toast. That's what I'm hearing. The shit they hit us with, fucking Sapphire warheads. You see that shit? Yeah, some nukes, too, mostly tactical stuff just to get our attention, but the goddamn Sapphires. They loaded some EMP cluster bombs on the old Darkstar hypersonics. That was likely just to disrupt communications and take down the financial markets. The biologics, though, they hit all the high value targets with those. I'm sure D.C lit up like a fucking Christmas tree." He paused for a few seconds to get himself under control.

"The working theory is that the nukes and the EMP disruptors were simply used as cover. Disable our response capabilities, so they could get those slower Sapphires on target. Whatever those were carrying is the real danger. We know they're biologic capable, viruses, nerve toxins, who knows what else."

"Sounds like a shit-show, Pops."

"So, where are you now?" an element of actual concern showing up in his voice.

I decided to test a theory. I had a working premise that my father had my comms system lo-jacked when they implanted it in my skull. "Kansas."

"Don't lie to me, kid. Why are you going to the capital?"

"I knew it. You bugged my comms, didn't you?"

"No, your grandpa's old truck is still on one of my monitoring systems. I thought you might have to use it. I was right, too. Now answer the fucking question."

"The protocols, Dad... the meds... I only have a few weeks supply." The line went silent for so long I thought we'd been disconnected.

"Maybe you should have stayed on base instead of out in the damn nether regions."

"I like where I live, Pop. If I had been on the base, I would probably be dead."

"Shit, no one could hit that place. It's a geographical oddity... two weeks from everywhere. Do you have any idea how much shit lies between you and those labs?"

"I..." I began before I realized how foolish my admission was going to sound. Something about speaking to Colonel Jackson 'Bones' Kovach always made me feel like a ten-year-old who'd just gotten beaten up by one of the smallest kids in class.

"You have no idea where the lab is, do you?" he said, clueing in way too quickly for my comfort.

"I've got a mailing address."

"No, you do not!" His voice cut through the bullshit, the same way he had done with his troops and COs alike. "You have a postal mail stop somewhere. It's a damn DARPA black site laboratory, dumb ass. You think they're going to put that on the fucking box?"

"Look, Pops, I know it's stupid, but I figure I can't wait. If they have a supply, I need to find them... to get to them before someone else does."

"Yeah, you need your fucking meds, otherwise you'll be shitting yourself and making me look like I gave you bad genes or something."

"Yes, Dad, let's do try to make this all about you."

"Stop being a smartass, Son. I'm trying to help you here."

I'm the smartass? How does he do that? "Yes, sir. Sorry, sir."

"I'm sending Ada an address. It's in Virginia. That's where you need to go. Fuck D.C., nothing there but dead politicians and those pricks at the Pentagon. Maybe the Sapphires turned them all into zombies... no wait, that would actually be an improvement."

"You worked at the Pentagon for twenty years."

"Yeah, and I was a prick then."

But not anymore? I thought it. Hey, I didn't say it, okay? "Okay, Virginia."

"Son."

"Yes, Dad?"

"Listen to me now, okay? Get your team together. You guys are going to be needed."

"Who hit us? Was it the Russians?"

"They're working on it, but no. It wasn't them or the Chinese. They were both hit too, worse than us. So were the French and India. Several strikes in North Africa even. This was well funded and precisely planned. They hit the normal stuff but also wiped out food distribution centers, shipping docks, and transport hubs."

"Terrorists? Terrorists with the funds to acquire that much high-tech armament?" I asked.

"A new player. That's what they're thinking. None of the missiles had significant range. That's why they mostly launched from sea-based platforms. It was old inventory. Surplus stuff really, but the warheads were all heavily modified."

"How hot are the coasts?"

"Major cities will be uninhabitable for years. Depending on the payloads in the Sapphire bombs, the smaller ones may have increased biohazards for even longer. Interior of the country is fine, but almost eighty percent of the population is immediately affected. Casualties may already range into the hundreds of millions. So, yeah, find a seat for that little fact to sit on."

"Shit..."

"Joe, this lab. The one that Dr. Reichert used to mix your meds..."

He faded out completely, and when it cleared up, he was unusually silent.

"What about it?"

"It's a DARPA deep site," he offered as an explanation.

"I know that."

"No, you don't know, dipshit. That's what I'm trying to tell you. This isn't your fucking neighborhood CVS. The site doesn't exist. It doesn't exist even for me."

"Oh," I said dumbly. There was nothing I was aware of that was off limits to him. Shit, he took me through the old Area 51 site on my eleventh birthday. It was boring, actually. Most of the good stuff had been moved or destroyed decades earlier. An old TriCraft prototype dropship was the only thing I even remembered.

"Yeah, oh," he said. "Watch your fucking back. It would break your mom's heart if I let anything happen to her baby."

"Mom's dead, Pops, has been for..."

"Stop being a dick, okay? The woman still has feelings."

The connection went dead.

"Did you get all that, Ada?" Despite her being hard-wired into every part of my brain and body, she rarely was aware when one of my dad's calls slipped though. This time, though, she was.

"Yes, I have made modifications to the route and updated it on your overlay. I might also suggest you find a place to rest for the night. We did not make as much progress as you estimated today."

The truck's batteries were draining faster than I'd hoped, too. I'd pulled power cells from a few of the vehicles back at Johnson's Gap, but they looked questionable. It was full dark when I pulled off into an isolated spot that seemed to suit my needs. Two days into the apocalypse and electricity was already becoming a rare commodity.

CHAPTER
TWENTY-FIVE
BANSHEE

Bayou opened her eyes to a sea of red... foamy, blood red. Something moved across her visor. She saw small, wriggling things. They coalesced slowly into fingers, then a hand.

"You there, Boss?"

That was... um... Priest? she wondered, her head still foggy. With a start, she realized she should be dead. "Sitrep," she called out hoarsely. She felt cracked ribs, and everything that wasn't flaring in pain seemed numb.

"Halo got him... her, Bayou. Damn shot had to be two-thousand meters."

"One shot?" She might still be half unconscious, but no one had dropped one of these beasts, even with a dozen shots. She leaned up painfully and wiped more of the animal's blood from her helmet. Riggs realized she was covered in the stuff.

"One shot, LT," Halo's voice came in over her comms. "I'm approaching now. AO looks clear."

"Yeah, he said he noticed a small indentation behind the ears," Priest said, clearly impressed with the man's shot. "Only about an inch across, but armor plating must not be as dense there. Nailed the fucker just before she was about to take your damn head off."

"Yeah, thanks, Halo," she said absently. The last thing she remembered was seeing the jaws opening wide. Inside that mouth were more than just rows of razor-sharp teeth. It had wriggling tentacles like things that seemed to want to pull her into its open maw. An involuntary shudder ran through her, sending waves of pain as it passed. "Oh, God! Everything hurts."

Priest triggered a pain patch from her battle armor's tactical controls. Bayou's eyes fluttered as the drugs swept through her system. The third member of the team broke through the trees nearby, trotting toward them, sweeping his rifle for threats.

"Good shooting, man," Priest said as Halo eyed the kill. Danny 'Halo' Jenkins was not the best shot in Banshee. Well, he wasn't prior to today. That honor belonged to Darko. Darko went down under the first attack by one of these prehistoric abominations. His sniper's nest had seemed safe until the damn thing ran right through it just before dawn.

"She okay?" Halo asked, seeing Priest lay the lieutenant back down on the ground.

"Pain meds knocked her out," Priest said, going through her suit's internal monitors, which were patched into his head-up display. "Probably cracked ribs, bruised organs, no significant internal bleeding. Concussion likelihood is, um... moderate." He checked through the medical readouts one more time to make sure.

"We need to get the fuck out of here, man," Halo said, obviously already thinking about the challenges of hauling there injured C.O. and going back for Darko's remains.

"This mission is a bust."

"Worse than that," Priest said, looking up. "Bayou couldn't get through to JOC at Space Command. We got no ride."

"Well, shit," Halo said. The Joint Operations Center handled all the logistics and tactical support for the teams.

The other man just nodded. "Any chance that was the last of these rhino-beasts?"

"No telling. Due to their size, I think there would be a limit to how many you successfully keep in any one area," Halo replied.

Protocols said to continue the mission, even two members down they were still combat effective. They knew the lab had to be close. These guard beasts were undoubtedly the last line of defense.

"Wonder how they keep them from killing each other?" Priest said, running a gloved hand over the rough hide.

"Good question. Probably the same way they train them not to kill their creators. Drugs, electric shock, mind control. Who the fuck knows?" Halo offered.

"That's a hard copy." Priest seemed to realize he was holding onto Bayou's hand and awkwardly placed it next to her prone body. Everyone in the squad knew he had a thing for her, but he would never admit it. Didn't work to mix pleasure with business, as they say. She was the boss, unless Kovach was with them, then he was top dog. "She talked to Prowler," he said, mostly to deflect the conversation into new territory.

"How the fuck he get through? The entire Milcrypt comms are down." The MCN was a tight channel band of the internet. It ran on a highly compressed secure band on any available network and tied together every military service on and off the planet. It theoretically never went down, but today... well, it was down.

"He's got Ada. Remember?"

"Oh... right," Halo said, nodding. "Any chance he can get us an extract?"

"He's working on it, but in the meantime, we need to put eyes on the target," Priest said. He saw the other man's expression. "Look, I know the rest of the world has gone to hell, but we still have a job to do. Darko died for this mission, and Bayou was one inch away from getting a complete frame off restoration like Joe did. That shit has to count for something, okay?"

The other man nodded. "I hear ya, brother." Like most war fighters, they knew you did your job for the man next to you, not the pukes back in the CIC. "Let's make this count."

CHAPTER
TWENTY-SIX

LUX

Lux listened to his stomach growl. It was loud enough to wake him up, even though he didn't believe he had ever gone to sleep. He was cold, scared, and tired; he didn't want to open his eyes no matter how hungry he was. Then the growl sounded again. It wasn't coming from him. It was coming from something close. Maybe his mom had...

His brief moment of hope vanished as he opened his eyes and stared into the dark, wolf-like eyes that were watching him. He was propped up on his elbows and he crab-walked back into the tree behind him, never taking his eyes off the animal.

The wolf moved closer, now only a few feet away. In the dim morning light, it was difficult to make out detail. Lux's eyes were mostly shut anyway. "Go away!" he cried. He felt the wolf's leg brush against his. He was crying, and he held his arms in front of his face. Whatever was about to happen, he didn't want to see. "Please," he begged. "Please go away. Marcie, make it stop!"

Alissa had been telling him monster stories all week. Even after her mom told her to stop. Now he was living a real one. He silently wished she was here instead of him. That would serve her right. But then she would get dead and that would make her mom sad and then his dad would be sad. *Would he even miss me?* he wondered as he swore he could hear the wolf's heart beating.... maybe it was his own.

Then it was on him, the monster's hot breath. He could feel it on his face, then wet saliva on the arms he was using for cover. He pictured long bloody fangs dripping the wet, foamy drops on him, then he felt... a tongue. The wolf, no... not a wolf. The dog was licking him. It was a dog.

Lux moved his arm down as the big, furry dog moved up against him. His silky soft hair brushed across his face and tickled. Instinctively, he patted the animal's neck and rubbed his ears. The dog lowered his head and nuzzled into the boy's chest affectionately.

Lux shared his meager breakfast with the dog, a cereal bar from the red bag. He'd already finished off the juice in his book bag. It was warm and kind of nasty, but he was so thirsty. The dog had run off a few times, which made Lux sad. He was glad to have some company, even though he'd been scared at first. He'd never had a dog. Always wanted one, but they were expensive and a lot of work, his mom had said. Thankfully, the dog kept coming back.

Having no other ideas, Lux decided to follow the dog the next time. The dog slid through hidden trails like he knew every rock on the hillside. He was a pretty dog, Lux thought. "Maybe you're a girl, though. Could boy dogs be pretty? His hair was long and a yellowish red. Every few minutes, the dog would stop and look at him with an expression Lux thought was, 'Hurry up, kid.'

"I'm coming."

They went downhill for a long time. Lux thought that would be easier than going up, but it wasn't. He kept sliding down, but the dog just skipped and jumped between trees and shrubs. At the bottom of the hill, he followed the dog as it ran down a long trail that looked like it might have been a stream at one time. It was damp, and he could see sandy spots in places. They walked for a long time, and he had to stop twice to rest. He was really, really thirsty now.

Now that it was later morning, he could see better. The dog was wearing a collar. He wondered if maybe it had been in one of the other cars on the road. If so, he might have belonged to someone. He tried to get close enough to read the tag. He could read most things now, but the dog would pull away every time he reached for it. He was playful and seemed to think everything was a game. Lux was okay with that. It was kinda fun and kept him from thinking about how scared and thirsty he was.

They were heading farther and farther from the road. Farther from where Marcie had been, but he had no choice... right? Marcie had told him to get away. Lux was tired and scared. The playful dog seemed like a friend; he would just trust him for now. Hopefully, the dog would look out for him.

CHAPTER
TWENTY-SEVEN
KOVACH

You know how in the movies and books where the soldiers say they can fall asleep anytime and anyplace, no matter the circumstances? Yeah, I must have missed that part of the training back in basic. No matter how tired I am, as soon as I try to sleep, my head fills up with random thoughts like a hive full of angry bees. After a restless night, I got up early and repacked the truck. Sumo was off doing his business, and I decided that was a pretty smart plan. As I finished up, some of the jumbled thoughts of the previous night came rushing back in.

I'd killed fellow Americans yesterday. I mean, I'd done it before. The Posse Comitatus Act, or rules against military action on domestic soil, went out decades ago. Right after the massive insurrection at the Tacoma power plant. Still, something was very different now. Those guys were virtually my neighbors. Yeah, they were stupid and greedy and totally unprepared for the fight they got, but a part of me almost felt bad for them. That is, until I saw the numerous cracks in my windshield and realized a dozen or more rounds had hit the old truck in various places. By the time I finished going over every inch of the vehicle, I was so angry I wanted to go back and kill them all over again.

Thankfully, the truck was okay, and after a cold breakfast, I took time to install the passenger seat Hank had given me. To his credit, the generic brackets attached easily, and before dawn we were back on the road, Sumo sitting proudly on his new, synthetic leather covered throne. He gave me a look I could have almost taken as approval.

"You're welcome."

The dog ignored me—he was not a morning person.

"Joe," Ada said by way of greeting.

I knew by her tone she was about to lay out my itinerary. You know, conference call at nine, emails about the lost shipment, dentist appointment after lunch. Yeah... no, not any of that.

"The route you are on has been modified since our original destination is now forty-seven miles away."

"Yeah, Virginia."

"Unfortunately, the direct route will go through several small towns between here and there. And..."

She cut me off before I could say anything.

"No, we can't take an alternate route. It would be much farther, just as risky, and the batteries likely wouldn't hold up."

Shit, I'd almost forgotten about the batteries. Looking down at the old-style gauge, it was hovering in the amber zone two bars below the green. Two bars above the red. As I watched, another section of amber light flickered off.

"It's dropping fast. Do we need to stop and hook into the solar blanket?"

"The forecast for today is overcast skies, so the energy you could collect would be minimal. I estimate at the current consumption rate, you will just make it through the first of those towns before batteries become critical."

"That seems sub-optimal. Likely not the place we want to be stranded."

She agreed but pointed out it might also be the best place to find spare batteries or possibly even working charging stations. West Virginia had been coal country and one of the last to embrace renewable energy, but they jumped on the mini-nuke plants. Much easier than stringing transmission lines up and down the mountainous terrain.

"Makes sense. See what you can find and let me know before we get to any populated areas." So far, there had only been a few stalled cars, but that would increase as we moved farther east and closer to any settlements.

~

Pittsview, West Virginia. Proved to be as memorable as I had expected. A battered sign at the city limits stated a population of 587. About a dozen, bleak looking storefronts that seemed to have weathered a few more winters than was fair. A garage on the opposite side of the road looked hopeful until we saw it was boarded up tight. The entire town looked sad and broken, and not because of the more recent events. The battle that had claimed this town was neglect, and it had started a good generation earlier.

"Anything?"

My built-in AI didn't respond at once, which was a good way of preparing me for bad news. "I'm monitoring local connections to the internet. That will let us know who has a working device and potentially a way to power or recharge them."

It was a reasonable plan, but comms units, data tablets, and such mostly ran off the universal p-cells now, and they could go ages without a direct power source. Still, the intel would be helpful, alerting me to...

"People ahead," she interrupted. "A large number of them a hundred yards ahead and fifty yards south," she amended.

"Yeah, people," I said, finishing my thought. The GMC crept silently up on the cross street. As the cab moved past the building on my right, I could see a small crowd of maybe fifty people all gathered outside a building that Ada helpfully identified as a budget food store. The kind that carried mostly staples, canned goods, diapers, and such.

A uniformed man was blocking the crowd from entering. *Brave soul.* Then, as a few people exited the building, he allowed an equal number to enter. "They're all carrying toilet paper," I said in total bewilderment. Every one of the people coming out had a few small bags of whatever and a massive pack of the rolled white stuff. "They're out here risking their lives to get that?"

Ada seemed perplexed as well but pointed out that common sense nor survival training was essential to the populace anymore. "They are panicking, Joseph."

They looked scared, but harmless. I'd seen before how quickly a mob could turn ugly, though. A few of them noticed the truck and began pointing. "We need to get out of here." Then the chime sounding low battery went off.

"Perfect," I said, moving the car to the curb and killing the power. "Sumo, out, guard."

The dog exited behind me and took up station beside the truck. I slung the MK4 into the slot on my back, the mag lock affixing it solidly. I holstered my sidearm and carried my tactical helmet as I began striding confidently toward the uniformed guard.

I don't know what the young deputy thought he would encounter this morning, but it obviously hadn't included seeing someone like me. The crowd in front of the store parted as I approached, and his right hand dropped to the butt of his own service weapon. I gave a slight shake of my head to the man. Whatever happened, I didn't want to undermine his level of control here. I also didn't want him to try to shoot me. That would fuck over my own plans.

"That's far enough, mister. Sorry, locals only inside the store. Council's orders, not mine."

Looking past the man, I could see the darkened interior of the store. "I don't want to get inside, officer."

I heard Sumo growling far up the street. "You may want to warn your folks not to try and steal my truck, though. My dog has been a bit grumpy today."

The deputy was nervous. That was bad. Nervous people do stupid shit. Nervous people with guns do stupid shit that gets people killed. The crowd behind me began to press in again; maybe they thought I was an ally, maybe they just wanted to see me take out the one man who was keeping them from there twenty-four pack of cheap toilet paper. I didn't know, didn't much care. I turned around and in the best imitation of my dad, politely told them to, "Get the fuck back or die."

The mob moved back; the lawman began removing his handgun. My hand shot out and grabbed his wrist and firmly forced it back down squeezing hard until he released the grip. Our eyes never wavered from each other's gaze. "I'm just looking for power. Anyone have electricity here? Batteries, charging stations, shit, a functional solar bank?"

"Mister, you're going to need to remove your..."

I hit him.

I didn't mean to, but well, my diplomacy skills suck. I have no patience for petty power brokers. "Let the people have their tissue, man." The deputy dropped, and the crowd surged around both of us and into the store. I drug his barely conscious body off to the side and sat him on a nearby bench. I then removed his weapon and sat it on top of an ice machine. "You can have that back when we are done," I calmly said.

"You fucking hit me, man. I could arrest you."

I shrugged my shoulders, "You could, but then you'd have to feed me, and I'm betting that's not really an option, right?

Look... what's your name?"

"Dan," he said bitterly after staring at me for a moment. He kept touching his lip that was already swelling nicely.

"Okay, Dan, first—sorry about the punch, but I did you a favor. Now, it's not your fault they overran the store. Some armored up military guy overpowered you and let them in. The fucking council was setting you up anyway. Most likely one of them owns the place, don't they?"

He laughed and nodded. "Yeah, she's the one in there screaming for them all to get out."

"Whatever she has in there, Dan, it's not enough to keep this crowd happy, not enough to keep this town alive, not enough to risk losing your life over. I just need some power. Any chance you can help me out?"

Turned out Dan was not the sheriff, who'd been out of town working a case. Dan was the lead deputy and the only one who'd shown up to work after the bombs fell. We sat and watched the locals looting the store as he held one of my first-aid cold packs to his face. "Mister, you have any idea what happened?"

I told him what I knew. He sat stoically and nodded. "I appreciate you showing up. Honestly, I thought I was going to have to shoot some of them." He gingerly touched the cold pack to his face again. "Wish you hadn't hit me so hard, though."

The deputy told me how to get to one of the remote charging stations close by. It was back up near a park ranger station in the national park forest a few miles away. He knew the battery bank was good as he'd used it to charge his security cart the prior day. "No one will bother you. None of these folks even know it's there. We haven't had a ranger stationed up here in years."

I thanked him, wished him well, and left. The man and his town were going to have their hands full. I could have given them some advice, stuff I'd learned about preparing and survival, but they would have to find their own way.

CHAPTER
TWENTY-EIGHT

It took me a while to find the dirt road heading up into the national forest. Several times, the old truck seemed reluctant to climb the next hill, but somehow it made it all the way to the solar array. The charger was an old-style system hooked up to only four of the panels. The deep cycle batteries lining the racks in the adjacent shed all looked as good as the officer had said. I plugged in the charging cable using one of the many adapters almost everyone carried these days.

This would be faster than the blanket, but yeah... it will still take several hours. Sumo used the time to go explore the woods. I sat on the edge of the cabin's wooden porch and contemplated the end of the world. Not really; I'm not that deep a thinker. The shit had gone tits up, that was obvious. If the capital was gone and the New York City metroplex, like they said, political and financial systems would have to start over from scratch.

I considered the why and the who, but mainly related to how it affected me and my team. Looking down at the flesh-colored med-patch on the underside of my arm made me realize I probably hated the U.S. as much as anyone. I'd gotten a shitty deal, but then again, I had disobeyed orders. Still, for the moment, I was alive. If I didn't get more of the drugs sometime next month, whatever we were fighting wouldn't matter to me either way.

I leaned back on the rough wood decking and considered my options. Even if I somehow could find the right drugs, how long would they last? How effective would they even be in a few months, a year, ten years? I had to face it. My expiration date was approaching fast. The man in charge of my enhancements, Dr. Reichert, had come up with the treatment protocols and implied they couldn't make them in advance. I always assumed that was bullshit. It was just one more tactic to keep me on a short leash, but what if it was true? Even if I found another treatment or two—that would likely be the end of it. Even if some of the labs were intact, would the technicians be alive and working —no. Would the raw materials, the base meds, be shipped in like normal — no.

"Fuck!"

Standing up, I reached into the rafters of the porch and pulled down a fishing rod. One of the rangers must have stowed it there. Where there were fishing poles, there had to be fish.

I enjoyed fishing, had done it all over the world. All special operators wind up in remote locations with a lot of downtime. Some read, others play music. I liked to fish. I'd stowed a small kit in my gear but assumed the rangers would have had tackle more appropriate for the local game fish. I picked the lock and went inside in search of a dry fly pack. I needed to think about something besides my coming demise.

A half hour later, I was standing knee deep in one of the most idyllic mountain creeks I'd ever seen. Sumo watched me patiently from the bank, unwilling to get down in the cool, fast-flowing water. The park ranger's cabin was stocked with everything I needed to go with the old fly rod. I whipped the line several times into a long loop and let it sail, the fly landing almost delicately in a shaded pool I had picked.

It quickly drifted with the current carrying it farther downstream. I played out line and felt hopeful for the tug of a nice brook trout. My battle suit's base layer kept out the cold and the water; it automatically sealed to the top of my boots and made an effective set of waders. I reeled in the bait and repeated the process. Long ago, I had discovered the magic of fishing was not in the catch but in the hunt.

Nearly two hours later, I had to call it a day. I had three small fish in my basket, and my arms were getting sore from the repetitive motion.

Sumo had gone to sleep; the truck was charging away, and the little green cabin on the hill seemed the perfect hideaway. Life could be worse, I decided.

~

It took longer than I expected for the truck to charge. Sumo and I were sitting by the small fire, our belly's full of fish. Everything I'd needed to put together a decent meal was in the cabin. "Think we will just get an early start tomorrow," I said, mainly for Ada and Sumo's benefit. Being honest, though, it was simply to justify my desire to stay put right here. It was quiet and peaceful, even better than my place, and somehow, I knew it would be much better than whatever awaited us out there.

"Ada, any contact with Bayou or anyone else?"

"I have an intermittent signal from Bishop. Not viable for voice comms yet, but I can probably get a text message to go through."

"Priest is alive, great. Debra won't be far away then." He composed a brief message, asking for an update.

The response came back quickly, "Bayou down, Darko gone, under attack. B-G hostiles, this is something new."

"Definitely South America, Joe. I would say Costa Rica based on the satellite triangulation"

Shit! Jack hadn't made it? Darko had been with us for years. Whatever was going on down there, it was obviously not the simple peek and seek mission Bayou had expected. *Something new.* I wondered what that part meant. "Ask them what they need, then see if you can raise my dad for help. Send him a text, too, if that works better."

"They are requesting medical evac," Ada said calmly a few minutes later. "Priest says no response on the Milcrypt comms."

I don't think I had ever felt so completely fucking helpless. My team was thousands of miles away, fighting for a country that wasn't going to be able to help them. Every mission had an exfil plan. All I could think of was the EMPs must have taken out whatever aircraft they were using. If the tactical communications were down, then no one was coming. Here I was camping out and fishing while my team... my friends were battling. What? Oh yeah, *something new.*

Ada told me the link had faded; she couldn't get any other messages through. "Do you have any additional details on their mission?" My AI was military issue. She had direct or back-channel access to things not even my father had.

"I have a preliminary report. No exact location, but I believe it was to raid a suspected bio-hacker operation. One of the Blanco Orquídea suspected labs."

I felt a familiar itch around the scars lining my torso, the seams where they put me back together again. That mission, too, was to recon a suspected bio-hacking lab of the White Orchids. The group had been around in one form or another for a hundred years. First, they fought against climate change, then the destruction of the rain forests and the oceans. Somewhere during the PetroChem War they decided on more direct action.

Unlike many of the other bioterrorists, the Orchids were well organized and well-funded. They even had a legitimate business selling the modified novelty pets that had been all the rage the last few years. Teacup sized tigers, flying snakes, even a goose that would lay a freakin' golden colored egg. Once most governments outlawed the genetic engineering after the war, they had taken everything they had learned and moved into the shadows. They made genetically sensitive designer drugs, offered illegal medical procedures, eventually moving into cloning, and, of course, specialized in the guardian line of creatures, natural predators that supposedly couldn't be killed, and sold them to billionaires as property security.

CHAPTER
TWENTY-NINE

"The batteries are almost gone," I said to no one. It had already taken the better part of two days to get even this close to my destination. From one of the higher vantage points, I caught glimpses of the capital in the distance. Not the Capitol, but the ruins of what our nation's capital used to be. Washington, D.C. is a mix of the iconic, historic, and the decrepit. I don't recall when the place lost its magic for me, but still... it didn't deserve this fate. I'd seen the White House and Capitol building destroyed in countless movies over the years, but nothing prepared me for seeing my nation's center of power totally destroyed.

Few buildings remained standing, but smoke from countless fires dominated the skyline. D.C. definitely took a direct hit. Ada informed me of the increased radiation levels, although not in the lethal range, still unhealthy for anyone without a battle suit. I tugged up the dog's collar and pulled his own helmet up to secure him as well. While both of us had rapid healing nanobodies to fight the increased cellular damage radiation could cause, I didn't see the need to take chances.

The road was becoming crowded with crashed and abandoned vehicles. Several times I also saw crashed air cars, and as I neared the turnoff south toward our destination, a crashed commuter jet was blocking much of the road.

The charred ruins of the craft were awful. Seat frames with some blackened structural ribs dripping something... maybe melted plastic over the blackened skeletal remains still seated in their upright positions. I looked back west, realizing this must be one of the approach vectors for one of the three local airports. The EMP blast would have likely knocked out avionics for all the approaching craft. After that, the blast's pressure wave probably took out even more. From the countless times I'd flown out of National and Dulles, I knew a passenger jet landed or took off every fifteen seconds. That would likely put another crash less than a mile and a half back from this one. Since AI piloted most jets, they likely would have kept flying directly into the expanding fireball until the very end. I pulled the truck to the shoulder of the road and drove slowly past. So many deaths.

Ada updated my map constantly; the roads were getting a bit more challenging to navigate, so I needed to change course often. This used to be rural Virginia farmland, but the sprawl from the D.C./ Baltimore metroplex now extended most of the way to Richmond, and everything out here was bedroom communities for the bigger cities. Millions of families lived here, and I did not want to see any of them, none that had died, and if I am being honest, none that survived. Many of the homes had blast damage. One large two-story had the mutilated front end of a freight truck sticking out of one side. There were signs of life, but no actual life. As soon as the road cleared ahead, I floored the accelerator.

Despite my years of training, I was not thinking strategically... barely even tactically. I had an immediate mission: don't die. To accomplish that, I needed drugs, a very special mix of drugs, preferably more than just the next month's worth.

What if I can't find the medicine? Mission failed. No actual need to dwell on that fact. I'd have maybe five weeks to get somewhere pleasant and say my goodbyes. Someplace where my dog could hunt and maybe have a life for both of us. My right hand was unconsciously scratching behind Sumo's left ear as he lay partially over the old console lid. He didn't seem to mind.

So, I find the meds, then what? After several minutes contemplating that, I realized dying would be much simpler. Pop had said to get Banshee squad back together. I was not seeing the military solution here, but strength in numbers made a certain sense, and there was no one I trusted more than my squad. I swerved to avoid... *Shit, what was that?* I slowed and looked in the rearview mirror. I clicked magnify multiple times.

From this side, I could now see a familiar logo. One I had stared at multiple times in my career with the Space Force. It was an Atmos deployment pod, or what remained of one. These were deployed from orbital defense platforms. Rapid deployment teams could be dispatched anywhere on the globe in minutes. The poor bastard in this can never had a chance. Now, he was just a few gallons of human flavored jelly. Looked like the braking thrusters had never even fired. More than half of the pod was imbedded into the roadbed. The rest had accordioned down to a fraction of its normal height. It really was now a coffin. I looked down at my arm, at the field of stars linked into my skin, and silently said a warrior's prayer.

Getting back on task, I thought again about plans beyond just surviving. Communications, rations, power. Yeah, a lot of power. Electricity had already been a major issue for me. It was also clear that the old GMC would not work, not long term. The roads were all clogged; currently my HUD said my average speed was twelve miles an hour. If I was to head toward Louisville see if I could find Bayou's sister, this just wasn't going to cut it. That reminded me.

"Ada, any update from my team?"

"Negative, Joseph, we are too close to ground zero. There is an umbrella of ionized particles blocking almost all comms signals. And to answer your next question, I don't know how far that will reach. It depends on the next closest city that was bombed and potentially favorable weather patterns."

Daylight was fading. I'd begun seeing the telltale flicker of candlelight in many of the homes. In every one I looked at, I could make out the silhouette of a head looking out a window. A body standing behind a glass door. Several times I thought I glimpsed frantic parents rushing small children back inside. In just a few days, seeing a passing car had gone from being completely routine to something so unusual as to be feared. I read off the numbers on my rad meter in the visual overlay Ada provided. They had been colored red all afternoon.

"Will any of them survive?"

Ada's silence was enough of an answer. I was enhanced; I had nanobodies coursing through my veins, clearing away damaged tissue, carcinogens, toxins. I was wearing the latest in battle armor. Hell, the base underlayer alone protected me from any actual damage. I wasn't special and... I didn't deserve it. Any of it.

My hand stopped on the dog's head. I looked down in horror.

"Sumo!"

Somewhere in the last few hours either he or I had pulled his helmet off. Probably me when I was scratching his damn ears. He stared at me with a look of confusion.

"He'll be fine, Joe. He's a combat dog, remember? He's got the Regenerax nanobodies in his blood systems, too," Ada reassured me. "Also, neither of you were in the initial blast waves. That would have been much worse. The background radiation probably isn't lethal on its own, but don't eat or drink anything from here. Hosing down and abandoning the truck afterward is recommended as well."

"You hear that, Sumo? Don't eat anything from out there. Don't even lick your nut sack, okay?" He stared at me again, still with the puzzled look. I know he understands English just fine, but he does like fucking with me.

An hour later I was convinced my father had been fucking with me, too. The wreckage of the suburban sprawl was well behind us. Now there was absolutely nothing. I'd driven for miles without seeing any cars, homes, or even anything resembling a working farm. "Ada, you have any evidence to back-up my father's claim on this place?"

"No, Joseph, and that is not due to the limited web access. I checked shortly after the colonel's call. The business and property records for much of this county have simply been erased. Back in the early part of the century, there was a small military base close to the coordinates he gave, but that was mothballed decades ago."

I nodded. Smells like a DARPA black site to me. Keep it off the books, make sure it's not on any highway to anything worth seeing, and strongly encourage the locals to move away.

Since I was wearing my helmet, I was using night vision mode to drive, leaving my headlights off to save battery power, but even that would not help for much longer. Granddad's old truck's power meter was in the red and just barely making it up some of the steeper hills now.

"It should be just ahead, Prowler. Two clicks."

Ada always went into battle mode when she expected me to also go into it. I was tired and grumpy and had been sitting in my own radiation saturated juices all day. Combat mode was the farthest thing from my mind, but I was ready to see something other than trees. As the GMC struggled to clear the next rise, the scene below took my breath away. It was a base or a town. Hundreds of buildings spread out along a once lush valley. The complex was massive, but it had not been ignored by the attack. Most of the facility appeared to have been destroyed as well.

"Shit, they nuked the place!"

CHAPTER
THIRTY

"Not nukes, Kovach." Ada said. "Standard radiation levels are near normal."

"Standard...?" I asked warily. "What about the other?"

"My standard sensors are not equipped to detect gamma radiation directly, but I believe I can assess from tangential evidence that possible bio warhead missile systems detonated here."

I had left the truck, and Sumo and I had picked our way carefully down into the valley and just crossed over the remnants of a barrier fence. "The place looks like it took a direct hit," I said, staring in awe at the obvious overpressure destruction.

"Agreed!" Ada offered. "There was an airburst nearby, but again, it was not nuclear."

"This place was obviously targeted; someone knew it existed. If they didn't want a nuke, that meant they wanted to leave it somewhat intact."

"That is one possibility. I am also getting readings consistent with something else."

Lovely, I thought. "Any clue as to what?"

"I'd rather not say. The residual signature of the weapon is very confusing."

The outpost was the size of a small city. In fact, other than the fencing and abandoned guard towers, it looked like a small town. One that had been through an F5 tornado, maybe.

"Over one hundred separate buildings," Ada said, as if she were reading my mind. She wasn't... well they assured me she couldn't, but... well.

"Where are the people?" We'd seen some bodies and some parts of bodies, but so far, no sign of any survivors.

"Unknown. The population may all live off base. Chances are, anyone left alive tried to go home."

That made sense. No one would want to stay here long. I saw what appeared to be an old hotel. One large section of rooms pancaked down into the lower floors. It had probably been for visitors or guest workers. I tuned up my helmet mics and listened. Dripping water, a groan of metal, a distant electrical discharge, and occasionally, a very faint mechanical tapping. No sounds of life.

I did not see any of the typical base housing or suburban neighborhoods a facility like this would normally have. This was more like looking at the industrial park instead of a secret military base.

I dialed my battle suit's sensors back to normal just as Ada informed me she had an outgoing connection. *Thank God*, something here still worked.

CHAPTER
THIRTY-ONE
BANSHEE

"Any chance you can help us unfuck this mission, Sarge?"

The voice of Sergeant Joe Kovach came back in waves of static. "Trying to get you guys a ride out. Give me a sitrep."

This was not one of his missions, but in the absence of a clear chain of command, Sergeant Prowler Kovach was the boss. Bishop gave him the rundown including the original mission objectives.

"Well, shit," came Joe's cold reply. "You guys were a recon team."

"Yeah, Boss, we got pea shooters against these freakin' rhino beasties they have guarding the place. No telling what else we'll come up against."

"Roger that," Kovach said. "Send me medical telemetry on Bayou."

Halo triggered the data patch on his sleeve to send the files directly into Kovach's AI. "She's stable, sedated. Mission ineffective for now. She'll need a few days with a Regenerax IV to harden up those cracked ribs."

"I'll have Ada go over the data, and we'll keep trying to get you some help. I put in the request earlier, but no one had your actual location, then comms went out again. Milcrypt comms seems out completely, but I have the colonel working on it. This lab you're looking for. Did CIC give you any information on its target value?"

"We're just the grunts, man. CIC doesn't talk to us. Hell, even the

TOC is quiet. We checked the place the rhino beast was guarding, though. It had been cleaned out, probably weeks ago by the looks of it."

"That's a hard copy," Kovach answered. The connection made it sound distant and small to the team awaiting orders. Truthfully, how important could this mission be now that half the world was burning? "Set-up poppers and bugs. Exfil to the backup LZ. I'm calling this mission a bust. If you run into unfriendliness, try hard not to get dead."

"Hey, Prowler, what about Darkman?"

Kovach knew what he was asking. Hauling a fallen brother out of the shit was the standing order. It was also a good way to get the rest of them killed. "Negative on retrieval. Sorry, man, but the playbook has changed. He's gone, Priest."

Bishop 'Priest' Taggert tapped his tactical comm and nodded to his teammate. "Guess that's it."

"Suits the shit out of me," Halo answered. "Chances are, whatever is going on down here doesn't even matter anymore. Someone just nuked half the planet."

Priest, who nominally outranked Halo, took charge. "Set us up a route to the LZ, not the same track we came in on." Carrying Bayou would make that route nearly impossible. The earlier route had been for stealth. This one was not. He got busy prepping the poppers, which were tiny autonomous mines. They would automatically deploy from a rack on his battle suit every hundred yards and lay in wait for anyone who might try to come up from behind.

He then brought up the surveillance menu on his suit and readied a swarm of the insect size drones. These would deploy up and down the nav route, cycling from high above to landing on trees to monitor things. Each was no larger than a yellow jacket, totally silent, and almost undetectable. The images and data they provided were fantastic. They should have had them out earlier, but the squad had a limited supply, and battery life wasn't the best, so they tended to conserve their usage.

Hauling an injured soldier in full battle rattle was difficult, no matter the terrain. A hilly tropical jungle full of mutant monsters...*well, yeah, they never taught this in basic*. After thirty minutes, they had only made it about two kilometers. The landing zone was nine more. Priest stopped and popped the visor on his helmet to wipe sweat from his eyes.

The suits had built-in thermal regulation, but the helmets did not. Instead, it had a small circulation fan, which today just blew hot air around his head.

"You think Kovach can get us a ride out of this dump?"

Bishop looked at Halo, who was suffering as badly as himself. "I don't know, Jenkins. If anyone could, he can."

They both knew that Master Sergeant Kovach had as many enemies as he did friends in Space Corp and here dirt side with the Rangers. Despite that, he was the most capable soldier either of them had ever served with. That was even before all the enhancements. Combine that with the pull his father still had with the corps, and well, Joe was a good man to have on your side.

"He said the coastal regions of the country are hot. Looks like they dropped some old tactical nukes, good number of Blackout 88s, as well as whatever those Sapphire's were hauling," Bishop said, buttoning his helmet back up and standing.

"Shit," Halo said, softly falling in behind his partner. "Full bio payloads?"

"That's an unknown, but my working assumption is yes. What else could the damn things be used for?"

The actual armaments system in question had come at the end of the last major war. Even though only a few were ever used, like the early atom bomb, it scared the shit even out of its creators. It was the culmination of everything that was wrong with global warfare. While the superpowers had the military might backed up by tons of armaments, threats of nuclear strikes, and ballistic drop teams, the enemy had hackers, teams, and teams of hackers. Not just computers, either, although those were some of the most talented. Biohacking was what they really excelled at.

From the first puppies that glowed in the dark back in the early twenty-first century, now you could literally program genetic code to make any creature you could imagine. Designer pets, miniature giraffes, and a popular line of multi-colored leopards. The domestic stuff was kind of cool. They had houseplants that could move to find sunlight and water. Flowers that filtered and perfumed the air. With every innocent creation, though, someone in some covert lab was creating hundreds of less desirable and total lethal life-forms. Vines that could wrap around you like a snake and choke you out before you even realized you were trapped. Trees that fired lethal dart shaped seed pods with deadly accuracy. Many of the missions they had been sent on had involved people developing shit just like this, or pharmaceuticals that were even worse.

At the halfway point, Jenkins relieved Bishop of carrying the lieutenant. Both men took a pull from the hydration tubes, then verified they were still on course and wordlessly began again. Ten minutes later, their suits' speakers picked up the first detonation by the poppers. First one, then several in rapid succession.

"We are about to have company, friend," Priest said, shouldering his rifle as he checked the bug cams for any sign of whatever was heading their way.

CHAPTER
THIRTY-TWO

KOVACH

Getting the confirmation that one of my team was gone, and Bayou... Debra... was injured, bothered me more than anything else that had happened. We were the brotherhood; these guys had my back, and I wasn't there for them. I couldn't identify, though, with the countless injured or dead I'd passed the last few days. Maybe that was just part of who I am. Maybe it's just human nature.

SpecOps programs from all the branches no longer take applicants with close family ties. No husbands, wives, or small children. Deb is a rarity with a sister; many of us were an only child. The military life is hard on family, special operations divisions even more so. You had no control over your duty station or missions. Deployment time varied, but with the UDT, at least up to six months of the year could be either off planet or in recovery.

As my DI in basic told us, "If the Army felt like you needed a loving family member, you would have been assigned one." Ultimately, family became your fellow soldiers, your squad. And yes, if you are wondering, Pops doesn't count. He is a non-standard ancient piece of military hardware that just so happens to be assigned to me.

A red beacon began flashing in my visor's readout. Earlier, I'd signaled Sumo to leave the truck and go on a search pattern. Now he was onto something. I activated my targeting system and raised the gun up from a low-ready position. Moving through the wrecked buildings was creepy. Not the ruins. That was no different from countless bombed out places my career had taken me to. No, this was something different, like someone was watching me, yet I'd seen no one living and only a few bodies so far. "Coming to you, boy."

The dog was a combat animal and had his own enhancements, including a tiny comms unit implanted deep inside one of his ears. Some of the rest of what he had was top-secret, even to me. Officially, I was his handler, not his owner. Sumo was 100% U.S. Government property. Just like all the shit I was looking at right now.

I heard a bark coming from the far side of the building I was circling. Some drone coverages or additional personnel would be nice right now, but this wasn't combat. It looked the same, though, and increasingly, it felt the same. I extended my rifle out past the edge of the building. The optical sensors on the end of the barrel would feed into the scope long before I had to expose myself to whatever was on the other side. The outer ring of the scope stayed green, indicating no hostiles detected.

Sumo was tense and staring directly at a metal service door. He glanced my way as I cleared the building, then returned his total focus to that door.

"Ada, what do you have? Is this my lab?"

"Not the right one, zero life signs, zero energy output, zero threats detected."

I knew her sensors coverage was limited; with the local grid down, she was relying primarily on Sumo's and my organic eyes and ears, as well as a few other goodies embedded in our gear. She had the advanced software, though, to make the most out of limited information. Still, she wasn't human, nor did I trust her the same way I did Sumo.

"Suggest you follow the dog's lead, Prowler."

Whenever Ada switched to my combat call sign, all my warrior senses went active. Sumo and I had worked on missions countless times. We knew each other's behavior and preferences in combat situations. I knew he didn't like me touching him when he was in game mode, or getting between him and a target. That was a lesson it only took once for me to learn. I posted up against the side of the door and made eye contact with my canine partner.

"Position your left ear to the door, please," Ada whispered. I did as instructed.

One good thing about having an AI system in your head is she can do some pretty nifty tricks, like amplifying what my ears picked up even if it was below the normal range of humans. She was now playing back for me in real time noises from the interior of the structure. I sensed a whirring, like maybe a cooling fan on a computer. Breathing, but not a pace or rhythm that sounded remotely human. Then the tapping again, very faint and distant.

I tuned in to the tapping. If it was code, it was not in any sequence I could quickly identify. Apparently, Ada couldn't either, or she would have let me know. I put my hand on the door. Sumo's hair bristled, and he began a low growl. My dog has a way of letting me know the level of danger better than any human soldier I've ever worked with. Despite the fact that this should be friendly soil, something behind these doors was eliciting a major reaction from him. Realizing discretion might be smarter, I removed my hand from the door. Sumo visibly eased several degrees.

I backed slowly away from the door and then away from the building entirely. "Let's recon this for a while before we do something stupid," I whispered. Sumo looked at me questioningly. "Yes, by we... I mean me, Dipshit." The four-legged little shit wagged his tail and smiled. And yes, don't tell me dogs don't smile. I am looking at him right now, not you.

Three hours later, the sun was dipping toward the far hills, and I was positioned under a window in a building across the street from the building I was watching. I'd attached several motion and sound sensors aimed at the door, but so far, nothing. Earlier, I'd circled the building and only found two other ways in. Both were loading dock doors, and each was secured with padlocks from the outside. Each time we neared the entrance, Sumo went on high-guard and got himself a good case of the willies. He currently was sleeping in a puddle of sunshine streaming in through the cracked windows.

"Not sure I can afford to wait out whatever is in there."

My ever-present AI responded, "That is not the address you told me to look for. What makes you think it's important?"

That was the real difference between AI and humans, or even dogs. Intuition, randomness... the ability to make leaps of faith based on nothing more than a feeling. I trusted Ada, but I would always rely on Sumo in a crisis.

"I dunno. It's probably nothing," I admitted.

"But you are intent on making sure," she answered.

I nodded. "Something about it seemed... almost familiar." I had her replay the sounds we'd heard, and here in the fading daylight they creeped me out even more. For some reason, I kept seeing an animal's claw tapping down as it waited for its next victim to open the door.

That might not be too far from the truth; biogenetic developers had been turning out designer creatures for decades. There were a few dinosaur prototypes, all in miniature, most coming out of China or Taiwan labs. They didn't have real dinosaur DNA, of course, but their PR stated they started with a fragmented base of actual DNA. From what the news reports implied, gene editors could literally build any creature you wanted from the ground up. *Why not a mini velociraptor?*

I signaled Ada to stand watch as I was going to get some rack time. She would let me know if any of the sensors went off, and Sumo would make his own rounds shortly. I lay back using my rucksack as a pillow and tried to get comfortable.

CHAPTER
THIRTY-THREE

There is a point between sleeping and waking that can be perfection or absolute torture. The damp, cool air clung to my body like soiled linen. It was still dark; my internal clock put the time at an hour before dawn. Ada had let me sleep. Something in this place felt wrong. Something beyond the obvious facts of what had transpired here. Outside was unearthly silent. My eyes reluctantly opened to see a room cast in shadows of black and gray. Without moving, I scanned the room, looking for any threats, anything that didn't belong.

Sumo's reaction to the door yesterday had clearly put me on guard. And, I felt eyes on me. It's something soldiers learn to pay attention to, just don't ask us to explain it. It just is. Be it spidey sense or hyper-situational awareness, it can give you a second's head start and possibly the edge you need to stay alive.

It took a moment for my eyes to stop scanning and center on the thing. A darker shadow in a sea of black plastered into one corner of the room's ceiling. It wasn't there when I went to sleep. *What would be hanging from the ceiling, though?*

I used a series of eye movements to alert Ada, who came out of sentry mode and began filling in details in my visual overlay.

"No signs of activity last night, Prowler," her internal voice whispered inside my head.

I remained silent, activated magnification, infra-red, then full spectrum sweeps of the room. The thing was still there but didn't show up as anything on any of the scans. Still, it was there. Fear began creeping into my brain, the fear of an eight-year-old me who was afraid to look under the bed. I wanted to raise up and get a better view, but somehow, I instinctually knew that would be bad. Where was Sumo? I didn't hear his normal breathing. The fingers on my right hand crept to my sidearm, which I had placed on the floor next to me before going to sleep.

My fingers quietly found it and moved over the grip; the cold composite alloy felt comfortable in my hand. I heard movement to one side and turned just enough to see a shape that had to be Sumo. It was impossible to make out any detail, but in my head, he was looking at the same spot on the ceiling. *Did he see it, too?*

This is getting ridiculous, I thought as I slowly looked back up just in time to see... something. Movement, a reflection or... shit! The thing up there was alive, whatever the fuck it was. I jerked the pistol up, thumbed the safety off and rolled to one side, then came up in firing position.

The shadow didn't move. It also didn't exist, not anymore. "What in the fuck?"

"Are you okay, Joe?" Ada asked.

Which was the machine's polite way of saying 'Are you nuts?' 'Screwed in the head?' 'Imagining things?'

"Sumo, guard," I whispered. I had a tactical light in my bag but turning that on would do more harm than good. Along with ruining my eyes' natural night vision, I would let anyone in the surrounding area know exactly where I was. Somehow, I also knew it would be pointless. Whatever I thought had been there was gone.

The fog in my head began to clear, and I had to face the fact that it could have been nothing. Probably was nothing, but that wasn't what bothered me. What was really freaking me out was my own panic. Lying on that floor, I had been scared shitless. What in the fuck could make me feel that way? I didn't like it. It made me angry, and angry soldiers are stupid soldiers. I forcibly slowed my breathing and waited while my pulse rate subsided.

Sumo's soft footfalls sounded as he circled the open room, then made for the exit door and down the stairs. I followed his beacon in my overlay just to be sure he didn't run into trouble. I began donning my gear; it was time to get this day started. So far, I wasn't overly enthused at what it would hold.

I massaged my neck and tried again to shake off the fog of sleep. Ada had assured me she would have detected any life forms in the immediate area, but again, she mostly used my senses, even when I was asleep. This had limits, as did the dog's. "This place is creeping me out," I said to no one. At this point, I just wanted to get my shit and get out. The drugs that would keep me alive were the only compelling reason to spend one more second in this place.

"Ada what's going on with Bayou?"

My AI had been struggling to get any useful information from the team. She had assessed Debra's telemetry and determined she was not in immediate medical distress. The injuries she sustained could be remedied quickly at any fleet medical center, but she had also lost Darko and possibly...*shit*, probably a sister. I knew how emotionally damaging that would be.

"We may have a way to get them out, Joe. I've located possible transport but need help getting clearance."

I smiled, "So you messaged my dad, right?"

"Yes."

"That's' good, just please make it happen. They are the priority."

Sumo and I shared a couple of heated breakfast MREs. Activating the small chem pack on the bottom warmed the contents thoroughly and brought a sense of normal back to my world. I watched the neighboring building through the open window while I shoveled food into my face. The food was good; soldiers used to always complain about field rations, but no longer. Technology involving biological manufacturing had progressed to where manufactured shelf-stable foods were delicious. Even the ones developed for space-borne missions were exceptional.

The dog finished his and sat there looking at me. "Stop it," I said.

"This one is mine. You ate yours." He raised a paw and put it on my leg. Apparently not getting the reaction he wanted, he buried his head into my side and began snorting and wallowing his way into my lap. I held the tray up and continued to eat. "Do you have no shame?"

Sumo rolled over and looked at me with a look of total helplessness. *He has none, no.* I gave in and set the rest of my meal down and let him quickly devour the leftovers. Yeah, I know you shouldn't feed dogs leftovers. Bite me! It's the end of the world.

The first glimmers of daylight were just showing as we made our way back out. I moved around the area collecting the external sensors I'd set, then approached the building that had caused both Sumo and me so much concern yesterday. I noticed a faint dusting of purplish powder on each of the doors. Running a finger over the building's exterior left a mark of the same color. I rubbed it between my gloved fingers, wondering what it meant.

"You ready for this?" I whispered to Sumo as I reflexively checked my MK4, then felt the hilt of my main combat blade. The Heidelberg Damascus, steel six-inch blade that had saved me more times than I could count. Sumo took up position on the right side of the door and I on the left.

Even in the early morning light, I could see his muscular body lacked the tension and concern from yesterday. I, too, no longer felt the same level of threat. That did not mean either of us thought the place was safe. *Tactical lights and full sensor sweep on entry,* I sub-vocally communicated to my AI. My hand on the door handle, I nodded to Sumo who crouched low like a spring ready to uncoil itself at whatever lay beyond the entrance.

Silently, I brought the handle down into the release position. I'd seen no locks on the door, but that meant nothing. Throwing the door open, Sumo charged in, as did I, both moving in opposite directions with movements honed over the past year of working and training together.

A scream cut through the open space, the amplified sound turning my blood to ice before my helmet's filters dimmed it. My rail lights danced around the space we were in picking up nothing unusual.

"The sound was from outside, Prowler."

"Pattern match," I whispered, still searching for dangers.

"Unknown. No matches within the known catalog of any animal," Ada responded quietly.

The room was large, but certainly not the entire building. I guessed it at fifty by maybe a little over a hundred. Sumo was now in the far-right corner near what looked to be an office. I was against the opposite wall, which held several computer workstations, all dark. Other than the lack of significant damage, the interior of this building mirrored most of the others in the complex. Several doors led out of the room, all at the back. I signaled Sumo, who was clearing a second office, and we met on the back wall. Something... someone had been here yesterday.

"Threats?" I asked, knowing Ada would have alerted me to anything on her sensor array.

"Negative threats."

The scream came again from outside, farther away this time. Yeah, the threats were here, just not in this room. What in the hell was this place? I pulled open the first of the doors. It was a washroom, sink, toilet, normal stuff. The next one had a small sign with a symbol representing stairs. This door was locked. We moved to the final one as I chided myself for not leaving sensors outside. That was where the threat seemed to be now. A bead of sweat rolled down the side of my face, leaving a cold trail of wetness.

We were being hunted or stalked. I wasn't sure, but increasingly, I felt whatever we were up against was no longer contained inside these walls. I motioned for Sumo and said, "Hunt," as I threw open the last door. He and I both moved with speed through the short corridor beyond, actively clearing as much of the building as quickly as possible. This was something only a multiple-man team would normally attempt, but I trusted my partner, and we were good. I moved into darkened rooms one after the other. In two of them, I found bodies. No obvious cause of death. Ada recorded their names from the ID badges. I knew she would also get fingerprint scans and retinals as well, as I raised a cold eyelid on the lifeless face of a once very attractive woman. Most of this was routine. We'd raided a lot of labs on missions, and you never knew what intel you might need later.

Sumo barked from farther back in the building. I was already moving that way. Sumo is a combat dog and has a range of barks. Over time, both Ada and I have learned to interpret many of them. This one clearly meant, 'I found something, but no immediate threat.'

Seconds later, as I looked over the blood-soaked pile of debris Sumo had found, I wasn't so sure. The debris was flesh and bone. One finger still wore a wedding band. A trail of tiny red dots moved away and into a hole in the wall. My finger smeared one of the dots. It was blood.

CHAPTER
THIRTY-FOUR

We'd found three more bodies within the hour, all mangled just like the first. The bite pattern didn't match normal predation according to Ada. She'd analyzed the arterial spray that painted the surrounding floor, the position of the bodies, and what appeared to be defensive wounds when they were fighting off, well...whatever it was.

"So, these people were alive when it attacked? They didn't die in the blast?"

"Yes, Joe."

I looked down into what remained of the ruined face of an older, olive-skinned man. According to the badge still attached to a remnant of lab coat nearby, he'd been a scientist, a doctor in fact.

"Why were the other corpses not...not ...like this?" I finally said. "Why were they not eaten?"

"These victims were not eaten, Joe, simply attacked. Viciously so, but like I said, not for predation."

"And the others," I began. "They were already..."

"Yes, dead. They posed no threat, or maybe no challenge to what-ever did this."

"So, this thing only kills the living. Kills but doesn't feed."

"Don't think you can kill the unliving, Joe."

I had a butt load of zombie movie references to prove her wrong, but I kept quiet.

"This is a DARPA site, Joe. As far as I can tell, advanced weapons development for the Alliance."

"A biological weapon," I whispered. This reminded me of some of the stories my dad told about what they fought near the end of the last war. Still, I'd never seen anything do damage like this. Some cuts were precise and neat, almost surgical. Others were ragged and torn.

Sumo and I cleared the rest of the building, even forcing open the door to upstairs, where we'd found row after row of smaller labs. Some were obviously surgical suites, others held giant medical machines whose purpose neither I nor Ada could guess. One entire side held racks of advanced computer servers. The roof had been peeled back there, probably by the bombs. I tied in one of my p-cells for power for the servers, but Ada said all the storage chips were melted slag.

Half the morning was gone and still no med pack for me. Nothing but dead bodies, invisible monsters, and even more questions. Dying prematurely from organ failure was no longer the most pressing threat I faced. The monsters were out there... whatever they were. This was indeed a new world. We would never be the same again.

"Joe, I'm picking up a signal."

"What kind?" I asked.

"Net usage appears to be on the crypto bands."

"Banking?" I said curiously. That was interesting because machines didn't need money. It indicated something human. All comms systems used the crypto internet bands for issuing payments now. The block chain security was still better than any of the more ancient financial systems.

"Someone attempting to make a purchase. The location is a little over four miles away. An automated food store."

"It still has power?" That seemed unlikely, but maybe emergency backup was still working. The big guys, like Amazon, Tesco, and such, had the small reactor units to power theirs, but those were only in major metroplexes. Nothing like that would normally be out here in the Virginia hill country.

"Plot a course and bring the truck down," I said. We had only investigated a fraction of the sprawling complex, but so far, I'd found no one alive. No one that could give me answers or point me toward what I needed. Anyone close by had to be associated with this place; there was no other reason to be here. Also, whatever had killed these scientists was out there, probably still hunting.

CHAPTER
THIRTY-FIVE

The truck's batteries were failing. I knew it was just a matter of time, but walking didn't seem like fun, or practical, and I'd seen no other vehicles still operating in the last 300 miles.

"We're going to need to turn west to get out of the devastation once we get my meds. Maybe then we can find fresh batteries or even another vehicle." I'd been thinking an air car would be really nice to have. Being here on the ground with whatever had been in that lab was an increasingly unpleasant thought.

What in the hell had they created back there? Strangely, though, it was what haunted my imagination that scared me even more. I knew something had been watching us sleep, something that Ada and maybe even Sumo hadn't noticed. That lab had lots of secrets, and now all of them had potentially gotten off the leash.

The level of destruction was less on the other side of the ridgeline. The little community beyond seemed largely untouched. The downed trees inside the blast zone blended into just down limbs, then leaves and scattered debris. Something told me there was damage here, too, though. Maybe not the same as the facility, but it wasn't unscathed. The truck crunched over limbs and gravel covering the road. A few abandoned cars were stalled in places, but the roadway was passable, and radiation was near normal.

I saw nothing noteworthy except some long-abandoned barns and overgrown farmland until a small auto charging station came into view. All the hyper-charger connectors were still in the racks; the cheaper superchargers were all connected to cars. I slowed the truck and pulled to the edge of the road.

"Is this the place?"

Ada answered at once. "No, it is a half mile farther. This service station has no power nor Wi-Fi readings."

I could tell she was right; the cars had been left right where they stopped. My assumption was one of the hypersonic blackout bombs must have gone off near enough to take down the local power grid. That would have killed the all-electric cars where they were. Apparently, something up here in these hills still had juice, though. And power was something I could use.

"Coming into view ahead, Joe. You may want to park before the bend ahead."

"Copy that," I said instinctually as I rolled the passenger side window down.

"Sumo." The husky looked at me questioningly. I put a finger to my lips, pointed ahead, and then made a patting motion with my palm. He leapt silently from the window and began a stealthy recon of the area.

I donned my helmet, the bucket starting to smell a little ripe after so many days without being cleaned. The MK4 clicked into place on my back. I wasn't expecting trouble, but that's usually about the time it shows up. Making my way along the edge of the woods, I tracked Sumo's sensors in my heads-up as he worked his way along the far side. Ada could also use sensors on the dog and his battle vest to detect heat signatures and could often make reasonably good assumptions based on his movements as to the likely threat level.

"No life signs present, Joe."

I peered through the brush at a quaint food store. The kind just the right size for a community of a few hundred people. The interior had several flickering lights and one of the glass doors was smashed in. I saw Sumo's head pop out of the wood line on the opposite side of the small parking lot. I signaled him to clear the building, still motioning my hand patting down. He knew what the non-lethal signal meant. Stay hidden, don't assume these are the enemy, take down without serious injury if you must. Sumo's training had been extensive, in many ways even more comprehensive than my own.

My boot crunched down on broken glass as I moved up against the wall. My old instructor would have made me run the fifteen-mile trail's course in full battle kits had I done that back at Ranger school. Moving into the store, I dashed left, knowing Sumo would take right. The lighting was erratic. Most of the LED panels overhead were out. Still, I heard the hum of refrigeration units. It was surprising that no one was here, no workers, no locals. My anxiety inched up a degree as I thought about the creature that was out here somewhere. Maybe that was why no one was here.

Sumo cleared most of the store before I'd moved through even a third of it. I nodded, and he padded off to the door to stand watch.

"No one in here," I said to my AI, who obviously knew that already. It felt like a combat mission, and I couldn't help but revert to battle tactics. I was reporting in. Okay, I was talking to myself... whatever, it's the end of the world. Have I made that clear yet? Yeah, the end— game over. Let's all get a juice-box and let that sink in for a bit.

Moving up to one of the autopay checkouts, I saw a list of groceries that showed 'Payment failed. Please try again.' Canned food, bottled water, bleach, matches, and more. It was a good list of non-perishable supplies. Emergency supplies. Not a lot, but if someone were walking, they would have been limited to what they could carry. There was a personal ident key on the shopper. The store's built in audit AI would have tracked everything the person put into their bags and probably already had them on file as a regular customer. Looked like the system worked as it was supposed to, except it was unable to automatically debit their payment method as they left. The Wi-Fi might be working, but the payment processors on the other end must not have been.

"Ada, can you get a name or address from the person's ident key?" I knew that was unlikely with the extreme privacy protections places like this employed, but it was worth a try.

"Sorry, Joe, local customer is all I can tell from the system. Regular web is still out, so I can't do any cross references for a possible match."

"Okay, let's head out then, if they're on foot, they couldn't have gone far."

"Agreed," she said. "You may also want to restock essentials before you leave, Joseph. They also have a supercharger station if we can spare a few minutes."

I already had one foot halfway out the door before grasping what my AI had suggested. I offered a meek "Duh" before going back inside.

Ada brought the GMC down to the entrance. I plugged it into the charger and loaded it up with way more than we needed. It was obvious to me now that opportunities like this might not be that frequent. I just hated that a computer had to be the one to suggest it.

Sumo watched me as I grabbed every pork flavored sausage pack in the freezer. I also added an armload of nice-looking steaks in the ever-wrap section. These would keep nearly indefinitely because of the way they were packaged. Ada fed some information to the Audit bot to keep it from sounding the alarms and trying to slam the broken doors when we exited. I was back on the road in fifteen minutes, much better equipped than I had been, and with a solid half charge on the battery pack.

She came into view within ten minutes. A lone woman pulling a red wagon with several grocery bags. I knew she could be armed but pulled alongside her anyway. My helmet was off to hopefully appear somewhat less frighting to her. Still, she flinched noticeably as she finally saw the nearly silent truck easing up beside her.

"Excuse me."

"Leave me alone, I...I don't have anything," she said nervously.

She was thin, probably late twenties, with a bookish but pleasant face. "I can help you get where you're going. I'd just like some information."

She stopped walking and narrowed her eyes at me. The doubt on her face rapidly turning to fear. Her eyes darted to the dog, which made her pull back more than she had to the beat-up, old truck. "You aren't from around here."

It wasn't a question, and judging by her southern accent, she wasn't from around here either.

"No, ma'am. I'm not, but I'm harmless. Do you work back there at the base?"

"At the facility?" she said, moving a bit farther off the road. "You had business there? What, with ADI?"

Apex Defense Industries, or ADI, was a group I was familiar with. I hadn't known that was who was contracting at the base, but it made sense. The group's parent company, Hammer Industries, was a significant player in the defense industry. "In a way," I offered in way of explanation.

The woman had walked again, one of the wagon wheels squeaking and wobbling badly as she pulled it. Her eyes were fixed on something invisible directly in front of her; she refused to look my way. I pulled the truck down past her and stepped out to meet her.

One look at the guy getting out of the truck in a battle suit and she panicked and sprinted into the woods. The child's wagon kept rolling several more feet until it rolled to a stop near my rear bumper. I motioned my head in her direction and Sumo took off after her. This was not how I wanted the conversation to go, but, well... shit.

CHAPTER
THIRTY-SIX

She was crying. Her hair had fallen into her face, and her clothes were a mess of mud, twigs, and leaves. Sumo followed a few yards behind her. I sat on the tailgate of the pickup drinking a canned espresso and enjoying the view. The dog perp-walked her up close before sitting down and gnawing at an itch on his underside. He'd done his job. Now it was my turn.

"Why did you run?"

She shook her head, wiping tears away with a dirty sleeve. It was obvious this woman had already been through a lot. And yes, I was being an ass, but I'm not exactly known for my people skills.

"I only wanted to talk," I said as calmly as I could. I offered her a bottle of water from my new stash of supplies. She accepted it with a shaky hand. Anyone could see she was terrified of me and the dog. "I'm sorry we frightened you. My name is Joe. Any chance we could start over?" I offered an outstretched hand to her.

She took a deep drink as she looked warily at my hand. She made no move to accept the handshake. I believe the simple act of touching me would have meant defeat to her. I let it fall to my side and looked off toward the nearby valley nonchalantly.

"I'm Carol," she said in a voice so low I could barely make out the words. Ada enhanced the sound, though. *Good*, we had the meager basis for a conversation.

"Hello, Carol. I'm sure you've been through hell out here. I'm just looking for some information on one of the buildings back at... at the Hammer Industries site. I'll leave you alone, but can you answer me that one thing?"

Her head cocked slightly; a shadow crossed her face. "What building?"

"J-7"

The look on her face was telling. "I can't help you." She looked back at Sumo, clearly contemplating another escape. Giving out information on the local Hammer Industries Apex complex was a deal breaker, as far as this conversation was concerned. I knew the NDA agreements that dark sites like this one operated under. Even the end of the world would not void the penalties for any associate talking about it.

"I have to get back home," she said, easing now alongside the truck.

I stayed seated, still not looking at her specifically. "You have family waiting?"

She stopped moving. Anger flashed in the woman's eyes; I could sense the rise in hostility even before glancing toward her. Whatever progress I had made in building trust seemed to vanish. She forced her emotions back down but still looked like a tea kettle whose whistle was malfunctioning. "Yes. I mean, no, they just won't let me back in if I'm gone too long."

"I have her name," Ada said quietly inside my own thoughts. "She is Carol Reynolds. She is thirty-two from Georgia, divorced. She has shared custody of one minor child. I list no advanced degrees of note; no residence nor place of employment."

Good to see that there were apparent internet connections coming back. Ada's info was useful, but mainly in explaining the woman's motivation. A single mother getting food for her child was a perspective on the apocalypse I could appreciate. Carol's last statement had my full attention, though.

"Who are 'they?'"

Ten minutes later, the truck eased to a stop near the makeshift barricade. I counted five men, all armed; several carried their weapons with the practiced look of former soldiers. I nodded to them and looked at my passenger, Carol, again who simply stared forward. She said some of the men in her community had decided to blockade the subdivision to keep out looters and such.

Ada found an online aerial map of the subdivision, and it was clear there was only one way in and one way out. Carol was clearly afraid of these men. "Do they have your child?" I asked quietly, making a show of raising my hands high before I stepped out.

She glanced at me with a look of surprise. She still hadn't confirmed any family to me. She shook her head before looking back straight ahead. She was terrified, but it was no longer because of me or the dog.

"Let the woman go," one man yelled. A tall, lanky man with a disappointing week's worth of beard trying to fill in the gaps of an already unattractive face.

"Drop your gun and surrender your key fob," another said as I stepped out and lowered the visor of my tactical helmet over my face.

Immediately, targeting reticles appeared over each of the men, and threat indicators showed more weapons in two nearby houses. "Sumo has another at your seven o'clock position," Ada said.

The men's demeanor changed now that they realized they were facing someone in full battle kit. I snapped my rifle back into the maglock on my back and approached the group. Ada identified each man. All had former military or government credentials. That made sense; this was a base town. Security and paranoia would be part of their DNA. Despite appearances, this was not a typical middle-class neighborhood. It was a clandestine community full of what I considered to be the dark underbelly of the industrial-military machine.

"Greetings, gentlemen. Just dropping off my new friend, one of your neighbors I found down the road." My hands were still up. My helmet's speakers modulating my voice in what Ada knew to be non-threatening tones and volume.

"That's far enough," one of the younger men said, shoving a rifle barrel past the makeshift barricade and toward me.

"His anxiety level is approaching dangerous levels, Prowler."

"No shit," I whispered. Looking over, I saw Carol was still just sitting in the truck, staring straight ahead. I had no idea what might have gone on between her and these men over the last week, but I had a strong feeling it wasn't good.

"We're going to need your truck, Son," an older man said in a relaxed tone.

I turned to see who was talking. He was mid-fifties, holding the barrel of a rifle that was propped against some steel drums. That one was relaxed, confident. He was going to be the one to watch.

"You see," I began, "that's what I like about these little communities up here. Everybody shares, right?"

"Just give us the key fob and start walking, or you'll be sorry."

I was already sorry I'd wasted this much time. *Coming here might have been a mistake.* I saw the calm man give a subtle signal, obviously, to the sniper at my rear. "Takedown," I said to Sumo before lunging to one side at a speed that few men would believe possible. I heard my partner tearing into the hidden threat just as a bullet whizzed through the space I'd previously occupied. It caught Sketchy Beard in the throat, and he flew back from the impact, his body dead before the brain even realized the danger. *These dumb fucks have no clue on firing angles,* I thought as my body went on autopilot.

My pistol was instantly in my hand and firing. A flechette round shredded a fat man aiming a shotgun at my head. I did a body roll toward the truck, dropping the pistol and coming up with the rifle. As I brought the MK4 Rattler to bear on the remaining men, the look of shock and fear were plastered across every face. They knew the damage a pulse rifle at close range could do. All of them eyed it, then me, then at the blood-soaked dog coming at them from the other side of the truck.

I could now see other people emerging from houses farther back in the neighborhood. This little scene was obviously not the normal way things went down around here. One man dropped his weapon and ran; another turned, lowering his rifle toward my partner. I punched a carnage round into him, separating his head from his torso. A bullet caught me in the shoulder. It bounced off the armor but fucked up my shot at the calm man who still seemed to be smiling. Ada alerted me to the house and the window the shot had come from. I brought the rifle up and pointed it in that direction while keeping my eyes locked with Mister Smiley, the lone man remaining in front of me.

"Hey, stupid, you want everyone to die?" I fired blindly, trusting Ada to help me with the targeting. A muffled grunt came from the direction of the house, followed by a woman's scream.

The man in front of me now had his gun up and the smile was gone, but not the arrogance. I could still see the smugness behind his eyes. He reminded me of all the high-ranking government assholes I had dealt with in my work. The spooks, the consultants, the shits that could force even superb commanders to make stupid, irrational decisions. They operated outside the law, unleashed from the bounds of human decency. Motivated by power, greed, or sometimes just a psychopathic need to inflict harm. Decisions that got some of us killed. I hated every motherfucker like him.

I wanted him to raise the gun. I prayed he would be stupid. He apparently preferred to keep breathing. Slowly, he nodded and placed his rifle on the ground with one hand. The other raised partially in a display of surrender. He then shouted to each side, telling his men to stop firing.

I trusted nothing this man did and assumed he was not done playing his part just yet. I bent a finger subtly motioning for Sumo to takedown with prejudice. The dog happily obeyed. Mister Smiley would still be breathing in a few minutes, but he would no longer be a threat. Not to me nor anyone else in the area. As Sumo cleared the barricade, I saw the asshole's expression go pasty white.

CHAPTER
THIRTY-SEVEN

I volunteered several of the people now out on the front lawns of their homes to help dismantle the roadblock. I'd half expected Carol to flee back to the safety of her own home, but she came and stood beside me. Her face shined with a new expression, a confidence I hadn't seen before. She walked over to where Smiley was sitting; Sumo had done a job on him. His back rested against a large metal trash bin. She kicked him hard, then spat on him. He began to wretch and we both turned away.

"I take it you aren't friends," I said, taking off my helmet.

She shook her head. "Government asshole. He proclaimed all the resources here as community property as soon as the shit went down."

"Did that include the women?"

She just glared, but it was obvious things were heading in that direction, if not there already.

"Being single in this neighborhood wasn't safe, even before the attack. Do you know what happened? These guys took all the local routers offline, said we could be tracked, so I haven't even been able to reach out to my son."

I nodded, unwilling to say more out here. Judging by the expression on the formerly smiling man, someone she had called Murphy, he was not well loved. No one was bothering to tend to his wounds. The deep cuts Sumo had left were weeping dark blood. I shrugged; he was no danger to anyone now. I left him with the trash. Carol was walking ahead, pulling her wagon full of groceries. I quietly asked Ada to secure the truck and then for Sumo to guard our own supplies. I turned to follow Carol; I was determined to get the information on the pharma lab. She walked just a few houses back from the entrance and turned into a modest two-story home.

She motioned me inside, much of her hostility toward me gone. I carried in as many of the groceries as I could manage into her kitchen. Another woman was there holding a kid's baseball bat. She and Carol hugged, then she turned to look at me. "You're Sergeant Kovach."

So much for all my attempts at privacy, I thought.

I was too stunned to even speak for a few minutes. I let the two women catch-up first. Soon I learned the other woman was Carol's neighbor, Damiana Voss. Ms. Voss had been previously assigned to Dr. Reichert's team as something like an administrative assistant, but that didn't quite fit her assertive demeanor.

"Reichert's not here, is he? I mean, was this where..."

Damiana cut her eyes toward Carol, then shook her head. "No, this is just a research site."

I could tell she was lying. This was a bio-weapons facility, and I was probably one of those weapons. At least partially built here.

"I need to find the pharma labs for building J-7."

Realization seemed to dawn on the other woman. She looked at Carol. "The Bio lab's on the east side." Looking back at me, she asked, "How long do you have?"

Damiana was attractive, brunette, glasses, with a runner's body and a look that could likely freeze men in their tracks. I wanted to be aloof, say something witty. None of that came out. The truth was quickly becoming too frightening for me. "Just over a month." I'd taken the last of my meds the previous day. "Assuming I keep my stress levels in check."

She nodded. "Yeah, that speeds it up, right? Could have been worse. I'm sure some of them were due within days of the attack."

"So, can you help me? Do you know where the med packs would be?"

She began unpacking the supplies her friend had brought. "Maybe, but no guarantees." She stopped what she was doing and turned to face me. "But I want something in return."

I motioned behind me. "I just got rid of your local thugs. Isn't that enough?"

Damiana gave a grim smile. "They were just a nuisance, Kovach, not a serious threat. Murphy is the only one with any brains. He was most of these guys' boss at Iron River."

"Iron River?"

"Yes, Hammer Industries, Iron River Research Center."

"Oh?' I said questioningly.

Her face broke into a smile. "Yeah, Murphy was co-director for one of the main labs in J-7"

No fucking way. Jesus H. Christ. Joseph Kovach, you are an imbecile. I struggled to regain some control. "So, what is it you want from me?"

"If we help you get your meds, you take us with you."

Before I could object, she continued.

"We aren't safe here. Not just because you killed all those guys either, although more of them are here. Murphy will regroup and come at us hard for bringing you here. Carol needs to find her son. He was spending the week with his dad down in Atlanta. I just need to get somewhere..." she trailed off briefly. "Somewhere else, somewhere safer."

She moved around the counter to look at me. "Most of the rumors I've been hearing. Well...I'm not sure any of us are safe here anymore."

I hadn't planned on going anywhere except maybe out of the immediate blast zones. Maybe to see if Deb's sister had survived. I sure hadn't planned on taking stragglers with me. Still, whatever had killed those people back in the labs was out here, maybe more than one. People in this subdivision knew the dark horrors Iron River held, and now they were all scared. I had to consider Voss's offer.

"My truck is on its last legs. The batteries are ancient. I just need to get some doses of my meds and reunite with my squad."

"What about your father?" Damiana asked.

She obviously knew a great deal about me. I pinged Ada to see if she could feed me the intel on Damiana.

"Isn't he down in Florida somewhere? Don't you need to check on him?"

The woman had an aggravating way of cutting right to the chase on everything. "We aren't exactly close," I offered weakly.

"You have my offer. I don't see where you have any options."

And dammit, she was right. Things were getting way more complicated.

CHAPTER
THIRTY-EIGHT

The two women quickly brought what they considered essential out to the truck. Damiana's house was next door, but Murphy's top man had forced her out days earlier, said they needed it for its strategically important position. It had been where one of the snipers had been posted. She didn't strike me as someone who would have been bullied easily. When I asked her about it, she just smiled.

"Just a house, Kovach. Sometimes you must pick your battles."

She wasn't wrong. Somehow, I felt she could have handled these men if she wanted. I got a vibe of hidden reserves within her compact frame. The two of them didn't have much to add to my own supplies but brought along bedding and spare clothes.

"Why did they let you go to the store alone?" I asked Carol.

"I didn't ask," she replied with a snort. "We weren't prisoners, not exactly. They kept telling everyone they had made a food order that would be delivered soon, but we both knew that was a lie. Most of the homes were well stocked. Not everyone came home that day so..." She left the rest unsaid. "Also, I had hoped I could get a connection so I could talk to Lux."

"Lux is your son."

She nodded; I could see the tears forming before she looked away quickly. "I'm sorry."

"Joe," Ada said in a soft, internal voice. "I managed to bypass the Wi-Fi firewall and access the satellites again, although the signal is noisy. I think someone here was running a jammer, but I am running a search for her child. Also, I see no information on any government associate using that name of the other woman."

Interesting, I thought. I subvocalized for her to go ahead and run the search. Minutes later, she gave me the update.

"I've found an autocar pickup in an Atlanta suburb for one Lux Reynolds last Wednesday, the day of the attack. Destination was here."

I did my best to hide the concern on my face.

The AI continued, "His nanny-bot posted an emergency message a few hours into the trip."

Ada read off the rest of the details, and it became clear. Carol's son was dead already or on his own out there somewhere in the north Georgia or Tennessee hill country. I stepped away from the women, who were grabbing final supplies and offering goodbyes to a few of the more friendly women who'd gathered to watch.

"Fix the crash coordinates and map a route from here."

"Already done, Joe, but that data point was nearly a week ago. One small boy on his own for that long..."

She didn't bother finishing the thought. I understood completely.

"Will you tell Carol? She deserves to know."

I looked over at the woman; she was a mother, and while she had not been particularly friendly to me, she was justified in how she felt. "I will," I finally said. "But I want to have a plan first. See if we have any assets we can call on down there. Anything you can find that might offer some hope. Also, please see if you can get an update on my team's evac."

Selfishly, I wanted the two women in a helpful mood until I found the drugs I needed. I knew if I said anything to Carol now, they likely wouldn't want to go back to the Iron River facility to help me look. What can I say? I'm an asshole? The thing is, five weeks from now... I still want to be an asshole, a living, breathing one.

∾

It surprised me that we got out of the neighborhood with no other shit coming down on us.

"Oh, my God, look," Damiana said, pointing.

I thought my fly was down, but no, she was pointing a little higher.

"It has a steering wheel."

I smiled. "Yeah, they are kind of handy now that the roads and cars can no longer talk to each other."

Carol was still quiet; I knew she had concerns about her son and leaving her home behind. She had no plan other than wanting to get to her child. I was a convenience, a means to an end—nothing more. Damiana was a bit of a talker, though; it was okay; I liked it. She was personable and obviously smart and, yeah, rather attractive, too. Honestly, both women were, but Damiana was more comfortable with it.

"Just call me Dami," she said. Her face wrinkling into a slightly adorable grin.

Was she flirting with me?

She sat up front in Sumo's seat, and Carol sat nervously in the back with Sumo.

"Can you get a move on? I don't want to be in that place come nighttime," Dami said with a tone of dread.

Nope, she wasn't flirting. Also, I agreed with her. I had no intentions of being there when the sun went down. "You said you had heard rumors. Care to share?"

Damiana pursed her lips, clearly unsure of what she could talk about. "Stuff went on in all of those buildings. We aren't supposed to ever discuss any of it, but well... you know, people talk. The guys especially. They love to brag."

"Did they do a lot of bio-warfare stuff? You know, like more of the genetically edited biologics?" I asked, hoping she would open more quickly. We were only ten minutes away. I wanted a better idea of what I might be facing.

She laughed. "Like you?"

"Touché."

She nodded. "At least a third of the base was involved in advancing biological weaponry in one form or another. Essentially, the ability to weaponize both flora and fauna."

"Fauna? You mean like plants?"

"Like everything. I know they have a vine that can wrap around a person in seconds and deliver a natural neurotoxin through tiny hairs on its tendrils. I had to write up the field trials on that one. Some of the other stuff... well, no one's talking about it. I saw the cages they had built, though, scary as fuck."

Visions of the dead scientist and the ceiling monster invaded my thoughts.

She went on, apparently feeling better about sharing now that she was away from Murphy and his minions. "Iron River is essentially an R&D facility, a skunk-works, so it had a little of everything Hammer was into. Being so close to D.C., it was a convenient air hop for influential senators and military brass to come out and get the full dog and pony show."

"Joe, the batteries are at twenty-eight percent and dropping," Ada said internally. I'd been too distracted to notice how fast the meter was falling.

"Shit."

"What?" both women said at once.

"I should have fully charged the truck back at your house. We may not have any juice to leave the facility afterward."

I couldn't see Carol, but the look in Damiana's eyes let me know that wasn't an option.

"Don't worry, it's okay. I'll come up with something. We can lay out a charging blanket, still have a couple of hours of sunlight." Right on cue, I noticed clouds building off to the west. We had a storm moving in. Maybe I could make it back to the little store and wait it out there. Have I mentioned that I wasn't thinking strategically? Whatever mental upgrades I supposedly got were obviously on vacation.

CHAPTER
THIRTY-NINE
LUX

"I'm really hungry, boy." Lux didn't know if the dog was a male, but that was what he thought of him as. The two had roamed the woods all day. He did not know how far away from the road they'd come, but it felt like a million miles, maybe more. He dug around in the red bag hoping to find something else to eat. He'd finished the last snack bar and water just after sunrise.

At first, he thought the dog must have lived around here. Every time they topped another hill, he just knew the shaggy mutt was going to start barking and racing for a house that he could just barely make out. It hadn't happened, not yet. They topped one hill, and then another seemed to rise up to take its place. The dog did run far ahead occasionally but always came back to wait on him.

The boy knew it was getting late again. He didn't want to sleep under a tree like he had the night before and the night before that. Ants had gotten down in his clothes and kept biting him, but he'd been too afraid to move. He did not like the woods at night. He wanted to be home; he wanted to be safe.

"I'm not going to cry. Dad said only babies cry, and I'm no baby." He stomped his feet hard to drive away the stinging in his watery eyes as he ran to catch up with the dog.

Two hours later, Lux's feet were dragging with each step. He'd tripped over a root and busted his lip. He tasted blood and could feel how much bigger the bottom lip was on one side. His stomach was growling so loudly he'd tried to eat some dark purple berries growing on a low plant, but the dog got between him and the bush. They looked good, but he knew things like that could be bad. Still, if he saw another one, he was going to try them. He needed something.

As they descended yet another hill, he began to slide; this one was much steeper than the rest. It was also getting so dark he couldn't see what was in front of him. "Hey, boy. Where are you?" He was nearly on all fours as he made his way down. He heard the dog but could no longer tell in what direction he was. Then the sounds of the dog faded, then were gone. It was only him and the woods and the strange night sounds that always scared him so much.

"Hey, boy!" Lux called out, much softer this time. He wanted the dog to hear, but not the other bad stuff that was probably out there. He was so thirsty, so hungry, and so scared. Giving up trying to walk or even crawl down the steep slope, he sat on his butt and slid. Mom would be mad about his pants, but it wasn't his fault.

After several minutes, the trees thinned, and he saw the familiar gulley that almost all the hills seemed to end in. He stood back up and caught a smell of something on the breeze. It smelled like food; his stomach growled again. It smelled good... really good, but he didn't know what it might be; mostly what they ate at home were the precooked meals or deliveries his mom ran through the food-prep machine on the counter. Whatever this was, he was smelling... he wanted it. He moved in the direction, his scuffed shoes sinking deeply into the sandy soil.

The house sat in a clearing; it wasn't alone. A dozen more that looked just like it lined the street, but the smell came from one with light flickering in the window. Outside, his new friend, the dog, sat wagging his big tail as a girl tossed him a ball. Lux wanted to cry, but his tiny body no longer had any water to spare for tears.

Strangers could be dangerous. His mom and dad both told him that —a lot. Marcie had warned him as well, but this place felt normal. He tried to call out and waved an arm weakly. The boy was so tired. He stumbled and fell as the forest floor turned suddenly into a thick green lawn. The dog barked again. He tried to rise, but the lush ground felt so good he just stayed there. Smelling the grass, the fragrant food, and hearing people again. His eyes closed as sleep took him.

CHAPTER
FORTY
KOVACH

I topped the last hill before the Iron River facility. As the sprawling complex came into view, Carol and Damiana gave an involuntary gasp.

"They're ruins," they both said.

I slowed to get a better view. The place looked even worse, much worse, in fact, than when I'd left earlier in the day. As the truck slowed to a stop, the reason became obvious. Thick greenish-violet vines, some as thick as my waist, covered the blast side of every building.

"Those weren't here earlier." I stepped out and pulled the rifle to scope the grounds. Green and lavender tendrils ran out from almost every inch of the thick vines. They seemed to writhe aimlessly until they touched the wall or a window, then they began burrowing into the cladding material. In places already breached, windows began falling out and large chunks of plasticrete fell away like paper.

A sudden noise pulled my attention to the left, where a low-rise building began to shake. The edges were covered in the ropy vines. Suddenly, it disappeared from sight with a tremendous crash. A cloud of dust and debris was all that remained. As the dust cleared, I saw even the rubble was disappearing under a thick mat of vines.

"The um...'flora' seems to be attacking your facility."

"No shit," Damiana said, gathering her go-pack, exiting the truck, and moving down a hill toward the ruins with a determined stride.

This woman wanted something here badly, nearly as much as I did. I quickly deployed the solar blanket and followed close behind, Sumo and Carol both somewhat reluctantly trailing after us.

"Hey, um," I said, catching up to Damiana. "I probably should have mentioned a few things. We might be in danger other than from that." I pointed ahead at a vine the size of a tall pine tree bent down to the roof of a collapsed parking structure. Through my helmet speakers, I could already hear the strained protest of rending metals as the plant forced itself deeper inside the structure packed with flattened cars.

"Like what?" she asked without slowing.

"Animal, fauna, megafauna, maybe more than one."

She stopped to face me. "Describe it."

I described the one on the ceiling, admitting that it could have been a mirage, then the shredded bodies of the scientists.

"You spent the night here?" She waved a hand around like I must have been insane.

"Look, you and I both know if I don't find replacement meds, I'm dead either way."

She started walking again, even faster this time. "Let's hurry the fuck up, then."

Naturally, building J-7 was on the opposite side of the Iron River complex. The upside was that was the farthest away from the worst of the detonation—and the encroaching vines. The damage was everywhere but slightly less as we wove our way through the warren of tumbled down walls. I saw Sumo dart to the side several times as ropy vines snaked out of piles of rocks toward him. After I jumped back moments later, I realized we were both more frightened than the woman. Something else occurred to me, and I decided to voice it.

"The bodies are gone."

"Huh?" both women asked.

"When we were here earlier, bodies littered the sidewalks and buildings." I could still see blood and gore but hadn't spotted a single corpse yet. That could mean predation...that something was feeding.

Those would have been these women's co-workers, neighbors, friends. Yet neither seemed overly concerned. I muted my external speakers. "Ada, any assessment on what is going on? Why all the changes since this morning?"

"Working on it, Joseph. This is a case where I have too much information instead of too little. Unfortunately, none of it is adding up sufficiently. My working hypothesis is whatever they were working on here was adversely affected by gamma radiation from the Sapphire bombs, or maybe the blast wave just freed the creatures and plant life, and the blast sped up their evolutionary clock. Genetic progression is taking place in minutes here rather than generations. This place will be a wasteland within a few days. I suggest you get what you need and get out."

Damiana had gotten us to the row of multistory buildings she'd indicated as where the pharmacy lab was. She had darted in and out of several of the smaller structures, clearly looking for something. As I moved to finally step inside the building marked J-7, I offered a small sigh of relief. The destructive sounds of the vines were more muted here. Still, I knew better than to let my guard down. Too many missions ended badly when you were getting close to your mission objective.

I swept my pulse rifle back to cover Sumo and Carol. The dog was staying close to Carol, clearly protective of her. I heard something grinding and leaped to the side, away from the building, and that was when the earth opened beneath both. Carol and Sumo disappeared from sight in an instant.

CHAPTER
FORTY-ONE
BANSHEE

"Stay down, Bayou."

The injured lieutenant was struggling to rise.

"Get the fuck off me, Priest," she yelled. Her teeth were clenched in pain. "Sitrep?"

"NaFu," Jenkins yelled over the comms.

Normal. All Fucked Up. She shook her head. "I have incoming hostiles on my HUD. What is it?"

"Unknown, LT, but there's a lot of it... whatever 'it' is," Bishop said, leaning in close to check her vitals readout. She struggled to take in a deep enough breath of air.

"Was Kovach able to find us a ride?"

"No word yet, Boss, but comms has been mostly out. I think the entire world done forgot about us."

"The world has its own problems to deal with. I think we must handle this one alone, Priest."

"Hard copy on that, Bayou."

"Priest, I need you to authorize a stim boost," she said, the pain of the last two days etched across her face. Her suit was still reading medically compromised. It wouldn't allow her to self-administer without another soldier's ok.

He looked at her questioningly.

"You're going to need my rifle in this fight. Give me the override."

Bishop swiped his tac-sleeve over hers, okaying the potent drug cocktail. "You'll pay for this later, you know."

Bayou nodded. "If I have a later." The drugs hit her system like a jolt of electricity. "Now what have you morons gotten yourselves into?"

~

Updated and alert, the pain still gnawing away in the background like a team of hungry rodents feasting on her ribcage, Lieutenant Debra Riggs scanned the video once more. "Shit, shit, shit, shit and shit," she muttered. "Deep, smelly, fever-baked shit."

Bishop smiled. "I like the way you Cajuns can have so many different ways of describing something so nasty. Kind of like the Eskimos with their fifty words for snow."

"Yeah, Priest. Well, the snow that's about to hit us is brown and smelly. I call it shit, and we are the fan." They were in the small clearing for the landing zone; to their rear was a sheer cliff face of two hundred feet of near vertical rock. The incoming sensor video showed hundreds of small creatures, possibly modified capybaras, the beaver-sized rats they had down here. Those animals were docile, slow plant-eaters. What the bug cams were picking up was anything but that. It was a snarling mob of gnashing, razor-sharp teeth and mouths full of foamy, pinkish saliva. The legs were sleek, muscular, and tipped with long claws that dug up the ground like a farmer's plow.

"Close those suits up. They'll be here in thirty. Watch your firing lines."

Halo had set out a series of tripwires, all attached to modified antipersonnel mines. It wasn't much, but they were quickly running out of time.

Bayou squinted as the first of the mines went off seventy-five yards back into the jungle. Body parts and rat meat flew upward like a volcano exploding. Halo had either pointed it too high, or the first ones had knocked it down before it even triggered. The little bastards were fast. The team was quiet. They knew their jobs. No words were needed. She loved these guys, but damn, she missed Kovach. These recon missions were all hers, and she was okay in combat, but the master sergeant, well, he was the best she'd ever seen. He was patient, analytical, and able to unleash extreme violence at a moment's notice. 'Asymmetrical warfare,' he called it. Hit the other fucks way harder than they can hit you.

She felt the rough edges of cracked ribs grinding together inside her chest. Despite the meds, this was going to hurt like a bitch.

"Ten seconds." Another series of booms echoed through the forest. She could make out the separate sounds of anger and pain in the mass of creatures. *We did this, we made these little fucks*, she thought. Not the United States, but man did. Man always fucked up nature, usually to suit our own agendas.

"Contact!" Priest yelled.

A shot came from Bayou's right. That would be Halo. She saw the front line of deranged creatures break out of the foliage, and they looked even uglier up close. She loosed a two-round burst of flechettes downrange. It cut a swath through the pack. The meter on her HUD showed 242 rounds remaining. Even if she could kill three or four with each shot, the suit's battle AI estimated 1500 plus of the things. It would come down to numbers, and the math was not in their favor.

She aimed, fired, moved on. It was routine, and it was awful. The wails of the dying animals reminded her of children. Children being sliced apart by pure energy. She kept firing until the ammo count clicked zero.

"Switching to MRA." She slapped in a mag rail ammo pack as the gun reconfigured itself for the new ammo. She heard Priest click on empty as well.

"Updating threat assessment," Bayou's suit's AI intoned. The 1500 plus number had been steadily decreasing in her heads-up display. They'd gotten it down to just above 400. "New data," as the count rose again to over 3000.

"Fuck me! Halo, find us an exit—this is not a fight we can win."

"Working on it, LT!"

The count on her rail gun was dropping even faster. Every shot was taking down one or more of the rodents, but several were breaking through. In one of her displays, she saw Priest backing up and literally firing at his feet to kill the first wave. Her back was against the wall, so she couldn't go any farther. She felt wind and a dark cloud moving in overhead. *Great— rain,* she thought. Every fucking afternoon in this god-forsaken place. That was just what they needed. She had to select the animals individually now. Unlike the carnage flechettes, she had to punch single holes with these almost like old school metal-cased rounds. The wind picked up, and she realized Jenkins was calling her.

"Go for Bayou. What do you have, Halo?"

When he answered, she stopped firing and looked back for the first time since the battle had begun. "Holy shit!" The giant black triangle sat stationary a dozen feet above them, the enormous white repulser disk glowing steadily with that unearthly bluish light they had. "Thank you, Master Sergeant," she whispered, almost as a prayer.

"Move your asses. Our ride is here!"

CHAPTER
FORTY-TWO

"Ada, locate Sumo!" I shouted as I ran toward the hole.

"Twelve meters below your position. Life signs are in the green."

The hole was a gaping slash in the ground a dozen yards across and twice that wide. The green and violet tendrils were already creeping up, out, and over the edge.

"Rappelling spike," I yelled at my AI as I aimed, fired, and leapt in one motion. The rail gun fired a specialized metal dart that imbedded deep into the pavement above. The spike trailed a thin line of carbon microfilament. I hit the ground hard, my boots crushing through something thick and wet.

Realization that it could have been Sumo, or the woman, came to me slowly. Then, with a jolt, I turned on the gun light and swept the surrounding ground. Sumo was against one wall; he was straddling a body. Carol.

"Hey, partner..." I began just as a vine began wrapping its way around my arm and neck. The vines were about as thick as my thumb but incredibly tough. They were fibrous and felt more like a powerful snake than the harmless ivy that might cover your favorite aunt's home.

In seconds, the goddam thing had everything on me locked up except my left forearm. My fingers strained to reach down to my side. I grimaced against the layers of vines that were feeling like bands of iron.

With one last push, my fingers finally touched the Heidelberg blade in its sheath. One tendril around my feet began circling up my leg, constricting more with each turn. I shouted in pain. My grip on the knife vanished, and I fought to keep that side of my body free. I saw liquid running down my visor as the tendrils swept over my helmet. Then I recalled Voss's mention of neurotoxins. "Stay away, Sumo."

I found the knife again, still hanging from my rigging. Freeing it, I began to hack down on the vine wrapping my leg and then did the same to the one encircling my neck. The battle armor prevented me from choking, but it had restricted blood flow. I moved to free my other arm when a giant trunk of the plant slammed me from behind. The knife went flying this time.

My vision tunneled to a pinpoint of light as my body stopped fighting. I was trapped in a spiderweb of the stinging vines. Soon, I felt even gravity disappear as I was hoisted off the ground by the ever-growing tangle of plants. These things took down buildings. What chance did I have?

Vaguely, I heard Ada counting down. "Three, two..."

A snapping pop, followed by frying sounds, brought me back to the tableau of horror. My HUD was dark, as were many other suit controls.

"You're on backup power now, Prowler. I used your suit's batteries to stun the attacking vines. You need to move, now!"

It had been a brilliant move. One I wished I'd thought of. I grabbed my knife, lying several feet away, and cut away the rest of the vines still trapping me. I could see the rest of the angry mass writhing away a few feet from me. Ada was right. It wouldn't take long for it to get over its shock and come after me again.

Quickly checking over Sumo, who appeared unhurt, and Carol, who was unconscious, I clipped the rappelling cable around her, then picked up Sumo. Ada signaled the spike above to retract. Two minutes later, I released Sumo and placed a hand on the edge of the hole and hoisted myself out. I could see Damiana there, enraged and yelling. My suit's speakers were out, and frankly, I was glad. Yes, I had left her friend, and I didn't need to read lips to know she was less than thrilled about seeing only me and my dog.

I unclipped and turned to pull up the rest of the cable. The thin hyperfilmanent was made of a hardened carbon-graphene composite and was ultra-thin. Without the armor, I would have needed specialized gloves when using it just to avoid it slicing through my hands. The spike round carries nearly a hundred yards in something the size of an old style match box. Damiana, realizing I had her friend suspended behind me, rushed to help, but I lifted my visor and told her to stand back. I needed her and Sumo watching for the above ground threats while I did this.

Carol wasn't heavy, but it suddenly felt as though she were caught on something. I flipped on my helmet lamps, and my blood froze. Two vines were encircling her neck. Her face was deathly white, and her lips were turning blue. I held her with my left hand as I carefully removed my sidearm with the other. I heard Damiana yelling at me, undoubtedly even louder now, as she saw me aiming the weapon down at her friend.

Carol was suspended ten feet below me, caught in a vicious game of tug-of-war. The game was life or death for her. I fired, searing off one of the two thick vines, but I saw hundreds more moving in to take its place. I fired again and again. Finally, I felt the cable give, just an inch, then a bit more. I holstered the gun and heaved again with both hands. Suddenly, she was free, and I had her out of the hole in seconds. I reached to feel for a pulse.

"We've got more trouble, Joe," Damiana said from behind me.

CHAPTER
FORTY-THREE

I wasn't ready for another fight. Not yet. Despite my enhancements, I was feeling lucky to get out of that hole in one piece. Sumo seemed good, but Carol was an unknown. Now, Damiana was glancing between her unconscious friend and out toward the ruins we'd passed through minutes earlier. I felt a chill run through me as I saw her expression.

"That other thing you mentioned," she said, her voice taking on a nervous quality that until now I hadn't heard from the woman. "Did it sound at all mechanical?"

I was still struggling to unhook myself from the micro-cable and get back to my feet. Her words were a shock. "No." The two encounters I had felt were creatures, living things. Although, seeing the tendrils of vine creeping around my boots made me wonder if I even knew the definition of creature anymore. My battle suit's sensors began picking up a sound, very faint, but rhythmic and familiar. A clicking tap, followed by three more... click, tap— tap, tap, tap.

Just like at the closed door yesterday afternoon, the sound sent an involuntary shiver through me. I'd pictured a drooling creature, something evil and prehistoric, tapping a razor-sharp claw on the floor just waiting for me to open that door. Looking back to where the woman was pointing, I knew that assessment had been very wrong.

"Kovach, we have to go now!"

Damiana's words were unnecessary. The glint of thousands of metal bodies moved almost as one, covering much of the western side of the complex, their metal legs tapping out in perfect synchronization. Each of the damn things were the size of a shoebox. The hoard swarmed over everything and were moving in every direction at once. I watched as they cut a swath through a thick valley of the violet-colored vines as if they weren't even there. "You had a division working on battle bots, too," I stated as I bent to pick up Carol's limp body.

"Swarm technology," she said. Her tone was flat and unemotional.

"Ada, plot me a course out of here and get the truck moved to somewhere we can meet it."

"Roger, Prowler. Be advised, though, the batteries have only partially recovered. Your range will be extremely limited."

I'd already assumed that. We would need better transportation, but right now, I just wanted to stay alive. That thought made me consider something. Building J-7 loomed above us as I ran by. My future, my ability to live through next month, was likely somewhere inside those walls, and I was giving that up in this desperate dash from danger. Selfishly, I considered stopping and going back to find what I needed. *What did I really owe these women, anyway?*

I pushed the thought out of my mind as a thick vine burst out of a window above. Its ropy tendrils immediately began covering the exterior. The plants were underground, probably in the sewers and tunnels between buildings. The bot horde now seemed endless above ground; the tapping sound now thunderous, even with my battle suit systems dampening the volume. I stole a look at the woman in my arms. Her color was returning. Maybe she hadn't been hit with the nerve toxin.

My life was probably over, but I could still do whatever I could to get them to safety, maybe even help her find her son. I'd chosen the path of a warrior in this life, and these were the people we served, not the politicians, not even the officers in our chain of command. I heard the J-7 lab beginning to come down behind us. A part of me seemed to die with it. Fat rain drops began to spatter against my visor. Looking back, the ground seemed to erupt as the plants sought the moisture. I began to run even harder.

~

"She's stable, Joe, her injuries are not life-threatening," Ada said.

My battle suit has the ability to do rough medical scans on anyone I can touch the suit's tac-sleeve sensors to. Ada had scanned Carol via the sensors in my sleeves and administered a sedative, antivirals, and pain meds while we were winding our way through the thick forest. My truck was on an unpaved road high on a bluff overlooking a rust-colored stream.

Sumo had already made it to the truck and sat watching us, seeming to ask why humans were so damn slow. I could tell, though, the shit we'd just been through had shaken the animal as much as us. This wasn't his kind of battle. An enemy with no throat to rip out was no enemy he cared to face.

I slid Carol into the back seat, rolled up the now frayed solar blanket still flapping behind the truck bed, and climbed inside with the others. Damiana leaned warily against the side of the truck, then climbed in and got busy checking over her friend. I'd already relayed to her what the suit's sensors had indicated.

"Will those things keep coming?" I asked.

Damiana shrugged. "No idea. I'd read up on the Thunder Vine, but the bots were never mentioned in any real detail."

The power levels on the GMC were reading barely ten percent. I put it into gear and began following Ada's meandering route overlay in my vision. I could still hear the relentless tapping. Maybe that was just my imagination, but if so, even the memory of the sound set my teeth on edge.

I flipped the helmet off my head, feeling better to be rid of it. Damiana looked up from her friend, then raised a hand to touch something on my neck. Her touch sent a shock of pain through me.

"It got you?"

I reached up and felt the twin ridges that were raw and hot to the touch. Now that I was aware, I could feel the intense pain. Until now, it was something that would not have done me any good to know, so my body compartmentalized it away from my consciousness.

"You should be dead," she said. "Not just from the nerve agent, but that jump down into that hole should have killed you."

Her fingers lingered on my skin a moment more. I had to admit, I didn't mind the feeling.

"Dr. Reichert really did the full program on you, didn't he?"

The man saved my life, but I was still coming to grips with everything else he'd done to me.

"I have a lot of enhancements," I said, nodding.

"More than that, you were augmented. I saw some of the reports." Apparently satisfied that Carol was just asleep from the sedation and not unconscious, Damiana climbed back up to the front. "Like, I know they use a nanocoating of carbon and kevlar mesh to reinforce your bones. Probably why you can jump into a hole that deep without injury."

"They told me some of it, but I'm not even sure of the full extent." I wasn't sure I liked this stranger knowing more about my body than I did.

"Some of your blood was replaced with something called respirosites. Essentially, artificial red blood cells, capable of carrying many times the normal amount of oxygen your organs need to perform at peak levels. I'm betting you can run for hours and not get tired."

I could, but I didn't enjoy attributing that to her former boss. "I was an Army Ranger before I became a Space Grunt or lab rat. I was already in reasonably good shape."

"I'm not talking about fit for duty. They were making you into a weapon, Joe."

She must have seen the look on my face. I had a strong sense of being violated by everything that had been done to me. They saved my life, but then they made damn sure I knew Joe Kovach was government property from that moment on. "They did a lousy job on it, if you ask me."

I felt her hand again, this time on my arm.

"I'm sorry we couldn't get what you needed back there."

We both knew what that meant. Just like the batteries in this old truck. We both had a limited shelf-life remaining.

I shrugged, unwilling to show how crushing the loss really was. "What about you? Did you find what you were looking for?"

Her eyes glanced back at Carol before she answered. "Why do you think I was looking for something?"

I smiled; she knew I knew. But I was ok with her keeping her secrets, for now.

CHAPTER
FORTY-FOUR
BANSHEE

"Where are we heading?"

"Lieutenant Riggs, I am RTB on the IAS Alice Springs," the pilot said.

"Since when do U.S. dropships base on Alliance Space craft?" The still classified TriCraft dropships were the taxis of the Space Force. Rumored to have been built using reverse engineered technology, they were unlike any other flying craft in the world. They were shit slow for flying from one spot to another, but incredibly perfect for going from ground to space in mere seconds.

"Since Space Command went dark, ma'am," the pilot said.

Even after all the rides up with Bayou's drop teams, she still couldn't get over how they could be on the ground one minute and in the dark of space the next with absolutely no feeling of movement. The acceleration had to be in the tens of thousands of miles per hour. The G-forces should have left them as greasy smears on the back wall, yet the TriCraft's inertia dampening made it feel like nothing. They were a one-trick pony, though, so only a handful existed.

"Thank you again, Captain, for plucking our asses out of that shit down there."

"Just doing my job, ma'am. Tips are accepted, and please leave a review." The man tapped a few buttons on his console and the section of a solid wall in front now showed an external camera. Sunlight reflected off a large and rather ugly ship coming into view. The carrier Alice Springs. It was one of the monolith class ships along with Denali, Stone Mountain, Everest, and Kilimanjaro. Banshee had been assigned to her once several years earlier, but Bayou lost track of the deployments. After a while, one section of ship's hull looked pretty much like every other. Generally, they were in the Hermes class anyway, more cramped, but more effective for an orbital drop platform.

"Better strap in, we will have to match spin."

She didn't bother. As long as she didn't have an outside view, the spin inside the TriCraft was undetectable. If she had bothered to watch, she'd likely be hurling her lunch in a matter of seconds. The thought made the pain in her ribs shoot through her again. She patted the pilot and stumble- walked back to where the rest of her team were seated. Both Jenkins and Bishop had their eyes closed; they were all drained from the narrow escape, but she had questions that needed answers.

"Banshee Actual to Prowler." They weren't in combat, but she wanted Joe to know he should watch his mouth, assuming he answered. Using his call sign was normally enough of a clue. Tactical comms were supposed to be private, but any soldier that believed that probably also still left cookies out for Santa.

Joe didn't answer, and that didn't leave Bayou with a good feeling. She left him a brief message relaying her thanks, and that they were safely off-planet. Now she wanted to know what in the hell had happened to her world down there.

Ballistic drop troops didn't rank too high in the hierarchy of the Spaceborne Infantry Division. So, when the senior flight controller for the Alice Springs summoned Debra a short while later, she was relatively sure it wouldn't be for tea and cookies.

"Lieutenant Riggs reporting, sir!" she said to the middle-aged woman seated behind the desk. Orbital charts, vessel loadouts, and various other hard copy reports littered the major's workspace. Every billet on Space Force craft was small. Few were private, with most people hot swapping with other shifts. The CAG's office was about double the size of the rest.

"At ease, soldier," the woman said without looking up from the tablet she was reading.

"You were on a recon mission in Central America."

"Yes, sir."

"By your report, that mission was unsuccessful."

The words stung, but Bayou had known they would.

"That is correct. Objective not reached, and we lost one member of my team."

"Sorry to hear that." The lieutenant wasn't sure to which point the major was referring, so she remained silent.

"Do you have any idea the magnitude of the destruction down there?" the woman asked, placing the tablet face down on her desk and making eye contact for the first time.

"No, sir, not really." She didn't want to mention the calls with Kovach. Those were off the books and against regs during a mission. To be honest, they were only hearsay, as Joe also only really knew what he himself could see.

Major Kerns pulled up a display wall. It was dominated by what must have been a real-time view of Earth. The scene showed a condensed version of the first wave of attacks hitting the East Coast of America, followed by the launch of a counterattack. Then, similar missile tracks over Europe, Russia, and the opposite American coast. Debra looked on as a red overlay started from each impact spot that began spreading out in the animation.

"In five days, much of our planet is now a wasteland," the major said. "I don't have time to give you a full briefing, nor do I think you are worth it. I do want to know how you could requisition a pickup from my Space Force assets. My assets. How were you in one of the few places on the globe unaffected, and how did you fail to accomplish a simple recon mission? One that might have prevented all of this."

Riggs was stunned. She had already felt like a failure, an emotion that was totally unfamiliar to her, but this woman was trying to lay this entire disaster on her command. *Not fucking likely.*

"Major, you are not a part of my command chain. I am here out of common courtesy. My team's deployment and its evac is above both our paygrades. Do you have anything helpful to add before I attempt to file my final mission reports?" Riggs asked with authority. The disrespect which female officers received hadn't changed much in the last century, and Riggs damn sure would not take it from another woman, no matter her rank.

The Combat Air Group commander was obviously not expecting that. The woman looked ready to snap, but her eyes fell on the arm patch. Bayou was an operator, Special Forces. Clearly not someone to get off on the wrong foot with. Kerns steepled her fingers on her desk and eyed the younger woman carefully.

"Maybe I was a bit rash, Lieutenant. You are correct, I do not know your M.O., it was classified, and as I said, we do welcome you aboard. Our carrier group rarely has RDT teams on board, but we may be the best place for you right now."

She stood and moved gracefully around the desk, movements that came only with years living outside Earth's normal gravity.

"Come with me, Lieutenant. I believe you will want to see this."

CHAPTER
FORTY-FIVE

LUX

The smell was back, and it was dark.

"Ah, you're awake," a woman's voice said from nearby.

Lux yawned, realizing that he was lying on something soft. A bed or sofa. "Where am I?"

"You're in our house. My son found you asleep in our yard. Are you lost?"

"Your son? I need... I need to go." He did. That's what mom would want, but something smelled like food, and he was so hungry. "I need to get home."

"Okay, honey," the voice said again. "Hey, Bill, can you come here?"

Flickering light started painting its way up the walls, and the shadow of a man came into view. The candle he was holding began softly illuminating the small living room. Lux saw he was lying in an oversized chair.

"So, our guest is awake? You get a name yet?"

The woman was younger than Lux's mom, pretty, with long, straight hair. It looked dark colored. His mom's was blonde like his, but the candlelit room was still so dim it probably could have been any color.

"Not yet, I was just asking him if he was lost."

"I'm not lost. I don't think I am. Marcie knows where we are but..."

"Is she with you?" the woman asked.

"No... she's, um... she stopped working when the car..."

The two adults looked at each other and nodded, something unspoken passing between them.

"Were you in a car... on your way home, maybe, when the cars stopped?"

Lux's stomach cramped and made a loud growl. "Do you have anything I could eat, please?"

The woman looked at the man, who seemed to shake his head slightly.

"We don't have much, but how does a bacon and tomato sandwich sound?" she said, rising and giving the man a glaring look.

"I've never had bacon, but I like sandwiches."

"Oh, so you come from one of those kind of families, huh?" the man said with a small laugh. "You only use the processed food from the machine, or are you vegan?"

The woman left the room down the same dark hall the man had come from. Lux heard voices in the other rooms, kids' voices.

"I don't know what vegan means, but we eat lots of stuff. My mom works a lot, though, so yeah, mostly delivered meal kits and stuff from the processor. It's good. I can make some things myself now."

"That's good," the man said. "I think we all have to do more for ourselves from now on."

He moved around, so the candle showed more of his face; he had a beard. Lux didn't think he knew any men who had beards. It was a strange thing to see, and it made him think of old-fashioned pictures where it seemed like all the men had them.

"I'm Bill, by the way. My wife is Laura." He saw the boy looking at him, then realized the reason. He stroked his beard with one hand. "You like it?"

"I've never seen anyone with one. Was it hard to get?" Lux asked. His stomach growled another protest.

"To grow, you mean? Yeah, it took a while. Lot of farmers up this way, several of them have gone back to the older ways of doing things. Beards, making bacon, and such."

Lux realized there was a face staring into the house through a glass door past the man. "Your dog saved me."

"No way!" the man said. "Timber brought you here?"

"Is that his name, Timber? Yes, he found me one morning. I thought it was a bear or something."

"Yeah, that's awesome. I named him that 'cause he loves the woods so much," Bill said without realizing the boy didn't catch the connection. "You were up on the main road then... that's quite a walk from here. Didn't know Timber roamed up that far."

The lady came back in and set a sandwich on a napkin with a cup of water. Lux downed the water in one long swallow. Then he bit into the sandwich and all thought of other food drifted away. It was the single best thing he'd ever put in his mouth. Even better than birthday cake.

"My taste buds are dancing," he said between bites. He was wondering if his mom had ever tried bacon. Surely not, or she would have made it all the time. "Sorry, ma'am," he said, having devoured the sandwich in minutes and looking down at the now empty napkin. "I mean, thanks. You know... thank you for everything."

CHAPTER
FORTY-SIX

KOVACH

I unwound myself from the steering wheel, my foot getting hung up in the strap of my rifle. We'd decided to sleep in the truck, which had only made it about thirteen miles before the charge was completely gone. Damiana was watching me from her equally awkward position, wedged between the seat and window on the other side.

"She okay?" I asked, nodding my head to the rear seat.

Damiana nodded, "I think so."

I opened the door and stepped out. My foot sank into mud. The storm had hit with force just as we fled down the rural mountain roads. Now I wanted food, and I needed coffee.

The other woman joined me as I built a quick fire. I wanted proper food, not the prepackaged stuff.

"So, what's the plan?"

"The batteries will need to recharge. We'll probably need to stay here all day and maybe be good to go tomorrow morning."

"What about the... you know." She looked back the way we had come.

Weird how neither of us wanted to talk about what had gone on back at the facility. "I don't know, Dami. Can those things move fast enough to catch up to us?"

"Yeah, maybe... I just don't know," she responded.

"Look, can you see if you can find some dry wood? I just need coffee." She wandered off, and Sumo hopped lazily down from the pickup. He gave me a look.

"Don't you start with me, buddy. I wasn't the one who fell in a hole with a cannibalistic kudzu vine." He snorted and left to go do his morning business. Truth was, I had no freakin' idea what to do. My plan ended when that building came crashing down. I was on borrowed time now.

"Sergeant, confirmation that the remainder of Banshee team was successfully evac'd off world. Bayou is on an Alliance craft."

"Good. Thanks, Ada." At least one less thing to worry about.

I moved the starter block around to ignite more of the fatwood I kept in my go-bag. By the time the woman came back, I had the coffeepot set up and was getting some of our food supplies cooking. She dropped the wood by the fire.

"You didn't even need this, did you?"

"We do... we will," I corrected. I placed a few of the still damp pieces closer, so they could begin drying out. "Truth is, I'm not exactly a morning person, or a people person. I don't really care for either."

She smiled. "Can't really blame you on either count."

We sat by the fire waiting for the coffeepot to boil. "All the technology in the world and suddenly we are back to camping out like the original settlers did hundreds of years ago," she said.

"In the Army, we had a saying that nothing ever really changes."

"Some things change," she challenged. "Flesh eating plants and zombie battle bots are new."

"Point taken. Just new and inventive ways of doing the same old things—killing your enemy. Names change, flags change, weapons evolve, but the goal remains the same."

Minutes later, she poured us both a cup, and I was glad to see she took it black. "I never really even thought about it... the killing, I mean. It was just a job. To see if we could make something better than the competition. They kept most of us away from guys like you."

I sipped my cup, savoring the familiar warmth. "That's the problem when wars become driven by money."

She eyed me suspiciously. A look in her eye, I couldn't completely place.

"The military industrial complex," I said. "There was a time when we made better weapons to fight wars. Now we fight wars to make better weapons. There is a sizeable profit in war... or used to be, last week, for example."

"Your dad was part of that system. One of the few who had gotten his hands dirty out on the battlefield," she said.

"And he hated it like most military commanders. The actual warriors, not the appointees who make decisions for their men, sitting behind a desk thousands of miles away from the battlefield. The system in place to wage those wars doesn't really take the men—our needs, into consideration. We're trigger pullers." I smiled at an old memory. "When I was fresh out of Recon school, I thought I was king of the jungle. Hell week is a brutal beast of a final exam. One of the instructors, a beast of a man named Stouten, asked me if I knew what I was now. I told him I was a weapon, a lethal weapon of war."

"Ballsy," Damiana said.

"Stupid," I admitted. "He pulled me aside and got right in my ear. 'You, Kovach, will never be a weapon. You aren't even the barrel of a weapon.' He then pointed up to the grandstand where my dad and a bunch of other invited military dignitaries were watching. 'They are the weapon. You are just a single round in their gun. They point, the gun fires, you go meet the enemy. You are a meat-filled bullet, nothing more.'"

Damiana laughed; it was a good laugh. I liked it.

"Then you joined the RDT and became a drop trooper."

I got her meaning. "Yeah, I literally became a bullet being fired out of a gun at the enemy. Irony is a bitch."

"So, you don't have any thoughts on what happened, the who, the why?"

"Does it matter?" I asked. "After all these years and, well... all I've been through, I know my lane. Figuring out shit like that is for people further up the food chain. I would like to know the how they did it as that could be useful to our survival... your survival," I amended sadly.

Her face darkened. "I am sorry about that, Joe. I know you need that med kit."

She got a distant look, and I could tell she was considering something.

"What?" I asked.

"Iron River wasn't the only site Magnus used."

I poured us both another cup of coffee.

"I'm listening."

CHAPTER
FORTY-SEVEN

I only had one problem with Damiana's news of another lab—she didn't know the location.

"She might." Damiana was pointing toward the pickup.

"Carol?"

She nodded. "All our work at Iron River is...was compartmentalized, but I know what she was doing was to be used for a new prototype weapons system. Something called the ZR-12s."

"And you think that was at the same facility?"

"Relatively sure. Magnus mentioned it several times, and over the last year, he spent more time at that facility than anywhere."

"Does it have a name?"

"A code name. I heard it referred to by Marcus simply as the Rainier site."

Ada cut into my thoughts, "The name has several possible references. Most likely connection is an ancient Germanic name that means army advisor or the deciding warrior."

I hadn't mentioned my internal AI to either of the women, and if it was part of what Damiana knew about me, she never brought it up. For now, I had kept it to myself.

"Never heard of it. I assume that was not one of the places I was treated."

She looked away, considering it, then shook her head. "I followed your case rather closely. Your enhancements... I mean, you were essentially a prototype. My job was to help document certain steps for the doctor. I know some things they did were classified beyond my clearance level, but I don't think any of those were at the other site."

Damiana rose to her feet. "I need to go check on Carol."

I looked at her and realized her silhouette was familiar. She could have been in the medical ward that day, standing by the door. I filed that away for later.

Sumo came over and lay down. I fed him part of my breakfast and rubbed his head. The dog turned and licked my hand. *Who would take care of him if I were gone... when I'm gone,* I corrected. Truth was, Sumo would probably be fine on his own. He hunted with me and had survival tactics hard-wired into his DNA. Humans were the weak ones. Even the enhanced ones like me.

I sat there enjoying the moment with him for a long time. Just looking out over the rolling hills extending into the distance. I could hear Damiana fussing over her friend but didn't detect any response from Carol. My battle suit had administered some pretty strong sedatives, so I wasn't surprised she was still sleeping it off.

"Any other official references to this Rainier, Ada?" I asked softly as I looked down at Sumo. Talking to your dog was more acceptable than simply talking to yourself, right?

"Negative, Joseph. Nothing by that name is in any of my references, although without a better connection, I can't access any of Hammer's internal servers."

"You know, since the world ended, you are being less and less helpful."

"That's a hurtful thing to say," Ada replied in her best fake, emotionally butt-hurt tone.

Sumo's ears twitched, then he stood quickly and looked back to the north, back in the direction from where we had come. "Ada, is he hearing what I think?"

"Get your helmet," the AI replied. "I can verify if it is, but my guess is yes."

Sumo glanced at me before turning back to the apparent sound.

Hair was standing up on the dog's neck. "I don't need my bucket to verify anything. Sumo knows. Ada, give me a way to boost these batteries right now."

"Okay, but you won't like it."

~

Well, fuck, she was right. As I stood next to the truck ten minutes later, I agreed. I didn't like it. Her solution required me jury-rigging eight of the P-cells in sequence with two completely dismantled ammo packs for the pulse rifle. The ammo pack was essentially just a super dense capacitor; it charged up high voltage and released a small portion with each trigger pull. The issue was that much energy at one time would fry every circuit and motor on the old truck.

I pried the side plate off the second magazine with my knife. "Don't touch the contacts," my AI said for the fifth time. It was good advice. A single flechette round from the gun could decapitate an enemy. The ammo packs had enough charge for several hundred shots. So, yeah, touching the contacts could absolutely shorten my already tenuous status as a live human.

Damiana picked up the side plate. "Do not remove— explosive danger," she read.

"Should I be worried?"

"Worry about that." I pointed my chin toward the growing noise. To her credit, she'd remained remarkably calm when I told her what was approaching. She packed up the solar blanket and the rest of the meager camp site while I hurried to complete the battery booster.

"The creatures would have overrun West Charles by now, wouldn't they?"

I remembered seeing a sign with that name outside her neighborhood's entrance. "Yep."

"You saved our lives, Kovach. Thank you."

"You aren't saved yet, dear. And I don't know if this will work or just turn us into pixie dust."

She bit the inside of her cheek. She looked worried, but not scared.

"Carol is coming around. She's hungry. I gave her some water and an energy gel pack. Probably best

not to overwork her system, you know?"

I felt relieved Carol was awake. Damiana liked to have things she was in control of. I got that. So much seemed so far out of our control right now.

"She's a good woman. Carol, I mean," she continued, "A good mom, top-notch at her job."

Did she think I was going to leave her by the road if she'd gotten a bad performance review? I just nodded and continued to follow Ada's silent and increasingly complex instructions. A tree fell, not close but close enough for us both to hear. Damiana was standing above me, her gaze back down the gravel road.

"Thunder Vines," she said. "I can see them crossing the road a few hundred yards back."

"How in the fuck do they grow so fast, and why does it feel like they're hunting us?"

"It's not really a plant anymore, something more like an animal with roots. It can absorb energy from almost any source: the sun, direct current, sugars, and proteins. They can literally absorb other life forms, like a giant Venus flytrap. They were designed to be resilient and aggressive."

"Too fucking aggressive," I said. "Get in the truck and lock the doors." I'd seen those damn vines get into sealed buildings; I had no doubt they could get into an old truck. But it was something, at least.

She looked as if she wanted to protest but nodded and left. I heard the door shut as I continued my work on the battery pack. If I fucked up, we were all dead anyway.

The sound grew steadily louder; it was like a roaring river. I didn't recall it being that loud yesterday, then remembered I was wearing my helmet then. I picked up the helmet and slid it on and checked my dwindling weapons status.

Full battle suits were great for a lot of things, delicate electronics were not one of them. I saw vines creeping around me on both sides as I did the last of the connections. Sweat was dripping down in my eyes. The suit's vent system seemed to be failing. I just needed to hook this into the power junction and see if I had managed to kill us all. The two leads I had left free were simple enough. I wired the first one to the frame of the truck with a stud and wing nut, then held the thicker hot wire above the jumper block where Ada said it needed to go.

I felt the vines encircling my feet; these were smaller than the ones yesterday. I could break free simply by changing position. "You sure about this?" I asked, my hand poised over the power block. Then I carefully slipped it...

Something hit me on my right side, and I found myself flying past the truck and a dozen yards farther down the road. Stunned, I was instantly back in a crouch, rifle out, looking for targets. I saw nothing other than the tendrils of thicker vines now beginning to cover the trees, the road, and the old GMC. Faintly, in my suit's sensors, I could hear a dreaded familiar tapping as well. "The battle bots." Wherever the vines went, they seemed to follow.

I turned in a full circle, but no targets came up. I glanced at my side and saw three deep scars across my body armor. I hadn't imagined it, and it damn sure wasn't a vine. I saw both women inside the truck motioning frantically for me to join them. "Ada, bring the car forward, it should have some power." I wasn't sure I had gotten that final wire connected or not.

The pickup began moving slowly toward me. Vines snapped with meaty pops as gobs of blue-green liquid oozed out. I noticed my hand was shaking, and my heart rate was abnormally high. "Ada, replay attack."

My vision overlay showed a black, gray blur briefly pass in front of me and then another view as I was upside down flying across the road. She tried rendering it multiple times to clear it up, but I couldn't tell anything about it other than whatever hit me was blindingly fast. This was my night visitor. It had to be. "You were trying to get away from those mutant hordes, too, weren't you?"

I reluctantly shouldered the weapon and finished making the last connection. Slipping into the truck, I took off, determined to put some serious distance between us and well...all that shit behind us. Sumo, sitting between the front seats, licked my arm affectionately.

It took several minutes for my heart rate to settle. Whatever the beast was, it affected me on a very primal level.

CHAPTER
FORTY-EIGHT
BANSHEE

Lieutenant Riggs studied the map. "Can I see it again?" The major had brought her into the war room as part of a larger conversation on Banshee team's possible ongoing role.

The scene started over, multiple waves of missile strikes on several continents. Although the attack was coordinated and widespread, the number of total targets was relatively small. She studied the time code superimposed above the time lapse graphic. Within three days, the area around a significant number of the targets was colored red, then faded to black.

"Red means lethal to organic tissue, black... well, black means no life signs remaining," an ensign standing nearby said.

"D.C., New York, Atlanta, Boston..." Bayou said in sad realization. Then she touched another black circle, this one farther west. She knew the city name without looking. "Louisville," she whispered in quiet desperation.

The major walked up and put a hand on her shoulder. "Along with Rome, Beijing, Paris, Amsterdam, and dozens more. We think it was a coordinated attack by the TWC."

That would make some sense. The Third World Coalition had lots of funding, a brilliant leader, and a fundamentally rational cause. Which was the simple fact that the superpowers seemed intent on destroying the entire world through war, greed, reckless manufacturing, or environmental collapse. The TWC was also very fond of terrorist attacks that made splashy headlines. This, though, was on another level entirely.

"What is happening in the blast zones? Why are they going dark?"

"That's the question we need answers to, Lieutenant. The destabilizing event was largely conventional. Either nukes, dirty bombs, and Darkstar EMP disruptors or some combination of the three. Those alone would have wiped out our government officials, banking systems, coordinated air traffic control, and cause a massive loss of life. Yet, scattered reports of a Sapphire bomb blast wave in many of the locations suggests something else. Gamma and neutrino detectors registered significant spikes during the attack."

"Sapphire bombs."

"That is our assumption, but the payload is very much a mystery," the major responded. "We dropped some drones over D.C. and Beijing. They had to stay above 15,000 feet or something caused the software to glitch. We lost a dozen of them before we figured it out." She handed Debra a data tablet.

The video was grainy, the cities barely recognizable, but in several places, Bayou could see something happening. Buildings that were covered with colorful plant growth, others that were collapsing, and piles of what appeared to be dead bodies. The city was in ruins and looked more like the ruins of a thousand-year-old city instead of a modern metroplex.

She handed the tablet back, shocked by what she'd seen. Debra Riggs had fought in some of the nastiest places on Earth, battles that would never be talked about in public, but this was something on an entirely new level. This was Armageddon level *shit*. "You want us to go down, don't you? Into one of those death zones?"

"Riggs, we have half a billion people down there in those zones. Maybe they are all dead, maybe nothing is coming out alive. We must know."

"What about assets already on the ground?" Bayou asked.

"Fleet Command operations is offline," the major said, as if that answer was sufficient. The senior officer moved to the corner of the room and motioned Bayou over. "Some admiral over at Gateway is trying to assume command, like Luna bases have anything relevant to add to our fight.

We have no contact with ground command. You are the few who were down there we have spoken with. And…"

"And we were deployed nowhere helpful," Bayou said, finishing the thought.

"Right. Let me lay it out for you, Lieutenant Riggs. This boat has enough supplies to last three weeks, maximum. That's 1847 souls on board that will starve to death soon after. The other ships out here are all going to be in similar shape. We've even broken protocol and called our Russian, Indian, and Chinese counterparts. They are reluctant to admit much, but it's obvious we are all in the same situation."

"You don't want to send anyone down until you know what the threat is? Are hostilities continuing? Is the threat neutralized? And with no intel coming back upstream, you have no way of knowing. Thankfully, fate just handed you a world class drop team of senior operators."

The major smiled. "Not to mince words, soldier, but yes. You need to get cleared from sick bay and prep for that mission."

The med-bay bots did their job, and Bayou was back with her men the following day.

"You're fucking shitting me," Bishop said, throwing a faded tennis ball against the wall. "Do they not understand what we just went through?"

"Oh, they understand," Bayou said.

"They just don't care," Jenkins said, finishing the familiar line.

"The more you do, the less you matter. Welcome to the military, boys!"

"Did you tell them we had a team member dirt side already?" Jenkins asked.

She shook her head. "That's the one asset that might keep our ass alive. Personally, I think if they knew Prowler was down there, they would let us starve up here with the rest of the fleet, waiting on him to do the job."

"I take it you haven't reached him?"

"Sorry, Priest, no outgoing comms on this boat," Bayou answered. "Also... I think it might be best we keep that bit of intel private for now."

"So, we going ballistic, or we taking the taxi?" Halo asked, standing and grabbing his pack.

CHAPTER
FORTY-NINE
KOVACH

Ada hadn't waited for instructions. The truck was blasting down the road at speeds the ole' girl hadn't hit in decades. I sat back in the driver's seat and slowly removed my helmet. What just happened unnerved me more than I wanted to admit. I knew that thing was not an enemy that we knew how to fight. Looking in the mirror, I saw Carol awake but scared. She might be my only hope of staying alive, but her priority would be her son. The kid could be anywhere, or more likely, already dead. I felt like a shit for not telling her already about what I knew.

"Ada, get us the best path away from that danger back there," I subvocalized.

"Routing optimum course based on available power levels."

I knew she would also avoid other blast centers. While we didn't know every place the Sapphire bombs hit, we could certainly avoid most of the other kind. I felt Damiana's touch again; she ran her fingers through the deep gouge marks on my side armor and then looked at me questioningly.

"You didn't see it?" I asked.

"What?"

She obviously had no idea that the creature from my nightmare had shown back up.

"Nothing," I answered. No need to alarm them more. "Welcome back, Carol. How are you feeling?"

The woman just held her head and stared out the window.

"She just needs some time," Damiana said.

Yeah, we all do. Trouble is, that's the one thing we aren't going to get. I steered the old truck onto a paved road, a state highway heading southwest, and let Ada handle the driving for now. We needed a better plan. Shit, who was I kidding? We had no plan. I had a name of a mystery place that may not even exist. If it did, it might be in the same shape as Iron River. Even if we could find it, and it was still intact, how likely would it be for us to find the exact medications I needed to stay alive?

Truth is, I am a soldier. I handle the battles as they occur. Right now, I was still licking my wounds from the last few skirmishes. Normally, someone else would advise me on what came next. That had never been a job I'd had to do. I mean, sure, when it comes to battlefield tactics, I could assess and react faster than most, but this was something altogether different.... *no, it wasn't.* This was life or death, just like all those other fights. This time, though, I was fighting for myself.

"Ada, whenever you have a signal, update Pops and see if he has an idea on that other facility, what did she call it... Rainier."

If Carol couldn't help, maybe my old man could. He seemed to be tied in to just about everything else.

We drove for nearly six hours before the batteries began to flatline again. If the map in my head could be trusted, we'd passed through West Virginia and were now back in Virginia, getting close to rural Kentucky. Looking at the map in my display, I had to ask an obvious question. "Why does Virginia extend father west than West Virginia?" Ada didn't bother responding.

Setting up the worn charging blanket, I thought again about Bayou's family. What was it? A sister.

"How far to Louisville?" I asked my AI softly as I moved farther from the two women.

"Two hundred twenty-five miles," came the immediate response.

That didn't seem so bad, but did we have time? I began breaking out our gear. We'd have to camp here overnight.

"Louisville is gone, Joe."

I stopped what I was doing. "Gone?"

"Affirmative," Ada replied. "I detect fallout from a direct nuclear blast, and despite the radiation in the atmosphere, I can get some internet access. Louisville, Charlotte, and Atlanta all took direct hits. Riggs' sister would not have made it."

"You can't be sure," I stated flatly.

Damiana was helping her friend lay out some sleeping mats under a tarp I'd rigged.

"Radiation?" I asked internally.

"In Louisville or here?" Ada asked.

"Both... either." Then thinking better on it. "Here. What is the risk here?" I said with growing frustration.

"You will be fine. Your suit will block most of it, and the Regenerax in your system should nullify any negative effects at the cellular level."

I nodded. "I meant them, Ada. Will they be, okay?" No matter how smart she was, she was still just a computer. She could miss even the most obvious of human concerns.

"They are in jeopardy. Nothing immediately lethal, but longer exposure should be avoided and treated," Ada replied.

I knew anti-radiation medication had come a long way in the last fifty years, but that was about all. "Can we find what I have, the Regenerax?"

"No, that is not commercially available yet. It was still in trials."

"Trials?" I said, concerned, looking down at my bare arm, my real arm, where the infusion had gone in over many days the prior year.

"Mostly in pigs and monkeys, but human subjects were to start soon."

I wasn't sure she was being serious and — I didn't want to find out. "What about more conventional drugs?"

"Yes, there are several with beneficial prophylactic properties. They will help mitigate all but the worst doses of normal radiation." She then scrolled a list of commercial and generic drugs' names, most I'd never heard of.

I studied the list again. "Limit results only to those I could possibly find locally."

The list shortened to two entries.

"Hospitals and pharmacies should have stock on these, but they will be in extremely high demand by now."

I had Ada map several likely places to try. One was twenty-eight miles to the north, and another a little farther to the southwest. She assigned a probability of finding the meds at less than sixty-two percent for either location.

"Well, shit," I said.

"How long can they stay in this area without glowing in the dark?"

"Thirty hours before mitigation methods would be inadequate to reverse the damage," Ada responded.

I thought on that as I watched Sumo searching the riverbank for... well, whatever it is dogs go sniffing for.

"Why Louisville?" I asked. The barest hint of an idea occurring to me.

"Unknown," the AI said. "Limited strategic importance, economic impact will be minimal. Seems to be simply to decimate the large population centers. This was likely one of the more westward metroplexes that was targeted."

"Bayou's sister. What does she do for a living?" I asked, an old conversation slowly bubbling up from my scattered gray matter.

Ada must have sensed what I was getting at, because the replay of that conversation played in my visual overlay.

"So where is she now?" I had asked.

Bayou had been gazing up at a brilliant sky. I remembered we were somewhere on the African continent but could no longer remember where.

"She's with Rivex. Manufacturing. She just got a promotion."

"There, stop there," I said to the AI. In the replay, Ada had posted up the corporate tree of Rivex Manufacturing. The locations, stock prices, and earnings. "They're a division of Atmos Defense Systems. The ones that build the ballistic pods."

"That is correct, Joe."

I pulled the collar down on my base layer battleskin. *Rivex makes these.* I could feel the manufacturer's logo stamped into the collar. I'd seen it nearly every day of every deployment. "They also make the battle suits. That would offer Carol and Damiana protection, right?"

"Not as much as the full body armor, but yes, it would be a significant advantage. There is also a distribution center outside the city, which probably is still intact."

"Plot the course and help me come up with some way of shielding them for tonight."

CHAPTER
FIFTY

The solution was an ugly one, but during an apocalypse, aesthetics are a secondary consideration. At least that's what I told myself. I used the original battery tray from the truck as a roof over the sleeping mats. It had a thin lead lining that would offer some protection. Then, Carol and Damiana used combinations of my body armor plating and two of Sumo's spare battle suits to shield their heads and chests. We ate a cold meal and drank only from supplies we'd brought with us. Sumo and I would be fine outside, but I did everything I could for my new companions.

The night wasn't cold, but I wished for a campfire just the same. I had a gnawing uneasiness that I couldn't tamp down. I wasn't alone; Sumo also seemed agitated and restless. Of course, we had barely escaped from some of the worst shit either of us had ever seen. We were currently outside in close proximity to one of the first nuclear blast sites on the U.S. mainland. I rubbed a finger across the truck panel. In my flashlight I could see more of the fine lavender powder coating my fingertip. We had reason to be 'out of sorts,' as my mom used to say, but none of that was it. No... something else was wrong.

I emptied the can of prepackaged coffee and decided I should probably switch over to decaf. I was getting a bit jittery. My fingers kept tracing lines to my handgun, my knife, and reaching over my back for the Rattler MK4. None of those items were where they should have been. They were close, but being out of my armor meant I couldn't easily keep them on me. It was an unaccustomed vulnerability for me. Sumo snapped at some unseen flying thing, then settled against my leg once more. I stroked his fur and lay back, trying to think.

I was a professional soldier, and no, I didn't get nervous before a mission. We were well-trained, well-equipped, and we reduced the risks as much as possible. Take that into account and add to it the fact that I am augmented and enhanced. Hell, one of my arms is more metal and circuitry than flesh and blood. My point is, I don't get nervous; I make the other dumb fuck nervous. So why was I sitting here, clearly not thinking straight... okay, yeah... nervous?

My eyes snapped open instantly. I knew I had only been sleeping a short while. Soldiers get a sense of their own internal clock, and mine was as reliable as they came. I felt the dog's steady breathing, his chest rising and falling, my head resting where it had been. I didn't want to alert the AI. I knew she was using passive and active sensors to monitor the surroundings. She would have awoken me had anything happened. Still, something *had* happened. I could feel it.

I rolled my head from side to side, scanning the truck, the riverbank, and the trees beyond. The night was relatively bright. A gibbous moon cast the surroundings in silvers and grays. My heart was beating as it sometimes did in the heat of battle. I consciously attempted to calm.

"Are you alright, Joseph?"

Ada had monitored my ocular nerve and knew this wasn't just part of my typically restless sleep pattern. "Something is here," I whispered internally. I felt a pulse move through my suit. I knew Ada was going fully active on all sensors. Sumo stopped breathing. To be more accurate, his chest stopped moving. He was awake now, too.

"Prowler, helmet," Ada commanded.

This can't be good, I thought. I silently donned my bucket, and the Rattler was in my hand before I even thought about it. Something else occurred to me as I was kneeling there, sweeping the gun across the area for targets. *I was terrified.*

"It's here," I whispered. It couldn't be, but I clearly fucking felt it. My personal boogeyman had followed us for hundreds of miles. Sumo began uttering a growl so low I felt more than heard it. I had faced over-whelming enemies multiple times in my career. Narrowly escaped a biological and robot horde in the last twenty-four hours, but this thing had gotten into my skull.

"There is nothing here," Ada said with the finality of a machine that has weighed all the facts and examined every piece of evidence.

"You don't know shit," I said, rising to my feet. I motioned Sumo left, and I went right, keeping the two sleeping women in the middle of us. My helmet jiggled on my head; without my chest armor to attach it, the fit was comically loose. I felt like a human bobblehead. Visible in my visual overlay, Ada scanned through every available wavelength, but nothing flashed the familiar red glow of a potential threat.

"I know what you are thinking, Prowler. Whatever that creature is, it couldn't have followed us from Iron River," Ada said.

"Maybe there are more of them. Perhaps it can fly? You consider that?"

"I consider all possibilities," she said calmly. "To be more accurate, I should say the chances are infinitesimally small that it is here, or if it is, that it would be the same one."

At least she was admitting that the damn thing existed now. Still, why was it giving me the fucking shakes?

Sumo and I met up on the opposite side of the campsite. He seemed to have no better idea where the thing was than I did. My scope was still clear. Nothing larger than a fucking frog was within a hundred yards.

I backed up to the truck and wished again I had my armor. Carol and Damiana were sleeping soundly. My helmet mic could easily detect both of the women's soft snores.

"Active patrol," I stated. "Sumo, you first. Wake me in two hours, Ada." Sumo trotted off, beginning his rounds. We were too tired and too few to do an effective sentry duty, but I was beginning to distrust that Ada alone could keep us safe. All she could really sense was the weird paranoid signals my body was giving off. Still, that soldier's sixth sense had saved my ass before.

The rest of the night was Sumo and I swapping out every few hours. Other than a lone rabbit with apparently bad intentions, Sumo tracked down nothing of note. Absolutely nothing out of the ordinary happened. In the early morning hours, I sat on the tailgate between sentry rounds. I realized the feeling of the threat. The sense of being hunted was gone. As a soldier, I had learned to trust my instincts, especially when it came to potential danger, yet now its absence had me even more confused and on edge. "I don't think I like this new world," I said softly. The upside was, it didn't look like I would be occupying it long.

CHAPTER
FIFTY-ONE

LUX

He missed his mom, Marcie, and even his dad and his new girlfriend, maybe a little, but Lux wasn't miserable. In fact, he was happier than he remembered being in a long time. Bill and Laura had two kids. Aleta was already eleven and a boy they called Peegee was just a little older than Lux. Since that first night, the three of them had been playing constantly. The parents had talked little to him, but they'd let him stay. The house wasn't as large as his mom's or dad's, so he'd been sleeping on a mat in the utility room. It was still way better than the woods. They also fed him, but sadly, no more of the wonderful bacon. Still, things could be worse.

"No one lives in those," Peegee said as they threw a ball down the small street.

Lux had been looking at the other homes nearby, one he now realized was just a barn or something. It had machinery parked underneath. "Yeah, we have some empty houses around ours, too."

"Dad said you could stay for a few days until they can get in touch with your parents," the girl said, racing up fast on her bike and sliding it, the back tire braking hard.

Lux shrugged and tossed the ball back. "I'm glad. I didn't much like the woods."

"You can't eat all our food, though," she said before speeding off and circling the big round area at the end of the street.

"I wasn't going to, Aleta," Lux said when she came back by. His voice had a clear edge of anger now. He appreciated how kind the family had been, but it wasn't his fault he was here. He forgot the ball and went and sat on the curb. Timber came over and dug his face into Lux's side. "Thanks, boy. I'm glad you found me, too."

Peegee didn't talk a lot, but when he did, sometimes, his words sounded funny. "Don't pay any attention to her," he said to Lux. "Dad's just worried we don't have enough food and stuff." He turned and watched his older sister's bike as she went around a curve in the road. "She's not just being mean."

"What does that mean? Why don't they just call and order what they need?"

The boy shrugged. "Probably same reason the power's out, and the streaming holochannels aren't playing."

That made sense to Lux, but how would they get in touch with his mom then? "Someone will come and fix it, right?"

Peegee just twisted his face and spat into the grass. "Beats me. Let's go play in the barn."

After a week, Bill started spending a little more time with Lux each day. Mainly just walking around the small farm, pointing things out. Lux got the feeling something was different, but he wasn't sure what had changed. They also weren't eating like they had been the first few days. Dinner the day before had been the only meal, and it was just canned beans and some homemade bread that tasted gritty.

"The crops aren't in yet, you see." Bill pointed, and Lux could see a small round object hanging off a vine that was filled with yellow blossoms.

"That's a tomato," Lux said proudly.

"Very good, kiddo. You pick up fast. It will be another few weeks for those, longer for some of the other stuff." Bill waved his hand around to take in the vast expanse. Lux only saw it as a couple of gardens.

The farm, as they had called it, wasn't that large, not even as big as the playground area in his mom's neighborhood, but Mister Bill seemed proud of it.

"Have you ever gone fishing?" Bill asked, changing the subject.

"Uh, uh," Lux answered, shaking his head. "Mom, didn't like me to get around water."

"Aww, that's silly. Tell you what, tomorrow all of us will go see if we can catch us some dinner. There's a great little spot just a mile or so away." Lux wasn't good at reading adults, but he felt that the man was not really saying what he was thinking.

"Is everything going to be okay, Mister Bill?"

The man smiled, removed his Atlanta Braves hat, and rubbed the sweat from his face. "I think so, Lux. Me and Mrs. Laura are just a bit worried. That's all."

"About food?"

The man's expression seemed to blank out, but then he recovered. "We'll be fine. Look at everything growing out here, and tomorrow we're going to reel in some giant fish."

Fishing sounded fun, but Lux knew there was more than what the man was saying. He was more than a little worried.

~

By the end of that following week, things had gotten even worse. Mister Bill and his wife were fighting openly now.

"You were never a farmer, Bill. You just wanted to play in the dirt," she yelled from the backyard.

"It's not my fault. I have a barn full of equipment that will no longer do nothing." The back door slammed as the man stormed inside.

Lux looked at the two kids. Both looked scared. Neither seemed to want to stay near the house because of the increasing confrontations. They also didn't seem to want to be around him much, either.

"They weren't like this before you showed up," Aleta said accusingly, walking by and bumping him hard with her shoulder as she passed.

Lux wasn't sure what was happening, but knew it wasn't good.

Maybe not for this family, but especially not for him. He didn't belong here—he knew that.

There was no dinner that night. They all went to bed hungry. The next morning, Mister Bill took Lux out early. "We going fishing again?" Lux asked. He didn't think so because all the man carried was a piece of iron. That, plus, the fishing hadn't been very productive. Lux had caught a fish and Bill had gotten two, but they were hard to eat, lots of bones, and very little meat.

Bill stayed silent and kept walking toward one of the other houses. The man went up and peered into the door. Lux already knew no one lived there, so he failed to understand the purpose of the man's actions. Some of what the man had shown him was cool, like the plants and mushrooms you could eat, even some bugs if you got really, really hungry. How to find water that was safe to drink and stuff like that.

"Follow me," Bill said, walking around the empty house to the backyard.

Standing on the patio, Bill looked around, studying the place. It looked a lot like their house, Lux decided. A swing set, some furniture, and a grill for cooking. People had once lived here. Where had they gone?

Bill took the metal bar and gave it a little toss, catching it back in the same hand. It looked heavy to the boy. It was black with one pointed end and the other bent around to form a letter 'U.'

"Kid, I need you to know something,"

the man began; it sounded like he was on the verge of tears or maybe just angry.

Lux worried he had done something wrong, but he couldn't think of anything.

"I mean, don't take this personal or nothing."

Lux heard Peegee and Aleta in their yard across the road. Timber barked; Lux imagined they were throwing the ball to big dog. He liked Timber the best he decided. When he looked back at the man, Bill had the bar raised high, and he was openly crying now.

CHAPTER
FIFTY-TWO
KOVACH

I didn't tell the women anything about the night's events, or non-events, to be more accurate. We packed up as soon as the batteries were charged and hit the road again. I let them know about the battle suit manufacturer. Unlike the drive yesterday, today we would have to go through some residential areas, as well as a few small towns. I didn't like it but saw few alternatives.

After being on the road over a week, I had yet to see another operational vehicle of any kind. No cars, no air cars, no work tractors even. A few bikes, a handful of people on horseback, but the old GMC pickup had the road pretty much to itself, other than the stalled vehicles we had to navigate around or occasionally pull out of the way.

I felt like I was traveling through a foreign country. Traffic wasn't the only thing missing. I'd seen no other dogs or cats. Most cattle fields were barren. When we slowed down or stopped, I no longer heard birds. The world outside was very different from a week ago.

One of my earlier drop missions had been into Tunisia in northern Africa. It was unusual because I had vacationed there once with my family when I was twelve or thirteen. I remembered how great the beaches on the Mediterranean were and how friendly the locals had been. It was one of the most progressive areas on the African continent and heavily dependent on tourism.

Years later, it was a battle zone. A civil war in a neighboring country had spilled over the borders, and now Tunisia was where most of the heaviest fighting was happening. We had dropped in to secure a diplomat. One who, ironically, had already been dead for days before we arrived. We had to fight our way back to the coast and wait for extract. The beautiful buildings they used to remind everyone of Greece now were tumbled down ruins. The shops were gone, the restaurants all vacant shells, but what I remembered most was how much the people had changed. Their world had disappeared, and now they, too, were just hollow shells, full of anger and loss and guilt. They wanted our help, and they wanted us dead, sometimes in the same instant.

Those same hollow-eyed stares now followed me as we moved through small town after small town. Death had not come swiftly to this area; they were far enough out to only get brushed with destruction, yet none of these areas had power. Lines were long outside any store that seemed open. Most now appeared to be makeshift food banks. I stopped twice looking for the anti-radiation meds, but the drugstore had been relocated, and the hospital pharmacy had never stocked it according to Ada's scan of the system.

Walking back toward the truck from the hospital, I saw a group of men squared off at the opposite end of the parking lot. They were all carrying rifles. Sumo was positioned at the rear of the truck where I'd left him to stand guard. Being back in my full body armor left me more confident than I really should have been. After all, one lucky shot was all it would take to put me down.

I bypassed the truck, both women watching me pass as if I'd lost my mind. My weapons stayed holstered as I made my way down to the group. I hoped they didn't want trouble, but I knew better than to expect that.

"I told you he was some kinda soldier," a kid in his early teens said loudly.

Ada was routinely marking targets based on a threat assessment algorithm that had proven uncannily accurate over the past year. She had a bright red number one floating over a slender man near the back of the group. I moved through the front of the pack and right up to the man. I didn't much like avoiding confrontation. If he was surprised, he didn't show it.

"Do we have a problem?" I asked softly.

The man was in his early forties, in good shape, and carried his rifle like someone who'd done it for a living at some point.

"We do, Sergeant."

The man knew his ranks. He almost certainly was ex-military. "Where did you serve?" Using the brothers-in-arms approach was a bit of a shitty move, but hey, I wasn't looking for a fight. The longer we stayed here soaking up rads, the more time we'd need to get rid of it. The three rules of radiation exposure had been drilled into us back in Ranger school. Proximity, duration, and shielding. So far, we weren't being successful on any of those three.

"Don't much matter anymore. The fuckin Ruskies won, didn't they?" the man said with a voice that was far too weary for his years.

"Don't think it was them, but I get your point. Whoever pulled the trigger, we let it happen."

"You let it happen," someone else said.

"It was on your watch," another chimed in.

I got the idea now. These guys were just pissed. They wanted someone to strike out against. A government official would have been best, but a soldier in full battle rattle would work, too.

"I was on leave, fellas. Just minding my one business, just like you."

Something hit me in the back of the helmet. I staggered forward a few steps. I heard my dog and knew he was about to go full psychopath on the closest man. "Hold," I ordered.

Another punch landed but did little other than glancing off my armor. I heard the man swearing as he moved away, holding his hand. "Non-lethal, Ada." I had no desire to hurt these people. They were dying anyway with no help from me.

A panel in my leg armor rotated out. I reached down and pulled the ten-inch cylinder out and held it in front of me. Ada triggered the rod which fully extended. In seconds, the six-foot weighted baton was slicing through the air at the oncoming men. One man went down with a broken jaw. Two more got jabs into a windpipe, which left them crawling and gasping for air. While I didn't want to kill them, I wasn't too concerned with how close they came to it.

"Weapon rear," Ada stated.

I ducked, spun, and swept the staff up with a swing for the outfield bleachers. The attacker's wrist cracked, and the gun fell limply in hands that would likely never work again. I whipped the weapon back and inadvertently caught a man trying to attack me from the other side. He went down with blood gurgling from his throat. My alpha threat had smartly moved back several dozen feet, and I could see he was taking aim with his gun. Not at my head or torso, but at my hip joint. The one place battle armor is traditionally weakest.

"Hit, hit, hit," I yelled, and seconds before the impact, I saw a white and grey blur flying into the man from the side. The round hit, and I felt a jab of white-hot pain lance up and down my side.

"Minor damage, Prowler," my built-in AI said, clearly not understanding how the human body works.

"My ass, you bucket of..."

"I have your dad on the line. Would you like to..."

"I've just been shot, Ada, and since when do you announce his calls?"

"You said to let you know as soon as I could reach him," the clueless computer said. "I reached him."

"Ada, run diagnostic. You are turning into a smartass."

"Diagnostic in progress," followed quickly by, "Nope, all good."

"That you, Joseph?" My dad's voice sounded unnatural and tinny. The connection sucked.

"Yeah, Pops, it's me." I activated the suit's trauma kit to disinfect the wound, staunch the blood flow, and administer pain meds.

"You sound tired. Are you not sleeping well?"

"Um, yeah, that's part of it." I watched the blood leaking from the leg and knee joints of my battle- suit.

"Were you in a fight?"

"Yeah, several." I motioned for Sumo to leave the dead man alone and come back to guard the truck. Most of the other men that could were slowly moving away.

"Well, leave them where they fall. Don't waste time burying their sorry asses. Buzzards need to eat, same as worms!"

"Yes, Pops," I said weakly, the drugs beginning to take hold.

"You did win, right? You showing those commie bastards who's boss?"

"They weren't Russian, Dad. Do you have any idea what's going on out here?"

"Hey, it's okay, Son. I know you suck as a fighter. But know that, win or lose, you know we love you... okay, that's bullshit. You lose, and you are dead to me. You have literally been hard-wired for victory. Lose and you are 100 percent dead to me."

"Are you done?" I asked, praying the bullet would move up my leg and kill me before I had to continue this conversation.

"Sure, Joseph, what's on your mind?"

Oh, hmm, end of the world, flesh-eating houseplants, killer robots, and something freaky haunting my sleep. Let's see. "What do you know of a secret DARPA site, code name Ranier?"

"Weird question to ask during a fight."

"The name, Dad. Do you know it?" My voice was getting groggy now. "Do you know of a secret base named that?"

The line stayed silent for a long moment. I was beginning to think he was gone. My legs suddenly gave out, and I sat down hard on the pavement. I was vaguely aware of Carol and Damiana trying to help.

"We had another name for that place, Son."

"Ow!" I yelled as the women helped me back up. I used the battle staff to walk back toward the pickup.

"The Nightmare Factory," Pops said coldly. "I don't know what you saw at Iron River, but Rainier is where all the bad shit was perfected and produced en masse. You do not want to go there—ever."

The line went dead.

CHAPTER
FIFTY-THREE

Ada had us moving out of the nameless town in minutes. I triggered the release on my armor, and Damiana tugged gently then with even more force to pull it off. I heard Carol gasp as she saw the wound.

"They shot you."

"Not the first time it's happened," I stated through tightly clenched teeth. "My upgrades help with a lot of things, but they don't do shit to ease the pain."

"Do I need to get the bullet out?" Damiana asked.

"It was an old metal jacketed round, probably split up when it went in. The Regenerax will either dissolve it or force it back out through the entry wound overnight. Best just to leave it alone." My blood was full of artificial nanobot machinery whose sole job was keeping me alive and functioning in battle-ready condition. That also did little for the pain, but I'd learned to compartmentalize that long ago.

"There's so much blood," Carol said, the panic clear in her voice.

"Look up here, Carol. Up here." I didn't want her watching what her friend was doing. "I have something to ask you."

She looked a little scared, as if everything over the last two days was crashing down on her, and I was about to make her pay up for the ride. "Relax, I need to get to another Hammer Industries facility. One called Rainier."

All color drained from the woman's face, and she began to shake her head slowly at first, then increasingly more animated.

"No, no, no...no."

Tears began flowing, and she looked again like the woman yesterday, someone on the verge of shutting down. Damiana suddenly slapped her across the face, leaving a bloody handprint.

"Snap the fuck out of it, Carol. Joe asked you a question. Help him, it's the only chance you have of seeing Lux again."

Carol's eyes met mine. *Yeah, what she said,* I wanted to say. Maybe I should have just slapped her myself and not wasted so much time. No... I decided that probably wouldn't have been smart.

"You've heard of it?" I asked.

She gave a small nod.

"You know where it is?"

The look of fear returned, and she glanced at her friend for support. None was forthcoming.

No," she answered.

My heart sank."Fuuuuuck!"

Then her mouth moved, making no actual sound. I knew she was working something out in her head.

"Maybe," she said slowly, her eyes still full of terror.

My eyes closed from the pain. My self-healing body was doing what it needed to repair the damage. I got to enjoy white-hot pain and other parts of my body going numb as I was slipping down a long slide toward unconsciousness. I needed to hear her answer, but everything went black, and what I wanted... no longer mattered.

"I just need to get to my son,"

I heard Carol say from somewhere close. My eyes flickered slowly to life. My dreams had again been filled with nightmare creatures and fear that I had let the entire world down. I never recall feelings like this, but something was off in my head. I had Ada run neural diagnostics. I was starting to feel seriously unhinged.

"You're back."

Damiana eyed me warily. She was behind the wheel of the truck, but I could tell Ada was still doing the actual driving.

"Yeah, for better or worse," I responded, sitting up and glad that most of the pain was numbed.

"We are heading west, Joseph," Ada said internally. "Carol has given general directions, but very little specifics."

"The grid must be working here," Dami said, pointing out to the road. "Your truck seems to have locked onto the smart road system."

I just nodded, not wanting to get into that conversation yet. I scrambled to find food. The one thing with a body like mine is the increased metabolism means increased intake. Especially when I was injured, I woke up starving.

Damiana seemed to understand and pulled the car over so we could eat.

∿

Carol became much more animated over the next few days. Damiana seemed to have moved in the opposite direction. She'd become more surly, less confident, and something else even less identifiable.

Ada had delivered us to the Rivex distribution center. I was still weak, the nanobodies still busy repairing my insides. Sumo took the lead, and Damiana went in alone bringing out four battle suits. The suits were made in only eight standard sizes and had enough flexibility to fit them easily. It wouldn't be as effective as the full body armor/battleskin combination, but it should be enough normal protection for them. We packed the spares into a storage box in the truck.

Carol modeled hers for me, and I had to admit the dark blue, form-fitting garment cast her in a new light. I saw her friend looking at her with a frown. Both then showed off to each other, then donned regular clothes on top of the new 'bad-ass warrior gear' as they called it.

I was still unclear on what Carol's role with the Nightmare Factory had been, but some of her work was apparently vital in some part of the development. Later, when I was feeling marginally better, we finally talked. The truck was parked behind an ancient store, something my dad would have referred to as a gas station.

"You did behavioral studies?" I asked, again hoping if she said it enough times, I would see a connection to these warfare labs.

"Yes and no," she began in a voice a kindergarten teacher might use with a particularly slow student.

"Do you remember studying the early days of social media? You know, back when everyone shared every minor detail about themselves on public websites?"

"Yeah, we studied it in school. They gave up all privacy just to be popular or trending or something."

"Rich," Carol said, looking out at the green pasture stretching out from the highway. "Back then, they didn't realize they were the product. To be more specific, the hundreds of thousands of data points they provided those sites with for free. Data that the algorithms used to predict with uncanny accuracy future behaviors."

"Okay, yes, I recall more of it now." Amazing how far back to the side of privacy society had retreated since then.

"Well, that's what they sold to their advertisers, and that predictive modeling grew into what my specialty is today."

She stoked Sumo's fur unconsciously while she discussed her work. The woman had relaxed significantly around my dog since their first meeting. "Joe, my system can analyze your behavior for a few hours and then predict how you would react to a particular thing with an accuracy of over ninety percent. If I give it more time studying you, or as we say, acquire more data points, the predictive relevance goes up significantly more."

I wanted to say we were not just ones and zeroes but thought about my own cerebral passenger and thought better of it. "But we have free will. We can change."

"Free will is an illusion, and humans are notoriously easy to manipulate. Advertisers do it all the time. So do politicians. We all like to think we behave rationally and have common sense. The scientific truth is that human brains are mostly designed to ignore rational thought. That's why the conspiracy theories or clickbait headlines work so well at drawing us in. Even if your conscious brains know this is a lie, you are driven to click on it just to see what it says."

"I can kind of accept that," I said.

"We call that social conditioning. We believe what we're told, even without desiring to believe it, even when we try not to believe it, and even when we know it is false. Even our educational system is built largely on this, so from a young age, we're taught to believe what someone says."

"So how are you weaponizing this, Carol?" Damiana leaned in, apparently also curious to hear.

Carol scrunched her face up into a frown. I know she was thinking back to all the NDAs and top-secret certification she'd likely had to endure to rise up the ranks of Hammer's Industries. After a moment, she continued,

"I did the behavioral modeling. Assembling the data points into reliable predictive behaviors for various scenarios."

"Battlefield scenarios?" I asked.

"Um, some, but not many. Battlefield tactics are relatively routine and less impacted by conscious thought. War fighters tend to be proactive as in 'Follow the mission directive' or reactive as in 'That guy's shooting at us, let's hide.'"

I had to nod in agreement. "That's a pretty accurate description in a nutshell."

"No, I built models on micro and macro events. How people will react to everything from major crises down to hearing a baby cry in a restaurant. Honestly, some parameters they had me run were so banal and boring I thought they were kidding. One was to see how long any random group of fifteen people would sit in a locked room before one of them tried the door."

The pieces weren't fitting for me, but her role with Rainier could be merely a sidebar on one of the many projects going on there.

"I don't think I understand why you were so scared when I mentioned the place. What else is it that you know?"

CHAPTER
FIFTY-FOUR
BANSHEE

Priest looked over the loadout and was duly impressed. "This is different."

"Don't get too comfortable with it. If that Wulf back there dies on us, we'll be hoofing it. All this gear will just slow us down."

The TriCraft interior was crammed full. The Wulf, or more accurately, the military's ground assault transport, was a rugged beast of a machine, but it was notoriously prone to frequent breakdowns.

Major Kerns walked in with a wiry, Asian man. "Banshee, you are down a man. We happen to have a suitable replacement for you. Please meet Staff Sergeant Dae Him-Chan of the ROK's Special Operations Division."

Adding someone to a team just before a mission was... well, it just wasn't done. The lieutenant saw the looks her other two men were giving both her and the major. These were unusual times, though. "Ma'am and Sergeant Dae," she said, stepping forward with an outstretched hand.

"Just use my call sign," the man said in letter-perfect English. "G-force. Or, more often, just Gi."

"ROK SpecOps, you guys have a reputation for getting the job done."

G-force bowed slightly. "Very kind of you to say. We do our best."

"The staff sergeant came to us by means not so different from your own journey," the major added. "Our war commander, Admiral Reese, believes he will be an asset to you."

More likely someone to spy on us, Bayou thought, but she would gladly take advantage of the man's talents. She knew they were about to jump into the shit. "Grab your kit, synch comms, and get with Priest over there to go over some of the specific signals and tactics Banshee uses that may be unfamiliar. What is your weapon of choice?"

G-force looked at the weapons locker on the far wall of the dropship.

"Any."

Halo and Priest walked up and stuck out a hand. "I like a man who isn't choosy," Priest said.

"Oh... no, sir. I am choosy, I am just equally proficient," Sergeant Dae said, shaking hands. The man's voice was not boastful, simply stating something as a verified fact.

Two hours later, her men were doing last-minute gear checks. Bayou called for the final briefing. "Command, and by Command, I mean the guys up there..." Bayou said testily, pointing above her head. They all knew that the Space Force had named one of their own as interim War Commander, as no Command elements on the ground had been heard from. They also did not know who they were fighting yet. None had ever met or seen Admiral Reese, but his bio suggested he'd spent most of his service time at Gateway and Luna. Kerns had not seemed receptive to his command earlier. Bayou wondered what had changed.

"Command has multiple targets for us to recon." She pointed the locations out on the large display as the others looked on. "The coordinates and specific deployments will be added to your tac units." All were on the East Coast. "Several of these are major population centers. We already know casualties are massive. We are not to render aid or engage with the civilian population. Our job is to assess threats, damage, and provide actionable intel. Are we clear?"

The TriCraft dropship was being piloted by the same man from days earlier. "Lieutenant, heading back to the shit?" the man named Packer asked with a grin as he went through pre-flight.

"You know how us ground-pounders are," Bayou answered. "Just can't get enough."

Packer eyed the Spaceborne Infantry RDT patch on her sleeve and nodded. "Right, ground-pounders."

She gave him the exact coordinates for the first insertion, an area just outside the blast zone for New York City. Turning back, she gave her crew and the load one final check, ordering Halo to double check the Wulf was secure in the cargo hold.

"Staff Sergeant, a word," she said softly, turning to her team's recent addition.

"Yes, of course," the man said, placing a hand in his jacket pocket.

"Gi, we don't have time for niceties. I quickly read over your file. You are more than capable. I just have one question for you. Do you have any agenda I am unaware of?"

He gave a thoughtful smile. "Me being here is unusual, troubling for you and your men. I totally understand that. I am not Spaceborne Infantry, never left Earth until now. I don't belong up here. You feel I am of no real use."

He removed his hand from his pocket and opened his palm. It contained a small paper photograph of an older woman.

Debra studied the image. She had the same eyes as he did, kind but determined. "Mother?"

He nodded. "She was in London."

Bayou smiled sadly and gently placed a hand on his rock-hard shoulder. "I understand. Don't go down there for payback, though. Go to do the job they trained you for, and we will be fine."

He forced a smile and a tiny nod.

"Launch when ready, Captain," she yelled before taking her seat.

Inside a TriCraft dropship there is no actual sense of movement. No acceleration or sudden drops. The ships use a proprietary inertial dampening system that no one seemed to fully understand. What is universal, though, to everyone who travels in one is a low pain in every joint in your body. Riggs could tell they were accelerating simply by the degree of pain. No one ever bothered to explain any of this. It was simply how it was. She gritted her teeth and wished like hell for it to hurry up and be over. Glancing around the jump seats, she saw the rest of her team suffering just as much, except the new man, G-force. He had the same stoic expression he'd worn since they met hours earlier. *The guy was a fucking machine.*

The ship came down at incredible speed. While it lacked much in the way of armaments, it could drop in silently with little to no radar signature. Bayou always knew if they'd had more of the little ships, the RDT troopers like her and her team would be unnecessary. Why they didn't make more was also a mystery that no one upstream every bothered to discuss.

"Ground floor in thirty," the pilot said. Bayou pointed at Jenkins, who was already poised to unstrap the tiedowns for the Wulf. Bishop moved to the cargo gate release. "Gi, get inside on the controls." Being on the ground was the most dangerous time for the dropships, so they wanted to be in perfect synchronization. When the pilot counted down from eight, the former ROK soldier had the Wulf ready to roll. Bayou and Halo were in the back. The gate touched down as the craft went from several hundred miles an hour to a full stop in just a few hundred feet. The change in inertia alone should have killed them, but inside the black triangle airship, they felt nothing.

Sergeant Dae moved the vehicle out with practiced ease. Priest grabbed hold as it went by and triggered the hatch to close after them. They were moving away in just over ten seconds, and the ship was soon a near invisible dot high above them once again. The pilot was not returning to the carrier. He was on assignment to them as cover and extraction. They had numerous targets, so they needed to stay mobile. Most likely, he would wait for their signal up in low orbit, but the lieutenant was not allowed to question TriCraft operational tactics.

They were 150 miles outside New York City. Debra knew the city well. Her sister had lived there while going to college. She'd visited her often, always amazed at the diversity and sheer density of humanity. As the Wulf sped over the grounds to the city, she braced herself for what came next. Her orders were to proceed to a set of coordinates, evaluate the scene, and report back. "Buckets on," she ordered. The rad meter was already climbing toward the red. The city had been hit by multiple dirty bombs. Each of her team placed the suit helmets on and switched over to the internal systems.

While the helmets always smelled and were claustrophobic at first, Debra wanted the privacy. She tapped her comms to change the frequency.

"Banshee actual to Prowler."

Kovach's voice sounded tired and distant. Still, she was damn glad to hear it.

"Glad to have you back dirt side, Bayou," he said after she caught him up on the basics.

"Joe," she said, abandoning the sometimes-ridiculous combat radio security protocols. "What in the fuck is going on down here?" This was her first time seeing the near destruction of her own country. The sensation was somewhat overwhelming even for a battle-hardened soldier.

"Bayou, watch yourself. There is shit out there that surprises even me. I'm not sure what we're even fighting or fighting for. These guys unleased a biological storm on our country."

Those words didn't sound like the man who'd led them into more battles than she could count. "What's wrong, Kovach?"

He didn't want to tell her about the gunshot, nor the fact that he was still scared to go to sleep. The fucking nightmares kept coming back. "Hammer Industries." he said. "Does that ring a bell?"

"Hell, yeah! Nearly every part of our gear leads back to Hammer in some form. You think they caused this?"

"Caused it, were the target, I don't know yet, but they were involved. Also, I think all those labs, all that shit we were recovering since... well, you know."

She knew full well he meant since Rollo had been killed and a sizeable chunk of Kovach got blown away in that shitty terrorist cave of abominations.

"The stuff Hammer was working on looks like a continuation of what all those bioterrorists had started. Mostly, what I have is just more questions at this point. Just watch your backs."

She involuntarily glanced at the Korean man helping navigate the troop carrier. He was still a question mark. Could he be a spy, someone working against them?

"Trouble ahead," Gi's crisp voice said over the internal comms. The Wulf slowed.

"Got work to do, Prowler. Send me an update on your twenty. I'm feeling no great loyalty to this peek and seek recon plan the major has us on."

"That's a hard copy, Bayou. Take care of our team. If you see some wild-looking vines, stay clear. They are deadly and fast as a snake to attack."

"Solid copy, Prowler. Be safe!"

Gun shots began pinging off the outer hull of the Wulf. It looked like not all the natives were under cover or dead.

CHAPTER
FIFTY-FIVE
KOVACH

I rubbed a hand over the week's worth of stubble. After the conversation with Debra, all those feelings of obligation and duty hit me once more. Despite everything Ada had told me, I knew I owed it to Debra to go into Louisville if there was any chance that she still had family alive.

"Ada, how much would it add to our trip if we went on to Louisville?"

"Louisville is a nonstarter," my AI said in her monotone voice. "It was hit by a full CBRN attack."

I knew that stood for chemical, biological, radiation, and nuclear, and indeed it seemed like they had gotten hit by all of those.

"I know. But we have armor, and I can leave the ladies somewhere safe. They don't need to go to this place with me. They'll be okay for a couple of days—right?"

"That may be so, Joe, but what I'm telling you is the two to three days it would take is in the best conditions, if you ran into no trouble and if the roads are even passable. I can tell you from what I've seen, Louisville took a direct nuclear blast. Possibly more than one."

I sighed and looked out at the pristine rolling hills and farmland. If America was destroyed, you couldn't tell it by this area.

Ada continued, "Have you not wondered where all the people are?"

I didn't actually want to admit that I hadn't. Most of Kentucky seemed rather sparsely populated, so it didn't seem like there would be many people.

"Not really."

"No matter the scale of the attacks, you would expect people fleeing from the destroyed cities. By car, horse, or on foot. These roads should be littered with the debris of a mass exodus."

"Where would they have gone?"

"Anywhere, Joe. Anywhere would have seemed safer than where they were. I am telling you there is no way her sister made it out okay."

"You can't... you can't just say that. It could be the same thing as Carol's son."

"No, Joe. He was in Atlanta but somehow got out. Atlanta also took a hit. No, Kovach, this one is a little more definite. In fact, I couldn't be more definite."

I did not like the tone my AI was using.

"Spill it, Ada. What do you know?"

She took one of her artificially long pauses before responding.

"I know because I monitor all your teams. I think you know that."

"You invade our privacy? You mean you listen in on calls and emails and shit?"

"No, I don't do that. I, or more accurately Central Command, do store them in case they're ever needed, as I have recently discovered cataloging all those communications, with their loved ones, their family, their extended family. It was part of my central programming, part of my core mandate. And beyond that, the government stores the conversations of nearly everybody, but especially those connected even tangentially to the government or military."

As a key leader on a special operations team, I began to understand where my trusty AI was headed.

"You know more about what happened to her, don't you?"

Ada's response was slow and muted. And even though I thought many times that Ada and Debra didn't get along very well, there was mutual respect. No matter what Ada was about to say, I still owed it to Deb to see for myself.

"Ada, they're the ones who pulled me out of that hell-hole with my guts hanging out, my arm gone. You understand I owe her my life?"

"Joe, I found something in the files. These are the final moments of her sister's life."

I heard a voice, obviously a recording, road noise and music playing in the background. It was a female; she was talking to someone.

"I'm pretty sure it's a comms conversation with the driver's brother out on the West Coast," Ada explained.

"Debra doesn't have any other siblings."

"That isn't her sister on the comms. Just listen... and watch."

An image resolved itself in my head. A shaky video image came in from the phone's camera. It was pointed ahead toward traffic heading into a city. The resolution was grainy, but I guessed from the skyline it was Louisville.

A shadow passed over the interstate and the scene ahead erupted into a brilliant blast of white-hot fire. The autocar slid to a stop, and I watched as a new Toyota just ahead was consumed by the roiling pressure wave. Then the picture went to snow, then black.

"This woman was in a car headed back to work when the blast wave hit the entire area. It was hit by the full impact of a megaton nuclear blast," Ada said.

"The car just ahead of her, the grey Toyota, was driven by Debra's sister, Jacey. She would have died instantly, even if she'd been shielded. The radiation there inside that blast zone would have vaporized her instantly. Your cells regenerate at record pace, and even with that and your technological marvel of body armor, you could have made it maybe five minutes if you survived the initial blast.

Jacey did not make it," Ada said somberly.

The video left me feeling gutted. I knew for a fact Deb hadn't seen it.

"There must be something we can do. Can we get some drones over the place? Any assets that we can pull in?"

"Joe, the roads within 100 miles of Louisville are a junkyard of wrecked and stalled cars. Roads are buckled, bridges are out. There is no traffic. There is no communication. There is no power. No food, no drinkable water.

Deb will do a flyover. I can pass this information along to her if you want. But I'm telling you, this will cost you your life. If you go after her, you will probably die and will miss your only chance to get the medicines you need."

Joe had made up his mind. He already knew he had to try. It was just baked into his DNA. Something he was going to have to do today. How would he break it to the women? That was the tough part. Not that Carol or Damiana had any great love to go visit this or Rainier factory. But that didn't mean that they wanted to sit around waiting for him to make a fool's run.

What if he didn't come back? And they're stuck here in the middle of Kentucky, trying to figure out what the hell to do? He felt the unfamiliar fear of uncertainty gripping him again. He could not shake this nagging doubt... things that he'd never had to deal with his entire career.

Should he betray his friend who risked her life countless times to save him or abandon the two women that had become his travel partners? Carol and Dami had held up their end of the agreement to get him to where he needed to go.

He just didn't have the answers. He did have an overwhelming sense of duty. He would have to calm down and talk to Deb. That's the only thing that made any sense to him. He couldn't just leave that question hanging. Fighting for our loved ones is what drives us and all soldiers. None of us did it for the honor, the pride, or the spirit of patriotism or any of the other bullshit they throw at us. We did it for the person standing next to us pulling a trigger. And we did it for our families back home. That's what a warrior does. That's what really drives us to be on the front line to hold that line. We want to make sure this shit never follows us home.

And yet, it had. That was the miserable ball of guilt I was feeling in the depths of my soul. It hadn't been on my watch, but it could have been. I definitely should have known something. Pops certainly had. How was Hammer Industries involved? How deeper up or down the chain did this go? Was it really an enemy? Or was it a false flag operation that just went horribly wrong? Could someone purposely want to make the human race go extinct? I had to admit these were damn good questions. Ones I simply didn't have the answers for. In my storm-tossed mind, I thought if I could just get some sleep, my decisions would be easier. Maybe it would all make some sense.

There was one thing I had to do first. I had to share what I knew with Carol. I'd been holding back this information, and this woman, maybe above all others, really needed to know everything I knew about her son.

CHAPTER
FIFTY-SIX

Morning came on me like a slap to the face. The 'slide,' as I had come to know it, was my body's screaming need for the pharmaceutical intervention every month. It had been the case every month since Doctor Reichert's team had saved my life. Immediately after getting the drug cocktail, I was fine, nearly as good as new, but that peak soon started slipping away. By the fifth week, I was much less sharp, barely capable, in fact. Even though today was only about my two-week mark, I could feel it coming on. That was part of what I assumed Ada's diagnosis would have concluded. My sleep irregularities were caused by something off in my body chemistry. But that was not what she came up with at all.

"Joseph, your neural patterns are showing a very specific and highly troubling wave pattern."

"My what?"

"I have been running a soma diagnosis on you for several nights and something is off. Your delta waves are nearly non-existent, your gamma and theta waves are spiking when they shouldn't be, and I am detecting an altogether different signal that almost looks more like a radio carrier wave than anything natural."

Okay, some of my upgrades helped increase my cognitive ability, but I was lost on most of what she said.

"So, I'm not sleeping well," I guessed. The news about Deb's sister had weighed on me until the early hours of the morning.

"Your sleep is not the issue; you are not getting a restorative sleep. No matter how long you are out, your mind is not shutting down. It is firing as if it is on high alert."

"Why... I mean, how could that happen? Something wrong with you know... my hardware?"

She took a while to answer. I'm sure it was a totally artificial pause simply to appear more human and show empathy or something, but I noticed. "You are not like others, Joseph. You have an organic computer in your head. A control system wired into your spinal column. Also, we are in very challenging times and traveling through areas irradiated by both gamma radiation and neutron saturation. I originally assumed some combination of this could be causing your issues... the night terrors."

"So, you don't think that creature back at the Iron River facility..."

"Possibly," she answered smoothly. "I didn't think it did anything to you. It is theoretically possible, but only if it possessed some psionic capability."

"A what?" I asked.

"If the biologist that likely created this creature had been able to give it the ability to essentially project fear into the minds of the enemy, a psionic or psychic broadcast, that would be an incredibly useful adaptation."

"And you think that's what that thing had?"

"Monitoring your stress levels from the first likely encounter outside that door, yes. I believe it was likely the case."

"I've never heard of any animal that could do that."

"No," she agreed. "Humans are the only ones to use fear in that way, but even they can't effectively convey it on a purely subconscious level."

I noodled on that all afternoon. If this was the level of dark-site research Hammer was diving into, I'm not sure I wanted to know what else they were doing. I thought about Banshee and what they were heading into. We were all working blind right now. Way more questions than answers. These attacks had loosed God knows what from the darkest corners of our nightmares.

What Carol knew about Rainier was largely anecdotal. Information reports she got back from the other lab's production to help refine or corroborate her own data modeling.

"Some of them were holos. Where they set up real-world scenarios and used test subjects or focus groups to see how accurate my predictions were," she offered.

That all sounded reasonable to me. "Like, how long it took the subjects to try the locked door?"

"Twenty-three minutes," she said instantly. "Sometimes they included other things... stuff I'm sure I wasn't supposed to see. Most of it was disturbing."

My injury was mostly healed already and beginning to itch. I took over the driving from Ada; all I knew was to keep heading west for a few more hours before turning south. The ruins of Louisville were to the north, and yes, I had decided to listen to my AI despite what my gut told me for once.

"Rainier is the primary production war lab," Carol continued. "All the rest of the locations are just development sites. All our research goes into whatever projects are active at that location. Exotic technologies, genetics, enhanced humans, cyborgs, propulsion, robotics... I could guess at some of the rest, but it would simply be a guess."

"Tell me some of what you saw."

She grew more anxious; her emotional state had seemed fragile before but now seemed to escalate even more. Over the next hour, the woman tried to relate to me at least some of what she'd seen. Then she added what she had pieced together from other bits of data she'd had access to.

"I saw a video of them testing prototypes of combat droids. All shapes, all sizes. First, they used them against animals, then against something that looked like a man but clearly wasn't. It was deformed or something. It could have been a genetically altered human."

She described it: large head, bony chest, massive torso. The description was way too close to a thing I had encountered myself years ago. A thing guarding an enemy lab thousands of miles away. Genetic enhancements with humans had been a growing business for many years, mostly in the cosmetic or health maintenance segments. Gene editing at the level Carol described was off limits and heavily illegal. The technology had been around for decades, but ethics laws strictly prevented almost all germline edits and anything as radical as creating a mutant human. We only saw that in the illegal baby labs like the one where I'd nearly been killed.

"Some of the weapons' systems seemed downright bizarre. After seeing the killer kudzu at Iron River, it makes more sense."

"What do you mean?" I asked.

"I thought some of it was, you know, animated. CGI for a virtual reality game or something. Like they were testing weird shit like trees that shot some kind of darts at intruders. I think they were modified cones or seed pods. Grass with poisonous barbs and, of course, the vines we already saw. When I asked a supervisor, he said they were doing some terraforming projects for NASA. You know, coming up with creatures that could live in harsh environments and change the atmosphere and soils to ones more suitable to our biosphere."

"But you said that Rainier was a production facility. They wouldn't be doing the testing there, right?"

She nodded. "Probably not. Judging by the department that handled it, most of these fell under the passive intrusion prevention. BioSecurity Division they call it."

"Yeah, I'm familiar with that. A security system that's always on works great as a perimeter defense." Also, from Hammer's standpoint, that could be weaponized to pacify wide swaths of the planet if needed. The byline for Rainier was they seemed to be into lots of fringe science. Exotic technologies and a few things that neither Ada nor I could make sense of.

"And all you know is that it's somewhere south of here?" I asked.

Carol shook her head. "I saw the same IP coordinates on enough of the files that I could guess the whereabouts of many of the other facilities. As you probably know, satellite IPs are assigned by grid, unlike the old school ones that were mostly random."

I did not know that, but I did now, thanks to Ada. "IP addresses are standard for any device connecting to the web?" I asked, parroting what my AI had just said internally.

"Yes, Internet Protocols," she said. "Been around since the early days of the web."

"And you somehow knew it was down there." I waved my hand in the generally southern direction.

"Nothing in the entire sector except a small town. Sparta, Tennessee. I even site-mapped it, virtually nothing that looks like you might expect."

That would make sense. Hammer wouldn't want to be obvious with a facility that important. I now had a destination. Now, if they just had the meds I needed. My finger twitched involuntarily. *It's nothing*, I told myself.

Ada let me know we would need to stop soon to recharge. I needed to get this next part out while I had the chance. Carol deserved to know what I knew. She'd been forthcoming with her information. Now it was my turn.

"Carol, there's something I need to tell you." I wrapped the truth in a lie, just a small one. I told her I had gotten a brief internet connection back in the last town and had used my military web search to do a trace on her son. I was hoping it would go over easier for me... It didn't. I let her know everything Ada had uncovered.

"So, you're telling me my son isn't with his father in Atlanta? That he was in an autocar when the missiles hit?" She had her hands on her hips, and her face was red with rage.

"When were you going to tell me this, Kovach? Huh? After you got what you wanted, what you needed?"

Yes, I thought. "No, of course not." My voice held just the perfect amount of righteous indignation at the accusation. Have I mentioned I'm an asshole?

Atlanta had been destroyed. If her son had stayed there, or the car never got out of the metroplex, then he would certainly not be alive. Unsurprisingly, that nugget of intel didn't help their feelings at all. Both women quizzed me relentlessly, but soon accepted I had no other useful information to offer.

I got only perfunctory nods of acknowledgement for the rest of the day and into the night. I knew they both were upset. Carol was on the ground rocking back and forth, hugging her knees. Damiana tried to comfort her, but it was hopeless. I could read their looks of hatred directed at me across the campfire. I took the first turn on guard duty and heard Carol softly crying long into the night.

CHAPTER
FIFTY-SEVEN

The morning air had a faint smell of wood smoke. It was an increasingly familiar smell as the nation's survivors shifted from restaurant delivery and modern kitchens back to patio grills or plain old campfires. I looked around for the women, both of whom were usually up by now. Carol would have had the last watch, but we'd gotten a bit lazy this last week maintaining the vigil. Nothing had threatened us since back closer to Virginia. Now that we were several hundred miles away, that fear wasn't as pressing. I unfolded myself from my sleeping bag and went to do my business.

"Ada, status update."

The call into my AI had also gotten routine. Ada didn't reply, not immediately, which was more than a little troubling.

"Sumo!" I called, softly at first, then louder.

"Ada, locate Sumo!"

"Sumo is outside transponder range," she replied in an oddly official voice. *What in the fuck did that mean?* He was never outside a range that she could locate. Not in the many remote locations we had been together since we became a combat team.

"Where are the women?" I had now made a full circuit of our campsite

"I am unable to say," Ada replied, also in the same cold mechanical voice.

"Ada, run deep diagnostic."

Something was clearly wrong with her.

"Yes, of course. On what?"

"On you, goddamit! You are fucking up!" My gun was now in my hand, and I was sliding my other arm into my chest armor now. I could feel the tension rising. I'd gotten caught sleeping on the job, and now the two people that I was supposed to be protecting were missing.

Carol's bedroll lay where it had been the night before. Damiana's was missing entirely. I checked supplies. Nothing gone as far as I could tell. I was the only one who had an actual backpack, but the women had found duffels to use, and both were still here.

I wasn't a fool; I knew Carol was pissed at me and they could have chosen to leave on their own, but that didn't feel right. Also, Ada would have known that and, well, shit... Ada was acting weird, too. What in the hell had happened?

Sweeping wide right, I almost yelled for Sumo to take the opposite side before remembering he, too, was missing. As much as losing the two of them, Sumo being gone was like losing a part of myself. I'd given up on family, given up on relationships, and started to even hate the Space Corps, but Sumo was the constant. I switched to his private frequency and started talking to him. The tiny ear bud implanted inside of his right ear should still pick up my signal no matter what Ada was saying.

"You okay, man? Tell me where you are. Bark."

I stopped moving to listen. My suit's audio sensors were highly sensitive, but I heard nothing. I circled in larger and larger arcs. No sign, not even any footprints. No bent grass or broken twigs. Even the covering of light morning dew seemed undisturbed. I was originally an Army Ranger. My tracking skills were a little rusty, but I was better than most, and I wasn't coming up with jack shit.

"Ada, status."

"Boot sequence at ninety-two percent," the mechanical voice said. *Boot sequence?* As far as I knew, my AI had never rebooted, never needed to. It had been upgraded twice and maybe then she was briefly offline. I was unconscious at the time, so I really didn't know. Yeah, I get a little squeamish about them doing brain surgery when I'm awake, even if it's to simply get me the newest version of Windows.

"Fuck, fuck fuck..."

"Joe," Ada's actual voice finally said, then nothing.

"What, Ada, what?" I couldn't believe how dependent I was on this thing in my head. How had I not realized that before? "Talk to me, goddamit!"

An overlay popped up in my vision. It took me a minute to recognize it as this place. It was a topographical map of the surrounding area with a single green line moving away from the center. So, my AI couldn't communicate yet, but she was trying to help... at least I hoped she was helping. Minutes later, I had crossed the road we had come in on and was standing on the bank of a wide, fast-moving river. Not exactly a river. Back home we would have referred to it as a creek, but the current was swift, white caps showing in many places. I'd seen it when we came in last night. All of us had refilled water bottles in it. The sound of the rushing water had been what finally lulled me to sleep.

I hadn't bothered searching on the other side 'cause I didn't see how they would have crossed it. But the nav line left little doubt that was where I was to go. If I trusted my AI not to be trying to kill me, that is.

Shouldering the MK4, I slipped off the bank into the icy cold water. The thermal response of the battleskin kicked in relatively fast. Still, the current was already pushing me downstream. The water level was up to my chest and then deeper toward the middle. The armor makes it hard to swim, so I simply walked across the sandy bottom. My head was quickly underwater, but the helmet sealed the water out, and the suit had a built-in oxygen supply. All I saw was a cyclone of brown and gray water and foam. I was being pushed downstream faster than I was moving across, so the visual nav line kept readjusting.

Just past the midpoint, I was leaning into the current, my feet driving into the soft river bottom. There was no way Carol and Damiana went through this, not willingly, at least. I felt my body coming up to a massive boulder. I could see the roiling water several feet above. If I moved to the lower side, the current would be less, but it might sweep me underneath it and trap me until my air ran out. I pushed myself up to the front and let the water pound me into the face of the stone. I moved a hand over it, my palm slipping along the mossy rock. My hand grasped frantically in all the mud tossed up by the turbulent water.

I was exhausted. The effort was draining everything in me. Finally, my helmet broke out of the water, and I hoisted myself up on the rock. I needed to catch my breath, to think this through. Then my suit mics registered a faint blip. "Sumo, that you, friend?" The faintest of barks came through my speakers.

I lunged from the top of the rock to the next one and then did it again, missing the last one, only to splash down in the water. I didn't care. I was re-energized, and Ada had me going in the right direction. Five minutes later, I was out of the water and moving up through the tree-lined hill bordering this side. The Rattler was out again, and Ada seemed to be coming back online.

"Headed your way, buddy!"

CHAPTER
FIFTY-EIGHT

LUX

"I'm sorry, kid."

Lux was uncertain what Mister Bill was apologizing for. He held the iron bar overhead and placed it into the crack between the door and the frame opposite the doorknob.

"I know this is going to be hard for you, but you need to know all this. You need to know how to break into houses." He put his weight on the bar and the door popped loose. Next, he inserted the crowbar lower and had the boy try.

Lux felt uneasy trying to break into another person's house, but Bill said he might need to someday. The wood didn't separate and splinter like it had for the man. The crack just got a tiny bit wider before he let off, and it went back to normal.

"It's okay, Lux, I was hoping it would do that. Remember, you can always break a window, too. I'll show you that next. Sometimes the windows will be too high or covered with bars. Getting into doors is always useful."

Bill searched around the house and came back with a piece of metal pipe that he slid over the crowbar. "Move out to the end of this pipe and try it again."

Lux thought that was silly, like much of the stuff Bill had been trying. He'd about decided that Laura was right. Bill wasn't good at a lot of things he tried. Reluctantly, Lux leaned into the pipe, and to his surprise, the hinge side of the door popped free.

"Perfect," Bill said. "The hinge side screws rarely go in as far. There are more of them but still easier than prying loose the lock side."

"Mister Bill," Lux began reluctantly, "things aren't getting any better here, are they?"

Bill pushed the rest of the door in, then sat on the side of the steps resting the iron bar under his chin. "No, they aren't."

"I guess I need to be getting home." Lux said the words, hoping the man would shake his head, tell him no.

The man's eyes looked up, studying the boy briefly before looking away.

"That's why you've been showing me all this stuff, isn't it? I can't stay with you no more."

Bill wiped an eye and nodded slowly. "I'm sorry, Lux. We're barely getting by as it is." He tossed the crowbar to the side in disgust. "I was supposed to send you off a few days ago. I just couldn't."

Lux went over and touched the man's shoulder. The first time the two had shared anything like a personal connection. "It's okay, thank you for helping me not get dead."

The man was crying openly now. Lux was moved by the man's guilt over sending him away, but he was still so scared of going on alone. He heard the two other children playing down the street. He wouldn't exactly miss them, but he'd enjoyed his time here. He would miss Timber. The dog had saved his life first.

Bill stood suddenly and said, "Hang on." He moved through the wrecked door and came back out a few minutes later carting something. "I made you a pack, a survival pack. It's not much, but it should help."

The man went through everything in the worn knapsack. He was right, it wasn't a lot, but it was better than his bookbag. Lux understood now, he wasn't going back over to Bill and Laura's house. They had come over here for Bill to send him away.

"Thank you. Thanks for everything. If..."

The man cocked his head slightly.

"When my mom comes looking for me..." Lux wasn't sure what to tell her. He'd been expecting her to show up every day. "Please tell her I love her, and I miss her."

Bill nodded and tried to give some advice on how to reach the main road. "You'll probably be better on the main roads. Houses will have people in them, some may be bad. Anyone still alive will be desperate. Lux, you can't just assume people are good."

That was something Bill had been repeating over and over all week. It was almost like he knew something the rest of them didn't. Lux hugged the man's neck. "Please tell the others I said bye. It was nice meeting you all."

"Look, little dude, this... this sucks. I mean..." he trailed off. "I'm no expert. Shit, Laurie tells me that every damn day. I guess I'm just saying you're going to have to do stuff, stuff you may not want to, just to stay alive. That's just the way it is now. Stay alive, survive. That's more important than getting home. That's more important than being a good kid. Do you understand?"

Lux put the pack on. "Yes."

That was a lie. He really didn't. Lux suddenly turned and began walking away. His eyes were filling with tears, too, but he refused to acknowledge them. He needed to be brave. He needed to be a big boy now more than ever. He walked until the houses were out of sight, then he began to run. He ran until his chest burned and his legs ached. Then he sat on the side of the road and cried. He would give himself this one time.

CHAPTER
FIFTY-NINE
KOVACH

I found Sumo almost a mile away from the campsite. He was tangled in what appeared to be a cargo net. From a hundred feet away, I could tell the dog was highly agitated. Someone had purposefully trapped him here. Why? Not only that, where were Carol and Damiana? Had they done this?

I had a thought, one I prayed I was wrong about. "Ada, status on the truck."

"Truck is operational, fully charged."

"Um... um," I stammered. "That's not what I mean. Is anyone attempting to do anything to it?"

"I don't have sensors on the vehicle." I was thankful she was at least beginning to sound like herself.

"Move the truck, take it down the road and back, just don't let it sit stationary."

If I was right, someone had led Sumo away, possibly just to get our supplies or our vehicle. Right now, I had two likely suspects.

"Unable to comply." Ada still didn't sound completely like herself, but it was closer. "The truck's auto drive feature appears to be offline."

Shit! It was an ancient system, one I had to manually update with current maps, but no reason it should be inoperable unless my worst fears were correct.

I finally had Sumo free, and he was blazing a trail back in the direction we had come. I scrambled over the last embankment and mostly slid down to the water's edge. On the other side of the river, I saw both women doing something to my granddad's truck. Carol glanced my way before saying something to Damiana, who nodded and got in on the driver's side. Sumo was halfway across before I leapt off the rocks and immersed myself again in the icy waters.

Crawling out on the far side, I could see the campsite was deserted. They were gone. My truck was gone, along with all our supplies. I didn't know how they had done it, much less how they knocked Ada offline. They shouldn't have even known about her, unless Damiana had been read in fully on what had been done to me. Somehow, though, I'd been suckered. "Fuck!" I yelled. That's what I get for trying to help anyone.

Sumo was sniffing around; he was just as pissed off as I was. I had been wrong about one thing. They hadn't taken everything. My sleeping mat was still there and my backpack and water bottles. They mostly only took the things they had brought.

"Ada, can you track the truck?"

"No, Joseph, I'm afraid it is gone."

I gathered up my gear and repacked it to keep the load low on my back. I also tossed several bulkier items that I didn't consider essential, not essential if I had to carry it for several hundred miles. Ten minutes later, I was headed down the road at a fast trot. Damiana was right, I could maintain this pace almost all day as long as I didn't dehydrate or overheat. Sumo could do almost as well, but I remembered to stop every hour or two to give his feet a break. I was definitely heading south now, toward Rainier, but also to pay back the two people I'd considered friends.

The afternoon of the second day on foot, I came up on a ranch. The field was jammed with black cattle, all looking at me like I was from another world. A man wearing battle armor probably does look that way, but I wasn't wearing the helmet at least. I'd clamped it to the top of my pack. I soon smelled grilling meat. *Hamburgers*, I thought. How long had it been since I'd had real meat? Back in the Army, I guessed. The military did a lot of things wrong, but they fed us well. Nothing stalled a fighting force faster than hunger. But real meat was a high-end luxury now.

I saw what looked like a family up between two farm buildings tending a small fire. My water bottles were nearly empty, and Sumo was beginning to look like he wanted to attack some of the livestock. I shrugged. "We can see." I moved up the dusty two-track drive with my hands raised high. Sumo somehow had physically transformed himself into the friendliest of puppies, dancing around in circles and looking like anything but the deadly weapon he was.

The act must have worked. The man visibly tensed when he saw me and made a move to send two little ones away before relaxing somewhat.

"Just passing through, mister. Wondered if I could get a water refill. I assume you have some with a herd this large."

The man pointed toward a trough near a metal building and an old-style lever pump that seemed to be a recent addition. An ancient car's hubcap lay on the ground, and I filled it for Sumo. I then repeated the process for the bottles I carried.

I washed the road grime from my face with a wet rag, and we moved over to thank the rancher. He was hovering over a large grill, flipping about a dozen of the best-looking burgers I'd ever seen.

"Thank you. I'm sorry if I scared your family."

The man, who could have been somewhere between twenty-five and his early sixties, just eyed me up and down. "We don't get a lot of visitors."

Ada announced a threat coming from the upper window of what I took to be the main house.

"I suppose not. However, the smell of those burgers carries, and well, no one has much to eat anymore."

The man gave a snort of a laugh. "You can have one, your dog, too, but if you try to take anything else..."

"I know," I said, cutting him off. "Your wife has a bead on me right now. Upper window, second from the left."

He turned toward the house, then slowly back to me. "You active duty?"

"More like reserve," I answered.

"That's a Glisson Rattler MK4, isn't it?" he asked, studying me closer now.

I nodded. The man knew his weapons.

"Tell you what, let me shoot that a couple of times, and you can have all the burgers you both want."

That was an easy enough trade and a good ploy on the man's part to disarm me without seeming threatening. I unclipped the rifle and handed it over. Ada could block it from being used against me, assuming she didn't go offline again. He called his family back out, and I put a burger into a bun and started wolfing it down while following him out behind his house to an improvised firing range. You have to love farmers.

Thirty minutes later, I was down half a pack of ammo, and the man seemed to be my new best friend.

"Goddamn, those things a work of art," he proclaimed. "Sorry, Jesus, but you know... damn!"

Jimmy MacLeod said his family had been farming this land for almost two hundred years. "I don't know what to do with the cattle. I have 250 head, almost a million dollars worth of working capital on the hoof, and it will die out there unless the trucks start running again. Add that to the mountain of bills I owe on the tractors, the seed licenses, and the carbon tax for the herd. Well, I'm finished... I know it."

I was on my third burger by then. Sumo had at least as many and now was rolling around on his back so the two kids could rub his belly. Seeing him play was almost as good as the meal.

"I'm not sure there's anyone to pay your bills to anymore. Might just be a clean slate."

"I always pay my bills," the man said, his conviction unwavering.

"Where ya headed?" the wife asked, seemingly eager to change the subject. She was a small, somewhat plainspoken woman with a fierce determination in her eyes.

"Sparta." Saying it out loud didn't seem wise, but I didn't want to lie to these people. Ada had worked it out days earlier from some of the information Carol had provided.

"That's over toward Knoxville."

"In the general vicinity," I said. "Middle of nowhere, really."

"We saw a blue glow that night, Jim… you know. It was from over that way," the woman said. "Thought it was lightning or something, but it was steady, you know. After a while, it just faded out."

I'd already brought them up to speed on world events. What Ada knew, at least. They'd had practically no information since the lights went out. If the Nightmare Factory site also got hit by a Sapphire bomb, I could be in some real trouble. Iron River had been no picnic, and this one was already rumored to be considerably worse.

"So, what's in Sparta?" Jimmy asked.

I didn't feel comfortable answering that, and I told them so. They took it in stride and moved on. They were okay with respecting my privacy, unlike many people I knew.

The MacLeod's offered to let me stay overnight in their hay barn. I was okay with that. My legs were sore from the last few days on the road.

The rest of the family went to bed, and Jimmy came out to the fire with a bottle. He never asked, just poured several fingers in two glasses and passed one over.

"You have a good thing here, Jimmy," I said, sipping the excellent bourbon from a local distillery. "You're in a lot better shape than most."

"Not sure how long I can keep it, though. Not just all the damn bills I owe. I ain't stupid. I know others will come." He looked at me, a question already on his lips.

"Why don't you stay on here with me, Sergeant? Help me protect the place until, you know, they get the lights back on and stuff."

My hand was shaking. The tremors had started in earnest earlier in the day. I'd been ignoring it, but I knew the slide down to the end was increasing.

"I got orders, Jimmy. Besides, I won't be any good on a farm. I know how to break other people's stuff, not how to make it grow."

"You would know how to keep it safe. How to help keep my family safe," he said, disappointment evident in his words.

He did have a point there. This farm was so far out from any township, I doubted anyone would come all this way just to steal something. I had Ada run a security plan for the place, though. On our third glass of the good stuff, I shared with him what I would do in his shoes.

Simple stuff like blocking the drive. Moving the cattle to a field that wasn't visible from the road and having shooting blinds set up in the main compound. After being on the road for two weeks, I knew the best defense was making the place look abandoned and nothing of use to anyone just passing by.

"So, no more grilling out?" he laughed.

A few minutes later, he tilted his tumbler. "What kind of world are we leaving them?" His drink hand motioned to the house where in the candlelight I could see small shadowy figures moving inside.

"Same world, Jimmy, just going to take some getting used to." I poured us both a splash more. "I've been in places around the world that have never had power, no cars, inadequate water. You know what? Kids there still grow up, they have fun, find love, get married, and make babies. Humans are a resilient bunch. If you don't base your worth on what you lost, you'll be fine."

He nodded. "We have to survive the craziness first."

"You got that right, friend, you do indeed." I covered my shaking hand and repeated it to myself.

CHAPTER
SIXTY

LUX

Lux tried to think about how many days he had been walking. Three. He definitely remembered two nights, so this was the third day since leaving Bill and Laurie's house. Honestly, they hadn't been too bad. He found he was less scared this time and had found a lot of abandoned cars along the road. He checked these for water and food and had also found they made good places to sleep at night. Not all the cars were empty, though. Some had, you know... dead people in them. That was gross, but that didn't bother him that much anymore.

The people he had stayed with had been good to him. He'd been furious when they sent him away, but things were just different now. Stuff like that was just part of it. The supplies Bill had made him take were coming in handy. It wasn't a lot; he couldn't have carried much anyway, but it had some food and a few supplies, including some fishing line that he was using now. He'd tied it to a long stick he'd cut off with the knife he'd found in the bag. He caught some crickets like the man had shown him, pierced one through the middle with a hook, and dropped it in the lake. In minutes, he had a fish up on the bank. It was silvery and kind of flat, with a reddish part right under the mouth.

Lux tied some twine through the mouth and gill and then looped it over a big rock, then let the fish swim until he caught another. This was pretty much how he and Bill's family had done at the creek. He was less sure about building a fire but thought he could. *He knew he needed to save the canned food.* It took a while, but he caught two more fish. One was like the first. The second was black with whiskers and a white belly. He couldn't feel any scales on it. He wasn't sure about how you cleaned it, but he would work on it.

He moved into the woods to find what he needed to build a fire. Bill had made him and Peegee attempt it over and over. You had to be safe. Clear out a spot. Get dry, small stuff to start with, then bigger pieces of wood. It took him a lot of trips back to where the fish were still swimming. He knew he needed to be ready to cook them when he killed and cleaned them. That seemed so odd to him, to be killing something and then eat it, but it also made him feel good. While he was gathering wood, he wandered up to where the lake seemed to form and found that a fast-moving stream fed it. Water moving faster is safer than water moving slowly. That was something else Bill had said.

He filled up his two water bottles, then used the weird color light on the lighter pen that was in his pack. Supposedly, that would make any water safe to drink, and best not to take chances. Using the lighter part of the pen proved more challenging to making a fire. It shot out a small beam of light that would make the twigs smoke and turn black, but they never caught fire. He needed some paper or something, but hardly anyone used paper these days. He tried some leaves, then some dry grasses, but none wanted to burn. "Dang it!" he yelled in frustration.

Lux stood up, mad and hungry. The fish were swimming furiously now, as if they knew what was coming. The boy's stomach growled. It was so much easier when his mom just had to push a button on the machine to get his dinner. The very thought of her brought tears to his eyes. He fought them back. *Not now, you need to make a fire.*

His eyes picked up movement, something small in the underbrush. Maybe a baby squirrel; there had been plenty of the adult ones around. Getting closer, he realized it was a mouse. The fur was almost black, and it was rooting around in some moss. Every so often, it would pull up something and eat it. When it noticed it was being watched, it took off running. Lux followed it. It scooted under a fallen log and into a hole at the base of a gigantic tree.

Lux took a stick and tried to dig the mouse out. Not to be cruel, but mainly just to have something to do. All he got was a bunch of fuzz and dry moss. He tried to figure out where the little rodent had gone, then realized he might be looking at the very thing he needed. He raked up the bits of wood shavings, fuzz, and moss and held them close to his chest. "Thank you, Mister Mouse," he yelled over his shoulder as he ran back to his campsite.

He carefully placed his prize underneath the twigs and leaves and aimed the lighter once more. It sparked and a brilliant flame started almost at once. Minutes later, he was busy feeding larger pieces of wood into the flames.

He cleaned the two fish like he'd been shown and placed them on sticks near the fire to cook. The last one he just couldn't quite figure out. He sliced up the middle and removed the stomach and stuff, then tried to cut the head off, but the skin was too hard. It felt almost like bone. He kept an eye on the first two. They were kind of small, but he knew they tasted good. Eventually, he just sliced the whiskered one all the way through and drove sharpened sticks through it to keep it spread apart.

The first two fish disappeared in just a few bites. They were more bone than meat, but Lux's stomach felt a little better. He probably should have tried to catch more. He carefully rewound the fishing line around a small piece of wood and secured it with the hook. He listened to the fire crackling and the smell of the meat cooking. It was nice. Maybe that wasn't the thing he should be feeling, but this wasn't terrible. "I really miss Timber." He also missed his mom, but not too much of the other stuff. He found he thought about his dad less and less. It just seemed like he had moved on, didn't want to be his dad so much anymore.

This last fish was tough, he couldn't bite through the skin even when it was cooked. When he went at it from the other side, though, that was a different story. The white meat was flaky and kind of sweet. It was so good, not as good as bacon—nothing was that good, but this might be like number two or something. It also seemed to have fewer bones. He wanted to catch more of these. He ate all he could, then tossed the rest into the lake. The sun was going down, and he'd already picked out a car to sleep in for the night. He kicked dirt over the fire and headed off to bed. This day had been a better one. Whisker-fish were now going to be his main focus when fishing.

CHAPTER
SIXTY-ONE
BANSHEE

Bayou motioned for Gi to tighten up the distance. She and Halo were on opposite sides of the highway. The Wulf eased up between them, scanners actively searching for more targets. They'd passed through part of New Jersey south of New York City. Every town was demolished, most looked like they had been in ruins for decades. Moving up toward Newark, they finally found an intact bridge into the city.

"This is some shit, LT."

"Cut the chatter," Bayou ordered, but she had to agree. There was no city, not anymore. What had been lower Manhattan was a giant smoking crater. Water filled the streets. Skyscrapers slanted sideways as if leaning into a strong breeze. Many had fallen. This hadn't been the result of any dirty bomb.

"Rad levels near normal," G-force said from inside the transport.

Everything seemed covered in the strange-looking violet vines Joe had warned her about.

"At least these aren't shooting at us," Priest said from somewhere high above.

Soon after landing, they had come under attack, but scans here showed no enemy, or no living human enemy. It had taken half an hour to identify the shooter, a bushy vine with exploding seed pods of some kind. They fired sharpened thorns that Halo had gone out and recovered. Sensor analysis showed it was coated with a powerful neurotoxin. The system identified the poison as a modified version of one occurring naturally... in scorpionfish.

"How many people in this city?" Halo asked his suit's AI.

"Twelve point three million prior to the attack."

One of the densest population centers in the world, and now it was a smoking ruin.

"Bayou, I don't know what's affecting the wildlife, but I think we all know what made that big-ass hole."

She had her own thoughts but wanted to hear her team's assessment. "Let me hear it, Halo."

"That thar's a kinetic blast hole, Lieutenant. See how it pushed up the land along the edge and how the buildings are all pushed away from the ground zero? The damage is mostly from the heat and the overpressure of the blast wave. Had to be orbital bombardment."

"Shit." She agreed but had been hoping that she was mistaken. "Priest, Gi, you concur?"

They did. "That means two things," Bayou said as she began calling the TriCraft's pilot.

"We have a potential enemy up there," Halo said, pointing up.

"Yeah, and we have to go get proof," Bayou said, finishing up the call to Packer, the pilot.

"We're going into that?" Priest asked, his voice showing none of its normal confidence.

"We're RDT specialists, boys. It's what we do. Mount up."

"Hoorah," they each mouthed with little real enthusiasm.

The Wulf could float and even traverse in water or mud if needed. Today it was required. They were riding along what was called Hudson Street the previous month. Now it was essentially part of the Hudson River. Water depth was nearly twenty feet. Chelsea was gone, as were most of the other areas Bayou had once known. They saw people staring at them from some windows. Small children waved at them, their haunted eyes wide with fear. There was no way to get them out, and that wasn't Banshee's mission. The doors to the apartment buildings that were still standing were down at street level. Street level was underwater or covered in yards of dirt and debris pushed up by the blasts.

"We could shoot out some windows on each building," Priest said, obviously looking at the same thing Bayou was.

"We going to drive all over the city doing that? Then what, Bishop? Then what..."

"I'm just sayin..."

"Can it. We know our job. This city has its own rescue ops."

Angling the Wulf into a side street, Gi fought to control the momentum. Underwater obstacles kept grounding the big transport.

"Must be the 4:00 rush hour," Priest said.

Increasingly, the streets were clogged with tangles of the thick, violet-colored vines that seemed to thicken even as they moved past. They saw people in windows much less often now. IR scans were showing up negative as well.

Bayou was riding in the second seat, where she flipped on a set of external microphones. The dual shotgun mics could pick up sounds from miles away on the battlefield; she wasn't sure how effective they would be here in the city. There were strange ambient sounds, but for the most part, the city was filled with an eerie silence.

They had been trying to angle over from midtown toward Queens and see what was left of the Alliance HQ on the site of the old U.N. building. So far, none of the routes they had taken had panned out. Faint sounds came over the speakers.

"Gunshots," Halo said.

Bayou was working with the boom mics to get a fix on it.

"We're going to check it out?" the Korean asked uncertainly.

She got the coordinates and nodded. "Move us closer at least. Maybe we can put some drones up to give us a look." She turned to look at Halo.

"On it," he replied, already moving to the back, where he began opening cases.

Minutes later, they were bobbing up and down at the corner of a low-rise apartment building, trying to understand what they were watching.

"Can you get closer?"

"Sorry, Boss, not without them seeing it. Their equipment is nearly as good as ours."

Half a dozen serious looking boats were anchored next to what looked to be a basic warehouse. The faded sign high up on a wall said it was one of the many New York Sanitation Department collection sites.

The fact of that location drawing so much interest was unusual, but not the most striking thing about the scene. Bayou had thought first that these were the Navy's light attack craft, but the armament let her know she was wrong. Civilian authorities. Must have a rescue mission that went sideways. She was about to order her team on toward Queens when more gunfire erupted. This time, it was obviously occurring between the boats.

"Look at the insignias on the boats."

Bayou followed where Bishop was pointing at the display. She could see it didn't look right, but his eyes were better than hers. "Not NYC," she said questioningly.

He shook his head. "Maryland, at least one other is from Harbor Patrol out of Newark."

She looked at him, momentarily perplexed. "Gi, move us back under that fire escape. Priest, get up top. I want you on overwatch."

She busied herself querying her battle computer on what was actually at this address.

"Shit, it's a disaster relief center," she said moments later.

New York was better prepared than most of the large metroplexes for a large-scale disaster. That included a lot of pre-stocked warehouses full of supplies, equipment, and even emergency medical centers.

"Those places have food and supplies for millions, don't they?"

"Yeah, Halo. Won't last the city long, but apparently the next-door neighbors are in a better position to get to them than the city's own rescuers."

"No need to prep yourself as long as you know where your friend's stash is, right?"

"Not our fight. It sucks, guys, but I don't..."

The Wulf lurched to one side and began moving out toward the open intersection. "Sergeant!" Bayou called, her voice full of nervous energy.

"It's not responding. Something seems to be pulling us," Gi answered.

She switched on external cameras, and the reason was immediately clear. The vines were a roiling mass in front of them. "Probably wrapped our axle.

We will be exposed in thirty seconds, people. Priest, you in position?"

"Ran into a little trouble, Bayou. Give me five."

"Overwatch, you have three," she responded.

Minutes later shots rang out high above followed quickly by two bodies hurtling down beside them. The Wulf was now emerging into a clear line of sight with the raiders at the warehouse.

"Those attack boats can inflict some serious damage on us, ma'am."

She knew the Korean Sergeant was understating the obvious. "I have control. Exit and find cover."

Halo popped the side hatch on the opposite side and hurried out with G-force close behind. Bayou heard small arms fire hitting the outer hull as she pushed the throttle hard forward and tried to go with the pull of the vines. The strong electric motors whined as they jetted water out the twin nozzles at incredible force. The Wulf gained speed only to slam to a stop as the vine caught. The weapons fire increased in volume.

"Banshee, light those fuckers up," she ordered.

There was an embankment of dry land on the far side of the road. She knew if she could get the Wulf to it, the tires would generate enough traction to break free. Unfortunately, she soon realized the vehicle was moving in the opposite direction. Toward the shooters.

Priest was up top of the adjacent building lying on his belly facing the warehouse over seventy feet below. Several other bodies lay behind him. Seemed the excitement here had pulled out a lot of interest in the neighborhood. He centered the scope on the uniformed woman manning the old style .50 cal on top of the attack boat. The first trigger pull removed her arm at the shoulder. The spray of blood nearly covered the boat's windshield. He then moved to the closest boat to Bayou. Men there looked to be readying an RPG. The grenade might not sink the armored transport, but it wouldn't do it much good. He stitched a line of rounds along the hull until he found the fuel cell. By the size of the explosion, it was probably hydrogen.

G-force and Halo swam to opposite corners of the building. Halo was going to signal the new guy to break in and move to the opposite side. That had been his plan, but when he looked for the Korean, he saw nothing. *Shit,* he'd been right there. Using the butt of his rifle, he broke through the panes of glass and crawled over the brickwork. The building reeked of mold and wetness. Smells he remembered from a flooded fishing camp back when he was a kid. He heard noises in the building; some of these apartments were probably still occupied. Judging by the smell of death and rot, many of them weren't.

Bayou stopped fighting the pull and let the Wulf transport be towed to wherever the damn vines wanted it. Instead, she recentered on the original threat. Only four of the boats remained, and they were in the process of scattering. Now that they had a common enemy, they'd apparently decided the military presence was the bigger threat.

"You, in the transport, cease fire and stand down! That's an order! This is an official police matter!"

They were on the loudspeaker and all official sounding. Did they really think that would work against an elite military squad? Bayou saw a carnage round slice straight through the boat she had suspected was the loudmouth behind the announcement. The torso of a man still clutching something white in his hand toppled over the side of the boat and into the water. This wasn't Banshee's fight, but they were in it, anyway. Besides, maybe providing one warehouse of supplies to this neighborhood was the one honorable thing they could achieve in this clusterfuck. *We are here to make a difference.* She brought the auto cannons online and picked out the first, second, and third targets. She hit the red fire button and let the combat command system do the rest.

CHAPTER
SIXTY-TWO

Gi moved in closer, seeing something no one else on the team had. His training in the ROK special forces had not been as diverse as the other members of Banshee, but he had excelled in what there was. Underwater combat held a particular lure for him. He'd grown up on an island just north of Incheon. The former DMZ ran right through one part of his island. Even though Korea had reunified over twenty years ago, there was still a lot of animosity. Some of that turned into underwater turf battles with the boys from the northern side. Many of the lessons of youth were learned at the hands of others. That was life on the peninsula.

He passed under one of the attack boats as it burst into flames. He felt the force of the explosion above. The damn vines kept reaching out to him as he swam by, and he saw more than one figure snatched from the surface by the ropey tendrils. He emerged from the water by the door of the warehouse. He'd seen two men enter in an inflatable craft before most of the shooting started. As he slid silently under the raised door, he heard Bayou open up with the transport's mounted weapons.

A mezzanine walkway encircled the large open space. Lines of shelving stacked nearly to the ceiling filled almost every inch of space. Rounds were pinging off the girders and wall cladding. G-force slipped silently from the water and knelt to scout the surroundings. His HUD showed a clear trail on IR, four pairs of footsteps going in several directions. It also showed something else, the presence of an explosive material. It was a version of the highly effective octanitrocubane called OCX-9. A bit of it could bring down the entire block.

He didn't bother to try and determine what they were up to. Steal what they could and destroy the rest. Destroy and deprive the locals. It could be something else entirely. He didn't care; he was a killer, and that became his plan, end this threat and get the hell out. He spotted one man moving near a wall unit, storing something that looked like portable energy cells. The guy was wearing body armor, so Gi's options were limited. Slipping back into the water, he swam over just beneath the man and pushed himself out, driving a knife up and through the man's unshielded inner thigh. He pulled back sharply on the blade, catching a major artery, and the man went down screaming. Sergeant Dae was already back under the water.

His HUD gave an indication of two more targets back in a far corner of the building. He radioed Bayou even though she would be watching the feed. The sounds of battle outside seemed to slow, the exchange of weapons fire growing less intense each second. He analyzed where the next target was and realized he couldn't get to him the same way. The mezzanine was comprised of metal grating; he could swim under it to within three meters of where the other police officer was working. He could tell by the symbols on the bottom of the crates that this guy was stealing drugs and medical supplies. Gi fired two rounds up through the grating, catching the man in the chest and the face. The officer's armor worked, but the man still went down from the impact. Gi then shot him at point blank range, the MK4 dialed up to maximum yield. The back of the man's head came off along with half the helmet.

The kill coincided with a pause in the battle outside. His battle AI alerts went off, followed closely by impacts on his armor. He was taking fire and in a bad position. One round clipped a power feed, and half his suit went offline. No movement, no sensors. He kicked and dove to the bottom. He tried calling the other team members, but his primary comms unit was dead.

A twirling twist of violet and green wrapped around the useless arm of the suit. The vine pulled with an unbelievable force. Oxygen warnings went off; the O^2 recirculation system was one of the parts offline. With the working left hand of the suit, Gi grabbed onto a shelving unit and locked the suit in place, then punched the emergency eject. The blast wasn't large, but he barely had time to grab the rifle as he was rocketed upward. Now he had no advantage over the enemy.

He tasted metal and salt and something else in the water. Also, men talking, someone moaning. Gi fixed the positions in his mind and assessed the battle space. He could get one of them but could see no way to kill both. If they were using any sort of combat discipline, each would cover the other. That was okay. Not all of his tricks required him to be wearing battle armor. He kicked across the space, deep underwater, to get a new firing position. A shadow passed over him along with a brush of current that hadn't been there. He was no longer alone down here, and what was up above was not just the twisting weirdly colored vine.

In the dim light Gi couldn't see what was in here, but with the amount of blood and bodies, he had a good idea. Sharks were opportunistic feeders, and right now downtown New York City, and this block in particular, had to be a feeding bonanza.

Without the battle armor, he felt more exposed, but also more agile, more natural. He slipped silently out of the water and up onto the metal walkway. The suit's base layer had a super-hydrophobic coating that literally repelled water. He paused only briefly to let all the drops cascade down and back into the water.

Lying flat on the edge of the walkway he activated the camo mode of the inner suit to match the dull gray metal. Both of the other men were actively sweeping rifles around searching for a target. It wasn't military precision, but it wasn't bad. All he needed was one of them to move a few steps toward him, and he could try something reckless.

A dark shape moved in the water beneath where he lay. Gi watched through the metal grating as it slid by effortlessly. As the shark neared a wall, it spun rapidly, making a small splash on the surface. That was enough to get both of the enemy looking and then moving toward him.

"Coming in," he heard one of his teammates say as Gi slid his backup earbud in. He wanted to warn them, but they would see it. They knew the risk. Besides, even a shark couldn't harm an armored operator. He kept his attention focused on the lead man. He wore a black suit; a civilian version of the battle armor Gi had abandoned meters below. The official police badge shone brightly on the man's chest.

Uncoiling instantly, G-Force sprang up on his hands, launching a kick into the man's chin that sent him up and over the railing.

"Holy shit!" Gi heard in his earpiece as he went after the other. He ignored the rifle and instead slipped out one of the two blades he always carried. *Move like water,* he thought. The other man was watching his partner, no doubt now becoming fish food.

Gi used the opportunity to launch himself from nearly a dozen feet away. Too far for any practical attack. He closed the gap, hitting the man in the face with an elbow, then drove the knife blade into the hilt at the base of the neck. It was the one of two known vulnerabilities built into the civilian battle suits. Blood spurted out of the man's mouth as he dropped to his knees in surprise.

Gi tapped his comms. "Clear!"

CHAPTER
SIXTY-THREE
KOVACH

I found the truck the middle of the following day. It was hot, the sun baking the roadway to hellish temps. Coming up to what seemed to pass for towns around here, I almost missed it. Granddad's GMC was in a parking lot full of other abandoned cars. Sumo checked it out. There was a crack in the windshield and blood on the seat. Most of the gear was still in the back, but no sign of my two thieves. I suppose whatever happened was some form of karmic justice, but I shared in that karma. I'd kept something important from them. It was selfish and wrong, but I kept justifying it because to not have, would have meant giving up on any hope for my life to go on.

Glass crunched beneath my tactical boots. The store windows, just like the world beyond, now simply fragments. Destruction here was some of the worst I'd seen. My trigger finger itched, but I left my weapons stowed for now. I was in a retail district, in a small town in northern Tennessee. I was closing in on what Carol's guess was as to the location of the Rainier complex, the Nightmare Factory. I also hadn't forgotten about what the rancher had said, a lavender blue glow in this direction. I stepped cautiously, something about this abandoned strip mall had my spidey senses on edge. Sumo was also taking extra care in his recon.

A sound of chittering was followed by an answering scratch on the other side. The pistol was in my hand instantly and looking for targets before I was consciously aware of the threat. A plasma round flashed out and killed the beast as it jumped from a high ledge full of women's purses. The deadly round ended the existence of the rodent-like creature mid jump. Its lifeless body slid up to my boot unmoving.

I bent down for a closer inspection. What I had assumed was a large rat, maybe a squirrel, was neither. Needle-like fangs in a head that looked less like a squirrel, maybe more like a shrew.

"Stay sharp, Kovach."

So, the mutations were here already. Those changed things, the mutated, were no longer confined to just the fauna, it appeared. This little bastard was probably just the first of many. Where had the women gone? What had gotten them? I knew they must have run into trouble. I hated myself for even giving a shit, but... but nothing. They double crossed me, abandoned me to the wastelands, and to death if I didn't find the meds. I owed them nothing.

Was this all just Hammer's bio-engineered threat response, plants, animals, insects, and other things that were now something else entirely? Genetic editing had gone underground the last two decades. Now it was the living graffiti, an underground art form for the biohackers who'd been left unemployed after the new ethics laws took effect.

Sumo growled. I knew that sound. In fact, I felt it, too. "Easy, brother." I spoke in low, steady tones despite the knowledge of what awaited. Sumo had my back as he had so many times before. A shadow moved in the corner straight ahead. I dove, just as a blur of movement passed within inches of my face. I peeled to one side and struggled to set hard sights on the target. My barrel tracked down until I saw the cluster of leaves and tendrils easing around a bit of shelving. This wasn't the same vine as in Virginia. Maybe it was mutating, too, as it spread. *Maybe this was something else altogether.*

I remembered something from my childhood. Something in the woods near where we had lived that looked a lot like this. We called that one Thunder Wood, too. Basically, a super fast-growing woody vine whose stems and leaves were covered with toxic hairs. These would leave a nasty burn like a line of wasp stinging you over and over. Or if your body chemistry leaned toward allergies... it could be fatal. Of course, the vine from my childhood didn't attack you, it stayed firmly attached to trees and only hurt if you weren't paying attention to where you leaned or put your hands.

"Sumo, circle left." The dog warily eyed the creeping vine and moved outside its reach in the other direction.

These mother fuckers who created this shit are going to pay. I was sure of that. I just didn't know who to blame. Hammer or whoever attacked us. Somebody who decided the planet would be better off without humans. I heard a sound like a soda can being opened, then felt something whiz by my cheek. I instinctively ducked as the sound repeated itself, and I saw several two-inch-long thorn darts shoot past my head with the speed of an arrow in flight. Several more of the darts came my way. Most bounced off the body armor, but one made it inside. Just the point of it reached my skin, but that was enough to immediately induce searing agony.

I had the MK4 in my hands now, and I unleashed with the Rattler on full auto. Fuck operational security, fuck alerting anyone close. In the flashes of blue light, I saw the bloated pods quivering on meaty stems high on the vine, the end of the foot long pod thing resembling a shriveled green anus. It fired another round of the quills in my direction. Another anus pod rippled and seemed to track Sumo. The rifle lit it up and sprayed all the pod's contents across the floor. Sumo barked, and I swiveled to see several more of the dangling ass-pods aiming in our direction. A chime sounded.

"Hey, sport, what are you doing, picking out a prom dress?"

"Little busy, Dad." I had to find out how to block him from connecting whenever he wanted.

"Go with the yellow one, it will match your..."

"Dad!" I cut my old man off as I made it to the far wall and a bit of cover. Sumo tucked in behind me.

"Would you like me to call back later?"

"No!" I began, wanting him to know I was not going to be free then either.

"Good, well, what I was thinking..." began the senior Kovach, oblivious to my situation.

"Dad!" I fired from the hip at a vine that was moving itself rapidly toward Sumo.

"Is that gunfire?"

I was busy ducking another ass-pod, firing darts of toxic wooden death.

"Yes, Pops. I wandered into the Little Shop of Horrors."

"I hated that movie," Dad said. "Fucking musicals. They needed John Matrix in there."

Oh, God, I thought.

"He would have ripped that fucking plant apart with his bare hands."

I couldn't remember which movie Schwarzenegger had played Matrix in, but I was pretty sure it was not the one with Agent Smith. *Shit, why am I even thinking about this?*

"If it bleeds, we can kill it."

"It's a plant, Pops. It doesn't seem to bleed."

"Well, it's still a great line. Arnold should have won the Oscar for that one."

I had no idea what an Oscar was, but I motioned the dog outside, and I was about to follow when I saw something. A shoe sticking out from beneath a pile of debris. Just above the shoe was the lining of something unmistakable. The battleskin base layer of a Rivex battle suit.

I tossed aside the racks of clothes and boxes until I could see the body. It was Carol, and she was in bad shape. One of the wooden darts had impaled her on the one bare spot on her neck. The blood had set, and I couldn't see if she was breathing, but I still felt a faint pulse.

Hauling her out just ahead of a trio of the running Thunder Vines left me wondering again if I owed her anything. They'd left me. Even so, it wasn't all her fault. She was just being a mom.

"Ada, scan interior for any other life signs." I applied a wound seal to Carol's neck where the giant thorn had been. "Human." I amended.

"You are going to Rainier, aren't you?" Pops asked. "Didn't Iron River teach you anything?"

"What's going on, Dad?"

The old man stayed silent for longer than normal. I expected him to tell me to get off my ass and go find out for myself.

"You need to walk away, Joe."

"You know I can't, Dad. You let them save me. You let these same people turn me into a living weapon, but unlike this other shit, I am flawed. I have to get meds to stay functional."

"There may be worse things than death, Joe."

"What the fuck does that mean? We are in the business of death, and business is fucking good right now. Tell me, Bones. What is worse than death?"

There was a long pause before my father answered.

"Not living, Son. Or... becoming what you fear." A chirp signaled the connection was closed.

"No other human life signs, Prowler," Ada said a moment later.

CHAPTER
SIXTY-FOUR

Her attractive face was bruised, with deep scratches along one side and across her forehead. I put my wrist computer on her and listened as Ada went through her vitals.

"Pulse is weak, breathing is shallow but regular. Oxygen levels are nominal. Heartrate is stable."

I checked her pupils as Ada indicated.

"I believe she has a concussion and may be in shock. I will deliver a mild shock to try and wake her," Ada said.

"Good, so this isn't neurotoxins from the vines?" I asked.

"No, I am not detecting anything that would suggest that, Joseph."

"Go ahead. I need to know what happened."

The shock did little in the way of waking the woman. She moaned and tried to remove the device from her arm. Ada sent a second pulse, and then after a longer pause, a third one. Carol's eyes flew open in an expression of terror. She tried to sit up, but my palm on her chest kept her in place. She fought against me.

"Get off me, get it off me."

I moved my hand, but she was still fighting and screaming. She ran her hands over her head, her side, everywhere she could touch.

"You're out of the vines. They are way back there," I said. Unlike in Virginia, these didn't seem to be interested in pursuit. I'd moved her out of the initial threat. Who knew vegetation could be lethal? Sumo circled farther out; he was still hyperalert to the dangers.

Carol started crying, and although no longer screaming, she was mumbling incoherently. "Carol, what happened? Where is Damiana?"

"Joe," Ada said, "having her relive the trauma may be detrimental to her at this point."

"Tough shit. They wrecked my truck... after they stole it." I might feel guilty about what led up to the theft, but I was far from forgiving them for leaving me stranded. They had to know I would likely die out there on the road.

"Carol, snap out of it. Where is your friend?"

She looked around blankly, her eyes distant and glassy.

"Damiana, is she gone? Are we in danger here?"

She was looking at her hands, then met my gaze with a brief nod.

"She's gone?"

She tried to speak; her mouth was moving, but no words came forth. I read her lips, though. *Danger.*

CHAPTER
SIXTY-FIVE

"Sumo. Pull back on me!" I lifted the woman, who let out a moan, but her eyes were again closed. She felt weightless in my arms. I didn't know what the danger was, but I felt it myself. I backed slowly away from the buildings. The wild clusters of Thunder Vine were writhing in the entrance but weren't coming closer. My eyes finally took in the full scene. Most of the buildings were covered in ever-thickening bundles of the woody vine, the thick toxic hairs digging deep into the permacrete walls. There was danger here, but it was not the weeds. It was something more primal, more basic.

I eyed the truck before realizing it was time to let it go. Trying to get it moving would simply be time we didn't have. As my eyes moved past to the road ahead, I caught the briefest ripple of movement. When I refocused, the vehicle was the same as before. Then I felt it again, a stabbing jolt of paralyzing fear. I dropped to one knee, and my vision blurred. One part of me was aware of something peeling itself away from the truck, but it made no sense. It looked like the old jalopy was unfolding itself into thin air.

I laid Carol on the ground and struggled to get the MK4 aimed toward whatever it was in front of us. The creature's camouflage was nearly perfect. I could see the scene beyond with only a small shimmer around the edges of what looked like giant wings but... not quite wings.

"You are the beast, the Wraith of my nightmare at Iron River." I tried to fire the round, missing it entirely.

Distantly, I heard Ada saying something about an ammo change. Then the rifle barked twice more. The Wraith was briefly illuminated, then it was gone. With it, the paralyzing fear.

"We brought that damn thing here. We brought it with us all that way."

I looked down at the limp form of Carol Reynolds, understanding some of what must have happened. "I'm so sorry."

Her eyes began to slowly open like shades being pulled open before you're ready to face the day.

"Kovach."

Her voice was weak and filled with fear, or maybe regret.

"I'm here. I think we are safe. The... the wraith thing is gone."

She seemed to know exactly what I was talking about. Her head gave a slight nod. I raised the water flask up, and she took a long drink.

"Where is Dami?"

Carol shook her head. "No idea, she was driving. I heard her scream, then I saw something, that thing. We both..." She shook off any more water and looked up at me.

"I'm sorry we left you. We stole your truck."

I wiped away a streak of blood from her face and looked for the source. She needed to confess, it seemed. My anger was gone, but I decided to just let her say what she needed to get out.

"Dami said she thought you had some way of communicating this whole time. Something they had put into your body. That you probably knew about my son the entire time. She also said you would never take me to see him. I think she wanted to get to Rainier before you."

That made no sense to me. The only reason we had come here was for me to get my drug pack. I motioned Sumo back and noticed the vines were now advancing again. We were going to have to move.

"How did she...?" I wanted to ask how she screwed with Ada but didn't much want to admit to what she had just said.

"How did she convince me to help her?" Carol offered weakly.

It wasn't my question, but I nodded. "Lux. She just made me focus on getting to him. Kept telling me he could be out there all alone."

That made sense. I really couldn't blame her—either of them. I had kept Ada on constant alert for any sign of the boy and Bayou's sister, but no one had popped up with any activity so far. Of course, there wasn't a lot of the internet left to access, but eventually, survivors would reach out even if it was just to buy a drink at a curbside vending machine.

I helped her to her feet. She seemed to be marginally better. Ada had run a full diagnostic on the truck and declared it beyond repair. I patted it as I pulled the gear out and added what I could to my ruck, strapping it back on. I carried Carol's and left the other stuff in the bed of the truck. The Thunder Vine had moved about fifty yards closer but seemed to slow. We began moving in the opposite direction. I didn't think we could outrun it, but maybe there were some natural barriers it couldn't cross. Right now, I was more concerned with our stowaway monster.

Our safe zone turned out to be a stretch of barren rock face about two miles to the east. I left sensors that would pick up the noise the vines made, and we made camp. I treated Carol's wounds again. Nothing appeared life threatening, but I hated the involuntary wince she gave as I applied the treatment.

"Why are you being kind to me?"

She'd slept several hours and now was eating some of the last of our food. I looked at her, then up to the campfire reflecting off her and the surrounding forest.

"Carol, Damiana is right."

The woman just looked at me with a look of incomprehension.

"I have a... my comms system is..." Shit, no way I could say this that didn't make me seem any better, any less an asshole. "The military put a comms system in my head. It can do things. I call it Ada."

"So, you do have a way of connecting, communicating with authorities?"

I nodded, "There really is no authority right now, and the sat links have been mostly down, but yes."

"You knew the whole time that my son was on his own, didn't you?"

I'd been dressed down by some of the toughest officers in the Corps, making me relive my many fuck-ups in painstaking detail, but I never felt as small and worthless as a human as this moment. "Yes."

I poked a stick at the fire, wanting to make an excuse, but the truth was I was a selfish prick. I wanted to live. I needed to find the goddam meds, and in doing so, I had kept a mom from looking for her lost child.

"It won't make you feel any better, but I do have alerts set-up to track any sign of him. Nothing has come in so far."

"So, we have no idea where he might be?" she asked as her eyes grew heavy with tears.

"He could be anywhere," I admitted. She wailed and leaned up against me. I pulled her close and let her cry. The wracking sobs of the mother wrecked me, gutted me, as my friend Highsmith would have said. It was the most heart-wrenching sound I think I'd ever heard.

"I was a terrible mother," she said after a while. "An inattentive wife and an absentee mother."

I dried the tears from her face with my hand. "I don't believe that."

"It's true, I loved my work. I mean, I love Lux, too, but the school and his nanny, Marcie, did all the heavy lifting. I didn't have to do much myself, just place orders and make schedules."

I kissed the top of her head, unsure of when or how we had suddenly become so close. "I know that's not true, Carol. You're tough, determined. I have a feeling Lux is a lot like you."

"He, he's a good boy. He likes to please, which makes being his mom great. His father was a bit of a rogue. I always feared he'd be more like him." She looked away for a moment. "I guess he's gone now, isn't he?"

I knew she meant her ex-husband. I nodded slowly, "Probably." I then added, "Definitely."

"Even if we found Lux... you know, learned he was still alive, we have no way of getting to him."

She was on the mountain of misery now, as my mom would have called it. Piling on all the bad stuff just to make one big heaping pile of sadness and failure.

"Maybe not," I said. "Let me worry about that."

She looked up; our faces suddenly seemed way closer than they had been moments earlier. Her lips met mine before I even had a chance to think about it. I decided I enjoyed kissing her, so I did it again and again.

CHAPTER
SIXTY-SIX

LUX

Lux awoke to a gray sky and a pale sun that offered light but little warmth. Climbing out of the car, he gathered his pack and dreaded the day ahead. He walked, he fished, and sometimes ate, and he slept. Occasionally, he passed houses with swing sets and toys in the yard. He wanted to be a kid again; he wanted to just play and enjoy being a kid.

He'd given up days earlier on trying to know if he was walking toward home or not. He was kinda sure he was pointed the same way the car was that morning when it stopped but had to admit it wasn't his primary concern. The car he'd slept in last night had been a good one. In one compartment, he'd found a pack of crackers and a candy bar. He ate the crackers but saved the candy for later. That was something he was slowly learning. He had to think ahead. There had already been several days when he hadn't been able to fish and a few when he hadn't caught anything. Yesterday was one of those days. His food was running low, and he knew what that meant.

The morning was cool, and he couldn't tell if it was fog or maybe about to rain. Up here in the hills, the weather was hard to judge. The mist was soaking into his clothes, though. "Don't let it get you, Lux," he told himself. "Think of something fun." He tried, but nothing came to him. Even the memories of playing video games or watching holovision with his mom seemed as pale and unreal as the sorry excuse of a sun hanging in the murky sky. He got a small jacket from his bag. It was an old one of the family's daughters, Aleta, he thought. It was pink and yellow, but he didn't care.

"Come on, fun thoughts."

He could see the road twisting down for miles and miles ahead. There were fewer cars stopped here.

"This would be a great place to ride my bike." He could almost feel the wind whipping past as he pedaled as fast as it would go.

"Why not?" he asked himself, and why had he not thought of it before now? "I need to find a bike." But that meant going toward the houses, maybe seeing people. Mister Bill had told him not to do that unless he had to. This seemed kinda like a 'had to' thing, though. Lux moved over to the edge of the road; there was a long drop off to a valley below. He could see in the distance a bunch of houses; they looked abandoned, some were partially covered in old vines. Maybe he could find a bike there. His feet began to pick up speed as he headed off the road toward the neighborhood.

Lux was close to the bottom of the hill doing the crazy run, skip, jump thing he'd picked up over the past week. He was going way too fast when his foot caught on a root, and he went airborne, crashing into a small tree. He was laughing despite the pain because it was just so much fun. Strangely, though, he didn't see the root that had tripped him now. He retraced his steps and could clearly see where his foot had left the ground, but whatever it had been had vanished.

The houses here all seemed different somehow. It was a neighborhood kind of like his mom's, but different. Old and beaten down. He stopped on the edge of a yard and listened for several minutes.

Nothing! There was no sound of life. That was it. Total silence. No animals or kids or even birds singing. No distant leaf blowers or autocars. He had to admit, he'd seen no people other than the family he stayed with, and that seemed really odd. The road he'd been walking on had high sides, though, so if there had been people or houses, he probably wouldn't have seen them. Still, where did all the people who had been in all those cars go? It gave him an uneasy feeling. He wanted to find a bike and was hoping for some real food, but Bill had warned him about people.

"I'm just a kid. Why would anyone hurt a kid?"

The thought echoed around for a second before Lux realized he was hearing something. A very distant sound, like raindrops on a roof but steadier. He moved to the road that bordered the houses. Farther down the street, he saw a tangle of weird colored vines. The sounds seemed to come from beyond that. He doubted he'd find a bike there. The place looked abandoned. Still, he was careful as he moved past each of the houses.

He slipped the knife out of his pocket and struggled to get the blade open. He wasn't sure what he could do with it, but just having it made him feel better. The only other thing he heard was the sound of his sneakers on the pavement, but the tinkling noise was getting stronger. Definitely coming from deeper in a cluster of houses. He studied each house as he passed. Did they have toys, bikes? Did it look like anyone might live there? Maybe he should find a suitable spot to just watch for a while.

Something shot out from under a fence. At first, he assumed it was a cat, maybe a rat, but then decided it must be a snake. The slithering thing seemed to come for him. Then he saw the leaves, the small branches looping off into smaller vines. This thing was a plant. Not only that, the cluster of vines down the street seemed to be moving as well. Plants don't do this, they aren't scary.

One of the vines twisted around Lux's ankle; he slashed down with the knife, lopping off a thick piece of the thing. Another was quickly trying to take its place. He ran for the steps of the closest house and hurried up them. He knocked on the door, then tried the knob. It was locked. Vines now covered the bottom two steps of the house, and more were coming this way.

He slid his backpack off and took out the tool. A smaller version of the break-in bar Mister Bill had used. Bill had called it a pry bar. He moved to the hinge side and wedged it in and pushed against it. One small crack showed, but nothing more. He heard the vines now, rustling and slapping each other as they neared. He pushed harder against the bar, but the door stayed in its frame.

"I need the longer pipe." That was something Bill said he would have to find, as it was too big to carry with him. No time to look for one now. The porch ran all the way across the front of the house. Lux ran to the far edge and was about to jump when he realized there was a window. He took the pry bar and broke the glass. The sound scared him, but he knew this was an emergency. He only had to break out two of the panes before he could get in. He rolled onto a sofa, then landed on the floor. A dead body lay on the far side of the room, an old man. His middle was swollen really big, almost like a balloon.

"Until a few days ago I... I never saw a dead person before." He decided right then he didn't ever want to see any more.

Looking back out the broken window, he saw the creeping vines inching down the railing. They almost appeared to be looking for him, but surely that was nuts. Plants couldn't do that, could they? Something on his ankle burned. He looked down and saw a bluish-purple stain on his sock. That was where the vine had wrapped around his leg. He quickly pulled the shoe and sock off and saw a ring of red blisters coming up where the thing had touched his sock. The burning was getting worse.

Lux couldn't stop the tears. He apologized to the dead man as he ran by. Drying the tears, he looked through the man's cabinets. Old people always had medicines and stuff. He did not know what might help ease the pain, but he would try it all if he had to. Thick, weird colored vines now covered the window on the front door. He knew it was a matter of time before they covered the entire house. He found the medicine cabinet in the bathroom. He moved to the tubes of clear stuff applying several until one felt cold and seemed to numb the pain. He threw these into his bag.

Searching the kitchen, he discovered some cans of soup. He grabbed them all, a manual can opener, and a small pot. He rushed toward the back and opened a door overlooking a neatly manicured lawn and garden. The tinkling sound came again, much louder now. He carefully made sure the entire area was clear of the creepy vines before venturing out. He softly closed the back door and crept down the steps. Moving toward the noise, the volume increased. It was something in the next yard.

He climbed up the ivy-covered wire fence and peered over, almost too afraid to see what it might be. Then he almost wished he hadn't. A small, black and brown dog had wrapped itself up in a chain or leash. It was tight against a metal post. The vines were within just a few feet of the animal, who appeared too terrified to make any sound. His shaking made the chain around him bump the pole every few seconds.

"Shhh!" Lux said, his voice no louder than a whisper. The dog looked at him, its mournful eyes clearly begging for help.

"Oh, man, am I going to do this?" His leg was burning again, and the fence was cutting into his ribs. Briefly, he thought how different his life was now. He tossed the pack into the other yard, then followed it over. He hit the ground at a dead run, knife in his lead hand. He cut away several of the vines to get to the animal, which suddenly looked more afraid of him. It cowered back and started growling. Lux didn't care, he was going to free the thing.

He felt around for the metal clasp and pushed it in, but the chain was wrapped too tight to slip out. He wasn't strong enough to muscle it. He felt the tendrils climbing over his shoes. He had to do something now. The dog saw the knife coming at him and ducked away. Lux slipped it under his nylon collar and sliced up. The collar and binding chain fell away.

"Run, boy!"

He jumped over the vines, grabbed his pack, and headed for the rear part of the yard where the vines hadn't converged. The small dog was already there, as if waiting on him. Lux hoisted the dog over the fence with some difficulty, then himself, and they dashed back toward the trees.

It took a long time to find the main road again. The dog stopped and drank a lot of water before following behind. He was not as big or pretty as Timber, but he seemed to be a good dog. He wasn't letting Lux out if his sight. They found an unlocked car and crawled inside. He offered a can of beef stew to the dog, who wolfed it down and licked the inside of the can. "How long were you trapped there, boy?" The dog just wagged its stiff little tail.

"Those vines were scary. I didn't know they had things like that down here," Lux said to the dog. He saw the public phone in its cradle on the dash. He picked it up, wishing he could talk to Marcie or his mom or dad. The phone briefly seemed to power up like a lot of them did, then went dark again. He ate a can of cold soup and rubbed more of the clear goo on the burn on his leg. Tomorrow, they would need to get past the plants. He didn't know how he was going to do that. The dog crawled up and nestled in against him. They could do it, though. He felt better now.

CHAPTER
SIXTY-SEVEN

I simply held Carol for much of the night. I wasn't sure which of us needed it more. My love life had never been a big part of my world, and I wasn't about to let it become one now, but I think we both needed this moment of mutual sanctuary. The world was coming apart. We were both facing a bleak future. Yes, she was vulnerable, and I may have inadvertently taken advantage of that, but I am also human. Increasingly, I realized I cared for her and her boy. Somewhere during the night, reuniting them became the most important thing for me to do. It might not be the happy ending Carol deserved, but maybe it would help.

Ada and Sumo had kept watch during the night for the creeping vines and the Wraith. She let me know she still couldn't detect it on sensors, nor could she isolate the apparently psionic broadcast that seemed to strike unfathomable fear in me. She could, however, detect my reactions to it. She claimed my brain would light up with every neuron firing if the beast was close.

I was convinced that was total bullshit, as the thing had hitched a ride with us for hundreds of miles. Only once during all those days had I sensed anything close to the stomach-churning fear of that first day and night in Virginia. The creature could obviously turn it on or off. It had a way to control it... to weaponize fear. What genius egghead came up with that one? Of course, my delightfully optimistic AI brought up another possibility—there were more than one of them. What I faced yesterday may not be, in fact was likely not the same one.

I tried in vain to steady my hand holding the steaming cup of coffee. Building a fire and making coffee was a risk, but shit...everything was a risk. I used my other hand to help steady the tremors. The headaches, the stomach issues, and, of course, the shakes, I knew what they meant. My expiration date was approaching faster than normal. Doctor Magnus Reichert, the man who had practically rebuilt me, warned me that would be a possibility. Over-exertion, heightened states of awareness, and lack of sleep could all speed up the organ rejection. That was also why I was routinely checked out after each mission. Now I was quickly becoming what I would deem 'mission ineffective.' If it was any other member of Banshee squad, they would be on the sidelines by now.

"It's getting worse... isn't it?"

I looked over at Carol; she had the sleeping bag pulled up to her chin. She was studying me; I wasn't sure how to read the look I saw. I gave a simple nod.

Sumo reported in with his normal tail wag and 'Where is my breakfast?' look. I poured Carol coffee and dug in the packs to find food for him.

The woman gratefully accepted it and took great care to keep herself mostly covered as she sipped. I wasn't sure what had changed between us during the night, but something had. My dad's words echoed back to me, though. Especially his line about not living as being worse than death. I'd never given much thought to my solitary life, to being alone. I'd always had the service, and it occupied nearly all of my time right until it nearly killed me. Maybe I just wasn't sure I deserved love, a wife, kids. I couldn't see Pops as a granddad. Mom would have been great, but Dad? The idea made me smile.

"There you go again," Carol said, standing up and letting the sleeping bag fall off her wonderfully sculpted body.

"What do you mean?" I asked, trying hard not to stare at her exposed skin but wanting to do nothing else but that.

She shrugged and did a few morning stretches, something she called Pilates. She had done them nearly every morning, but always when she was wearing clothes. Today it was presenting a whole new set of challenges for me. Doctor Reichert would be pleased that not everything was as broken as I'd originally thought.

She walked over, gave me a friendly kiss on the cheek, and then went through her bag for a granola bar to eat.

"Just, you disappear into yourself, sometimes. I've noticed it. You keep things pretty close, don't you?" she asked.

I shrugged. "Maybe... I guess. Not that complicated. I just don't feel like others would be too interested in the crap that goes on in my head."

"Not a big over-sharer, huh?" she asked, nibbling away at her breakfast bar.

"My dad raised me old-school. Handle your own problems, quit your whining, and, well... a lot more stuff like that."

She pulled some clean clothes out of the bag. "I'm going to get dressed." She stepped into a pair of panties, then grinned. "Unless you want to take care of..." She pointed at me with a finger.

I may have been confused, but I'm not completely stupid. I nodded.

"What about her?" I asked. Carol and I had been walking for hours and finally seemed to be clear of the main concentration of Thunder Vine. Now we were encountering something new. Some of the grass along the roads seemed to have developed a stinging barb. I'd accidentally flopped down on the ground and felt like I had landed in a nest of yellow jackets. My suit administered an agent to block the toxins and mute the pain, but it had been a wake-up for me. The entire fucking planet was turning against us.

"She's pretty," Carol said. "I could see the attraction."

"She's gone, Carol. You're not jealous, are you?" I asked without realizing I had unwittingly stepped into a minefield way more dangerous than poison grasses.

"Damiana's my friend, and I know she normally gets what she wants."

"She didn't seem to want me," I said without breaking stride. "She stole my truck, left me for dead."

Carol just looked at me. "Men," she said, mostly under her breath.

I let the silence fall over us for another mile or two. "Look, I'm not good at this. Relationships, I mean."

She looked at me with a look of something... horror, maybe.

"Okay, not relationships... bad word choice. Really, really terrible choice. I like what happened between us. That's all I'm saying. I think we should just concentrate on getting to Rainier now. If I don't get some help, I'm not going to be any help to you in finding Lux."

She stopped and looked at me. Her face scrunched up as if contemplating something, then she nodded. "That works."

Am I safe? Did I win? Am I screwed? Adult level topics had never been a strong suit of mine, and—well, women were essentially enemy territory and not a place I seemed to belong. Ada was very unhelpful in all of this.

"How did you guys manage to slip away?" I asked Carol. "I mean, I tracked you across that river and you had doubled back."

She smiled. "I had found a downed tree crossing most of the river the night before when I was on watch. We simple walked to the water's edge, then went up the river in the shallows and crossed over."

"Then you came back down on the far side and continued as if you had gone straight across. What an idiot I am."

I could see her shoulders shaking, and I knew she was laughing. I deserved it. I was once an Army Ranger, and I'd been outfoxed by two women who worked in an office.

"Smart," I said.

"Still something bothering me, though. My AI was knocked offline. Did you see Damiana do anything?"

If I expected my admitting to having an AI would catch her off guard, it did not.

Carol said she hadn't and appeared ready to move on from the topic. I was somewhat contented in just watching her walk. Wearing only the cobalt blue Rivex base layer did amazing things for her figure. A half hour later, we left the road to detour around a mass of stalled cars when the smell of death encompassed us like a fog.

"Oh, my God," Carol muttered, trying not to gag.

I could have slipped my helmet on and blocked it out, but that seemed unfair. Sumo seemed to have no problem with the smell and was checking out a house just ahead. It was an upscale, newer one, clad mostly in real brick from what I could tell.

"We should check it out," she said. "We need supplies."

We debated it for a few minutes, but the woman was becoming increasingly vocal and forceful. I had to admit; I found it rather sexy. In my kit, I found simple filter masks for us to wear. It blocked just enough of the odor that we could function.

'The Johnsons' the sign by the door read. I knocked and looked at Carol, and I could tell just from her eyes that she was grinning.

"Such manners," she said as she thumbed the knob and the door swung open.

Unlocked was good, *right?* The smell got instantly stronger. By now, we were both familiar with the odor of rotting bodies, but the smell of rotting corpses inside a house was new for us. The home was really nice, the kind most people would have worked their entire lives to live in. Richly furnished, with real wood paneling lining an elegant den and library. I could see a chef's kitchen over to the right. High-end appliances and granite counters framed the perfectly designed and now mostly useless room.

"Hello!" Carol called out. The silence answered her back with a dreary nothingness.

"This place is a crypt," I said, looking down at a pile of fur that might have once been a cat. Or judging by the size, it was more likely a dog.

"Check out the pantry, see if there's food," I said. "I'll go, you know..."

A quick circuit of the ground floor yielded no bodies and nothing useful, not in the current world at least. Expensive Holovision sets, high-end video game systems, and something that might be a virtual workout machine. The visual of Carol doing naked Pilates popped into my head again. *Stop that,* I voiced internally. I saw Ada pop up a visual of a question mark on her ocular overlay. I shook my head. "Nothing."

The second floor was where I found the first body. An older woman, her skin was leathery and puckering in places from the decay. The discovery in the master bedroom suggested the woman was likely living with the family, maybe she was the grandmother or mother, it was hard to tell the age. The couple lay in a bed; the duvet was covered with dried vomit and what looked like shit. Death is not tidy, not even when you bring it on yourself. An empty bottle of pills lay between the man and the woman.

Carol made it upstairs and came to me, taking my arm. She held up a bag showing her find from the kitchen. I moved out of the room and almost headed down the stairs. That's what I should have done. Instead, I slowly opened the door at the end of the hall. It was a girl's room, judging by the decorations and posters on the wall. I would have guessed her as a teenager. The tiny lump on top of the covers made me realize she had been younger. Carol gasped and shielded her eyes.

I carefully unwrapped myself from Carol and moved over closer to the bed. The tiny body had a thick head of still bright blonde hair. One part of her skull was missing. A widening arc of brownish spray seemed to erupt from the girl's skull.

"They shot her," I said in disbelief. "They shot their daughter, then took pills. What in the fuck was wrong with these people?"

Carol ran from the room, and I followed closely behind. We hurried away from the house, my lack of compassion for the dead parents inside growing with each step. They had food; they had water. They could have held on. What in the world would make someone do that, do that to their own daughter?

Ada's warning and the sound of a round ricocheting off the pavement reached my brain simultaneously. The next round pinged off my chest plate, followed by a shouted command.

"On the ground. Now! Surrender your weapon or you will be shot."

CHAPTER
SIXTY-EIGHT
BANSHEE

Hell's Kitchen was nearly in as bad a shape as lower Manhattan, with less flooding, but more ruined buildings. Midtown was better, and the Northside looked to be in good shape. Still, the team had seen very few people out. Now that they were on dry land again, they had to avoid the crush of abandoned cars and delivery trucks that were packed into each slice of road like pickles in a jar. The entrance to the Holland Tunnel was a festering mess of corpses, cars, and more of the damn vines covering everything.

Sergeant Dae pulled the Wulf to a stop near Columbus Circle. Riggs climbed out and signaled to the others to stay alert.

"I'm telling you, man, G-force is a beast," Halo said to Priest as they both used the transport monitors to scan opposite sides of the street.

They had been discussing it since the scene with the cops. Gi, for his part, downplayed it; he was not a fan of being singled out just for doing his job. He had a long way to go to earn the trust of Banshee team, he knew that.

"I'm not kidding, dude moves like Prowler. Super-fast and just as deadly. Fool even went back down to get his armor even with those damn sharks in a feeding frenzy!"

"Dae, you get upgraded, too?"

"Only by nature," he said, the hint of a smile on his face. He hoped to meet the one they called Prowler. He knew the master sergeant was the official leader of Banshee team but also knew he'd not been with them on the last mission. Master Sergeant Kovach had a reputation that extended far into the corps. Maybe not to the degree that the more senior Colonel Kovach still held, but as far as reputations went, Joe's was getting damn close.

Bayou was surveying the growing piles of bodies in Central Park. Several blocks back, in Times Square, the venomous vines were covering every solid surface. "This city won't be coming back from this one," she muttered. She also could see no way to cross over into Queens. The bridges had fared even worse than the tunnels. From what she could see, though, everything out in the direction of Alliance Headquarters was just ruins.

"Packer to Banshee, Packer to Banshee."

Bayou tapped the tac channel on her comms. Why was the dropship pilot calling them on the all-company channel?

"Go ahead, Packer, this is Bayou. Did you pass along the intel?"

"Yes, lieutenant, just like you said."

The TriCraft pilot seemed disoriented and confused. Something dropship pilots never were. "So, what's the issue?" Bayou asked.

"Something cut off our comms just as the major was acknowledging receipt. She'd ordered a battle alert."

"Comms are down? That's it? Captain, we are on a miss…"

"Look to the west. Seventy degrees from your location."

Bayou saw the others emerging out of the Wulf. They were hearing the pilot as well. They all moved toward the park entrance, where they had a clear view of much of the western sky. She saw a white contrail with specks of orange and yellow.

"It's the Alice Springs," Packer said. "They were just attacked!" The massive carrier was already stationed in a dangerous low orbit; it was clearly visible and now directly above the city. "That's thousands of souls on board."

"Who did it?" Halo yelled into his suit mic.

"Ignore that," Bayou said as calmly as she could. "Are you safe?"

"I believe so, yes. I am in a LEO, well clear of the debris," Packer answered.

Low Earth orbit, or LEO, was still considered space, just not the higher and safer altitudes of longer duration craft.

"Can you render aid? Do you see any lifeboats?" Bayou asked.

The lifeboats were little more than larger versions of the ballistic pods Banshee used on their drops. They would save lives, though.

"No, to both. I have no vacuum lock, no way I can take on survivors. Also, I was relatively close when the attacks came. I don't think anyone is getting off that boat. Not alive."

The pilot was calming down finally, signs of the normal cool demeanor returning. Bayou watched the Alice Springs flaming out as it descended to the east, pieces of it already raining down into the Atlantic.

"Captain, get down here on the deck. Pick us up. This mission is a bust. Let's go somewhere we can do some good."

"Gi, get us into a clearing in the park. Send Captain Packer the coordinates."

CHAPTER
SIXTY-NINE
LUX

Something woke the boy before the sun came up, a sound. It was the dog; he was whining to be let out of the car. Lux cracked the door, and the puppy scooted off into the nearby woods. Lux looked into that dark tangle of vines and trees, thinking about all he'd seen the day before. He'd hoped it was just a bad dream, but deep down, he knew it had been real. The plants were attacking. That might not be completely true, but it sure felt like they were.

He reached down to his leg and pulled the stretchy bandage down. The burn from the vine wrapped all the way around his leg now. That much was real. He'd been in the woods off and on for weeks, and nothing like that had happened. Countless vines and roots had tripped him up, but the worst that had happened was a scraped knee.

"Come on back, boy. Where are you?"

Maybe the dog was heading back to his house. That's what dogs do, isn't it? He wasn't sure, but that sounded right. That was what Timber had done.

"Hey, boy!

Maybe it wasn't a boy. How did you even tell? He recalled a show where a vet flipped one upside down. Was it written on their belly or something?

"Hey, girl!"

The puppy peeked its head out of some bushes; it cautiously sniffed the air before walking back over and sitting down at Lux's feet.

"Girl?" Lux asked.

The dog wagged its tail.

"Okay, girl, it is, but you need a better name. 'Girl' won't do it."

He'd already checked the dog for a tag. She had a collar, but nothing but a bunch of letters and numbers on it. They sat back inside the auto-car. Lux took some of the food he'd saved and split it with the dog. She devoured everything he put in front of her.

"What about Lucy?" He looked at the brown eyes, silently pleading for more food. "You know, like those really old cartoons?" The dog didn't seem to recall.

"Okay, no Lucy." He thought some more. "Junie?"

He thought the month was June, but he liked the name, anyway. She wagged the thick tail again. Junie it was. They packed up, and they were soon back on the road in the blue-toned hours of early morning. He wanted to be away from this place. It was all wrong here, and now he knew why there were no people.

"We gotta avoid the vines, Junie. Don't just go running off, okay?"

As the road turned away from the cluster of houses far below, he heard a sound and turned to watch one of the houses crash down. He'd heard the sounds the night before, too. Thick, violet vines choked with clusters of blue-green leaves were already covering over half of the little subdivision. In time, they will wipe away any sign that people ever lived here. Lux still didn't understand it but knew he should avoid them.

At the next intersection, he turned onto a road that moved farther away from the stinging vines. His limp was getting worse, and he sat for a minute to catch his breath and cautiously removed the bandage. The burns on his leg had raised, red lines spreading out from them. They itched and were warm to the touch. He knew this wasn't good.

Junie came over and licked his face. He felt the tears trying to come again, but he gritted his teeth and fought them back. He cupped his hand and gave the dog some water from a bottle, then took a deep drink himself. Ahead on the side of the road, he caught sight of something reflecting in the morning sun.

As Lux hobbled over, Junie investigated. The metal was sticking out

308   BY J.K. FRANKS

of a cluster of vines, but not the mean kind. Junie would have let him know. These were just the regular kind with long flowers. Honeysuckles, he thought they were called.

"It's handlebars. Maybe from a bike."

He pulled and pulled, but the vines had it wrapped tight. Every inch he gained, the vines took back when he eased up. Finally, he walked back to where he'd set the pack down and dug out the pocketknife Mister Bill had given him. Carefully, he opened it, being respectful of the sharp edge, just like the man had taught him. He began cutting through vines until he could see the front wheel, then back along the frame until he saw pedals. It was a girl's bike with a bright pink basket on the front.

The chain was off and rusting, and one wheel scrubbed a little every time it went around. Still, with a little work, he could pedal it around in a circle. He used a tree and his pry bar to straighten the bent wheel enough for it to rotate freely.

"We got wheels, girl!"

He scratched at his leg, which was already throbbing. Below the burn, his foot tingled like it was asleep. "Come on Junie. Let's ride."

The puppy appeared much less enthusiastic about the contraption the kid had pulled from the overgrowth, but her ears perked up at another noise from deeper in the woods. The sound evoked a flight response, and she eagerly jumped into the pink basket, ready to be far away from it.

Lux noticed the dog's attention shift and understood the danger it represented. "We're going, girl. Just hang on tight." No longer would his trip home be a peaceful romp through the woods. He strapped on his pack and pedaled away from the intersection, away from the morning sun, and away from the evil vines creeping up from the valley below.

Soon he noticed other animals fleeing. Two deer, then five more, came out on the road and ran beside him. Later, a line of turkeys chattered out in front and a big one flared its wings and scared him so badly he nearly fell. They were all more afraid of something else. Something back there.

Lux followed the animal migration, trusting they would know where safety was better than him and Junie.

He had to push the bike up a very long hill. At the top, he rested a minute and let the puppy go to the bathroom. There were less of the fleeing animals now, the larger ones having easily out-distanced him, and the smaller ones probably not fast enough to escape the creeping vines. Still, he watched a continuous line of black ants moving along the side of the road in the same direction. These woods would be silent tonight. His blood ran cold at the thought. The only sounds would be the plants choking the life out of whatever was left behind.

He helped Junie back into the basket, then straightened the bike, climbed on, and resumed pedaling. Almost immediately, he heard a loud nose.

"That was a gunshot," Lux whispered to the dog as he tried to slow. The road was slanting sharply down now, and he was picking up speed. A small off-road vehicle was parked ahead, partially blocking the road. Through the wind racing past, he heard excited voices, then saw three men, all with guns. One was holding up the front part of a deer; blood covered the side of the animal's head. It made Lux sick to look at it. He raced toward the men who heard the bike and started yelling for him to stop. One of them raced into the road and held his arms wide.

Lux was scared of them. Mister Bill's words about some people being mean echoed in his mind. He eyed the puppy, who had been perched with two paws on the edge of the pink basket, anxiously looking forward. Then, she turned to look back at him. He'd rescued her, now he was responsible. He wasn't sure that was the way it was supposed to be, but it was what felt right.

"I won't let them get you, girl!" *I won't let them get either of us*, was what he thought.

The bike continued to pick up speed at an alarming pace. The downhill seemed far steeper and longer than the other side had been. His eyes watered from the wind whipping past, and then the man with the gun was suddenly right there, reaching out for him. Lux swerved the bike, nearly running off the road, but ducked beneath the man's outstretched hands.

He pedaled even harder, the bike racing away from the gunmen, who he could now hear were chasing after him. The sound of pursuit faded as he got farther and farther down the mountain. The front wheel, which had been the bent one, began to wobble worse. The more speed he had, the worse the wobble. Soon, the whole bike was shaking, and he was weaving all over the road. He knew he was about to crash just as the wheel left the pavement. He leaned over the basket to protect Junie as they plunged over a steep drop-off. Tree limbs grabbed at him as he fell through the forest, then a low branch caught him in the chest and separated him from the bike. He flew back, landing hard and unable to breathe. He heard the bike continue its journey without him for a few more seconds before it went silent, and Junie gave a tiny yelp of pain.

CHAPTER
SEVENTY
KOVACH

There are times in every soldier's life when you question your career choices. What kind of idiot would take a job for lousy pay? A job where other people are allowed to try and kill you? If you're like most people, you probably make good money, maybe you're still a student, or maybe you're retired, but did you ever go to work and have one of your competitors try to stab you down in the break room? Maybe a sniper round to the brainpan at a trade show. Right... yeah, this was one of those cathartic moments where I reevaluated my life's choices.

My hand edged slowly out and gently touched Carol's foot. She had hit the ground about the same time I did. Unlike me, she hadn't been shot at. At least I didn't think she had. Her foot was trembling. I took that as a good sign.

Ada had gone to combat mode. Why she hadn't spotted the attackers before me was a mystery. I scrolled through the HUD to see where Sumo was. His beacon came up on the far side of my field of view. It was stationary; no doubt he was behind cover like he was trained.

The voice told me in no uncertain terms to push the rifle away from me with one finger only. They were not advancing, not being reckless. These guys had some training, possibly military. Ada bracketed nine combatants, all spread out on a well-formed arc, each with a clear

312 BY J.K. FRANKS

shooting line on me. So, these were not just the locals jonesing for a fight.

I pushed the MK4 away as instructed. Yes, I probably could have ended them, but I was less certain I could protect Carol. I saw boots approaching, legs in forest green camo. That could be anything from the national guard to the local deer hunting club.

"Is this the guy?" The voice came from somewhere above the pair of feet.

Then a familiar voice said quietly, "Yes."

Damiana Voss, that conniving bitch, stole my truck, left me for dead, and now she was in with these guys who apparently wanted to make sure I was dead.

"Watch out, he has a dog… had a dog."

Dammit, she was giving away my ace in the hole.

"We'll be fine. The sergeant and I are just going to have a little chat. Ain't that right, Sarge?"

My view of the boot was replaced by a face. He was middle-aged, crew cut, missing a right front tooth.

I'd had enough. I raised up on my hands and then lifted my body up to a prone position, although still on my knees. "It's Master Sergeant Kovach, and why in the fuck are you shooting live rounds at us?"

My sudden assertiveness took him by surprise. He was indeed military, as were at least some of the others. He carried a formidable weapon, an old school Stoner 63 autofire that he must have found in a museum. My instant recall updated as quickly as Ada's battle maps. It fired a 5.56×45mm NATO round that could punch through my armor at this distance. Ada was analyzing the rest of the weapons; only one other was as formidable as this man's Stoner auto.

"Whoa there, friend, we just want to understand things. The little woman here says you have been raping her and her friend. She said they got away, but you would be coming to find them. Looks like she was right."

Now I had a decision to make. Were these idiots just trying to do the right thing and being duped by a beautiful woman, or were they evil pricks who were spending their last precious breaths pretending to be noble?

"Look, friend." I overemphasized the word back to him. "You can believe what you want, but I am not in the mood to kill anyone today, and you probably don't want to be dead."

I was paraphrasing a line from one of my dad's old movies. A western, I think. It was cheesy, but it seemed to fit. The boot hit me squarely in the chest, rolling me onto my back. It was beginning to seem like they weren't going to leave me many choices.

On a good day, I could probably take all of these guys with little trouble. I was better equipped, better trained, and highly motivated. Today was not one of my better days; I'd been feeling the coldness of my body turning in on itself all morning. The doctors had told me increased adrenaline could speed up my body's metabolism and cause the onset of symptoms sooner.

"Don't do that again," I stated quietly but firmly.

He tried anyway, and for his effort, he lost part of a leg to my blade. One second my hand was empty, the next the Heidelberg knife was carving out a sizeable chunk of his lower calf. The tendon sliced through; the man dropped the gun, which I caught, flipped, and fired, all in the shattered slivers of a second. The leader was down.

If any of the others had any combat discipline, they would have A) sought cover and B) returned overwhelming fire. Instead, they chose option C) which was essentially yelling and firing at everything that moved. The only one I was worried about was carrying a vintage model Glisson Mark 1, a solid weapon that could also punch through my armor, depending on the load-out. A silvery gray blur swept in on the man before I could even bring the heavy Stoner around.

Sumo hit the man, biting into his neck, leaving a gush of red that painted the pavement and the man beside him in hot, sticky gore. I dropped the clumsy machine gun and retrieved my MK4, letting loose multiple shots on several targets. Several small caliber rounds pinged off my suit before one massive blast hit me just under the chin.

Shit, the screens flickered, and I coughed up blood, coating the inside of my visor. The recirculation system gave a shriek of protest and died. I pushed the helmet back to its storage position. It was now more of a liability to me.

I saw the man with a single shot hunting rifle, chambering another round. My weapon was no longer in my hands, so I simply charged the man. Not great tactics, essentially nothing on style points, but sheer aggressive audacity sometimes wins. He raised the weapon and was about to fire when I heard a shot from behind me. Red blossomed on the man's chest and the fight went out of his eyes. I turned and saw Carol holding a rifle. She was trembling, but she might have just saved my life. I nodded and proceeded to kick the next man in the nuts; he went down like a sack of dog shit.

Sumo was just removing the life force from another of the soldiers when I called for a truce. The remaining men knew they were outmatched and seeing Carol shoot one of their own must have made them question their original motivation. They had lost four men, five if we are being honest. I could tell the last one wasn't going to make it much longer. He had a sucking chest wound. It was probably from me.

"He never raped us, he was helping us," Carol said, her tiny voice showing a strength I hadn't heard before.

The men just stood there, confused. I motioned for them all to drop their guns. The fight had clearly gone out of them. It was then I realized she was gone. Voss was no longer with our little party. I'd never even seen the woman, only heard her voice.

"Sumo, hunt." Then I had to let him know who.

"Find Damiana."

The dog took off.

"We didn't know the guy," one man said as he nursed a nasty gash across one shoulder. He'd clearly just missed getting fatally clipped by a shot.

"So, you were just following the random soldier for no reason?" It didn't sound plausible to me, but they trained soldiers to follow orders, even stupid ones from people that should not be in leadership roles.

"The girl... she..."

"She was damn convincing, right?"

I tried a different tactic. "Where were you stationed?"

Each of the four remaining men looked at each other. I knew that look.

"Can't tell me, right?" I had a feeling I knew, not much else around here except maybe a local guard armory, and that wouldn't typically be staffed by just a patrol squad. These guys were green, probably new recruits.

"Where were you headed then?"

"Louisville," a skinny, black-skinned woman said. "I got family there. We could hole up and at least eat, you know?"

I shook my head. "You need a better plan."

She leaned forward, both wanting and fearing the question she had to ask.

"What do you know?"

"I'll tell you, if you tell me about Rainier."

They looked confused. "The Factory."

They told me. Like I thought, I didn't get much, but it might be helpful. They were clearly terrified of the place and simply wanted to be anywhere else. I learned that this was less than a third of the original sentry force. Some of what they had been through sounded even more gruesome than our encounters.

My leg started going numb as I told the young private that her hometown had been nuked, her family most likely all dead or soon would be. She walked away slowly to the north, silver tears cutting trails down her face. I had just pissed on the one chance of hope she'd been clinging to since the missiles fell. I told the others they were free to go but to stay out of fights they didn't need. I would not be the worst thing they found on the road.

Sumo returned, his head hanging low. Damiana had somehow slipped past him, and he was unaccustomed to not getting his prey. In the distance, I thought I heard a vehicle moving away. There was more to this woman than she was letting on. My arm twitched, and the coldness settled in even stronger now.

The signaling chime from Ada interrupted my thoughts. "Master Sergeant, we have a possible fix on the child."

CHAPTER
SEVENTY-ONE

My brain may be supercharged, but when it came to decisions like this, it felt like it was working in slow-motion. I needed to tell Carol that Lux may have been located, but that wasn't enough. What was she going to do, walk there? I tried to activate my helmet again. It attempted to boot, then went dark. The dent in the exterior of the polyceramic shell had killed the built-in circuitry. I clipped it back to its receiver as we began walking south. Thanks to the good doctor, though, I had a back-up. Ada triggered the map I wanted in my internal view, the scene showing up directly in her connection to my brain's ocular inputs. The locked-in coordinates were on the map. The Rainier location pulsed with a purple dot.

"Distance?"

"Sixty-two miles to the location," Ada said crisply.

"No. Distance to the boy."

The map zoomed out; he was only a state away. In fact, it looked like he might even be on the Tennessee side of a mountainous line.

"One hundred seventy-eight miles," the AI replied.

I had her send a message for me.

Carol had remained mostly silent since the encounter with Damiana and the soldiers. I wasn't sure if it was the seeing her friend in a new light or taking someone's life. People deal with betrayal and killing a person in similar ways, but both are rough if you aren't used to it. I was fighting off the effects of my organ rejection and lagging behind. Carol was far enough ahead that I'm sure she thought I couldn't hear her crying. *Where had Damiana gone, and where was that damn Wraith?*

I jogged to catch up with her. I must have looked rather bizarre, as my back was on fire from the pain. Then, my right leg gave out, and I went down hard. I was twitching badly, and a new pain in my stomach felt like I'd been stabbed. My first thought was another of those damn creatures had attacked, but then I knew this was just my body taking its next step in the slow and agonizing process of dying.

Carol must have heard me fall, as she was quickly back, cradling my head in an instant. Through the pain, I mouthed almost silent words. The pain was tearing its way through me. It burned and ached and caused every nerve to fire its pain receptors in sequence. Strong tremors rippled through my body.

Sumo ran over and drove his nose into my neck. His concern was obvious, and a gentle lick told me volumes. I only vaguely sensed him, but the familiarity was comforting despite the untenable agony my body was offering.

"We..." I tried again to get the words out. Blackness was shrouding my thoughts. I stared up into the trees lining the road. Open pastureland to one side, more of the upscale homes on the other.

"Lux."

That word at least got out. It took nearly five minutes to make Carol understand what I was saying. She kept brushing the sweaty hair from my face, her concern for me obvious, but her thoughts clearly hundreds of miles away with her boy.

"We... we have to get your meds," she finally said.

"I think," I had to suck in a breath, "I think it might be too late."

"No... no!" she said with more conviction.

I drew in a breath and felt a slight reprieve from the attack on my body. "Yes, we have to go find Lux. If he leaves that spot, he could be impossible to locate again. It's hundreds of miles of Appalachian Mountains." I didn't want to admit that Ada's evidence seemed pretty thin. I had to give this mother hope.

She snatched her hand away from the ground as one of the stinging barbs of grass had found exposed flesh. I, too, was feeling them on the back of my neck, but it was insignificant to the agony I was already in.

"What if *there* is like here?"

I knew what she meant; the increasingly wild plant was trying to kill us all. The people, the survivors all with their own fucked-up agendas, as if the violet Thunder Vines weren't deadly enough. "I don't know." I gritted my teeth, determined to get my thoughts out. "We... you have to try."

She nodded; I think she finally realized I might not be coming with her. I heard the chirp in my earbuds and knew what that meant. She cried,

"It will take me days, maybe weeks. No way he will last that long."

"No." Her eyes followed my arm and then out in the direction my finger was pointing. "It won't."

She gasped. I knew what she was seeing, even without turning my head. A thick black triangle of solid matter was now suspended a half a dozen feet above the ground. I felt her hand begin to shake as it rested on my head.

"It's my team. They'll help get you to your boy."

"Jesus, Kovach, you look like shit."

"No shit, I'm decomposing. Still enough in me to kick your ass, Bishop," I answered back, feigning a significant level of overconfidence.

I'd already introduced them to Carol and given the coordinates, but Riggs insisted on checking me out first. The painful episode was improving marginally. I was sitting up again and hadn't thrown up in a good ten minutes. That was a win in my book.

"Who's the new guy?" I motioned with my head to an Asian soldier standing off to one side. He wore our standard kit but had an ROK battle patch on his breastplate.

"I am Sergeant Dae, sir. It is an honor, sir."

The soldier stepped forward and somehow bowed and saluted in the same motion.

"Your call sign happen to be G-Force?"

The man's face lit up; he gave a curt nod. "Yes, they call me Gi."

Bayou stabbed a needle into my neck and pressed the plunger home. "You know of him?"

I was familiar but didn't want to go into it right now. "He's a good man, Bayou. Change out that squad patch, though. He needs to be part of us." I took her hand. "I'm sorry. You know about Smith."

She nodded. Truthfully, Smith, whose call sign was Darko, was under my command, but mission commanders take on that responsibility, and Debra was showing the burden not just of his loss but of everything from these last weeks.

"He was a damn fine soldier, but we've all lost people. We will find a way to remember him later, not today," she said.

"That's an affirmative, Bayou."

"So, what's the story, Prowler? What can I do to make this better for you?"

I looked at my second, unsure exactly how to respond.

"Take care of my team, get the woman and her son reunited. I'm not sure I can expect much more in the win column."

"The soldier I know doesn't give up like that," she said quietly, putting away her med kit.

"Not giving up," I struggled to say. "I'm just being a realist. You were there last time. You know how bad it got before they evac'd me." She had been there; she had held onto my hand through a night and a day waiting for the damn dropship to finally locate our beacon.

"I'm going to that other facility. I'll do my best to get the meds, then we can make some decisions. Maybe head back up to the Alice Springs."

She shook her head. "Someone dropped her out of orbit earlier today. All hands lost."

Shit, so the war was still on. Someone was still shooting, but who?

"No matter what happens, it looks like Banshee squad is on its own for now."

Whatever Bayou had given me was taking effect. The tremors, cramps, and pain were all subsiding, at least temporarily.

I saw the look in her eyes. She had reached a decision. She was team lead now; I was unable to make Command decisions. She tapped her cheek to activate the squad comms.

"Halo, get Prowler's tac helmet repaired. Gi, bring the Wulf out. You're with Prowler for this next part of the mission."

Then, to me, "Now you have some backup, and your mutt has some firepower. We'll do a skip crossing to pick up the kid and be back by 0900, deal?"

We both knew it wasn't likely to happen, but I nodded in resignation. She leaned over and hugged me, then grabbed her gear and started running back to the TriCraft where that beautiful Wulf transport was rolling down the ramp. No more walking, at least.

"What if you need the transport?"

She smiled. "We can use the dropship. Not enough people around to matter anymore, even if keeping it a secret were still a thing."

She was right. There were way too few survivors around for what had happened. That was just one of the many questions I had.

"I know you've encountered the vines." She had already told me they seemed to be taking over every part of the countryside to the east.

"Yeah," she nodded sadly, remembering some personal horror.

"The guys we ran into this morning were from the factory."

"The factory?" she asked.

"It's the Hammer facility named Ranier that I need to get to. The common name for it is The Nightmare Factory."

"Lovely, just what I needed to hear." She looked back over her shoulder to watch Carol climb up the ramp. "The other woman, her friend. She's the one who told you about it?"

I nodded. Thinking about Damiana did raise a lot of questions. Maybe she had just needed me to get her here. Maybe it had nothing to do with them possibly having the meds I needed to stay alive.

"The plants were not what the guard unit had been worried about. They say they are attracted to movement and sound. As long as you could mask these, you should be okay," I told Bayou.

"What were they worried about?" she asked, genuine concern creasing her face.

"Mechs."

"Combat bots?'" she asked.

"Yes." I then told her about our encounter at the Iron River facility.

"So, the bot horde was battling the... the hostile plant life. You guys were just caught in the middle?"

I shrugged; the slight movement caused a brief spike of pain down my spine. "Possibly. It didn't seem like it at the time. The point is, I have no idea what all we are up against. I think it's humans versus whatever the hell comes at us. Just be ready, Deb."

"We're just waiting in the weeds at this point, Prowler."

So many occasions we had found ourselves doing exactly that. Waiting, watching, just praying for our targets to show themselves.

"Never had to worry about the weeds eating us before, though, Bayou."

"We're war fighters. Our environment has always been a battlefield. It's still the people behind the scenes that are the true evil, though."

CHAPTER
SEVENTY-TWO

I slept most of the drive to the presumed coordinates of the Ranier facility. Sergeant Dae informed me the others were already at the location but had no additional information. He eased the Wulf down a rural road, wary of an ambush. Gi was up to speed with everything we had encountered at Iron River and the Wraith, although I was hoping we had left that demon far behind.

Since all we had was a set of GPS coordinates, we took several turns trying to find the spot. Roads don't line up well with map coordinates, and even with Ada helping, it still seemed mostly guesswork. The Korean soldier tapped the display on the dash.

"We're here, Prowler."

I looked out via the eight displays arranged around the cockpit.

"No signs of the woman or the Wraith?"

I had described both, and the Korean shook his head.

"No, Master Sergeant."

I liked Dae, but we needed to quickly get to a better working relationship.

"No one calls me that. I'm Kovach or Prowler."

"Ne! Master... I mean, Kovach."

"Ne means yes, no?" He nodded, and I was still confused.

We had pulled off the state highway some miles back and proceeded through mostly rural sections of Tennessee before turning onto a dead-end road with a faded sign optimistically welcoming us to the Sparta Technology and Industrial Park. The buildings were probably originally built on spec with taxpayer money in hopes of attracting occupants. From the looks of it, they had only been marginally successful. Of course, if this was a Hammer location, all of this may be subterfuge.

The place looked nothing like Iron River. "This can't be right. This is simply an industrial park."

Large, generic, grayish-beige buildings scattered down both sides of the roads. Most looked like warehouses or manufacturing, with small offices on one side and docks for shipping and receiving on each end. I could see a few had signs out front with names and logos, none of which were familiar. Most appeared unused. No trucks waiting at the docks, mostly empty parking lots. Parking lots with cracked pavement and regular, old, normal Tennessee vegetation reclaiming the site. There was, however, a dusting of the lavender powder coating everywhere. Almost like the yellow pollen of spring, but there was nothing natural about this stuff.

"Are we in the right place?" I asked.

Ada responded, "Indeed, an excellent job of hiding in plain sight. Think about what you aren't seeing, Prowler."

I looked even closer at the buildings, especially the ones with the well-manicured grounds. I saw nothing unusual, and that pissed me off. I'd spent my entire career paying attention to the smallest of details, yet the comprehension of how this could be a top-secret military facility eluded me. I shrugged my shoulders.

"We did not pass through a town, nor did we see any signs of the town that apparently used to be here. Sparta is simply a spot on a map now. There are also no major roads or railways in the immediate area," Ada said.

She was right, any complex like this would have been sponsored by a local township and obviously would need to be able to provide a work-force and ability to move goods in and out easily. "Well, shit. That's ingenious." Anyone that happened down this road would see exactly what they wanted them to see, a failing industrial park in an impoverished area of the state.

Fifteen minutes later, Ada had identified a full sensor grid overlaying the entire complex. Not just camera, but IR, audio, motion, and more.

"They'll know we're coming."

I nodded to G-Force, who was using the time to make friends with Sumo.

Who are they? was my question. So far, from where we were hiding, I'd seen no activity, no people. "They still have power?" That in itself would make the place stand out, as we'd seen virtually no places with a working grid. Only a few charging stations using solar and an occasional house or store whose local reactor was apparently still functional.

"Yes, but they hide it well. My guess is, if we came here at night, the entire facility would be dark, at least from the outside."

Someone had the location of Iron River and probably many of the other research facilities. Rainier, though, was not on anyone's radar. The guard soldiers had already said no bombs landed here. What drove them away was fear. The blue glow the farmer's wife had seen must not have been this location, still could have been close, though. Perhaps the terrorists got the coordinates wrong or, even more likely, the old missile simply didn't perform as intended.

This place was trouble. Hell, it was death. This was not a happy place. Everyone seemed to know that, and yet, despite that, here I was. Death no longer frightened me; I'd nearly died several times, yet here I was. There have been moments in my career when I doubted myself. Doubted my abilities. Doubted my team. But I can't say I ever faced anything like this. Today there was genuine doubt, maybe fear. Something was going to go horribly wrong, and I would not be able to fix it. Once again, I would not live up to expectations. I would not be ready for the challenge. How would I fuck this up? Hey, that's who I was... am. Just can't get around that fact. Still, the mission is what matters... the purpose... the plan.

All these things have been drummed into me at the hands of a colonel, my father growing up, and at the hands of every C.O. I'd had since signing my enlistment papers. I knew I had no choice. I knew what had to be done. And the deep, cold blackness in the pit of my stomach could do nothing to stop me.

I took that step, and then another one and another one. That's how you get through tough times. You just keep walking. You keep moving, hopefully forward, occasionally getting shoved back or knocked down. Tough times are tough for a reason. If it was easy, everybody would do it. This was one of those moments. Those are the life-defining moments when I knew I had to be better than myself.

If I am being honest, that was something I'd rarely achieved. I wasn't really sure I could do it now. But I was damn sure going to try. I had to make this work. Not to save the world. Not to save the planet. Not even to possibly save my own sorry ass. I was doing it for a woman I'd only known a week and a little boy I had never met. For some reason, they were all that mattered and me staying alive was what she wanted.

CHAPTER
SEVENTY-THREE

Gi called me over. He was behind a series of storage tanks. The micro GPR he held was giving a subterranean scan of the surrounding area.

"It's all open space," he said, turning the screen to me. "It won't scan out far enough, but this entire site is sitting atop a massive underground complex."

That seemed to jibe with what the soldiers had told me, so we had to be in the right place.

"Find us a way in."

The man began zooming in on various points. "Ada, a little help." I knew the AI could deduce things from clues far too random for us mere humans to catch. Still, she lacked intuition and didn't have an immediate plan, either.

Sumo and I wandered off and do what we do best—explore and knock shit over. Ultimately, our way worked, although not quite how I'd imagined.

"You're determined to do this, aren't you?"

Pop's voice on my comms shocked me to a standstill. Now, there were a lot of things I might have said at that point, but truthfully, I was tired of him second guessing me.

"You really don't care if I live or die, do you?" I answered, my weariness clear in my voice.

"We need you to be the hero, the good guys. You are the military out there now. Do you understand what that means?"

"Good guy, bad guy. I'm the one with the guns... that's what I know, Pop" And yes, that was a movie line, too, but I'll be damned if I know which one. Something about talking to my dad made me descend to his level. It was a major character flaw, something my therapist should have been helping me get past. If I had one, I mean.

He sighed. "You don't have enough guns for this mission, Son."

I have to admit; he sounded genuinely concerned, in a detached, artificial sort of way. "Okay, Dad. Well, I don't know how, but I do have to find a way into this little shop of horrors."

"No, I'm serious. You're going to need more guns, a lot more guns. Big damn guns."

I heard a sound like ice cubes clinking in a thick glass tumbler. The image of him sitting there with a bourbon in his hand flashed in my head.

"Find the landing pad for the airfreight. Should be a keypad embedded on the western side. Ada can hack the codes."

Then he was gone; the silence returned to fill my head. I spotted the pad in the aerial view Ada was now providing. "G-force on me," I whispered. Sumo followed my signal and swept wide as I crouch-ran to the thick slab of concrete just outside one of the smaller buildings. The keypad was simply a part of the concrete. You wouldn't see it unless you knew where to look. I placed a remote sensor just below the number pad. Seconds later, Ada confirmed she had the code.

"I can get us in, but there is a biometric lock just ahead. I can't get you past that as easily."

Okay, by not as easily, my AI meant not at all. As soon as I entered her numbers, a large section of the landing pad rolled back to reveal a ramp heading down at about a fifteen-degree angle. The three of us went in, and the concrete slid back into place with a resounding click of heavy-duty locks. Ahead of us was a solid steel wall with warning signs of

'Absolutely No Admittance.' It was written in red — all caps and everything.

The sloping road was clearly built for large vehicles to use. I searched one side and G-Force the other. High on the wall, we found another sensor. It required a matching thumb print or DNA sample. No way we were on the approved list. To one side, a thick window offered a glimpse into an empty guard room. The glass was inches thick, the multi-laminate stuff they use in armored cars.

I looked at the Korean and winked. "You know what to do."

He smiled as he fished in his pack and came up with an even smaller pack. He unrolled it and removed one strip of adhesive with four silver buttons, each a little smaller than an old American dime. He placed a button on all four corners of the window, then stepped back.

The buttons were sonic generators specially designed to set up a resonant harmonic frequency that would match the natural frequency of the substrate, then alter it until the molecular bonds failed. It wouldn't work on metal, but on glass like this... well, it was perfect.

The window shattered into thousands of harmless bits. It was loud in the confined space, but I doubted the element of surprise was on our side, anyway.

It took some doing to get both of us, Sumo, and all our weapons through the two-foot opening. I think my new partner took every weapon the Wulf's arms locker contained. The door leading out of the guard room wasn't even locked. All that elaborate security and they failed to secure the weakest link. Typical government operation.

"Power is still on," Gi confirmed, doing a quick scan into the space beyond.

"Ada, any chance you can find a layout or do something to help me find the med labs?"

"In the official DARPA database, this place doesn't exist, Prowler. If you find an active workstation, though, I may be able to help."

We stepped through the door, Gi darting to the far wall about twenty feet away. The road here appeared much as it had on the other side of the barrier, but the incline was less, and it quickly opened up into an underground parking area. On the far wall, I saw loading docks; these were nearly all filled with the same generic looking freight trucks. The autonomous kind with the low squat cabs up front.

I heard sounds, the telltale whine of mechanical servos. Was the entire place automated or simply just abandoned?

"You are being targeted," Ada said. I saw twin lasers lighting on Gi and knew they had to be on me as well. The laser reticles didn't budge off target once they locked. A human's hand would have shaken, the lasers would have moved around to find the best place to shoot. Machines didn't think like that, though. These were from an automated weapons system. They found a firing solution and waited until whatever command system algorithm had enough data to say whether to fire or not. The color of the laser on my chest changed from the icy blue to a fire engine red. That was probably not a good thing.

"Move!" I yelled just before an arc of brilliant red sliced through the air. I saw Gi racing like a cat, low and agile. My body no longer flexed like that, and today, simply walking upright was a struggle. Still, I made it to the far wall without serious injury.

"That was an automated defense system." I said it as a statement, not a question. "Where is everyone?"

"This factory appears to be nearly completely automated, Kovach."

The voice came from above me. I spun around, MK4 at the ready. Damiana Voss stood in a darkened alcove a dozen feet above the floor. I had a rule, okay, more like a mandate: 'When in doubt, Take them out.' Killing an enemy before they got a chance to do the same to you had been a winning position my entire career. Still, I hesitated. Switching to IR view, I saw no weapons. In fact, confusingly, she appeared completely nonthreatening.

"What do you want, Voss?"

Sumo began a low growl from somewhere in the darkness. I knew he and Gi would have my back.

"I want to help you, but first, I should apologize."

"That could take a while. You've gone out of your way to betray me, multiple times, when all I did was offer to help."

She disappeared momentarily and a section of wall in front of us soon began to retract silently to the side. She was walking down several steps, turned, and stood in the doorway.

"I wasn't the only one keeping secrets, Joe."

She reached out and placed a hand on my arm. It might have been a friendly gesture, but yeah, I still wanted the bitch dead. It would have been easier to do if she had been a little less beautiful.

"I'm sorry I used you, but I had my reasons."

"Not an apology, Voss." I turned and motioned for Sumo to sweep the corridor the woman had just come out of.

"Are the lasers off?" I asked.

She shook her head. "Sorry, no."

"How did..." Then I saw how she had gotten in and avoided the defense system. A lanyard with a badge and a holographic image of her face. She had clearance to be here. I nodded. "You wanted to come here the whole time."

"I was supposed to be here. This is my job, Kovach. Sorry if that doesn't square with your idea of how things work. I did my best to keep both of you out of here."

"But you don't work for Hammer, do you?"

She ignored the question, but I thought from her expression I had struck a nerve.

"Joe, surely you realize there is more going on here than just some enemy missile strike on key targets."

I just stared at her, my face barely hiding my growing rage.

"They knew where our labs were. They used exactly the right warheads to create chaos. Have you not wondered why so many people are dead or missing?" she asked.

I had wondered about that. At first, I assumed they were just hiding. Sheltering in place or maybe bugged out to a remote location somewhere. Ada had stated at one point it appeared eighty percent of the population was absent. In the affected areas out closer to the coast, it was even higher.

"What about the rest of the country?" she continued. "Chicago, Dallas, St. Louis. Why are we hearing nothing from them? We have military bases there, but have you seen any hyperjets or bombers or, hell... relief planes dropping supplies?"

I hadn't. Bayou and I had discussed something similar. Where was the Navy? Where was the help from any of our allies?

"Two of the three remaining monolith carriers were destroyed in the last two days. You're a military man. Tell me who has the capability to do that?"

I knew the answer. No one. Our enemies were fragmented, never reaching a threat level adequate to pull off simultaneous attacks on multiple domestic ground targets, much less on our marine or space-based ships. Banshee's primary missions had been to play whack-a-mole with these other would-be players and keep them underground and off our threat matrix.

My newly repaired helmet's speakers began picking up a sound. Something different emerging from the slightly mechanical background noises. A tap... tap, tap tap sound that repeated and grew. The look on the woman's face let me know she heard it, too.

"The bots," I said.

She nodded. "We need to move," she echoed, turning and moving fast back down the corridor.

CHAPTER
SEVENTY-FOUR

BANSHEE

Bayou studied the woman. She couldn't help but wonder who she was to Kovach, but it was obvious her only concern was finding her son. Carol's expression as she looked around the top-secret TriCraft was typical of everyone's first encounter. There was something otherworldly about the ship. It was the stuff of myth and legend, especially in the UFO community.

"Coming down on target now, Lieutenant," Captain Packer yelled from the Command seat.

Carol met her gaze. "How far away will we be?"

"Not far," answered Debra. She unbuckled and moved over closer to the civilian. "Kovach said he got you out of a pretty bad situation down there."

Carol just smiled. "Yes, he did. He saved me more than once. He's a little moody, and he talks to his dog and himself a lot, but they both looked out for me. Both are excellent protectors."

Riggs felt there were layers to the truth in the woman's answer but didn't press her.

"He's not going to make it, is he?"

The words were low, but in the eerily quiet confines of the dropship, Bayou heard them clearly. Carol's eyes were heavy with tears. This wasn't about her son—she was asking about Kovach.

"I was with him the first time he ran long on his meds. I didn't think he would survive then. He was in so much pain, I don't think *I* would have wanted to survive."

Carol gave a small nod. "He said he'd been injured on a mission; he didn't have a choice, is that right?"

"Are you asking if he volunteered for the surgery?" Riggs asked. "No one in their right mind would volunteer for the shit they did to that man." She leaned back against a bulkhead, remembering the battle. "Kovach made a choice, a decision. One he felt was for the greater good but went against our orders. Our bosses made him pay."

"That sounds awful," Carol said, tears now making silent trails down her face.

"It is, but the master sergeant was a hard man to kill, even before the upgrades. Now I feel sure he will figure something out. You must have 'faith in the everlasting brilliance that is Kovach,'" Bayou said.

"Is that one of his lines?" Carol asked, a small smile creeping through the tears.

"When he starts referring to himself in the third person, you need to look out," Deb offered as she began to carefully study one of the wall displays.

Carol's eyes danced with a sparkle now. The tears were gone. "Thank you, Debra. Thank you for doing this for me."

Riggs nodded.

"LZ is hot, sir," Packer yelled. "Ma'am," he amended. "Biologics only, but they're all over."

"Stay here, we'll check it out," she said to Carol, knowing the woman would probably still try to race her to the hatch.

"The vines, they can kill," Carol warned.

"We know." Bayou then motioned for Halo and Priest to join her at the door.

Priest carried a large backpack, and a mean-looking device they hoped would help clear a perimeter. The hatch lid opened onto a scene of absolute hell. The ground was a writhing mat of the snakelike Thunder Vines. Autocars were being overrun by the overgrowth. The mewling of a baby deer being suspended by the violet stinging vines was the loudest sound they heard.

"Look!"

Bayou's eyes followed to where Priest pointed.

"Shit! It's not just the plants anymore."

The mass of plants was interspersed with other living things. Things that might resemble animals if they had been designed for a Hollywood monster movie. Snakes with thousands of pairs of legs scrambled over downed trees. Creatures the size of a dog with a bony ridge on their backs and a series of elongated teeth lining a rounded face. Whatever was causing the plants to evolve and attack was now altering the other creatures on a genetic level.

"Priest, clear us a spot near that car."

The soldier stepped out onto a ramp that was still ten feet above the ground and unleashed a gout of flame from the tube he carried. The gel-based fuel covered the ground and instantly scorched an area clear. Bayou was on the ground with Halo beside her in seconds. Halo quickly opened the car that had been identified as the boy's last location. Bayou stood guard, sending cutter rounds through plant and animal alike.

"Empty, ma'am."

She looked back, disappointed but not surprised. Who would stay here with all this shit moving in around you? The sounds of the baby deer had drowned out her own thoughts. She shot it just to end its suffering.

"Grab the phone and anything else, you see." She bent down and scooped up some samples of the vine and one of the smaller animals. It was larger than a rat but smaller than a squirrel and was covered with colorful scales.

"Gotta go, Boss. Flame pack is running low," Priest said from high above.

She tapped Halo on the back and they both jumped onto the remnants of the closest car and then up to rails on the TriCraft's ramp. Priest hauled each of them up and onto the platform, the pilot already moving the dropship up and away. Riggs had the misfortune of landing face down with her head hanging over the edge. She saw the deer she had killed being torn apart by both vines and other animals. "They're working together." Vines, or some other sort of parasites, could be seen and were writhing under the animal's fur. More of the smaller creatures were using teeth and claws to effectively unzip the flesh from the skeleton. Bayou turned around to get up, only to see the boy's mother looking down at the same horrific scene. Her face frozen in a look of pure terror.

They followed the road, assuming Lux would go in the direction the car had been facing. Also, assuming he'd made it out of here alive. Riggs placed the specimens in an onboard analyzer. She then took the car's phone and placed it on the ship's AI interface.

The phone hadn't had service, but it had still recognized Lux and tried to synch. The ship's AI overrode the phone's simple security, and a display of the boy appeared on several of the ship's display screens. Everyone heard Carol suck in a breath followed by a painful shriek. It reminded Riggs of the sound the deer had been making.

"Oh, my God, look at him!"

The kid's face was covered in dirt, scratches, and bruises, but to Deb, he looked to be in good shape. The clip was only a couple of seconds long. Just enough for the phone to unlock and attempt a synch.

"He's alive, Carol," Riggs said. She couldn't understand how, though. If he had been on his own since the attack, he was indeed remarkable.

"Loop that and enhance," she told the computer.

She watched it again and again. Lux's face filled most of the screen. The camera wasn't great — just a simple system designed for the generic car phone. Despite that, she was seeing something of a shadow behind the boy.

"There, stop and replay, expand here," Riggs gestured in the air for the AI.

"What do you see?" Carol asked, her voice about to break and looking for any sign of hope to cling to.

"I don't know."

The small portion of the video expanded and expanded but was still just a fuzzy shadow. Was it somebody in there with him? Maybe one of the mutant animals had gotten in the car.

"It's fur," Riggs said, moving in close. "It's...it's a dog."

Carol shook her head. She was glad her son wasn't alone, but how did that help, and why was Bayou smiling?

"Match sensors to the timestamp on this video, then track," Riggs told the ship's AI.

Turning to Carol, she said, "For the last two decades, all domestic pets have been chipped automatically by every vet in the country. It's illegal to even have an unregistered one."

Carol had never owned a pet but didn't think that sounded true. "Isn't that just so the vets can identify them if they turn up somewhere else, like a lost dog recovery aid?"

Riggs nodded. "That part is true, but the sensor chip is fully functional. We can activate it to show a location. All we have to do is find out what animal chip was in that vehicle yesterday with Lux and activate its tracker."

Left unsaid was the big 'if' of the animal still being with the kid or even still alive. After seeing what those little dagger rats were doing to the deer, who knew?

"We have a marker," she said seconds later. "It's about seven miles ahead."

The TriCraft's displays all showed the ground below. Seeing the huge soundless black triangle moving slowly across the treetops had to be surreal for anyone who might still be alive. On the top of the next ridge, the vines were less dense, but you could tell they had been here.

"Look there," Priest said, motioning off to the right side of the road. An old-style, off-road vehicle lay on its side. The remains of a body lay in a smear of red on the ground. Several dozen yards farther down the road was another. The bodies were human, or had been.

A shower of thumps hit the hull of the ship. "Is that what I think it is?" Debra asked.

Packer zoomed in a video. "It appears the trees are shooting some kind of dart things at us."

It wasn't the trees. They had already run into these things before. Another of the vines that liked to climb high into the trees and used a modified seedpod as a lethal dart. Every living thing in this new world seemed bio-engineered to kill.

"Preliminary analysis complete," the ship's computer stated. Bayou flipped over to the screen on the forensic analysis of the vine and the dagger-rat.

"Coming in on the beacon, Boss," Packer said.

"What is it, LT?" Halo asked, moving over to the screen she was using.

The creature's autopsy report had been heavily redacted by the ship's AI. Along all the edges was a red border with "Classified" in bold type.

"What does that mean?" Halo asked, but the gears were already beginning to slip into place.

"No...shit no, please tell me, no!" Debra yelled.

She tapped her comms squad channel. "Bayou to Prowler." Kovach needed to know this.

CHAPTER
SEVENTY-FIVE
KOVACH

The corridors seemed endless, with countless others crossing at regular intervals. The sound of the tapping sounded more like muted thunder here. It was something we felt more than heard. Sumo raced ahead; I kept looking for the next level of defenses. I knew the brief laser fire in the shipping area couldn't be all they had. This was a Level-1 DARPA facility.

Voss came to a sudden stop at the next intersection, and I nearly crashed into her.

"What..."

She held a finger to her lips and had an expression that required no other explanation.

Why was I following her? She could certainly be leading us all directly into danger or certain death. Still, she seemed familiar with the massive complex.

In a voice that was low but not quite a whisper, she pointed to a steel door down to our right and said, "We have to go down."

I'd assumed the factory was multiple levels below ground. That didn't mean I actually wanted to explore it. I nodded to her before switching to internal comms.

"Gi, you don't have to do this. You got me here, and I have no idea what is waiting down there."

I could see the man's round eyes look at me, and then at Voss, who was using her ID card to presumably call the elevator car.

"I don't trust her. I'm with you, Prowler."

And that was that—we all stepped into the elevator. The damn thing was huge, like three times as wide and high as a normal one.

I raised my visor to talk to Voss. "Where are you taking us?"

She looked annoyed, her mind obviously focused somewhere else, somewhere... deeper down this shaft.

"Why did you try to have me killed? I was bringing you here."

She shrugged, "The soldiers had a vehicle. I needed it. I didn't want Carol to come, and well... you were showing signs." She sighed, "I doubted you would even make it, and honestly, I figured you would eventually make the decision to go find the boy."

That told me a lot. She didn't ask where Carol was, and she was unaware of Banshee team still being in play. She didn't want Carol here, but she had abandoned her to the Wraith. The woman's words didn't match the facts.

"Is there even a med lab here?"

She turned to me; her exasperation was clear—I was right there with her. Nothing was stopping me from reaching out and crushing her windpipe. In fact, the simple thought of it brought me an uncomfortable amount of pleasure.

"The enemy is here," she offered as a non-answer. "You need to see what is going on here."

I held my arm out toward her. She stepped back in surprise.

"You see that?" The arm was moving and the hand shaking almost uncontrollably. "Me learning anything new at this point is irrelevant if I don't survive. My best guess is I have about three hours before I am in a near comatose state." I didn't share the level of agonizing pain I would be in just prior to that point. "After that, nothing will save me."

My hand lowered, and Sumo licked it. "Believe me when I say my last order will be to have you taken out." I gently rubbed the dog's ears. "By whatever means I can still manage."

The car stopped dropping, and the doors opened.

"I'd expect nothing else." She strolled out into the darkness beyond with the confidence of someone who clearly had all the leverage.

Our suit visors instantly went to NV mode, casting the cavernous space in an eerie bluish-green hue. The tapping of the bots now seemed to be mostly above us, distant, but still a constant evil, fucking heartbeat of this place. I motioned Gi to go right, and Sumo left. I followed closely behind Voss, who was appearing a little less confident with every step she took. I wasn't sure how she could even see where she was heading, but soon it became apparent she was using landmarks, columns and machinery. Several times, I watched her reaching out blindly for something she felt was close. Her fingers fluttered and clinched until she made contact.

"Ada, give me intel on this room," I mentally asked.

I felt a pulse emit through my body and knew the AI was using a subsonic sonar wave to help her map out the space. The dimensions updated in my HUD. It was indeed enormous. Almost ten kilometers long and two wide. That can't be right...*can it?*

"Purpose?" I asked, hoping she had a theory.

"If this is the lowest level, I would assume it is raw material storage. Perhaps excess production inventory."

There were thousands of crates, drums, and assorted containers stored on racks that seemed to run the entire length of the space. High overhead, the ceiling appeared to be solid rock. I couldn't see enough detail to know if this was a natural cave or not, but that seemed less important.

"Here," Voss said, her voice snapping through the darkness like a bullwhip.

The wall where she pointed was filled with prefab rooms and offices. All seemed abandoned.

"Compounding labs are there; I don't know what you need, but you have ten minutes before I pursue my own mission."

Holy shit, I couldn't believe the woman actually seemed to be helping me for a change. I was confused. This woman was a threat. She was the enemy... I think. I let one part of my brain calculate the odds of this being a trap, but ignored it and made my way to the labs. Voss blacked out the windows with shutters, then alerted G-force and me to lose the NVs before flipping on banks of overhead lighting. My hand still shook, but this time from nervous optimism as we went through hundreds of shelves of chemicals and pharmaceutical material. Ada had interfaced with Gi's suit cams as well. If either of us saw any of the exotic compounds I needed, the AI would register it and have us secure the entire supply.

He and I raced up and down the rows, scanning each shelf in seconds. So far, I'd only located one container of a minor element in the drug mix. It was now in my backpack and my brief sense of hope seemed to be drying up like a desert puddle after a storm.

"Here's one," Gi shouted, tossing me the oversized plastic container. It had a name that was almost too long to fit on the label. I had no idea what it did, but Ada said we needed it. I now knew the entire compound had thirteen different base ingredients. A handful of others were added to make storage better and lessen side effects. We didn't have time for any of that. Of course, nothing said we had to leave when Voss did. Her reasons for being here were her own concern, not mine. Then the tapping abruptly stopped.

It had been such a constant that I'd no longer even noticed it. The rhythm had simply become part of the environment, and then it suddenly was no longer there. Voss, who had been keeping a vigil at one window, pulling back the metal shutter every few minutes to peer out into the darkness, turned to look at me.

"Times up."

My heart raced, the tremors in my arms were spreading. We were nowhere near having everything. "What? The bots?"

"No, something worse," she answered. Her voice was filled with a sad regret.

"What else? What in the fuck did you people make down here?"

In answer, a terrible crashing came from outside. Then the sound of rending metal.

"Warbots," Voss whispered. "Titan class, most likely."

Gi looked at me for guidance, but I was as bewildered as him. We'd been on battlefields across the planet, but neither had ever encountered a battle droid that carried that designator. I keyed the mic and asked Ada for help. She indicated a computer terminal nearby.

I silently moved over and placed my gloved hand near the row of input ports. Seconds later, she confirmed a connection, and her data began to update.

"Oh, no..."

When an artificial intelligence begins to sound scared, that is usually a good sign something bad is about to happen. Ada's reaction was the right one. The entire front wall of the labs was sheared away by what looked to be a giant claw. It didn't appear to be mechanical but gleamed with a deep shimmering blackness in the flickering LEDs that were still struggling to illuminate the space.

I grabbed Voss just before a second claw swept down from the ceiling. Gi and I were sealed in armor and might withstand some of this, but the woman and Sumo would be chopped in half. I pushed desks and shelving out of the way and raced back toward the elevators. Almost at once, my enhanced brain realized two things: (one) the one giant MechaDroid wasn't alone, and (two) we had no chance of making it out. Lights started illuminating around the outer perimeter of the cavern. Each was an alcove, and I could see more of the enormous warbots unfolding themselves and disconnecting charging cables.

"Find us an exit!" I'm not sure who I directed that command to, but Ada was first to respond.

"Elevator is offline, emergency stairway is straight ahead."

"Boss, what about your meds?"

ROK soldiers are an elite bunch. Some of the toughest warriors I have ever encountered. And Gi was as committed to the mission as anyone I'd ever fought with. This time, though, the MO was out of reach, unattainable, and I knew it.

"Forget it!" I yelled. *These mechanical demons are going to end me way before my own body has a chance.*

We both were reverting to battlefield tactics intended for a larger force. I stopped to lay down, suppressing fire while Gi and Voss ran ahead. Gi would then return the favor, covering me while I ran to catch back up.

So far, we hadn't seen any returning fire from the robot warriors. They were just hulking giants smashing their way toward us. When I caught back up to Voss, I intended to quiz her on the load-out for these things, then something caught me in the chest, flinging me back a solid fifty feet. The impact felt like getting hit by a truck.

My breathing became labored, and looking down, I saw a large dent in my chest plate. My armor was not supposed to deform like that, no matter the impact. This indention was so deep I could no longer expand my chest fully to take a breath. Slowly, I leaned up only to see one of the Warbots unleash another of the objects. It spun out of a side on the arm of the thing. It looked like a grappling hook but flew with tremendous speed. Then, the heavy metal hook retracted just as fast. I ducked just below it, or it would have removed my head at the shoulders.

"These are considered unarmed. Most down here are mainly used for loading and unloading." Ada said, in response to my unspoken question.

I recovered my gun from nearby and unleased several of the carnage rounds at the bot that was positioned closest to me. The plasma rounds dissipated harmlessly against the black exoskeleton.

"Can you shut them down, find me a weak spot... something?"

"They are all autonomous, no central command in their system architecture," she responded.

"Shit!"

"Prowler!" Gi was yelling for me, then I knew why. One of the Warbots was uncoiling itself right behind me. Its full height had to be close to twenty-five feet. I was scared shitless, and I was impressed. Whoever designed these things had been a genius. Every joint moved independently, allowing them to change direction on a dime. Shoulders looked just as maneuverable as the hand joints, which on this one also ended in a claw. Others possessed pinchers, and a few had what looked to be forklift blades. They were adaptable, tough, and worked together as a team.

I saw the movement of the open claw, which this close looked more like a giant serrated carving knife. Just before it hit, I saw Sumo lunging for the thing's groin. The arms sliced down, just missing me, but getting hung up momentarily in a shelving system that had toppled over.

"Move it, Sumo. We gotta haul ass!"

Running headlong for the door Gi was holding open, I glimpsed

Voss already running up the stairs. This woman's loyalty was only to herself. Had to respect that in an evil bitch kind of way.

"I have an important update from Bayou. Would you like to hear it?"

I was covering the rear as we side-walked up the steps. "Well, shit... why not? Send it."

CHAPTER
SEVENTY-SIX

I listened to the message and immediately wanted to call Riggs back, but this wasn't the time or place for a conversation. We could still hear the mechanical beasts outside in the corridor. We'd climbed at least four stories but still hadn't cleared the bottom cavern.

My legs were trembling, and the gun I held was nearly useless in my failing grip. A crash a dozen yards below us shook the metal stairs loose on one side of the shaft.

"The things are breaking in," Gi said. This was the first time I had seen the man's stoic demeanor show any signs of stress.

I smiled. "Welcome to Banshee."

I pulled him closer. "I am about to be a liability; my body is shutting down. If that happens, take Sumo. Get out, shoot Voss if she gets in your way. Bayou needs to know about these Warbots." I sucked in a painful breath, the polyceramic casing pressing in on my sternum still making that difficult. "Riggs also has some news for us. The plant and animal life that is mutating, apparently, we created it... our government."

"It's Alliance tech?" Gi's face showed the evident shame of that revelation.

"Transgenic or transmorphic genetics, something like that. Too many pieces, too little time, friend. None of this is making sense, and I have no idea who the good guys are. We look out for each other from here on out, screw the rest."

"Ne," he said in agreement. "By the way. The girl. I no trust her."

"Smart kid," I answered. Voss was a very big question mark, but I was beginning to come to terms with my suspicions about her. I would never trust her, but she had answers I wanted to get before I faded away.

"Follow her." I pointed up the steps, the woman's footsteps still echoing on the metal stairs. Gi looked at me, then took off at a run. I slowly began climbing at my own pace. The tapping sound was back, as were the sounds of obvious destruction from the Warbots below. Sumo looked at me from the next landing as if to say, 'Hurry the fuck up.'

"I'm trying, partner."

I was grabbing the rail and pulling myself up each step. My legs were feeling like leaden weights. I heard a crash and a woman's shriek from high above. Then the tapping was louder and even more ominous.

"Ada, I need something. I can't quit now."

"I've been monitoring your deterioration, Prowler. The best I can do is give you a stimulant. It won't help you for long, and when you come down, it will be even worse."

"Do it!"

I felt the needle prick from my suit's med pack and the cold liquid draining into my veins, then a flush of heat as it began to mix with my bloodstream. The pain began a slow retreat, but a baseline ache remained. The tremors also began to fade, but I knew I was walking on a virtual landmine. How long would this reprieve last? How much would it cost me in the end?

The end... I was literally facing that now with every step I took. Somehow, I had to pack that away along with all the other events of the past few weeks. I'd always done that with missions. No matter how bad they had been, I never thought about anything but the end result. Did we succeed, did we fail, could we have done it better? Now I had my entire life to pack into that same box... was it worth it? *Did you improve your tiny piece of the planet or just make things worse?*

My mind was drifting. The pounding wreckage going on below was being matched in intensity with the thunderous tapping of tiny metal claws up above.

"Weapons free, Gi," I said, reminding him not to worry about me, take care of himself and get to Voss if he could.

CHAPTER
SEVENTY-SEVEN

Sumo raced up the rapidly crumbling staircase. "Take down," I yelled up to him. He would not leave me like this unless it was a direct command. He knew I meant Voss. His ice-blue eyes briefly met mine, and I swear he nodded before turning and running on, his footsteps lost in the heavy metal echo chamber of the stairwell.

The adrenaline hit my system like a sledgehammer, anchoring my feet back to a standing position and forcing my body to climb. I heard a section of the stairs collapse with a thunderous roar behind me. We may have made the monsters, but was I the enemy that turned them loose on us?

I moved faster.

Above, the rhythmic tapping was getting louder and more ominous. I heard a gunshot, then another. That had to be Gi. I tried to run, then my feet were detached from the world as the stairwell caved in on itself. The only chance for escaping this hell hole disappeared in a cloud of dust and concrete as I fell back toward the ominous black machine beasts far below.

~

I landed with a crunch that I knew would ruin the rest of my day. I was, however, not at the bottom level of the chamber as I'd expected. I was on top of the growing rubble pile. One side of the stairwell had collapsed at an angle, revealing a tear in the wall leading to another dark chamber. Feeling the rumblings of the machines somewhere below me, I achingly rolled over. Ada was assessing my damage, but I ignored her. I know damage—we are old friends. I wasn't dead, so I raised up on my good arm, then pushed up to a knee, then finally to both feet. I sipped water from the suit's tube and stumbled forward into the crack of darkened space.

Turning around after climbing through a gaping hole in the polycrete wall, I saw I was in another chamber. The beam of my helmet light cut a pale line that pushed the shadows back, but not much. I stumbled forward and quickly ran up on a solid rock wall. Turning to either side led me to a similar dead-end. With no other hope of getting out of this dungeon, I began exploring every inch of the space. Some walls had tool marks and seemed to have been made or at least enlarged by humans. That was good. There had to be a reason for the chamber. After ten minutes, I was ready to abandon the search, but my eyes had taken in something that my brain was trying to process as a clue. Not sure if it was the meat-sack part of my brain or the computer portion, but either way, it worked. A scuff mark at the base of one section of wall. To be honest, it was more of a line that was nearly devoid of dust and loose rock.

I tapped on the wall with my armored fist. It felt like the real thing. It looked like the rest of the wall, but when I applied all my weight, it shifted. Just a fraction of a centimeter, but I noticed it. Within minutes, I had located the release. There was something behind this wall, something they preferred people not easily find.

The entire wall swung inward on silent hinges, revealing a long narrow corridor ending in more of the metal stairs. These went down into blackness. An odor of death wafted up at me. My suit's filters cut in at once, but it was already inside my helmet. Putrid decaying meat. Human waste. And... something else. A smell of chemicals, ammonia, urine maybe, and something that reminded me of a hospital., antiseptics that were failing to do their job perhaps.

My auditory sensors picked up unfamiliar sounds, too. The familiar tapping was subdued, but other machine noises took their place. The whir of electric motors. Rhythmic gurgling of pumps. There were other mechanical sounds, a confusing mélange of soft, unnatural noise, all muted. At the very faint edge of even the suit's auditory range I thought for a moment I heard.... music? Tinny, old, and very surreal in the dark place of horror.

I drew my pistol as I descended the first step. "What's down there?" I asked my super AI. Ada offered no answers.

The stairs were long, and at each landing a metal grated floor zigzagged away into the darkness, and with each step the putrid smell of decay and an acrid ozone smell increased. My spidey sense gave my system a little jingle as sweat ran down my back to make a puddle at the base of my spine. It would be nice to just pretend and say it was because the corridor was hot down here, or my suit's ventilation system was failing, but that would have been bullshit. I was scared. Oh, yeah, really damn scared. Anyone that tells you tough-guys don't get scared is out of their mother-fucking minds. We just learn to work through it.

The Nightmare Factory, whatever it might be, lay ahead. Whatever horrific form the madmen at Hammer with their perverted science, had conceived, was down here. I had a feeling I had not seen the worst of it yet. My dad had warned me not to come here... he had been right. I didn't find my meds; I didn't even find anything helpful. These dicks were bioengineering weapons of war.

What kind? All kinds... every kind. From what I could tell, there was no area of exploration off limits to them. And they were on our side, or at least had pretended to be. I was standing inside what was likely a multi-billion-dollar facility that our tax dollars had paid for. A place so vile, so evil, that I was about to shit myself before learning what psycho-horror beast was going to jump out at me next.

Since I joined the special operators of Banshee team, my optimism for humanity, decency, and basic common sense has taken a real beating. After seeing the bizarre shit in some of the labs we'd raided and eventually what my own people had done to me, I knew our abilities had outgrown our capacity to control it.

That thing Jeff Goldblum had said in that old movie about the dinosaurs rang true, every time. "Our scientists were so preoccupied with whether they could, they didn't stop to think if they should."

As I moved through the labyrinthian maze of walkways, the darkness seemed suffocatingly close. My tremors were back, and I wasn't sure if it was my body reasserting its scheduled death march, or if it was just the sheer terror. I must be the worst super-soldier in the history of super-soldiers. Which sucks because, as far as I know, I'm the only one.

I'd tried to get G-Force on comms, but our systems were satellite based, or line of sight. Down here, they were utterly useless. I could only hope he and Sumo were nearing the surface.

Ahead, the darkness became fuzzy and indistinct, and slowly it gave way to the glow of a flickering, sickly, green light in a metal cage mounted on the wall beside a big metal door.

Really? Billions spent in research money, and this was the best lighting you could come up with? Hell, I bet the Holiday Inn down the road has better emergency lighting.

The door was a massive ugly piece of metal, easily a foot and a half thick. It was solid and as impenetrable as a vault door. Beside the odd colored security light was a bio scanner for entry. I was certain Ada could bypass it, but that was not going to be necessary. The massive door was already cracked open, and the remnants of a bloody arm were hanging through the opening.

The foul-smelling air was much worse here—this was the source. Even with my suit's filters, the stench was strong enough that I had to consciously force the gag reflex back down.

I pulled the door, and it smoothly opened. The thing lying just inside was very dead. I think it had once been a man. But it was impossible to tell. The arm did not go with the body, unless he'd originally had three, which, as I considered it, wasn't totally out of the question.

The body was shredded with deep wounds which had flayed the muscle right down to the bone in various places. Other wounds were scorched, the flesh blackened to a crater of red meat seared by something hot and deadly. The body was swollen, and just under the skin a spider web of purplish-black veining showed, the putrefaction process having had days to dissolve the tissues and horribly swell the corpse.

The more prominent thing was the head... it had none. The shoulders ended in a very clean, very precise line of flesh that seemed to have been removed with surgical precision.

"Jesus," I said. "Did the battle bots do this?"

Ada said nothing. I was beginning to seriously wonder if Voss had some sort of leverage over my built-in AI. It was definitely something I was going to find out... if I survived, that is. And if Sumo didn't kill her when he tracked her down.

"Hello, Warrior."

I tore my eyes away from the body, my light barely penetrating the darkened space ahead.

I knew that voice.

CHAPTER
SEVENTY-EIGHT

"My God," I whispered.

I moved deeper into the room; more bodies littered the floor. Bodies and... um... remnants of bodies. Overhead, lights flickered on as I moved closer. They glowed with the same sickly green as the one outside. The ceiling rose high above, fading out into shadows. I holstered my sidearm and switched to the MK4. The night optics on the scope lit up the room even better than Ada could currently do.

The lab was a charnel house of death and destruction. Desks, chairs, and more bodies littered the passageway. "I think we know where the missing staff are," I mumbled.

In the middle of it all was a man sitting awkwardly in a chair. As I moved in closer, who he was became clear.

"Doctor Reichert?" I asked.

I heard a rasping intake of air, the breath a ragged and jutting sound ripping out from the sickly green shadows.

"Yes, my boy. Please come closer."

The last time I had laid eyes on this man was over a year earlier, as I finished up the last of the tests required to be medically cleared to return to active duty. Tests given to make sure his enhancements on me had not produced any anomalous results.

I cautiously advanced on the man, increasingly doubting myself and my AI. She'd been strangely silent and hadn't giving me any advanced warning on immediate threats. Perhaps whatever Voss had done to her had left her damaged as well. Right now, though, I had other issues.

The smell of death was everywhere. I did not know how the man could still breathe this air. He sat partially slumped to one side in an old metal folding chair. Blood stains riddled the white lab coat, and one mangled arm rested in his lap.

"Love what you haven't done with the place," I said.

"Ah, Joseph, glad to see it is you."

The man seemed delirious. "What the hell happened here?" I asked.

"They're out...."

"What's out?" I demanded, but he simply shook his head.

"Everything... all of it."

He was in pain, more so than even me. The weird lighting made green, jewel-like beads of sweat glisten on his forehead.

"What happened here, Reichert? What were you people doing?"

If the man heard me, he didn't bother to answer. He was in his own personal hell. I placed a gloved hand against his neck and the suit's bio scanner gave me a basic diagnosis on him.

Low blood pressure, insufficient O^2 levels, multiple neuro toxins, and a rapidly spreading response to internal trauma. The tissue on his neck felt oddly detached. As I pressed harder, part of it seemed to slough away to the floor. I jerked my hand back.

If it caused him more pain, he didn't show it.

"Master Sergeant, you were my most fun creation."

I didn't enjoy thinking of myself that way, but it was clear that parts of me were designed or created in one of these war factories. Mine resembled a hospital, but the research came from somewhere like this. I was sure of that now.

"Doc... Magnus. I need the med packs. Or the compounding drugs. What do I need to do to stay alive?"

He smiled. "Don't worry about that, Kovach. I've taken care of everything."

What in the hell did that mean? "My body is shutting down; I can't even get out of this place."

"Is Voss with you?" he said weakly. "I was told by Nevis she would be here."

My face had to show my confusion and my irritation. Who the fuck was Nevis, and what difference did Voss make? "Yeah... she fled after we encountered your MechaDroids down in the basement."

He looked genuinely concerned, which was hard to imagine for someone in his shape. "You went there? Why on earth..."

A large crash behind me cut his words off.

"They are our Titan class mechs. If they are armed for war, we designate them by loadout." He wheezed but was clearly still proud of all his work here. "The staff here call them by several names, but most often it's Decimators. The operational ones simply do the heavy lifting down their in the storage bay. You should be fine as long as the others weren't activated." The man's voice was weak and distant.

My insides went watery as I recalled all of those alcoves lighting up around the enormous cavern. Inside each one, a Titan class Decimator was coming to life.

"Ada, can you do anything for him?" I asked silently. I wasn't exactly feeling compassion for the man but he could be useful especially if I didn't find the drugs.

"I'm sorry, Prowler, but no. I can ease his suffering if you wish."

I looked around the lab. More horrors awaited me, I was sure. "No." This man had helped create horrors. Yes, he had saved me, but only to let me suffer an even more painful death.

Somewhere below me, I heard the muffled thumps from the mechanical beasts hitting something solid. "They're making monsters." The thought came out, although it had been there the entire time. These were not war machines; this was something else entirely. Of late, I've come to realize that when it comes to keeping in front of the global arms race, there is virtually no line of research that's definitively off limits. So, without government oversight, where had the twisted minds here at Hammer Industries gone? What's worse, I was recognizing some of the experiments going on here as things Banshee had recovered from mission raids. Illegal shit that Space Force Drop teams had been sent in to shut down. Missions that ended my friends and nearly me.

The sounds behind me were growing closer. Doctor Reichert's head lolled to one side, unconscious or dead. I didn't shed any tears. My fingers searched his pockets removing a key fob, ID badge, and a small black hexagon that felt like marble or onyx. I pocketed it all and moved past him and toward the flickering green-lit walls.

The massive chamber was different. It looked more organic as if it had simply grown out of the earth. It also had a definite Gigeresque quality of ridges, coils and spikes that immediately reminded me of the alien movies my dad was addicted to. Even in 2D those things gave me the creeps. It must have stretched hundreds of yards under the abandoned industrial park. The ceiling was at least twenty-five feet high, supported by large polycrete pillars a good five feet across. I pushed past another steel door, just as massive as the first. There were racks of computers—the high-end kind. I knew they would use supercomputers for whatever genetic mapping and editing was going on here. There were tables filled with unknown scientific equipment, and a dozen stainless-steel dissecting tables. On one was a clearly mechanical limb, but attached to it were muscles and tendons that looked clearly human. There were also more bodies in this room.

Many, many more bodies.

Like in the prior chamber, most appeared human, and none of these were whole. Legs and arms, ragged torsos, bodiless heads lay scattered across the floor.

I stood there, aghast at the scene. I'd gone into battle in some of the worst hellholes on the planet. I'd come face to face with my share of humanity's worst. People who would do anything for money or to expand their ideology, but this was worse than any of the things our enemies had ever cooked up. I was appalled at the science and couldn't wrap my head around the slaughter. What had done this?

But then, my eyes were drawn to the far wall. Even with all the death, the smells, and the gruesome tableau of horror in every direction, how could I not look? How could anyone not stare at what was there?

Aisle upon aisle of large transparent cylinders, each a dozen feet high and as thick as a dining room table. All filled with a green, algae-colored liquid that smelled vaguely of ammonia and death.

Most of the tanks were otherwise empty. In some, the contents had gone dark, and my light wouldn't penetrate. But in others, creatures floated inside. These could have been humans at some point. The heads, arms, and feet were clearly something else now. They were all naked, powerfully built with bulging muscles under a skin that looked oddly artificial. Each arm ended in a long appendage that ended in a claw, or more accurately, a blade. A label at the top read FU-Y288. In my mind, they instantly became known as Furies.

They floated in the green liquid; cables ran down and attached to the connections buried in the creatures' skulls and spines. I froze as one of them twitched. It wasn't dead. The interface at the base of its neck activated, and I could see a faint blue glow under the skin radiating down from the base of the brain stem to the spinal cord. The device was not unfamiliar to me. It was exactly the kind they added to me when I was augmented with Ada.

"This is me, would be me," I said out loud.

"It is not you, Joe."

Ada's voice surprised me. It had been so long since she had done anything approaching a conversation.

"What is it then?" I asked.

"I'm still processing. There is an enormous amount of data in these computers. Some of it I can access. I believe they were using a new form of transformational genetics to create augmented life forms."

"How...for what purpose?"

"War would be my assumption. Transformational genetics is useful in searching for methods of changing specific DNA and essentially rebuilding it so that a new custom-made code can be developed."

She paused as I moved in closer to one of the tanks. A female with dusty rose-colored skin peered out through the glass.

"I am detecting something else, Joe. They are using XNA."

"I remember that term from that earlier mission. As in no source code?" I asked, my voice rising in pitch. The female suddenly kicked out, causing a deep thump to sound through the room. I jumped back and likely pissed myself just a bit. These things were horrendous but oddly mesmerizing to look at until I saw the first one with an open mouth. It was just a gash with thick rubbery lips, between which I could see row upon row of dagger-like teeth. Instead of a tongue, undulating waves of tentacles lined the mouth. Once they bit down, I knew getting away would be impossible.

"Artificial or synthetic DNA," Ada continued. "Meaning they don't have to combine existing species to make their creations. They can design one from scratch. Each of these seems similar but different, as if they are iterations on a common baseline of XNA coding. They can experiment freely, picking out the most desirable characteristics."

"Shit..." I let that one just hang there for a moment.

The Furies I could see were indeed all slightly different, with scaly skin that ranged from an emerald green to a deep purple. As they moved, the colors seemed to vibrate and shift to other iridescent tones. Then one stretched its limbs, which caused a row of hidden spikes along the curve of the back to arch up. The things looked lethal but still mesmerizingly elegant.

This place was evil. Not satanic evil, no possessed or inhabited but just devoid of anything remotely human. As if someone had bleached away everything but the pure essence of life and then decided what components to keep and what to discard. Idly I thought that mankind had been destined to the discard pile.

CHAPTER
SEVENTY-NINE
BANSHEE

"I've lost touch with Prowler and G-force," the ship's AI informed Lieutenant Riggs. "Telemetry and comms are both offline. They are on a sublevel of the Hammer facility."

Bayou tried hard to stay on task. Yes, she was busy looking for a proverbial kitten in a tree, but it was important to Kovach and therefore important to Banshee. Ada had passed along the video of her own sister, but she would have to deal with that later. The world was shit and maybe saving one kid would help balance things — at least a little. Still, she was glad she got the autopsy report to Joe; that might help him in that damn place. He needed to know these creatures were based on Hammer Industries' biological patents.

The TriCraft settled in directly over the roadway. Bayou, Priest, and Halo exited in a staggered defensive line. She hurried down the hill, following the marker in her heads-up display. Activating external comms, she called for the boy, then the dog. The target location was near the bottom of a deep ravine. She saw the bicycle first, the wheel bent sideways, and the frame mangled beyond repair.

Bayou's heart sank as she pieced together what must have happened. She glanced nervously back up at the towering hill they had just flown over. The downhill had to be nearly a half mile at a good nine percent incline. *This kid had some nerve to take that on an old bike.* Then she remembered what was on the other side of that mountain and the bodies at the top. Lux knew he'd had no choice.

"Lux, can you hear me?"

Bayou fine-tuned her battle suit sensors but picked up nothing, no kid, no dog, no sounds of life even. She pulled the bike out and saw blood covering one of the handlebars and a bright red smear of it across the faded pink seat. That was when she heard a soft whimper.

Minutes later, she emerged carrying the puppy. The animal's limp body felt like nothing in the warriors' arms, but she treated it like a fallen comrade, passing it off to Halo, who rushed it up the embankment and inside the stationary dropship. Seconds later, Carol came down the ramp, jumping the last few feet to the road.

"I'm sorry, nothing but the dog. Help me look," Bayou offered. She didn't want the civilian out here, but she was trying hard to put herself in the mother's place. What would she do to save her own child? If she ever could have had one.

"There's blood on the bike? Do you think he was..." Carol couldn't finish the sentence and Bayou preferred not to share her theory. There was no body, so the crash must not have been fatal.

"Packer, give me a perimeter sweep, all life signs," she ordered.

"Yes, Chief."

The ship's systems were more sensitive than her suit's and located higher up, so they could see farther.

"May have something, a faint trail slightly warmer than the surroundings, sending to you now."

Bayou studied the image and agreed it was better than anything she had.

Minutes later, they were all back aboard and drifting just over the treetops on a slight southwesterly course, following the meandering trail indicated on the infrared scope. It might simply be more deer or a bear, but the size of it suggested something large, much larger than a young boy. Bayou had a bad feeling.

∾

The call from Gi was garbled, but the context was clear enough. He and Kovach had gotten separated, and they were under intense enemy fire.

What enemy?

Bayou eyed the IR scope; they were hunting for a kid while the rest of their team was engaged. She needed to be there; this was a lost cause. "Packer, lay in a course to Gi's location, expedited routing."

"That's going to be a high-g ride LT. Short geo-hops are the worst for a beast like this."

She knew it was going to be tough. The gravitational dampers cut in, making the ride to orbit gentler than an elevator, but when you added lateral movement at the speeds the TriCraft reached, you began encountering inertial shearing forces. Forces more than what the dampeners could handle and rather unpleasant for humans, too. From across the flight deck, the mother made eye contact. Bayou knew she understood, but the anger and frustration were clear on the woman's face.

They would be abandoning her son to whatever came across those mountains. After the kid had somehow survived the fucking apocalypse on his own for weeks, salvation would evaporate just when it was so close. She heard a mewling whine from the puppy. *Goddammit.* Debra hated being put in this position.

"Course plotted and ready to execute," the pilot said.

"Hold! We have something," Halo called out.

"Belay that jump," Bayou yelled. "Show me."

Lux was aware of the movement, but very little else. His head jostled from one side to the other, and he smelled something foul. He coughed, only to feel every bone in his face ache.

Where was Junie?

He tried to open his eyes, but they seemed almost glued shut. He struggled, and painfully, one slowly opened. He saw only blackness. It wasn't dark out—no, something was covering his face. Lux attempted to move the blindfold, only to find his arms wouldn't move. They were lashed together behind his back. He remembered Mister Bill's warning about 'bad' people. He was lying on something hard; it was moving, and he was a prisoner. He'd made a mistake, and now the bad people had him.

The men. The hunters from the top of the hill. It had to be them.

The thought hit him hard; he thought he'd gotten away, the puppy and him, but something had gone wrong... a crash, a tree coming at him fast, then pain and nothingness. He tasted vomit and knew he'd been sick. Now he wanted badly to wash his mouth out.

"Not good, Lux, not good at all," he whispered to himself.

He'd been through some tough times the last few weeks, but this one trumped them all. What would they want with a kid? His pack had a few things in it, but they could have just taken that. He didn't understand. Of course, he didn't understand grown-ups that well, anyway. Marcie always tried to explain things to him, but it rarely made sense. Like when his dad and mom used to fight, which was about nearly everything. It always seemed to end up with his mom hitting the end button on the screen and burying her head in her hands. The tears always came, and there was nothing he could do to stop them. Deep down, he always felt like it was his fault. The arguments always seemed to start with something to do with him.

Lux struggled with the bindings, but the rope seemed to be around his wrist and another higher, around his elbows. He tugged the arms backward and felt his legs move as well. They tied his arms to his feet? *That's weird.* It almost didn't feel like rope. His fingers brushed over the thin, hard strands. Some kind of wire. Even if the men had not found the knife in his pocket, he wouldn't be cutting through this stuff.

Man, his jaw hurt, and he had a monster, gigantic headache. It was so bad he was having trouble concentrating on what he needed to do next.

"Oh, you're awake," a voice said from behind him. "You whacked the hell out of 'em trees back aire."

The man's voice was odd, like a cartoon hillbilly, but even harder to understand.

"You coulda warned us about that shit coming," he yelled. Lux could tell the man was clearly angry. "My dad and my cousin Jessie..."

Lux couldn't hear all of what he said, but he got the feeling the man was alone and that he was somehow blaming Lux for what... the vines attacking? That made no sense, but clearly this man was ticked off. He knew firsthand that when people were hurting, they sometimes did stuff that made little sense.

The movement of whatever they were riding slowed, and the sound of the machine puttered to a stop. Lux felt hands on the wire restraints. He was lifted up and out by the wire, his arms pulling back painfully, causing him to scream in agony. He didn't want the man to hear him hurt. That's what gave bullies power, that was some of what Marcie had always told him. He gritted his teeth, flexed his tiny arm muscles and fought down the anger. He would find a way out of this. He had to get back to Junie and then somehow find his mom.

The man dropped him face down on the ground, then snatched the cloth bag off his head. The bag had been stuck with dried blood, which ripped open fresh wounds. Blood began seeping down Lux's face and into his eyes.

"Damn, that's gonna leave a scar," the man said, grinning.

He was skinny, but Lux couldn't tell his age or much else about him. He was probably one of the men on the hilltop, but he'd been too scared and going too fast to pay much attention.

"What do you want with me?"

The man's expression let Lux know he didn't really have a plan.

"Dunno, but it ain't gonna be good. You going to pay for not giving us any warning about what was coming."

Lux managed to rub his face on his shoulder, clearing one of his eyes a bit. They were in a clearing with a small house, or maybe just a barn. It was run down, not like the ones back home. He saw what must have been pens for pigs or something. It smelled, but then again, so did the man. The animals were making a lot of noises. It reminded him of all the ones fleeing the killer vines earlier.

"I... I'm sorry about your friends. I was just scared."

The slap surprised him. "You don't fuckin' talk about 'em... they is family. You... you ain't nothing. In fact, you less than nothing."

He dragged Lux across the rough ground; rocks and roots dug into his skin, but he choked back the sounds of that pain, too. The man pushed him up against a board fence. Lux heard the sounds of animals behind him. The grunts and squeals of hogs. That much he had learned in the last few weeks. He'd watched a wild hog in the woods chase down a possum and just trample it to death before feeding on it. Mister Bill had said that was where bacon came from, but he had a hard time believing it could be true.

"Food for my hogs, that's what I'll do with you. That way, I can get some use out of you. You feed them, and then they feed me. Poetic justice, I think it's called."

Lux felt the cold, wet snout of one animal pushing against his back through the fence. "No, mister, please!" He hated himself for begging, but the terror was taking hold. He saw no way out of this.

The man laughed as he picked Lux up like he was nothing and tossed him over the low board rails of the pen. "I'm gonna have fun watching this shit."

Lux looked up to see the hogs crowding around him, their mouths making horrible sounds. A large black one bit one of the others to get closer. Blood spouted from the other pig's neck. Lux felt something release inside and knew he'd wet himself. Mom would be mad, but it wouldn't matter, anyway. He heard the man laugh and then suddenly stop. The hunter's head had a black hole in the middle of it, and he slumped forward over the top rail of the pen, then tumbled noisily inside with the hogs.

Back behind where the man had been, a large black wall sat nearly motionless. *That hadn't been there a minute ago.*

All of the hogs moved over to investigate the new body, the one that always had brought them food. Now it appeared he was food. Lux's eyes moved behind the hogs' disgusting meal and back to the thing by the trees.

The black wall was moving closer. It must be some kind of ship, but it appeared to just be hanging there in the air.

"Lux!"

He knew that voice. He loved that voice. Then he heard a small bark. His eyes filled with tears.

CHAPTER
EIGHTY
KOVACH

Wispy, pale hair floated around the creature's inhuman face. Its eyes were half-open. There was an internal ring of white surrounding over-sized black irises. Scaled eyelids that seemed to shimmer with an iridescent hue. I could see the almost unmistakable human influence. The skeletal framework, the muscles and tendon layout beneath the strange skin, but where had these madmen gone from there? *Artificial DNA,* Ada had said. That seemed to indicate no limit to the madness they could build.

"So, they just designed these in a computer program or something? Match up the traits they want and presto, designer monsters?"

"That would be an imprecise analogy, but likely not that far off the mark," Ada replied. "Some of the files seem to indicate original source DNA was used, although the host subject's classification is very strange. It's completely unknown to me."

"Well, shit, so they may have modeled it after something else, some other creature?" I stepped back, taking in the entire scene at once. There were at least a few hundred tanks in here. Dozens of them were empty, the thick tubes shattered, the specimens' connections hung limply, their attachment points dripping oily blood.

"Christ on a bike," I whispered.

Knowing there was a connection between what they had done to me and these creatures pushed me onward. I needed to find something that would keep me alive. It had to be here. I felt myself taking stumbling steps like a man emerging from a coma. It was surreal; it was painful to consider... maybe I should just give up. Go quietly before...

I looked back through the adjacent chamber at the trail of dismembered bodies. "Is that my future?" Maybe Dad was right. There were things worse than death.

My hands grabbed the side of my head to block it all out. The smell, the sounds, the horror, and the pain. Yes, the pain was coming back stronger than ever.

Let me be clear on something. Pain is something I am okay with; it's part of my job description. I've been shot, stabbed, and partially run over by a truck. It all fucking hurt. That's just damage; that kind of pain I can pack-up until I'm either unconscious or the mission is over.

What my own body was doing to me is something altogether different. I'd been unable to describe it the first time I went through it, but let me assure you, it takes agony to all new levels of outrageous fun. Right now, I felt like someone was shoving a glowing, hot rod through my intestines while simultaneously flaying the skin from my bones. Now, I had a glimpse of what I might have been or maybe still would become. Could that be what the drugs are stopping, a complete metamorphosis? I briefly considered going back to rouse the doctor and make him answer my goddamn questions.

There was going to be a serious butcher's bill coming due for what was going on down here. And I thought I knew who was going to do the settling. This place, this tech, was an abomination. I was an abomination, and today we were all going to be destroyed. I slammed a chair against one of the tubes. It simply bounced off. The damn thing was solid. I picked up a piece of one of the shattered ones. "Armorglass."

"How do we destroy this place?"

"That would be in direct violation of Alliance Uniform Military Code of Conduct number 108," Ada stated.

"Screw that. This isn't government property," I yelled.

She continued, "Also, destroying the containment vessels might not be wise, Joseph. That appears to be how the first ones were able to escape and kill the staff."

I took a moment to look over at the empty tubes and realized she was right. Some of those units had fractures, perhaps where chunks of the ceiling had crashed into them, allowing the liquid inside to drain out. Others appeared to have been smashed from the inside.

"Well, shit... Ada, tell me you have something. What can I do to bring all this shit down?"

She never got a chance to respond, or if she did, I couldn't hear it. Up at the entrance came an enormous crash as one of the Decimators bulled into the lab. The mechanical behemoth moved through columns and was collapsing the ceiling like it was tissue. Its head was flattened, and I could see a ring of sensors; the damn thing could literally look in every direction at once and undoubtedly could see in every spectrum that I could. It briefly stopped in front of the chair where Doctor Magnus' body sat like a limp rag doll. It bent close, then stomped down with an enormous metal foot, leaving nothing but a grisly puddle of flesh and blood behind.

I may be wrong, but there seemed to be something oddly personal in the machine's actions. That thought had to wait as I was running now. I didn't have a destination; I was simply moving away from the threat. Yes, I am an enhanced soldier in an elite squad, but I have to balance my abilities against the realities of the moment. The reality right now was I was about to also get my ass stomped by a two-ton metal foot. I'd already seen what that could do to a body and preferred to go out on my own terms, thank you very much.

"Did I ever tell you why your mom had to change the drapes out in the bedroom?"

"Dad?" *What the actual fuck? How in the hell did he do this?* He could connect to me anywhere when the computer inside my own skull couldn't even reliably do it. "Not now, Pops."

"Yeah, I guess not. That one is probably still a bit salty for your innocent ears.

So, you having fun saving humanity?"

"Not really!" The fucking machine was smashing through rows of the glass tanks, spilling the mutant creatures onto the floor like commercial fishermen emptying their nets on the deck.

Pops continued, ignoring the sounds of destruction. "Hey, I'm all for saving humanity. It's the people I have trouble getting on board with. They just pretty much suck."

I didn't exactly disagree with that.

"You went down there, didn't you? To the sublevels at Ranier."

"Yes," I admitted, rounding a corner like a major league all-star rounding second base. I couldn't wait to hear how much of an ass reaming I was going to get for this stunt.

"And you lost your grandpa's truck. The sensor on it is showing up a hundred miles away from you."

Wait, that was what he was upset about? And... he had sensors on the truck and me? That would have been helpful to know yesterday. Several of the Furies were rising to their feet. Their bodies moved in ways that were very unhuman like and... well, just wrong.

I set up on one of the solid metal racks and clicked the selector on the Rattler MK4 to the plasma double flechette rounds. I took aim center mass on the first of the Furies and squeezed off a round, the familiar reverse pong echoing throughout the chamber.

"Oh, hell yeah, I know that sound," my dad shouted. "Get some!"

The round sizzled into the creature's flesh center-mass, then seemed to stop. The Furie looked down, seemingly more confused than injured by the plasma blast that should have sliced through its body like butter. It then raised its oversized head, centering its eyes on me. I'm no expert on reading alien expressions but, well... I think it might have been pissed.

"So, we're running, that's your plan."

"You're not here, Dad. It's a good plan," I panted.

"You remember when I told you not to go there? I know. I know, never listen to your father. Just like when you were five, and I told you not to put the fork in the outlet. Like a dumb fuck, what did you do?"

Something hit me from behind, sending me sprawling. I rolled out of the way as the creature slammed a claw down so hard the rock-hard floor shattered. I rolled up between two of the growth tanks and pulled my blade.

The Furie looked down at the weapon, then waved his own claw. The green light reflected off the chitinous blade, giving it an ethereal glow. Yeah, his knife was longer and looked way cooler than mine.

Maybe I shouldn't have shot him first. The smoking hole in his chest looked painful. I could understand why he was... agitated.

The creature clicked his claw closed, and I watched in horrific fascination as the curved blade-hand snapped closed into a serrated groove on the other side of the claw. It was damn fast. Like Mantis shrimp level of speed. I was sure if I watched this at super slow-mo speed later, it would still be too fast to see. Note to self, don't get between the claws of a Furie.

I made a careful show of sheathing my Heidelberg blade, at the same time drawing my sidearm and shooting it in the face.

That did some damage.

Not enough. The thing backhanded me so hard I defied gravity and sailed across the room. The back side of that claw hand is no better than the front. I could see my rifle but barely made it a step before the thing's freakishly long arm snapped out directly toward my head. The powerful claw snapped just in front of my face as I went low and slid under the blow. I punched up into what I hoped was a groin as the fingers of my other hand found the familiar grip of the weapon. The Furie didn't even flinch. That punch would have laid a marine out cold, but it barely noticed. Grabbing up the MK4, I sent two more of the high-power rounds into the beast, staggering it back. God Almighty, these things were tough to kill.

"Try the legs," the voice in my head suggested.

My shoulders shrugged as if to say, 'Why not?' I shot at where a femoral artery in a human would be, and the thing dropped to a knee instantly. That was helpful knowledge. Then the damn Decimator stomped it. Just when I was about to learn some useful intel on the enemy, the damn battle droid smeared it into paste. I shot the Warbot in the face as well.

"That was stupid," I heard Dad say. Was he watching all this? He can see everything I just did? That scared me more than the twenty-foot android bearing down on me.

Then, my shoulder exploded into white hot, searing pain. Oh, yeah, they have lasers, of course they do. Earlier, when I compared the pain in my belly to a white-hot rod, yeah... I was full of shit. The real thing made me realize the error of that comparison. My suit's armor had dissipated little of the blast, and now I had a clean hole drilled through my shoulder.

Thankfully, it was not in my dominant arm. I fired off two of the plasma rounds before Ada switched to explosive projectiles. The Rattler seamlessly switched into rail-gun mode and sent its deadly barrage toward the hulking metal giant.

I would tell you in glorious detail of all the damage the rounds did, but my feet were determined to carry me in the opposite direction at an increasingly reckless level of speed. I heard it crash down behind me, which was a good thing, then I heard it crash again... which I took as 'less good.' The third crash let me know it was not down. It was pursuing.

"About the truck. You just going to leave it there?"

I wanted to give the old man some witty comeback, but I was too fucking scared and too damaged. A door flashed into view, and Ada alerted me it was stairs. I swung wide and entered it at a flat sprint, gaining three or four steps at a time. I heard the impact as the giant mech warrior slammed into the rock wall below where the door had been.

By the sounds of breakage below, I knew the one Decimator was not alone, and in the next few minutes the rest of the Furies would also be unleashed. Yeah, instead of destroying this place, I had freed all the freaky, murderous beasts, but hey, I was still alive, so that was a win, right?

So far, I had angered a horde of giant killer robots, unleashed a mutant army of alien looking monsters, and maybe killed the doctor that had saved my life. Anything else... oh, yeah, finding the lifesaving medicines had been a fail... an epic fail. Still, the day was young. What else might I fuck up?

"I'm calling a service—they can get the truck. Can't count on you for jack shit, Son. You're irresponsible."

The call ended. I held my arm as Ada did something to help dull the pain. Grunting, I placed one foot after the other. I needed to go find my dog and a way out of the fucking nightmare and go maybe find a quieter place to die.

CHAPTER
EIGHTY-ONE
BANSHEE

Banshee Team dropped out of a darkening sky like a yoyo on a string. Packer had been right; the ride hadn't been smooth. The deep ache in her bones was unsettling, and Bayou could see the effects on Carol and the boy had been worse. For his part, though, Lux had been exuberant and for the most part, very healthy. His mother had held onto him constantly since being reunited. All the worry had drained from the woman's face upon seeing him there in that valley.

Bayou had treated his leg, a deep angry gouge that looked painful but seemed free of infection. She also gave him the meds for a concussion and closed the gash on his forehead. The kid had tons of questions, good questions, at least in her mind. She didn't know how the boy had been before the missiles fell, but she recognized he had the makings of a survivor. Could she have done what he did at that age? She doubted it.

The ship's AI plotted a rough course from the autocar's last known position and calculated Lux had traveled nearly sixty miles in just over four weeks. He'd told them about the family he'd been with for a good bit of that time. He was resilient, and his only worry had seemed to be about the dog and his mom.

Based on some descriptions Lux had offered and quickly cross-referencing the family names with public records, the ship's AI found the home of Bill and Laura Johnson. Packer had done a quick flyby of the rural neighborhood on his way to Rainier. As feared, the neighborhood had been swallowed up by the predatory vines. The ruins of demolished houses were the only thing visible. Lux had watched it pass by on the monitor, his face a solemn mask. Clutching the puppy to his chest, he let his mother pull him back into her arms.

"They're dead, aren't they?"

Carol was unused to this child; he was not the same as he'd been when she'd last seen him, but the same could probably be said of her. She thought of using some other euphemism, but the fire in her son's eyes let her know he didn't need shielding. The world is the world. He knew its horrors even better than her. She nodded.

"And Dad?" he asked, the puppy's tiny face scrunched up tightly into his own. Despite his strength and courage, Carol saw the eyes filling with tears and threatening to erupt.

She pursed her lips; she'd hated his dad but also had loved him once. That was how life was. Together, they had made this wonderfully strong, brave creation sitting in her lap. She gave a tiny nod. "Yes, the entire Atlanta metroplex was destroyed." She studied him closely. "I'm sure it was quick."

The boy looked away, then nodded. "That's good, I guess."

"On the deck in thirty," the dropship pilot called out.

Bayou pulled herself away from watching the pair and returned to battle mode. None of this was by the books anymore. Survival was the new mission, and getting her people back was the only thing that mattered. Halo and Priest flanked her at the edge of the ramp, awaiting her signal. They checked helmet seals, then lowered visors. On Packer's signal, she pressed the switch on an overhead panel to lower the door. The ground was coming up fast. She could see traces of the weird vines and what looked like an abandoned industrial area.

The ramp stopped just as the craft came to an abrupt stop two meters off the ground. Banshee was on the ground and headed to preassigned coordinates in under four seconds; the craft was out of site far overhead in six.

Priest located the transport hidden off to one side and pulled the Wulf into the compound. Bayou wanted its firepower in close, plus it was a safe refuge if it all went to shit. She tapped her comms.

"Banshee actual to Banshee-6. G-Force, you copy?"

She heard a hiss, then nothing. She tried Prowler and got the same.

"Looks like we're going to have to do this the old-fashioned way, boys. Let's break out the party favors."

They were above the landing pad. She knew this was where her other two had entered the base. They had the footage for them until they went inside. While Halo and Priest keyed the massive doors, Bayou studied the surrounding area. The woods had a blue hue that took her a moment to understand. It was the stinging vines; Thunder Vines was what Kovach had called them. They were surrounding the perimeter of the complex, but only a few were in the clearing. *Why?*

"We're in, Boss."

The down ramp showed a darkened space at the bottom. Her suit picked up a foul smell and faint sounds, both of which evoked a primal urge to flee. *Dammit, Joe, what have you gotten us all into?*

"Bring in the Wulf."

Water dripped from cracks opening overhead. Gi stepped around the debris with the precision of a cat stalking its prey. Ahead, a flash of movement showed he and Sumo were thinking the same way. That woman had led them to this sub-level, but he hadn't seen her again. She was cunning and capable. A small voice whispered warnings in the back of his brain. He knew it could be a trap. Still, he had to follow orders.

Most of his missions had been straight combat. Suppression skirmishes when one faction or another started getting out of hand. He'd heard some tales of Banshee, Red-7, Viper, and X-Squad. Shit, who hadn't? He'd always assumed they were largely fabrications. Now... he wasn't so sure. This op showed all the signs of the world coming apart at the seams and all of its buried secrets about to spill out across the floor.

Ahead, Sumo stopped at a cross tunnel and waited for Gi's signal before moving on. The dog started, then stopped, his enhanced hearing picking up on a faint sound. Gi followed the dog's look, and he, too, heard it. Music, very faint and very poor quality, like a scratchy record played on an old-world phonograph. There had been one in the village where he'd grown up. The song was in French and very old and very much out of place in this weird scenario. Slowly, his suit's audio picked up enough of the faint music to offer a title and artist. Edith Plaf's *Non, Je ne regrette rien*. He knew enough French to understand the significance of the song. "No, I do not regret anything." He shuddered involuntarily. Whatever happened here had been done on purpose.

Gi slipped into the next room to clear it before moving deeper. The music was louder here. It took several minutes to understand what he was seeing through the night optics view his HUD was showing. This was a weapons cache of sorts, but some, hell, most of these he'd never seen before. Instruments of battle that he couldn't understand how to even hold, much less use. Giant curved- edge bladed weapons with no safe place to hold. Heavy clubs that must have weighed a few hundred pounds. But others appeared better suited for a human warrior to wield. If this was a production facility, who were they building these for? Then he knew the question should be 'what?' not who.

He cleared the room and was about to exit when two items caught his eye. Picking up an enemy's weapon was rarely a smart move. This one, though, he knew, might come in handy. He marveled at the exquisite craftsmanship. It seemed to hold a place of honor among all the other killing devices here. He reconfigured the back slots on his armor and reverently raised it, felt its balance, its heft, then dropped the sword into the slot on his back. Swords were always associated with the Japanese, but they had fascinated him since childhood, and he'd been a master by his early teens. He moved to the opposite side of the case and retrieved its twin. Seconds later, he left the room with slightly more confidence that he would find success this day.

Gi and Sumo had Voss cornered in a series of corridors that seemed to go on forever. The constant tapping was a constant pressure on his concentration. He'd hated to leave his partner, his commander, behind, but the stakes on this mission seemed much higher than simple survival. The dog charged ahead in a classic pincer movement. Gi smiled and moved to counter it on the woman's opposite side.

Instead, something peeled off the wall and seemed to fly at him. He pivoted and sliced down expertly with the sword. It felt natural to grab the weapon, and it was perfect for this space. The creature literally seemed to disappear into nothingness. That had to be the Wraith that Kovach had described. He searched both ways up and down the rough-hewn tunnel. A scrape of foot on rocks caused him to duck just as something fast impacted the wall where he'd just been.

Gi did not panic. That was one thing the ROK got out of its operators. You faced every battle head-on. The shape in front of him was not the woman. It slowly resolved itself out of shadow into a horrific creature, more nightmare than reality. The thing was only vaguely humanoid, although the face was clearly that of a man. He looked Middle Eastern, with dark hair and a beard. The arms were mechanical; Gi could see the artificial tendons, the joints, even an odd kind of fluid running through small pipes, not blood... not even red. The chest looked more like that of a bear, or perhaps a gorilla. It was too large, too dark to be anything natural.

His soldier's mind tried to put all the separate parts into some logical assembly and utterly failed. Clearly, this thing should not exist. He noticed an ID badge clipped to the damn thing's chest fur. It was part of the staff... or once was. The face on the plastic card matched, so it hadn't just taken it from a body. He heard metal on leather and saw the beast had drawn a knife from a hidden sheath. Gi knew he should switch to his Rattler but already had the sword, and it still felt right.

The man-beast smiled an evil looking expression, then it charged. The Korean had to make a split-second decision on whether to stick to defense or attack. He chose to attack, then opted to go low as the mechanical arm came flying toward his throat, knife-hand expertly extended. Gi slid through the creature's legs, slicing up and into the thing's groin with the sword.

The beast looked down; blood was cascading over a pair of relatively normal looking legs. It did not seem to register the injury with any great concern. It spun and attacked once more, this time wiser to its prey's tactics.

Gi parried the attack, then let it move in as close as he dared, feigning weakness and emboldening the creature to make a mistake. He knew if this battle lasted ten more seconds, he was doomed. No way he would win, no matter how good his skills. He gripped the sword in a crossed two-hand stance with the blade near his own ear. Without looking down, he knew the instant the thing had over committed. It had crossed some invisible line on that dirt floor, now within reach of the long sword. It would never be able to move out of the way fast enough.

The movement of the sword in Gi's hands was little more than a whispered blur of motion. Never had he fought with such purpose or precision. He sliced; he did not plunge or hack. The thing was so massive that he might break the blade or get it lodged in the beast's thick hide.

One of the mechanical arms struck him from his undefended side, sending him sprawling across the floor, but Gi could see the damage had been done. This was not to be a death by a thousand cuts, but more like seven or eight, all hitting very specific targets on the damn thing's body. It fell to one knee, the mechanical arms going post rigid to hold the body upright even as the man... or thing, inside finally died. The song was just reaching its crescendo in the background. "Truly epic day," the Korean said aloud.

He turned and walked away, keeping the sword out in front. The heads-up display was useless down here, as no battle data was coming in. Still, his instincts as a hunter hadn't ever let him down. He heard the dog woof from a corner just ahead, readied his weapon again, did a low dash around the corner, and came face to face with Sumo.

"Where is she?"

The dog looked just as confused, his head cocked to one side, and then he looked at the wall to their right. The tapping was coming from the other side of the wall.

"You think she went there?"

The Korean officer didn't know what was making that sound, and he was less than eager to find out. A scream came from behind them, several hundred yards back in the direction from which he had just come.

"That was her." He was about to order the dog to pursue, but Sumo was already on his way. Gi ran after him. The dog was a truly capable soldier and was quickly earning the man's respect.

CHAPTER
EIGHTY-TWO
KOVACH

Ada spoke softly, "Whatever's in those tanks, that does not need to get past you, Prowler."

She was worried about the Furies. *What about the Decimators?*

"It would be bad. They are mutants designed for war. Seeing what happened to the staff, I think we can assume they are going to be a problem."

You did see when the first of the Decimators crashed through that adjoining wall, taking out at least a dozen of the tanks, he said internally. Yeah. Containing them wasn't going to be easy. I could still see the glistening bodies of the creatures slithering across the floor.

"Did those things start out as human?"

"They were likely test subjects," she said. "The ones that were not completely synthetic."

"What, prisoners, captives?

"Possibly—or volunteers," she said.

"Why?"

It was a stupid question; I was just trying to catch my breath and give her most recent injection of painkillers a minute to work. I knew why. They did it because they could and because no nation on Earth can face the Alliance military in a stand-up fight. Unconventional tactics called for new and unconventional countermeasures The other side ups the ante. We follow suit, or maybe this time it was our side that upped it. Whoever 'our side' was. As Bayou had confirmed, this shit was all Hammer Industries designs.

The thing was, I knew a lot about what the other side had. Hell, I had busted into many of those facilities. This shit seemed decades beyond anything I'd seen that our enemies had. The magnitude of these biological and technological advances seemed all wrong. The equilibrium was off, but then again, someone had just punched this country right in the fucking face... hard. Maybe these... weapons were exactly what was needed.

Problem was, the weapons were eating the creators. Correction... past tense. They had eaten all of them already, now they were starting on their dead and looking for any other snacks that might be nearby. To make matters worse, the monolithic Warbots simply stomped or drove over whatever was in their way.

"There has to be a way of controlling them, the Furies and the Decimators. These scientists would have had a final option to prevent a breach. Find it, Ada."

I heard a sigh from my AI. Not one of someone who is tired or even sad, but one filled with pity.

"I don't think they got that far, Joseph."

I was moving again, slipping around an office that had to be Reichert's. It was pompous and arrogant, just like the man. Filled with mahogany shelves and walls full of awards. My hand ran across a massive live edge desk made of the same material. I missed my workshop. I missed touching simple things like wood without fearing it was going to try to kill me with poison darts.

My legs buckled, and I went down hard. Pain, fatigue, a body that was giving up. I heard and saw the mayhem that was heading my way. The horror I knew would haunt me and every other living being if these things ever got out of this underground crypt of evil.

My hand grasped futile for the edge of the desk. Lifting my weight back up to rest on the surface. I saw a scientific journal. I thumbed through page after page of the vibrantly illustrated manuscrip with strange sketches, odd notes that refereed to DNA grouping and names that sounded both fantastical and terrifying. I flipped the journal through multiple times so Ada could record it then slid the whole thing into my storage pack.

There is a special place in hell for people who create monsters. Every kid who is old enough to talk knows that it is wrong. It's evil, it's the way to the dark side. Those instincts aren't wrong. What I saw out there on that floor could wipe the rest of humanity off the map.

I couldn't let that happen. This might be my last day alive, but I was going to do my best to give them hell before I went. Something unexpected calmed me. Not the absolute truth that this was my last day on Earth. Not the fact that I had a team somewhere out there that could not only avenge me but continue this horrible mission for humanity. Not even the ever-crazier one-liners from dear old Dad. What came to me in that moment of absolute darkness were the words of my senior drill instructor at Ranger school. An absolute beast of a soldier made from slabs of muscle forged into an incredibly solid frame.

It was on one particularly rough day of Ranger training. My face buried in steaming hot red Georgia mud, bugs eating me from every corner of my wrecked body, exhaustion that would have made the Virgin Mary weep. The DI knelt beside me and bent his head close to my ear. Sergeant Adders, in a voice that did not match his outward appearance at all, said, "Rangers, lead the way."

It wasn't shouted; it was not boastful... it was not a question. Simple statement, simple fact, and I had carried those words carved into my very soul that afternoon and through nightmare after nightmare since.

I said the words—said them out loud. "Rangers, lead the way!" I needed that warrior's strength right now, his fighting spirit, because my own was broken and lying somewhere below in a crumbling elevator shaft surrounded by monsters.

Yeah, it was cliché; it was corny, and no, I was not instantly imbued with super fighting strength. I did, however, finally manage to get back to my feet. Wobbly... sure. Sometimes... most times, that is what really makes the difference between winning and losing, just getting back up one more time than your opponent.

My opponent today was not as impressed with my resurgence as I was spotted almost immediately. One of the Furies leapt on me from somewhere high above. The impact nearly dropped me, but my battle suit's internal stabilizer kept me upright. The scythe-like arm was closing down on my left arm, my injured arm. I twisted my wrist, causing waves of agony to burst in my brain. By doing so, though, I brought the thickest part of the armor, where my forearm bone was, inside the creature's grip. Something clawed at my side, causing me to howl in pain. I twisted and heard something snap. I wasn't sure if the sound came from me or the Furie.

I felt its vice-like grip begin to crush the composite armor, knowing that once the suit failed, that bladed hand would cut through my wrist like soft butter. For her part, Ada was throwing everything she could into the fight. She enacted an electrical discharge from special panels built into the suit that should have fried the beast. It had no effect. She emitted high-intensity strobe lights that turned the cavern into a horror movie scene, with each of us appearing to move in a horrifically comical stop motion. Nothing helped until she started going through an audio spectrum.

Having a super intelligent computer in your head does come with a few nice advantages. She had evaluated every nuance of the creature in the files. Apparently, there were many iterations of the Furies that the staff science team had undoubtedly tested for weaknesses and tweaked the genetic code to eliminate them one after another. Still, Ada assessed all of this data in seconds and produced an oscillating sound that was thankfully not within the hearing range of humans, although I could faintly detect it. I am, after all, not entirely human. Not original equipment human, at least. It reminded me of the music I had heard earlier.

Unfortunately, it didn't cause the creature to race back into the shadows or make its head explode. It did suddenly change its attention, its large dark eyes furtively glancing around the space, following the sound waves as they bounced off solid surfaces. It seemed confused. The one advantage it gave me was the grip on my wrist loosened.

Not by much... just enough.

I whipped my Heidelberg blade out of its sheath and across the Furie's throat as I jerked my trapped arm free, doing my best to ignore the obvious damage it was inflicting for the moment. A gout of very red blood spouted out of the thing's throat, covering my visor and much of my suit. I threw the giant body off in disgust.

As suddenly as one was gone, another took its place. This one tried to bite me... on the neck. This bite had force, too. Those lips that looked so wrong held fast to the collar of my Rivex underlayer as the thing kept trying to get through my crunchy outer shell to the gooey, nougat center underneath.

As my shoulder ruptured and more bones broke, that part of me that had been a warrior got pushed aside. In that instant, Joseph Kovach stopped being a man. A man would fail at what came next. I knew it; the monster knew it. Instead, I became the thing I needed to be in order to get out of this fucking fight alive.

The rage, the fury in my own mind surfaced and exploded. I, too, became that thing I feared most. I was a monster.

With a growl that even Sumo would have appreciated, I flung the thing off of me. "Suck on something else, asshole!"

Instantly, it was coming back to finish me. I pivoted and launched myself, driving a mechanically augmented knee up into its groin. I followed that up with a hard elbow into the thing's ugly ass face. I hit it so hard I could feel the cartilage tearing and bone splintering.

Great gouts of blood were covering us both. I knew we both had significant damage, but I could see his. Mine was contained for the moment, packed down and waiting for later. Ada could still help use the suit where the man was too broken, but she was not me. I was in the zone; my purpose was singular. Fiery pain radiated throughout my body. Still, it was fighting back. It was as unconcerned with its own safety as I was. I reached for my blade, but it had disappeared in the fight. What I saw was a piece of the other Furie's claw still buried deep into my suit. Pulling it out, I realized it was not just embedded in the suit. I felt every serration as it carved its way back out of my abdomen.

I stomped back over to the creature, its back spines radiating menacingly. It leapt just as I drove the fragment of sharpened claw deep into one of its hideous eyes, bursting it into brown goo. Then I launched a hip throw, launching its writhing body back into the darkness.

My left arm hung loosely, covered in blood and virtually useless, the wrist and hand feeling like they were still being gnawed off by an alligator. My sidearm was gone, as was my knife. I had no idea where.

Movement caused me to refocus on the thing. For some reason, the other mutants had not attacked, instead letting this one do their bidding. Now it was struggling to get off its back. Its gruesome head turned its one working eye toward me, and I could feel its hatred radiating from yards away.

My eyes only saw red, hatred, anger. I ran at the thing that lay on that floor. Its claws were raised, maybe to shield its one remaining eye, maybe as a sign of surrender. I did not care; I was offering no truce in this battle. Monsters don't get the luxury of mercy. These things were bio-engineered killers. They had murdered every other living thing in this room. To be honest, this one had come late to that party. It had probably just been awakened by a giant robot slamming into its watery bed. Now it was vulnerable and being attacked by something it did not understand, something that ignored its remarkable power.

The weakened Furie raised a damaged claw and made a piteous mewling sound. I looked at it in disgust. Then stamped down hard on its misshapen head.

"Ranger's lead," I said, turning away. The others seemed to reappraise the lone human as more of a potential threat than they first considered. Somewhere deeper in the cavern, I heard more of the Warbots entering the space. I recovered my weapons with my one good arm and started moving along the shadows of the far wall. My adrenaline levels were receding, and in their place, pain and exhaustion rushed back in. It was time to make a tactical advance to the rear. Right. Retreat!

"Exit twenty meters to your right."

I turned and ran, only realizing minutes later that had not been Ada's voice in my head. As I pulled the door open, another of the creatures slammed into it from the other side. I pushed it back solidly against the wall until I heard something crunch and saw more blood seeping under the door.

Behind me, more of the Furies were joining the chase now. *Time to move your ass, Kovach.*

"Frags and smoke," I yelled.

Ada automatically deployed the mini grenades stored in specialized slots along the edge of my rear armor.

I slammed the heavy door, then braced my body against it. The sound was muffled, but the concussive wave hit the steel door like a truck. It bowed in as the frame deformed under the intense blast. Still, I heard the sounds made by the mutant beasts as their hatred of me grew in intensity to match the name I'd given them. "I don't think I'm going to be on their Christmas card list."

CHAPTER
EIGHTY-THREE

I took the stairs, as that was the only thing on the other side of that door. The shoulder where I'd been shot and the deep abdominal wound had joined my useless arm in the serious damage column. The suit's internal muscles enhancements gave me some movement but only with excruciating levels of pain. All of this on top of the fact my body was fighting against itself as my organs were being attacked by my own immune system. Ada helpfully displayed my body temp in my health meter. Currently, it was at 102 and climbing, although I knew that the augmented immune systems in my body were still hard at work doing the jobs they'd been designed for. Rapid recovery, combat readiness, accelerated healing, and higher pain tolerances for damage were the only reasons I could still move.

At the next door, I could hear the now familiar tapping. Everything in me said, 'Do not open this door.' I knew nothing good would happen if I did, so I kept climbing. Next floor, housewares and ladies' lingerie... maybe not. The stairs ended, so I didn't have many options except to take door number one.

My pain and drug induced mental fog cleared momentarily as I took inventory of the space. "Who was that before, telling me where the door was?"

"The voice print matches that of the woman you know as Damiana Voss," Ada said.

"How did she do it? Is she still connected?"

"Unknown," was the simple reply. Also, why did Ada phrase it the way she did? 'The woman you know as...'

Whose side was that woman on? And *well, shit*, now I apparently have two assholes that could call me and track me whenever they wanted.

I opened the door onto a brightly lit corridor with doors on each side. The space screamed barracks to me, but that was probably a bias from my years on military bases around the world. I swear they all have that same green paint. You know, the same shade as sewer sludge if you shake it up a bit. I personally think they all also have the same smell. Too many sweaty bodies, testosterone, and hopelessness in a confined space.

I reloaded my weapons with fresh magazine charge packs, then peeked into a couple of the doors. Indeed, rows of bunks, all empty, common areas for toilets, and somewhere on this floor would be a galley and probably medical. I looked down; my left arm still dangled uselessly, blood dripping steadily from the gloved hand. Other parts of my body were in nearly as bad shape. Medical bay might be a worthy stop, but I didn't have the time. I instructed Ada to tourniquet the left arm and cauterize the wound. I braced myself as she did it, and mother!!!!...fuck, it hurt. Intense, but brief, heat seared my body closed in several places, including the claw stab wound in my gut. It stopped the external bleeding, but not much else.

As I entered another corridor, a sound caused me to bring my gun up. A door opened ahead of me, about twenty feet farther down. I could see rough walls and darkness behind as a friendly IR strobe blinked on in my HUD.

"G-Force?" I asked on comms.

The door opened wider, and he stepped out, followed closely by Sumo.

"Yes, Prowler. Good to see you again, my friend."

"Is that a sword?"

He nodded proudly, and I could see it was already stained with blood. Although, the man and my dog looked rather pristine, which made me feel both relieved and pissed off at the same time. He rushed over to assist me; he could see the damage and the pain etched across my face.

"I... I'm okay."

I waved him away, but I bent down and hugged the dog, who had been waiting patiently. Sumo knew me, knew the bravado was bullshit. I was certain he could smell the death hanging around me like vultures circling roadkill.

"Where's Voss?"

Gi looked pained. She had gotten away from him. I knew that had to chap his Asian ass, but she'd apparently gotten away from Sumo as well, and that is no simple task.

"I am here."

The voice was in my head and from somewhere in one of the rooms behind me. I was really tired of this woman fucking with us.

"Locate." I gave the command to both Ada and Sumo. The dog took off, knowing he was still on task.

I no longer trusted the voices I was hearing. That was when the lights went out. The silence was immediate and suffocating. The darkness was complete. But there was something in that darkness. Something evil, something that was hunting us. Something that had tasted my soul before.

Despite what people think, fear is a good thing to have, as long as it doesn't render you stupid or impede your actions. Fear sharpens your attention to needle points of focus that can mean the difference between winning or losing. Between living or not living. Some fears were common; I had gotten used to them over the years. Like doing the ballistic drop, still scared the shit out of me, but I knew it. We had made peace, and it hadn't killed me yet.

The fear I now felt was a more recent addition to my haunted collection. This fear was more acute, less apprehensive than a total loss of hope. It was unnatural, it was external. It was also fake.

I said the word aloud, hating the passivity of being right and knowing with total certainty that I was.

"Wraith."

~

Here's the thing: fear cannot kill you... not really. I guess if you had a weak heart or something, maybe it could, but for most of us, the only play it has is making you do something stupid or running away in terror. When you think about it, if you could weaponize fear, it would be a nearly perfect offensive armament. I was certain that was what the creature had done, and I assumed it, too, was a product of this hellish place.

The psionic waves affected something very primal and basic in us. I could feel my bladder trying to release. Every fiber of my being wanted to flee. My visor had automatically gone to night vision, and I studied Gi's face. He was standing a few feet away. If the man was feeling the same thing I was, he showed none of it.

I was a borderline quivering baby wanting to climb up in his momma's lap. The Korean looked like he was ready to order some Dim Sung and enjoy the afternoon. Dim Sung isn't Korean, is it? Shit, I always get those mixed up. I'm uncouth, but that's irrelevant because I did just piss myself. To be honest, in the battle suit, you are supposed to do it that way. It takes too long to get out of the damn thing for nature breaks, so I'm going to say it was just a convenient time to do it, not that I was fucking terrified and, well... you get the idea.

I motioned Sumo to stay close; Gi moved off to my weak side without being told. Good soldiers inherently seem to know where they are needed. My left arm was for shit, so that was my weak side now.

"What's the mission, Boss?"

I thought about that. Had there ever been a mission? "We get the fuck out of this place."

"Banshee Actual to Banshee-1."

"That you, Bayou?"

"On site and coming in, package is secure," she stated confidently.

"Have I mentioned how much I love you?"

"Not today, Boss, but the day is young."

I heard some intermittent gunfire over the comms.

"Hate to ask this, Prowler, but how do we determine friend or foe?"

I didn't know what she was encountering, but in my odyssey, back toward the surface, I'd adopted a new battle plan. One both my dad and most of his eighty's movie icons would have supported.

"If it moves, kill it."

Everything down here was designed to hunt, attack, or kill, and I wasn't even convinced I'd seen the entire product line yet. Maybe I should have picked up a brochure in the showroom.

"We have your beacon; Halo pegs you half a klick out and a hundred and fifty feet below the surface. What's your status?"

If she had my beacon, they had access to my transponder, which gave them every bit of info my suit had on me. Low on ammo, significant damage to both arms. Running a high fever. Body on the brink of total organ failure. If you saw all this on an autopsy report, you wouldn't be surprised.

"I am absofuckinglutely great, LT!"

And then my world disappeared in a blast of rock and metal. Not the massive arms of the Decimators. Instead, a cascade of a much smaller battle bot. An entire side wall of the corridor had given way, spilling them into the corridor. The opening was into one of the numerous caverns, and there, taking refuge on the far wall, was Voss. She looked straight at me, then pointed toward the left.

I had no time to consider what she was up to as the swarm of battle bots was coming at both Gi and me. Sumo was staying well out of reach. This was my first time seeing the damn things up close, and they looked about as friendly as a wolverine getting a razor blade enema. They were oddly angular. The sizes varied as did the appearance, but most were about the size of a crab, a crab with a front and middle limb that looked remarkably like a folded, old school razor blade.

As they extended the limb, the bladed edge reflected the light. What was it with these people and bladed weapons? The back legs were thick with bundles of what I guessed might be some sort of artificial tendons. It was obvious they could jump or push with those back legs while slicing down with the front. Only then did I realize the things also had other, smaller appendages that allowed them to spin in place or roll back over if they wound up on their backs. Then there was the constant drone of the tapping. Hundreds, no... more like thousands, all in nearly perfect horrific synchrony.

But it wasn't the sound or even the numbers that were so unnerving as much as their actions. Every few seconds, they would all pause and do the same motion at the exact same time. It was like a giant conga line of MurderCrabs. They jerked and swiveled in a deeply disturbing snap upward. Stop, jerk briefly to a halt, then pop back down. It was a well-planned showpiece of horror as they moved as a unified mass.

"What is this? What are they doing?" Gi asked. He was trying to grasp the danger and significance of the horde, as was I.

"Beats the fuck out of me. I think they used to call it the Macarena."

Somewhere inside my skull, I heard my dad start singing the damn song. Was he listening to everything now?

"Hey, Macarena!"

They had dark black, wedge-shaped heads and bodies that were more trapezoidal than anything else. I assumed the designers had a specific reason for the shape, but it was lost on me. The underside of most was a dull, unpolished, silver gray. Others were a blood red, and a few, toward the rear, seemed to have blue colored undersides. Some sort of rank? Different purposes? I did not know.

They didn't move fast; they didn't need to. Once they swarmed, there was nowhere to run.

"What's the play?"

I didn't bother looking at Gi. Shit, the good idea fairy hadn't paid me a visit. I was clueless. He started swinging with the sword. I dropped and started unleashing carnage rounds into them. Off in the distance, I heard even more of the things coming. They were breaching the walls in multiple places now.

We would not be able to win this round. "Ada, EMP... anything?"

"Pops, do you know how to stop these battle droids?"

"Sorry, sport." He was still humming the damn infectious tune to the ancient song.

The arm blades were slicing wildly now, and each of the damn things kept tapping down as they moved. It was freakish and unnerving. I saw Gi falter once in his nearly robotic swings. The man was tiring, and I was running low on ammo packs.

Several of the MurderCrabs shot forward, getting past Gi's sword arc. The Korean officer muttered something unintelligible that Ada offered to interpret. It wasn't necessary, as I was pretty much thinking the same thing. 'Oh, shit' in either language is said with the same levels of pitch.

The MurderCrabs closed in on my human partner. The thick fiber bundle on the rear limbs seemed to coil, then release as the damn things jumped in unison at Gi, the bizarre leg knives carving the air as they headed toward various parts of his body. Gi had expected the lunge and sidestepped while expertly plucking one of the metal beasts out of the air by its rear legs. He ripped it down onto the floor, where he stomped it. That did not stop it, but it slowed it down. I placed a round into the thing, then turned back to the rest of the advancing menace. These were just scouts; they were testing our defenses. What would we do when they all came for us?

CHAPTER
EIGHTY-FOUR

The fucking things were tough. Because of their size, I'd initially downplayed the threat. We were in armored suits, and yeah... I was an idiot. Simply through sheer numbers, their aggressiveness, and the realization that they were determined to stop us, made me quickly reevaluate our response. Add that to the absolutely freaky way they moved as one, and I think they scared me as much as the Wraith.

"Sumo, get the woman." I saw the dog looking at me from a distance, unsure what his mission priorities were. The combat dog was great in a fight, but I didn't think he would be helpful against this inhuman enemy.

I continued to unleash lethal rounds into the mass, offering up mass casualties to the robot god of war. Still more poured in from the fallen wall. It seemed like for every one I killed, two more took its place. All the tapping I'd been hearing since I'd arrived must have been the things trying to break down the walls of their containment room.

That gave me an idea, a crazy one, but one worth considering. I signaled it to Ada, who started working on the problem as I played defensive cover for Gi. A group of MurderCrabs hit me from my blindside, their momentum spinning me around. Their mass surprised me. The damn things were made of a dense alloy. My feet got tangled as another of the bots hooked a limb into my boots and spun it in the opposite direction. I went down hard, my helmet bouncing off the floor with a loud crack.

Immediately, I felt tiny limbs trying to unlatch my tactical helmet. *Shit!* The little fucks were smart, too. They had gotten me down and knew the first thing they needed to get to. Not my gun, but my head. Whoever programmed these bastards had done his homework. I'd worked with a lot of battle-bots over the years from Gen-4,s that were mainly demolition droids, right up to the latest Gen-X models, but they were all slow, unreliable, and rarely useful for anything offensive except as an ammo hauler.

Most of them were even more limited by their weak AIs, more so than their limited power supplies. Whatever was powering these things seemed limitless. I had yet to see any slow or stop on their own. And the programming seemed fluid and natural. It was orders of magnitude ahead of anything I had seen in the military or commercial spaces.

A metal crab body banged into the tunnel wall beside me just as Gi stumbled past me on my left. Blood coated one of his arms, and I could see the machine army had done a number on the joints in his battle suit. His eyes locked briefly onto mine. I could see the weariness, the fatigue of a battle that had gone on too long.

"Got your back, brother," I said, my voice weary with exhaustion.

"Me... also," he said, pulling me to my feet. He was out of breath and, I knew, hurting almost as much as I was.

Gi raised his Rattler MK4, the sword back in its sheath for now. A rapid-fire burst of 'pong' followed by the tap-tapping rise and dip response of the herky-jerky crab army. I swung in beside him and flipped the selector to single shots. I was down to my last two magazines and didn't think that was going to be enough.

We picked off outliers, trying to keep the main group bunched together.

Suddenly, something dropped toward me from the ceiling.

The damn things could climb?

My hands shot up in a feeble attempt to block it, but the Murder-Crab was dropping too fast to stop. The razor arms snapped open as it landed squarely on my face and neck. Spindly arms began encircling my head in a vice-like grip as I felt the bite of one of its blades into my flesh. The neck seal of my suit had been breached; the thing had its blade to my throat. Fiery pain lanced up my face and down my spine. Ada began sending alerts, and I knew she was going to do a suit discharge. I blocked it. I couldn't afford for my suit to be offline in battle.

I saw Gi turn his gun on me and fire. The beast's hooked metal limbs that had clawed deep into my flesh were torn away under a fusillade of rounds. The suit offered me a wound seal, which I slapped into place. I raked the ceiling with my rifle, bringing down dozens more of the murderous little bots who had also gone for the more tactical high ground.

"I have a firing solution," Ada finally said.

"Oh, thank God!"

"It will require the armament in both of your suits."

"Understood." I entered the command to slave Gi's battle suit armor to Ada. He looked at me with a shocked expression as he suddenly found himself unable to move on his own. I then ceded control of my suit to the AI. Each of us simply riding along now in our own suits moved in opposite directions, then she launched specialized demolition charges at the far wall. The rounds were in our stores of specialized grenades but were coated in a molecular adhesive that activated on contact with atmosphere. They stuck on the walls where Ada had directed them.

Then she released us from her control.

"Run!"

The wall beside us detonated in a specific pattern that the AI had deemed would cause the most damage. We plowed over and through the mass of MurderCrabs to get to a relatively clear space beyond, but the wall came down on us as well as them.

However, the robot army was immediately in the path of the much heavier sections of stone wall. They fared much worse than Gi and me.

I was on the floor, one of the damn crabs on my visor. I could see every detail of its underside and filed that away for later. I flung it off with a hand. It was dead weight, its misshapen body torn apart by the blast of the wall.

I cleared the rubble first, then pulled the Korean out. "Destroying the corridor? That was your big plan?"

It hadn't been a plan so much as a... 'What else can I do,' sort of play. "It worked."

Stone walls are the only thing I had seen that slowed them down.

The soldier looked at me funny. "Is that more music?"

Shit, my bucket was busted up. The helmet's external speaker was now playing my dad's playlist. I guess it had been going the entire time. My concentration had obviously been elsewhere. Some eighties rock song was blasting out, pumping bass and a chorus about eyes of tigers.

"Yeah, kid... you don't have a fight song playlist?" I said, feigning as much machismo as I could.

Sumo had Voss cornered, but I'd already seen that fail. She was more dangerous than the corridor full of metal monsters.

"That was impressive," she said. The smile on her face offered no warmth. "Almost."

This lady liked her barbs, and that one stung. Or maybe it was the flap of skin the goddamn crab bot had carved off my neck that was burning.

"How is it you are still unblemished?"

She was, too. Truthfully, she looked fantastic, distractingly so. Carol may have been right when she suggested inevitably I try something with her. That was before, though. Before she tried to get me killed, then helped save me, then led me into a pit full of killer bots. Then maybe saved me. Shit... I couldn't keep up.

She turned her back on all of us and walked toward a door. Sumo looked at me as if wanting permission to take her down.

"I already told you to do that, yet she's still standing."

As if in response, I felt a wave of fear that melted my resolve. Glancing up, I saw the Wraith peel itself off a wall and fly through the door behind the woman.

Stumbling up to Sumo, I patted his head and gave an ear a small scratch. His head turned into my hand. I rubbed his face.

"I know buddy. She has weapons."

"Hey, Macarena!" my speakers suddenly blaring at twice the normal volume.

Gi moved his arms in a relatively good impression of the old dance. I shook my head and followed Voss. "I hate my life."

～

"They won't stay buried; you do realize that, don't you? Plus, that was only a small part of the inventory."

"It was an exit strategy, lady." She hadn't actually fled but made her way to an area that she deemed safer and waited for me to catch up.

Truthfully, I didn't know any of that, but I wasn't about to let her know.

"Why were they attacking us? Why is all of this shit attacking us?"

She gave me a withering look of pity, then shook her hair out and pulled it back into a ponytail. Voss produced a band from one arm to keep it bound up. She was no more bothered than if she was changing workout machines at the gym.

"They are security. You are an intruder. They are programmed to stop you."

"Why are they active?" I growled. "Nothing else in this goddamn world works, but these things still do, and what about the staff? The mutant freaks down there slaughtered them."

She was sitting on the edge of a crate. Her tight-fitting jeans and loose blouse were distracting me. I am man enough to admit it, and is that sexist? You're damn right it is. Still, I was on an artificial adrenaline high and probably couldn't have done anything, even under normal circumstances. This was very definitely not normal.

Gi and Sumo were guarding the entrance. We'd followed Voss upstairs one floor. I wasn't sure, but this seemed like maybe a receiving room that could have also been used for staff training. I had Gi make contact with Bayou while I attempted to interrogate Voss. I wanted answers. She saw where my eyes were looking, and her smile warmed slightly. At some point she'd ditched the battleskin.

"Yeah, the Furies, as you call them, they are not part of his mandate.

Not exactly. Reichert was given some latitude but clearly had underestimated the transgenic changes. They should have been moved to one of the research sites, but he wanted them here."

"What were you looking for here?"

She pursed her lips and crossed her legs. I wasn't getting answers to that question. Not today, maybe not ever.

"This facility needs to be destroyed. I'm going to order my team to take it down"

"Feel free to, Master Sergeant. It won't matter."

I stood up, wobbly from the makeshift chair of boxes I'd been using. I got up in her face and did my best interpretation of my old drill sergeant. I walked over and gripped her shoulder tightly. I could feel the strength beneath that lovely exterior. She was every bit an operator as I was, and she'd kept it hidden until now. I felt something beneath my grip, cables and straps. She was hiding something there; I felt sure.

"What in the fuck does that mean?"

She smiled and she batted her eyes at me. Coyly, I believe is the term. She knew the effect she was having on me, and she was letting me know she wasn't afraid of using it.

I saw a flash of color in my peripheral vision, and I swiveled my targeting camera to a blank section of wall.

"Your pet? The Wraith, is that how you survived in here?"

"It's not a pet, and yes, it is a formidable protector, as you yourself discovered. We have mutual interests... much as you yourself, Joseph."

"You are full of shit, lady."

"I deserve that." She stood and made a show of smoothing the nonexistent wrinkles from her clothes. "I have a mission. I do not fail. I manage this by using whatever and whomever I need to be successful."

"Half the country is in ruins. Was that your mission?"

"Don't be absurd. Who do you think did all this?"

"Russians, Chinese, the coalition?" I answered, clearly guessing.

"You are assuming it was only one. Why not all three?"

I thought it through—the reason our uneasy truces with the other superpowers held as long as they did was they needed us. Having a common enemy is good for business, especially one that is not such an enemy that they won't also do trillions of dollars in other business with you. No, none of them would trust the others enough to ever team up.

"It wasn't them," I answered. I'd already heard someone had hit them just as hard as the Alliance had been.

"You were here to do something. If not to stop this, then what?"

I'd made up my mind now that she was not what she originally claimed. An agent, a spy, maybe just a bit of inside leverage from within DARPA's own bureaucratic hierarchy. No one trusted anyone anymore.

"The enemy is here," she whispered.

I wanted to challenge that. To tell her she was out of her mind. What I'd already seen here was enough for me to keep my mouth shut.

"The War." She made air quotes. "Not sure who that was. Maybe these ass hats, maybe The Third World fanatics. What I am talking about is all this tech. The genetic bioweapons. You've only seen the tip of the iceberg. These people built it, and now it's loose. It will do far more damage to us as a species than the rocks and stones being hurled up there."

I considered all I had seen in this place. Yesterday, the worst of it had been a family that committed suicide together. Now, when I closed my eyes, I could see the faces of dismembered scientists. I could also feel the ground shaking under the powerful treads of those Decimator warbots, and I could see the mutant bodies spilling out of that foul brine onto the floor in the green lab. All of that added up to a simple conclusion and one that my tortured brain didn't want to accept. My view of the world yesterday was no longer relevant. Today... well, it was going to get much worse.

She looked at me, her eyes showing the sadness now.

"Sergeant," she said, then thought better of her approach. "Joe... you realize that this technology is out there. They developed nothing in isolation. Others have it and will most definitely use it. Plus, every other Hammer facility on the planet will be like this little piece of hell or Iron River or worse."

I said nothing.

"You've seen it," she continued, ignoring the growing sounds of chaos in the outer corridor.

I silenced the comms and checked in with the team. They were busy, so Ada interfaced with each of the other battlesuit AIs and came back in near record time with, "We're fucked."

Okay, to be honest, she phrased it slightly more professionally, but my sideways thinking, meat sack mind gave the rough interpretation.

"Gotta go, Voss. Every nightmare in this shithole is breaking out."

CHAPTER
EIGHTY-FIVE

She headed for the exit, not the one I was aware of. Not the one Gi and Sumo had been guarding. *Dammit, this woman is slippery.* That was fine, as I'd slipped a small tracker onto her when I grabbed her shoulder. I wasn't taking any chances with her from here on out. The only reason she was alive was I still needed answers.

"We have a firing line set-up a hundred yards south of your position," I heard Bayou say.

"Damn good to see you guys," I said moments later as we slid in behind the stacked crates. G-Force and I both had laid down a withering barrage of fire just to make it this far. My gun registered sixteen rounds left. I had a feeling Gi was about the same.

"Mags!" I yelled.

Halo pointed to a hard case that had rolled up to a stop nearby. I thumped the key-lock and passed out fresh ammo to the team, filling every nook and cranny of my suit with the black bricks of condensed power. I also grabbed several belts of the railgun ammo. These had done more damage on the Furies. Finally, I saw a replacement for my prized Heidelberg knife. I slipped it back into the empty receiver on my chest rig.

"Grenades?" I asked.

They didn't have any of those. I got it. They had to make choices on what to bring down. The most versatile weaponry first.

"What's out there, Prowler?"

I looked at Bayou quickly. I knew I was a mess, but the way she looked at me tore my heart away. She could obviously see where I was headed.

"They made monsters."

I sighed.

"And killer warbots."

"And cyborgs," chimed in Gi helpfully.

"I hadn't seen that, but thanks for completing the party list."

"The woman?" she asked.

I pulled up the map on my HUD and shared it with my second in command. "I have a tracking dot on her. She's moving up through some back access. She knows this place, but whatever happens to me, I don't want her walking away from here. You got me?"

"Sir, yes, sir."

"Don't kill her and don't underestimate her. Treat her like an asset. A potentially hostile asset."

She nodded and went back to sighting downrange at the shadows moving in the distance.

"Contact!" Priest yelled from off to our right. Just as quickly, Halo opened up with his specialized MK4-B. That version had several added features, including a predictive targeting system. It sensed movement and threats fed into it by the user's battlesuit AI. If the last shot appeared to kill, it instantly moved to the next highest priority target. The algorithm was so good it could synch with all the squads' weapons systems, so no one was targeting the same enemy.

We had encountered the MurderCrabs when we came out into the tunnel, but that wasn't what was heading toward us now.

"Shit... Decimators."

As they came into focus, my heart sank. What I had battled down below must have been the basic Titans. The fucking things had nearly destroyed the place and ended me, yet they were essentially the warehouse workers. What we were looking at now was the same... but so much worse.

It was in its compact form, everything retracted down to about twelve feet high. The legs were folded up and armored treads moved the body forward. I could see gun ports, targeting lasers, Dual Plasma Cannons mounted on each side of the massive 'head.' The damn things could reconfigure themselves to whatever the battle space demanded. Here in these tunnels, it looked more like an armored tank, with arms and, well... even more guns. As my squad began targeting the thing, its arms snapped open, revealing a rotating plasma gun that reminded me of a GAU-8 cannon they used on the old A10 Warthogs.

As it opened up, firing on us, the comparison was even more pronounced. If the Titans came at us looking like this, I was going to call them Warthogs.

"Cease fire!" I ordered. "We brought knives to a gunfight. Make it difficult for them, but let's get the hell out."

Banshee was here because of me; I wasn't willing to risk them in a battle we couldn't win. Halo, Priest, and Gi all plastered proximity mines on the tunnel's walls and ceiling as we made our way back in the entrance's direction.

"Do we have any assets overhead? Can we call in a strike?"

"Like... nuclear?" Bayou asked. "You want to nuke Tennessee?"

We were running now, not jogging, but flat out sprinting for daylight. It wasn't that I wanted to nuke Tennessee, but well, fuck...

"Yeah, doesn't everybody? This shit gets out, we'll never stop it."

A blast sounded from behind, followed closely by three more. Rock and dust rained down everywhere, and a section of wall collapsed just ahead of us.

"No joy, Boss. None of our hardware up there is responding on Milcrypt comms."

"Anything on the dropship that could do it?" I knew the answer, but I was out of ideas.

Bayou offered a nervous laugh. "Nothing, Boss." I heard the mechanical whine of the Titans moving through the rubble. I could feel their movements vibrating through my combat boots. Jesus, these things were powerful. Then, the tap, tap tapping joined in.

"Shit, shit, shit... both of the mechanical fuckers are coming at us."

More likely they were just trying to break free, and we were standing in their way.

"The Wulf is close," Bayou said, urging me on. I knew my steps had gotten increasingly unsure. That last little sprint had tapped out the last of my energy reserves. I felt her arm on mine. She was pulling but I pulled back.

"No."

I stopped running. I could see the underground garage area just ahead.

"I'm done, kid. We both know it."

"Shut the fuck up, Prowler."

"I can slow 'em down some, maybe even collapse this place."

I had the shakes again, much worse than before. My gun hand was shaking so badly, no way I could hit anything I shot at. The rest of the team raced past, heading for the transport.

"Joe...no!"

"I'm not trying to be a hero, Deb... I'd love to stick around and help you sort this shit out, but there is nothing here that will save me. But there is a lot here that can fuck up the world. Up there, you just have killer vines. Down here we have that."

As if on cue, the monstrous Warthog pulled itself down out of the tunnel entrance with two huge mechanical arms and swung around toward us.

"Go. Leave me your gear. Get back into orbit and call in a strike on this position. I don't care if it's from the Russians or Chinese or whoever's left up there. Just do it."

She hugged me tight. I could see the remnants of my battered soul in the reflection in her visor. She quickly unlatched her helmet, removed it, leaned in close, and pressed her forehead to my helmet. My visor was up. I could smell her sweat, her shampoo, and her need for me to come with her. The monster who lived down the tunnel whined, and I knew that was its blasters warming up.

Bayou nodded and was gone. A line of rounds arched toward me. The lead bot's targeting was clearly off as it simply tore long gouges into the walls. Sumo woofed. I turned to see him attacking some of the MurderCrabs coming through. "Sumo, leave it. Go with Bayou."

The dog looked at me, confused, then ignored my command. The little bastard had been insolent before. At times, he would obey reluctantly or with attitude, but not completely disregard what I said.

"Sumo, you have to go, boy." Another volley of rounds struck beside me, one dislodging a baseball chunk of stone that ricocheted off my chest plates.

With my visor opened, I smelled something, something that rekindled memories of me as a boy. Staying with my granddad, watching the July Fourth Holoparade where the VR spaceships came cruising down Main Street, and something else.

"Ada, scan surroundings for fuel storage. Petroleum."

No one used fossil fuels anymore, but this was a garage, and I knew that smell. Grandpa used to call it diesel, I think. Said all the old trucks used to use it.

"Multiple storage tanks, several thousand gallons, and a synthetic catalyst compound," Ada suggested.

"The catalyst?" I asked, already heading toward the location she had showed.

"It would make an excellent oxidizer. Down in the tunnels, the fuel may not burn if it doesn't have a significant amount of oxygen."

She knew what I was planning. I raced past the spot the Wulf had just vacated. I resisted the temptation to look over to the ramp, afraid my heart would break if I saw them leaving.

"Voss!" I yelled into my comms as I pulled hoses and piping that Ada indicated would work. "Damiana, you need to get out of wherever you are. I'm about to light this thing off."

I don't know why I warned her. If I was being honest, it was probably the jeans.

I had multiple lengths of hose heading back to the tunnels, and Ada triggered the fuel and catalyst release immediately. It wasn't a good plan; it was a Kovach plan. Now, if I could just keep the Warthog from killing me or triggering the fire too soon. I needed that fuel to go all the way down that shaft to the very bottom. I mentally willed those tanks to drain faster. Puddles of the stuff ran like blood around my feet and ankles.

The Warbot stopped firing and suddenly backed up, one of its treads hung up on something behind it. The thing seemed almost confused. It rocked back and forward but had ceased firing. Could the thing sense danger? Did it understand the threat this fuel poised to it and its mechanical brethren?

I had both guns leveled at it, my targeting reticle dancing all over the head and upper body, Ada clearly finding nothing that might be a weakness or a control system to shoot at. I had to use the gyros and stiffeners in my suit to keep my arms steady, but I wouldn't have to maintain it for much longer.

"Sumo, outside!" I yelled. "Go on, I'll join you in a minute."

I wasn't sure that was true, but I would do my best.

The dog's more sensitive nose had to smell the fuel by now, and he, too, seemed to know the danger. He barked, and then ran for the ramp. I made sure the hose was flowing well and ran to follow. I made it several steps before something snagged my leg and grabbed my feet. I looked down to see a steel braided rope. It bound my legs tight and was slowly being wound back to the Decimator. One panel on the front was opening, and inside I could see an empty space.

"Not going to happen."

The damn thing was pulling me faster now. My suit was nearly completely submerged in the fuel. I'd also dropped both of the rifles when the thing had lassoed my legs; I still didn't know how it could have managed that little feat.

I was within five feet of the Warthog before I got my blade out. Tapping down on the handle started the hypervibration that made the Heidelberg blades so deadly. The supersonic vibration happened at nearly the molecular level. If you looked at the blade, you couldn't tell it was moving, but it was like a chain saw made of titanium razors. It sliced through the metal rope bindings instantly. I blocked an incoming arm from the Warthog and dropped a magnesium grenade into the open cockpit. I noticed seats in the thing and realized they designed these for human operators.

I heard the dog yelping for me far ahead. My confused body seemed almost under the control of something else entirely. I didn't have long; I knew that. My awkward stumbling gait turned into a shamble, and then something sort of resembling a run just as the grenade cooked off. The

Warthog Decimator seemed to balloon outward, then in on itself. Fire exploded out in every direction. Flame engulfed the tunnel, the garage, and defined the confines of my new world.

Explosions rang out throughout the space. Detonations that had to be ammo packs, bright intense flares of battery packs exploding. My suit protected me, but only up to a point. The inner level of the Rivex base layer provided both a ballistic and thermal barrier, but I had to be approaching its limits.

A massive fireball came skyrocketing out of the corridor, blowing what was left of the Warthog past me. A massive chunk of the heavy polycrete ceiling collapsed, knocking me sideways into the old guard booth we'd entered only hours earlier, although it now seemed like a lifetime ago. I pushed myself back up with my one almost good arm. Daylight no longer shone down the ramp to the outside. I couldn't see more than a dozen feet in that direction. The thick concrete landing pad now slanted down, closing off that exit.

I stumbled through the wall of flame, my entire suit catching fire as I did so.

"That was fucking stupid."

I could feel and hear the silicone gaskets at my neck and wrist as they melted into my skin. I could smell my body beginning to cook. The damage I was enduring was beyond even what a billion-dollar enhanced super-soldier could withstand. I thought about being back at my cabin in the mountains. Building something magical out of the wood slabs I still had curing behind the shed. I thought about my mom, and grand-dad, and Sumo. Not my whole life, but enough of it to remind me I had done some good...not enough. But some.

Then the flames in front of my face disappeared in a spray of white mist. Suddenly, Voss was in front of me, fire extinguisher in hand. She somehow managed to drag me into a side door just as another round of explosions rocked the underground parking deck.

"Why? I croaked.

"Some monsters we need." She set the red extinguisher down heavily. "You are mine."

CHAPTER
EIGHTY-SIX

"Don't look at me that way."

"I'll look at you anyway I want. You are something I clean off the bottom of my shoe," my voice hoarse and dry.

She laughed, not just a gesture, she thought it was funny. That unnerved me more than nearly anything else she had done.

"Thank you. For back there."

She just nodded; I could tell she'd been through more trouble, too. Her clothes were ripped, and she had a fresh cut down her jawline.

I was busy prying the charred remnants of my now useless helmet off. I dropped the pieces to the floor where they rolled away, stopping at a wall that was canting inward at the top. I felt Ada coaxing the suit to supply meds and burn ointment, but she was just prolonging the inevitable.

"Did you get what you came for?" I asked.

"Some."

I was too tired to want the details. "You need to go. Get out while you can."

"They'll make monsters, too," she said. "Now they know what all we did here. They know all our bloody secrets. Warbots, cyborgs and worse, things you didn't even see down there."

"Monsters," I echoed. "Nightmares." Both names made the bile rise up in my gut.

Pain shot through me, and I shook from the trauma. Then it passed, and in its place was a sense of serenity and clarity. *Am I dead?*

Voss was motioning to something on the other side of the wall. I turned my head slowly but saw nothing.

"The Wraith," she said in answer to my unasked question. "Broadcasting fear is not its only ability."

"Cool trick," I said, understanding flooding through me. "It's just blocking the pain, though. My body is still a wreck. I've been here before. I know what comes next."

"Kovach," she said, totally ignoring my statement as she walked over to a brick of data storage cubes. "Hammer was not just working in opposition to the U.S., they were working against humanity. War is good. Wasn't that Arlen Hammer's motto?"

"Sounds right," I said.

"All of these data systems here have been breached, every one of them." She looked as defeated as I was. "Yes, they will make monsters, too."

"You don't know that."

"Yes, Joe, I do know it."

"Shit... who's left to do it? How can you possibly be so sure?" I asked.

"I'm sure."

Her words were evident of something deeper. A hidden knowledge that, again, she was not about to share. The war, it seemed, had just begun, and this was not the end, but merely the beginning. She grabbed my good arm and pulled me toward a wall, and I could see a shaft of light coming down. Some sort of ventilation shaft.

"We need to go."

I entered the slanted tube first, struggling to make it up the incline. Looking back, I saw her waiting for me to get clear. My suit barely cleared the last section, and I had to remove my sidearm and tactical belt for my hips to slide through. One good kick to a grille cover, and I was standing out in the misting rain. Pain began radiating through my body again, then Sumo was there bumping against me hard. Smoke billowed from dozens of hidden openings, obviously leading down to the underground facility.

I pulled a coil of narrow steel rope from the dog's tactical pack. He didn't carry much, but that one had come in handy several times. I tossed it down the vent shaft.

"Banshee is requesting permission to make a recovery drop," Ada said. "They are two minutes out."

The murderous plants bordering the complex were moving in; no longer was the tree line a defined edge. Whatever had been holding them back was gone. I also saw a line of the black mechanical crabs moving off in the direction of the road. Others appeared to be finding energy taps to recharge. Fucking little power vampires. Sumo bumped my leg again; he clearly no longer liked the neighborhood.

"Yes, tell them the LZ will be hot."

I leaned over to pull Voss up when a sudden violent rush of air came at me. *The fucking Wraith.*

I felt weight on the line, and just as suddenly, it relaxed again. A brief shout and then Voss's voice from the other end of the shaft.

"You're an abomination," Damiana said in a shout. "This is the end of the line."

Even without the helmet, my eyes were still damn good. I saw a shadow pass by the small circle of light on the other end of the vent. Then spikes and an arm, an unmistakable arm. It was a Furie.

I wanted to go back. I wanted to be her champion. *Was that me or the Wraith pulling on an emotional trigger?*

I heard the creature and could picture those rows of teeth.

"Stay up there, Master Sergeant!"

Could she handle herself... handle it? I heard myself yelling, then screaming at her.

"Fuck this!" I tied off the line and was about to go down when I heard a shout and a grunt of pain. Then, Damiana Voss was coming up the shaft, barely touching the line I was holding.

It was damn hard not to be impressed by this woman.

She took my hand as she lightly climbed onto the lip of the shaft, then jumped, touching down lightly beside us. I saw a flutter nearby and knew it was her pet alien manta ray thing.

"I have us a ride coming," I said. "What happened down there... all of that... thanks." I saw something slip out of her hand and retract quickly back into her sleeve. *What the hell was that?*

She smiled. "We all have our jobs to do."

I laughed and then winced at the pain it caused and sat down abruptly.

"I believe we failed."

"Not yet, Joe, but yes... we still might."

"Look, Voss, the planet is fucked."

"The planet is fine. It's humanity that's fucked, Joe."

She walked over and extended a hand to help me to my feet. "Same thing," I offered.

"No—it isn't.

Look, Master Sergeant, despite your beliefs and the optics of my recent behavior, we are not enemies." She moved several feet away before turning to face me. "Not yet."

"So, what, we're partners now?"

The Wraith watched closely from its perch; I could just make out the cold eyes following its master as she moved along the edge of the building.

"Let's say our goals are mutually aligned. If they ever are at crossed paths, that will lead us to a different outcome."

"My path is ending, lady. You know that better than anyone."

"Ah... yes. I am aware of your... predicament."

She said it like I had misplaced my car keys... which reminded me I had. Dad was right, I was never getting Grandad's truck back.

"There are a few things you should know, Kovach."

"Seriously, just a few? Look, honey, stop the ride. I'm ready to get off." My legs gave way again, and I dropped to one knee.

"First, this is not the only site. Hammer and others have similar facilities all over the world. We don't know how many, nor do we know what they are all producing. We do know that the Decimators were shipped in here for final assembly. Also, I'm sure by now you have figured out the terraforming shit...a rather different take on the old scorched-earth battlefield tactics."

I tried to speak, but my throat had started cramping on me. Sumo watched from close by; I knew he was unsure as to what to do.

"Terraforming? What, the plants?"

She bent to look at me, lifted an eyelid and stared close. I was unable to do anything. If she wanted me dead—I was dead.

"Consider this as well. sentient machines do not exist, never have, probably never will. Everyone knows we crossed the threshold years ago. The 'singularity' where the number of computations on each chip and the level of AI sophistication should have allowed it. It simply did not happen."

A sound foretold the destruction going on below. The Warbots.... large and small, were highly pissed off now. Apparently, there were other horrors on the verge of escaping, and I had no way to stop them.

She squatted down, bringing our faces just inches apart. Despite the blood, the bruises, the dirt, and streaks of black soot, she was damn pleasing to look at. And yes—even in death, I am still an asshole guy. Millions of years of having an evolutionary mandate can't be stopped simply because it's considered politically incorrect.

"Think about it, Kovach. Your line of command is gone. Your access to intel, good intel, is compromised at best and probably totally unreliable at worst. For a soldier, you are in a unique position. You now get to choose whose lies you believe or at least whose orders you follow. Despite that, your team may be the last line of defense for the survivors. Do you understand what I am telling you?"

I tried to nod, but truthfully, I did not... my nod looked more like early signs of a stroke, which it probably was. Why on God's green and slightly violet Earth was she still talking?

"You and your squad are off the leash. You must start making decisions for yourself. If you want to battle these monsters," she paused as if considering her next words more carefully, "or whoever is controlling them, we can help. I do still have some resources."

My face finally figured out how to move a few of the muscles in my mouth.

"Last month, you were a secretary in Virginia, looking for a ride." That, at least, is what I tried to say. The reality was far less eloquent and involved a considerable amount more of saliva exiting my mouth than is polite even in these trying circumstances.

Her smile was genuine, it was a good smile. "I wanted to protect you, I wanted to protect dear Carol. You are right, though. I used you to get what I required. By the way, did she find her boy?"

I nodded. "They're in the dropship."

"Good, he's a bright lad. I do feel a genuine fondness for them both... and for you. You are a tremendous fighter, but..." Her words trailed off momentarily. "You will have to be more."

I thought I detected just the faintest whiff of a British accent in her voice now. I wanted to tell her I was headed to Valhalla; I wouldn't become anything except dead.

A loud metal grinding was followed by a thump that shook the wall beside us. The Decimators had found us. Damiana obviously knew that but remained oddly calm. This woman acted like she had all the time in the world. I've worked with a lot of special operators, and I don't think I've ever encountered one this cool.

"This is going to hurt." She pointed her empty hand at me and mimicked pulling a trigger, and then her hand was suddenly not empty. She shot me.

"Sleep now," she said, leaning over and kissing me.

She fucking kissed me. On The Lips! Then she was gone. I was vaguely aware of Sumo giving pursuit.

All I could do was use my one good arm to pull myself out toward the fractured landing pad. I stuck a finger in the hole in my armor. It was in my upper abdomen. My armor was weak there, and the base layer battleskin must've failed entirely.

CHAPTER
EIGHTY-SEVEN
BANSHEE

"Watch it,"

"There, no, there, goddammit."

Barking... lots of barking.

"Going to be okay."

Why was Bayou barking?

The voices mixed together as my view of the world jostled back and forth. Gun firing and something black overhead. Then... nothing. No pain, no... Macarena music.

"Joseph! Son, can you hear me?"

Dad's voice was so far away. Too far for me to ever respond.

"We're losing him."

Bayou was shouting now.

"Get him in the med bay. Packer, get us in orbit, now!"

She moved around the gurney to get another IV started. It was all futile; she knew. His enhancements had kept him alive until now, but now they were killing him.

"Kovach, don't you fucking die on me." She yanked a charred piece of armor off his chest, taking skin and tissue with it.

"Fucking thing is melted to his skin. What in the hell did he do down there?" Priest asked.

Gi helped Bayou hook him into the specialized trauma sleeve and lower their commander into the pod-shaped med unit. The ship's medical AI would take over treatment from here.

"He never expected to make it back out," Bayou said.

G-Force was the closest one to her. He put an arm out and touched hers lightly. "He is a warrior. No matter what, it is better that he is with us."

She fought back the tears and looked up and around. The ship's display all showed reports of more crises gripping the planet.

"Why Joe... why?" She said it softly. Mostly to herself. Then she saw the mother and child looking on with concern. Maybe something more. Lux was a wonder. He had already familiarized himself with the ship's controls, many of the weapons, and never stopped asking those damn good questions.

"You did good, Boss." Bayou carefully kissed his forehead and moved to let others make peace with their fallen brother. The monitor showing the master sergeant's respiration and heart rate fall for another forty minutes before seeming to stabilize.

Bayou and Packer had come up with the essence of a plan. It was crude and risky as hell. Since they had no one to report to and nowhere safe to go, the solution was both simple and fortuitous.

They matched orbit with the IAS Stone Mountain, and the TriCraft entered the darkened warship. It had been parked in high orbit awaiting its next crew. It was one of the older Monolith class carriers, not as big as the Alice Springs but by no means a lightweight. Packer had scoped it out earlier, finding only a small maintenance crew aboard.

The TriCraft slid into a docking cradle. In minutes, they had the medical pod out and Kovach hooked into the more advanced systems in the ship's surgical suite. No one spoke, no one left the room. They sat with him, knowing the end was close. Carol touched Joe's broken body tenderly, her face a mask of pain and tears.

Lux ran his fingers gingerly over the scarred arm. "He's the one who saved me."

Bayou nodded. "He ordered us to come find you, no matter what."

"But if you had stayed, you could have saved him," the boy said.

"No, despite the damage, he isn't dying from what happened down there in that awful place."

"So, what was he doing there, trying to save himself?"

"He was trying to save all of us, Lux."

Kovach drew in a deep breath, then several shallow ones. The monitors flashed red as the levels all suddenly dropped to zero. The side guards on the bed slid up, preventing anyone from reaching in, and the medbot began performing CPR, then periodically shocking the heart. It did no good, nothing changed. No signs of life remained. This continued for a while.... too long. Bayou eventually canceled the resuscitation order. She was aware of Joe's wishes. The lifesaving attempts whirred to a quiet stop, then shut down, the mechanical arms retracting back into the machine's housing with a snap.

"Master Sergeant Joeseph Kovach is officially pronounced dead at 9:48 PM Earth Standard Time," the shipboard system said with appropriate solemness.

The lieutenant continued to hold Joe's hand long after the others had turned and left. Sumo lay under the edge of the pod and occasionally looked up at her. The dog's eyes weren't sad. In fact, they seemed oddly unconcerned with what had just happened to his partner.

"Nice to be a dog right now," she said through her tears.

"You left me a mess, you bastard. I know it wasn't your fault, but Jesus, Joe, I need you here. I can't stop those things down there."

She ran her hand over his personal effects. His clothes had all been cut away. His body lay beneath a pristine white sheet soaked with blood in various places. Gi had reverently taken the meager possessions from his pockets. An ID badge for some doctor, a wooden figure that looked remarkably like Sumo, and a strange black, multisided object that she was clueless about.

She leaned back in the chair, looking at the obsidian object. "What am I going to do now?" They had a ship, food, a dropship for as long as it kept working, but not much else. Someone out there had taken out the Alice Springs. Would this ship be next?

The squads all had a tradition. They stayed with their fallen until the family got the body or until the funeral. It was a simple task, just a final way of paying respect to a fellow warrior. First, she'd had to abandon Darko, now Joe. Bayou left reluctantly after a couple of hours.

Halo came in next. He'd brought Sumo a plate of food and some water. The dog stayed rooted under the bed. All the lines and monitors had been removed, and the body had been cleaned by the bots. A fresh sheet was now covering Kovach. He would not be embalmed, no one ever did that anymore, but his final request had always been cremation. Looking at the burns and scars, it looked like something had nearly cremated him prior to death. Halo bent closer; he would have sworn the wounds had looked worse earlier. The bots had done a nice job cleaning him up.

Priest took the next watch and read to him from a book. Kovach had never been much of a reader, but somehow, the story reminded the sniper of his sergeant. *Glory Road* by Robert Heinlein, an ancient classic. "It's a hell of a note when you can't even kill a dragon and feel light-hearted afterwards."

Priest smiled; he'd seen his boss kill everything but dragons. What Gi had described down in that hole had sounded even worse. When his time was up, he patted the arm. "Going to miss you, buddy."

Gi's shift was in the company of Carol and Lux. He liked them both, and although he'd only known Kovach for a day, he couldn't deny the bond forged in the pits of that awful place. Lux had brought in a small puppy and introduced her to Sumo. The two dogs were instantly nipping and playing. It was a side of the dog that seemed completely alien. Gi had fought beside the husky and could attest that it was a killer. Now it was rolling on its back, nipping at the smaller dog.

"He looks good," the woman said.

"Huh?"

"They did a good job on him, I mean," Carol said.

She moved back so Lux and Gi could see. Lux stood by his face and brushed the hair away from Joe's eyes. If dead people bothered the kid, he didn't show it.

Gi realized the woman was right. Joe looked better than he had all day. The boy was swinging on one of the rails the med bots had used earlier to travel up and down the bed. He was humming some ridiculous tune as he did so. The innocence of children.

Sumo stopped his playing and cocked his head, looking over Junie and toward the bed.

Lux eyed his mom and then Gi, before breaking out into song.

"Hey, Macarena!"

ABOUT THE AUTHOR

JK Franks is the popular author of numerous post-apocalyptic and near-future techno-thriller novels. He is an admitted tech geek, science nerd, cyclist, and storyteller. JK Franks' world was formed by a childhood growing up during the Space Age when he developed a love for books. He became an avid student of history and science and a regular reader of everything from reference books to dusty, old biographies. Once he discovered science fiction, he never looked back.

His work is mostly near-future thrillers, characterized by meticulous research, hard science, and a gritty, seldom-matched realism. "I hate stupid characters," states Franks. "Or even worse, smart characters, acting stupid." All of his work combines his passion for hard science fiction, well-crafted characters, and superb storytelling.

No matter where he is or what's going on, Franks tries his best to set aside time every day to answer emails and messages from readers. You can visit him on the web at www.jkfranks.com. Please subscribe to his newsletter for updates, promotions, and giveaways. You can also find the author on Facebook or email him directly at media@jkfranks.com.

OTHER BOOKS BY JK FRANKS

The Catalyst Series

Book 1: Downward Cycle

Life in a remote, oceanfront town spirals downward after a massive solar flare causes a global blackout. But the loss of electrical power is just the first of the problems facing the survivors in the chaos that follows. Is this how the world ends?

Book 2: Kingdoms of Sorrow

With civilization in ruins, individuals band together to survive and build a new society. The threats are both grave and numerous—surely too many for a small group to weather. This is a harrowing story of survival following the collapse of the planet's electrical grids.

Book 3: American Exodus

This companion story to the Catalyst series follows one man's struggle to get back home after the collapse. No supplies, no idea of the hardships to come; how can he possibly survive the journey? Even if he survives, can he adapt to this new reality?

Book 4: Ghost Country

Since the solar superstorm and CME almost two years before, the Gulf Coast town of Harris Springs, Mississippi, has suffered from gang attacks, famine, and hurricanes and has battled a crusading army of religious zealots. Now, they face their greatest challenge: outsmarting a tyrannical president and escaping an approaching pandemic.

Cade Rearden Thrillers

Book 1: State of Chaos

He's exhausted and brutally traumatized. Now, Spec-Ops Captain Cade

Rearden must finally listen to the voices in his head...or everyone on Earth may die. If you like near-future technology, complex heroes, and high-octane action, then you'll love JK Franks' explosive new adventure.

Book 2: Midnight Zone

Nightmares are real in the cold, dark waters of the deep. National Security Agent Cade Rearden is used to secrets. Assigned to protect the ultra-dark-ops organization known as The Cove Project, he grapples with his role of defending a country still in crisis after a deadly super AI has devastated much of the U.S.

But when part of his team mysteriously disappears beneath the idyllic waters of the Caribbean, Cade finds himself thrust into a web of lies and mystery, at the heart of which lies an eons-old secret that somebody will kill to protect. Grappling with his inner demons and struggling to locate his friends, Cade stumbles upon a government cover-up...and terrifying creatures, hidden miles beneath the surface of the ocean.

The Fade Novels

The Night Gate

Since losing his daughter seven years ago, Pike Shepard has struggled to maintain a normal life for himself in the coastal community of Blackwater. It's a quiet life, until a beautiful scientist shows up on his doorstep with a desperate plea for help. Dr. Kate Cassidy has uncovered a new aspect to quantum entanglement: the ability to not just see the multiverse but a way to travel through it. Her device allows them to SideSlip between parallel dimensions that are at once familiar and quite bizarre, wondrous, and terrifying. Pike learns they aren't the only ones with this ability, and the others want them gone.

Savage Earth Series

Book 1: Nightmare Factory

In the not-too-distant future, a devastating global attack takes place and planet Earth is on the brink of extinction. In this sci-fi thriller, Master Sargent Joe Kovach has been through a personal hell as he struggles to adapt to his new enhancements. As battles escalates, so does his determination to uncover the group who triggered this brutal extinction event that has left the planet overrun by mechanical and genetic horrors.

Book 2: Eradication

In a world ravaged by a devastating attack, the remnants of humanity are barely clinging to existence. Months have passed since the enemy unleashed hordes of murderous creations that now engulf the planet. Amidst the chaos, One renegade group takes refuge on Earth's last remaining space vessels, orbiting above the desolate wastelands. They are Banshee Team, and they are alone beacon of hope in the face of annihilation. They are committed to uncover the truth behind the brutal attacks and lend their expertise to turn the tide of this merciless battle.

Connect with the Author Online:

** For a sneak peek at new novels, free stories, and more, join the email list at jkfranksbooks.com.

Facebook: facebook.com/groups/JKFranks/

Amazon Author Page: amazon.com/-/e/B01HIZIYH0

Goodreads: goodreads.com/author/show/15395251.J_K_Franks

Other Sellers https://books2read.com/catalyst1

Websites: JKFranks.com or JKFranksbooks.coim

Twitter: @jkfranks

Instagram: @jkfranks1

Made in the USA
Monee, IL
16 June 2023

35963936R00236